Baby & Bump

Book one in the This & That Series

Brooke Moss

Cover art by: Brooke Moss

Edited by: Meggan Connors, www.megganconnors.com

Published by: Brooke Moss, CHP
ISBN print: 978-1939976024

The author acknowledges the copyrighted or trademarked status and trademark owners of the following wordmarks mentioned in this work of fiction: Dora the Explorer; 16 and Pregnant; My Little Pony; The Muppets; Eastern Washington University; Fifty Shades of Grey; Cabbage Patch Dolls; Red Door; Jello; Tic Tacs;

The Lawrence Welch Show; Food Network; YouTube; Alka Seltzer; Doppler; The Bachelor; Doogie Howser; QVC; Funyuns; Hermes; The Maury Povitch Show; Disney on Ice; Aliens; Sesame Street; Micheal Korrs; Graceland; Dungeons & Dragons; Oldsmobile; Valentino; Little House on the Prairie; BMW; Carrot Top; Dancing With the Stars; Volkswagen; Red Cross; Hot House; Kotex; Libman; Washington State University; Taebo; Cosmopolitan Magazine; People Magazine; Hamburger Helper; Sex in the City; Lifetime Network; Beverly Hills 90210; Gatorade; Tupperware; Chicklets; Real Housewives; Levis; Angus Beef; iPod; iPhone; As The World Turns; Kool Aid; Toyota Sentra; Chuck Taylors; CNN; CIA; Victoria's Secret; and Michael Kors, Gap Kids.

For my mom.

(Not as nuts as Patsy Baump, but every bit as devoted to her

children.)

Chapter One

Peeing on a stick isn't nearly as simple as the women in the commercial make it out to be, especially in a pair of four-inch heels and a pencil skirt.

In the commercials, women emerge from a perfectly clean restroom wearing head-to-toe virginal white, while carrying their positive tests across their breezy living rooms. They pause by the open windows, where air lifts the gauzy curtains and blows back their long, flowing hair. Gazing off into some distant, sun-filled meadow, they smile serenely and wrap their arms around themselves as if relishing their God-given gift of procreation. Their faces seem to say, "*I am a giver of life. My husband and I have created tangible proof of our undying union.*"

Never once in those commercials do the sticks drip urine all over their hands like mine did. And those women aren't late for a meeting with prospective clients. They don't collapse onto the floor with their skirt jacked up to their waists crying, "No. Oh, please, God. No. No, no, no, no, no…"

And in the commercials the women don't smell their friend's breakfast and dry heave.

"And so help me, *if you fry one more egg on my stove, I will choke you with the toaster cord. Do you understand me?*"

Still chewing on said fried egg sandwich, my friend and coworker, Marisol, popped her head through the creaky bathroom door. "What's your problem?"

Upon finding me in a heap on the floor, curled in a ball with my backside covered in mint-green granny panties, she added, "Good Lord, you're never going to find yourself a man wearing drawers like that, now are you?"

Yup. That was how I found out I would be a giver of life.

***

"You should go see my obstetrician. He's fabulous."

I looked up from my plate of saltine crackers at my cousin, Candace. She was stir-frying tofu and pea pods, the steam rising off the wok just enough to make her skin glisten and her wavy blonde hair dance. Candace was the only woman in the world who made being a housewife with three children under the age of five look hot. Seriously, it was a wonder we were from the same gene pool.

"I literally just found out this morning. This baby is approximately the size of the eye of a needle, and you're wanting me to go to an obstetrician?" I shuddered at the aroma of fried tofu, and stuffed a cracker into my mouth.

"You need to get on some prenatal vitamins stat," she announced wisely. She went back to chopping onions and tossed it into the mix.

My nostrils flared when the scent hit the air. "I really don't want to think about seeing an obstetrician right now."

"So, does that mean you're giving some thought to an abortion?" Marisol asked as she emerged from the bathroom. Her glossy curtain of mahogany hair swung as she sauntered to the kitchen table and sat next down to me.

"Shush." Candace pointed her spatula at her. "Could you be *any* more cavalier about this?"

Marisol plopped down in a chair and looked around, her caramel-brown eyes fluttering with feigned innocence. "What? Oh, sorry. So what's the deal, Lexie? Are you gonna keep it?"

My stomach whirled like a dryer on spin, and I grabbed another cracker. "I haven't really had very long to think about it, but I think so."

Candace put down her spatula and pressed a hand to her heart. "I can't believe this is happening. You're going to be a mommy."

Marisol rolled her eyes. She didn't have the "maternal instinct that Candace did. Growing up, Candace worked in the nursery at church and babysat for all of the neighborhood kids. Marisol spent her adolescence sneaking cigarettes in the girls' room and practiced tongue kissing with the neighborhood boys.

Me? I was somewhere in the middle. I'd enjoyed watching little kids for extra money, but also enjoyed the attention of an occasional boy, as well.

"Yeah…" My voice shook, and I took a sip of the ginger ale sitting in front of me.

I couldn't believe it, either. Not that I didn't want to be a mother. I'd spent my fair share of time gazing at baby booties and bassinets as my thirties approached. But when my marriage went down in a ball of flames before I'd even hit twenty-five, I'd assumed my chance at motherhood was permanently out of reach.

Candace gasped, jerking me out of my thoughts and back into her steamy kitchen. "Have you told your mom yet? Oh, Aunt Patsy is going to love being a grandma."

I felt the color drain from my face. "She's going to love being a grandma after she gets done raking me over the coals for being a single, unwed mother to her only grandchild."

My mother had been waiting for entirely too long for grandchildren. I have two brothers, and she'd expected procreation from at least one of us a long time ago. Since my brothers hadn't reproduced yet, all of the pressure fell on my thirty-year-old eggs. My little brother, Darren, who was five years my junior, was less interested in children and more interested in dating every single woman in eastern Washington. His job selling cell phones at the mall paid his bills just enough to keep the electricity on and a plentiful supply of beer in his fridge.

Corbin was five years my senior. He and his wife, Andrea, ran a successful house-flipping company. Now that their business was thriving, thanks to their eye for detail and the local buyers' market, and their own home was completed and designed to perfection, Corbin and Andrea longed for a child of their own, and had been unsuccessfully trying for years.

Reason number 462 why telling my family I was pregnant would be almost as unpleasant as dipping my face in acid; though my mother craved grandchildren with the same urgency as someone fighting to stay out of the electric chair, she certainly didn't want me to have them outside the bonds of holy matrimony. Patsy Holiday Baump was nothing if not traditional. She was the choir director and Bible study teacher at the First United Presbyterian Church, after all, and Pastor Irm—whom everyone in the family knew my mother had a crush on—expected better choices from us Baump kids.

"Oh, yeah." Candace grimaced. "I guess she will be a little disappointed in you, won't she?"

"Disappointed?" I snorted, and some cracker crumbs flew. "When she found out I lost my virginity in college she cried for a solid week and sent me three copies of *The Scarlet Letter*."

Marisol snickered. "In college?"

I cast her a dirty look. "Not everyone can develop as early as you, Mar."

"I remember." Candace smiled sympathetically at me.

Candace had lived at home with her parents while I'd gone to stay in the dorms, so she'd been there for the entire melodrama. When I'd told Candace over the phone that I'd finally done it with Bo Anderson in the Phi Beta House over Halloween weekend, my mother's sister, Aunt Dory, had overheard the conversation. She'd promptly called both my mother *and* Pastor Irm. The aftermath of those stolen thirteen minutes lasted approximately two weeks longer than my relationship with Bo Anderson, and my mother *still* brought it up every Thanksgiving over pecan pie.

"So what if you're not married," scoffed Marisol, tossing her hair. "You're thirty years old. It's not like you're going to be on an episode of *16 and Pregnant*. Er, unless the dad is sixteen." She looked at me pointedly. "He's not, is he? You dirty cougar, you."

"Geez, no! Give me some credit." I rubbed my stomach. It ached like it was empty, despite the seventeen crackers I'd eaten.

Candace set down her spatula and sat down across the table from me. "Listen, about that. You need to tell us."

The crackers in my stomach curdled like milk. "You need me to tell you what?"

"Well, who the lucky daddy is, of course." Marisol stole one of my crackers.

"Come on, Lexie. Spill it." Candace nodded. "I didn't even know you were dating anyone."

"I'm not." Looking down at my plate, I avoided their heavy stares.

"You're not dating anyone?" Candace asked. I could practically feel her frown on the side of my head. "But you're pregnant."

I nodded. "Precisely."

"Way to go!" Marisol held up her hand for a high five, but I didn't move. "I told you that you should cut loose more often."

Candace shook her head. "This is really out of character for you."

I nodded and pushed my short red hair behind my ears. Candace was right. It *was* out of character for me to be pregnant outside of any sort of relationship whatsoever. Actually, that was the understatement of the year. It was out of character for me to forget to set the timer when I made a soufflé at work, or to misfile a CD in my classic rock collection. To sleep with a man, and consequently get knocked up, even though I had no interest in having a relationship with him... now *that* was a departure.

"We just want to know who to buy cigars for, that's all." Marisol rested her chin on her hand and batted her eyes at me. "Come on, Lex. Spill it. Who's the lucky dad?"

This time Candace didn't shush her; instead she leaned forward in her seat and watched me closely.

I opened my mouth, not knowing what the hell I was going to say and not really sure how to articulate it, but the thundering feet of Candace's children interrupted me. Before I knew it, there were three children crawling all over us, each of them screaming in a different pitch. Candace's children—four-and-a-half year old Ellie, three-year-old Quentin, and eighteen-month-old Aubrey—redefined cute. It made me wonder if all of the cute genes had been used up in my family. Because, if so, my poor baby was screwed.

"Mommy, when's dinner? I'm starving!" Ellie announced at the top of her voice. She'd not spoken at a normal decibel since uttering her first word.

Candace bounced up from her seat, hiking the two little ones off of the table and onto her hips like a superhero. "Soon, soon. Where's Daddy?"

"He's watching the game." Ellie wound her tiny fingers into Marisol's long sheet of hair. "He said that the Seahawks are a bunch of friggin'—"

"Stop right there." Candace put a hand up and turned to the kitchen doorway. *"Brian!"*

Both Marisol and I jumped. "Ellie, darling, as much as I love you, could you get your hands out of my hair." Marisol untangled the little hands from her pride and joy. "You smell like peanut butter."

Ellie shoved a finger in her nose. "You're weird."

"Likewise." Marisol made a face. "Kids. Oy. How does she stand it?" She glanced down at my midriff. "Oh, whoops. Sorry."

The kitchen door swung open and Brian walked in, his tie loosened and collar unbuttoned. He plucked the baby off Candace's hip and picked a pea pod out of the stir-fry. "I lost track of them. All I did was blink, and they were gone."

Candace rolled her eyes and returned to stirring the food. "You sure it didn't have anything to do to with the Seahawks playing the Dolphins tonight?"

He shooed the kids out of the kitchen with promises of *Dora the Explorer* playing in the living room, then faced the table with a wide smile. "Marisol. How's it going? Working hard these days? You look tired."

"What?" Marisol turned to the nearby countertop and examined herself in the side of the stainless steel toaster. "I do not. Shut up."

Brian threw another pea pod into the air, catching it with his mouth. He and Marisol had a love/hate relationship that consisted of insults and the occasional crass joke. They mostly tolerated each other because of their connection to Candace, who'd introduced me to Marisol in college. But it wasn't until Marisol and I started our catering company, Eats & Sweets, that our lives became so intertwined. Now Marisol and I spent more time sitting around this kitchen table than we spent at our own places.

Brian laughed. "Made you look. Hey, Lex. Heard your good news. I guess congratulations are in order, eh?"

I smiled weakly. "Thanks."

"Does Patsy know yet?" As soon as he asked me, Candace slapped her forehead.

"She hasn't told Aunty Patsy yet, so you keep your mouth shut," she hissed.

"So, what's the scoop?" He sat down in the seat his wife abandoned. "We didn't even know you were dating anyone."

"Neither did she," Marisol snorted.

"Brian, would you grab the plates out of the cabinet?" Candace turned off the wok and tilted her head at me. "You're overwhelmed, aren't you?"

I cringed and looked down at my crackers. The smell of Chinese food, mixed with the weight of my newfound role as human incubator, and everyone's curiosity about the father of my offspring, contributed to a monster headache. As much as I wanted to answer my friends' questions, I couldn't. I just couldn't. In fact, simply thinking about how I got myself into this colossal pickle made me want to crawl into a pair of sweats and cry it out for a week. Or two.

My stomach roiled at the thought of pickles.

No more food analogies for a while, I thought to myself.

"Overwhelmed doesn't even begin to cover it." I stood up, the chair scraping along the tile floor noisily. "Listen, thanks for the crackers. I've got to go now."

"Oh, come on. Stay for dinner." Candace wiped her hands on a dishtowel and scooped me into her arms. "It'll be good for you. You're pale."

"Stop fussing." Marisol stood up and put her hands on her hips. "She's pale because she puked three times during our meeting with a bride-to-be today."

"It was food poisoning." I mumbled, pulling my sweater on.

"It was the baby." Candace rubbed my arms lovingly. "You poor thing. You've got morning sickness."

"It's not morning sickness. She's terrified. Good Lord, her whole life changed in the time it took her to piss on a stick." Marisol tossed her hair again.

"I've got a bug or something." I pulled away from my two best friends, who stood shaking their heads at me in unison. They weren't falling for my excuses. They knew better.

First off, Candace had been pregnant three times in four years and had her obstetrician on speed dial. And Marisol owned and operated a business with me, meaning she could sense my stress from fifty paces. And lastly, they were *both* right. Hands down, this had been one of the most stressful days of my life, topping the day my father died of an aneurysm when I was in eleventh grade, *and* the day I came home to discover that my husband had moved out while I was at work.

And it was only going to get worse.

Chapter Two

I took the folded blue paper from the nurse and smiled, even though the smell of her perfume made my stomach rock back and forth. It wasn't her fault. I felt nauseated by random smells lately. The other day, Marisol had opened a can of water chestnuts at work, and I'd vomited into the sink.

"Go ahead and get undressed from the waist down, and the doctor will be right in to see you." She nodded encouragingly, then slipped out of the examination room, leaving me with Candace, who bounced little Aubrey on her knee. The other two kids were in preschool, so Candace had deemed it the perfect time to introduce me to Dr. Haybee, obstetrician extraordinaire.

Dr. Haybee's office shared a building with Brian's ophthalmology practice. Apparently after six years of sharing a hallway and three pregnancies, Brian and Candace had become friends with the noble doctor. Now she'd made it her personal responsibility to guide every human with a uterus to his office.

"I already had a gynecologist," I muttered, unbuttoning my jeans.

Candace's nostrils flared. "You mean the old hag your mom and my mom both see? Yeah. She's the one who called to tell your mom when you went on the pill."

"Okay. So she's sort of…" My voice trailed off and I bit my lip.

"Dr. Smith has no respect for privacy laws." She pulled a bottle out of her diaper bag and popped it into the baby's mouth. "You'll like Dr. Haybee much better."

"Privacy shmivacy." I started to pull my pants down. "Hey, look away for a minute."

She shook her head. "You don't have any parts I haven't seen. We used to bathe together, remember?"

A memory of fighting with Candace over a rubber duck in my grandmother's bathtub while both of our mothers took pictures fleeted through my mind. I scrunched up my face. "That was twenty-five years ago."

"Oh, come on, Bump. Don't be so grumpy." Candace turned and faced the wall, then immediately whirled back around. "Oh, wait—"

"Hey!" I moved to cover my naked bits.

"Yeesh. Sorry." She faced the wall again. "What I was going to say was, isn't it funny that we call you Bump, and pretty soon you're going to have a big bump?"

Candace laughed at her epiphany, and I looked down at my still flat stomach despondently. My stomach would undoubtedly betray me soon and pop out like a volleyball. Or a beach ball. Or worse.

Sadly, she had a point. Having the last name of Baump had cursed me for thirty years. The kids in grade school called me *The Four Eyed Bump* for wearing coke bottle glasses. When I was a flat chested sixteen-year-old, they'd asked me, *Where's your bumps, Bump?* And in college, when spotted across the courtyard by a friend, I was often summoned by an ear-piercing cry of *BUUUUMP.*

I never liked my nickname. The irony that I would shortly be sporting a bump was just enough to make me loathe it.

"Are you decent?" Candace asked.

Settling myself onto the examination table, and ignoring the metal stirrups on either side, I did my best to cover my lap with the paper. "Yeah. All covered. Sort of. This thing leaves little to the imagination."

"Don't fret. Your OB will be so familiar with your girl bits after a few months that you'll be dropping your pants every time he walks in." Candace adjusted Aubrey on her lap, and offered me a wicked grin. "Of course, it helps that the doctor is hot."

My head snapped in her direction. "He's what?"

"Fletcher is hot." She shook her head. "Er, Dr. Haybee. Yeah, he's edible."

"You mean the man who is going to look at my unmentionables in a few minutes is hot?" I wanted to head for the hills and not come back. I could do it alone, couldn't I? Pioneer women had babies in the plains without prenatal care. Of course, those women weren't addicted to microwave popcorn and dependent on their DVRs, either, but I would manage.

"That doesn't freak you out, does it?" Candace giggled.

"No." I shifted underneath my paper. "Well, yeah. A little. Or maybe a lot. Okay, a lot."

"Oh come on. You've seen plenty of gynos in your lifetime." Aubrey popped the bottle out of her mouth and sat up on her mother's lap, appearing refreshed. "It shouldn't bother you that the doctor is young, cute, and single."

"He's single, too?" I cringed. "All the other doctors have been women, or much older than me, or married."

"Now's not the time to get shy, Lexie," Candace teased. "Being shy certainly didn't get you into this situation."

"You sound like my mother." I gritted my teeth.

"Sorry." Candace frowned at me. "I just wish you'd tell me who the dad is. That's all. I won't tell anyone. Not even Brian. And especially not Marisol. She'll go crazy with information like that—"

"It was immaculate conception," I said flatly.

Candace narrowed her cerulean eyes at me. I'd always envied those eyes. She'd inherited them from our mothers, who'd once been referred to in high school as the "blue eyed twinsies." She'd also gotten their blonde hair, another reason why I'd snarled with jealousy on more than one occasion as a child. I was blessed with my father's feathery, flyaway hair that was the same color as a new penny, and had his brown eyes, too. I'd eventually learned to control my Muppet hair by keeping it cut short and edgy, rather than trying to grow it long and luxurious the way Candace and Marisol did. So what if they looked like a couple of glamour-pusses, and I was their geeky, red headed tag-along. I told myself I didn't mind. Anymore.

"What are you doing noticing Dr. Haybee's hotness, anyway?" I scolded her before she could press the subject further. "I'm going to tell Brian."

She didn't react, and I hadn't expected her too. Candace and Brian met in an economics class at Eastern Washington University fourteen years ago, and hadn't left each other's side since. They'd been married by Pastor Irm in the Presbyterian Church twelve days after their college graduation, and when he went to medical school in South Dakota, she'd worked at a diner in Sioux Falls to pay for their tiny apartment. They finished each other's sentences, picked out each other's clothes and found the perfect balance between friends and lovers.

It was sickening, really.

"Go ahead, tell him. He knows already. Fletcher comes to our house for Monday night football every few weeks." She sighed and straightened her sleek blonde ponytail.

I watched as she turned the pages of the cardboard book patiently with her daughter and felt a tug in my chest. My hand instinctively went to my belly, and warmth spread under my palm.

There was a quick knock at the door, and when it opened, most of the—well, *all* of the—air in my lungs released in one long whoosh.

I'd been expecting someone handsome. After all, Candace and Brian were an extremely handsome couple. He was half Asian, so with his almond-shaped eyes and chiseled cheekbones, and her golden hair and perky boobs, they had the whole modern-American couple thing happening. Most of their friends were doctors and nurses, professionals and suit-wearing types. Lots of wayfarer glasses, and monochromatic shirt and tie sets.

But Dr. Haybee went past handsome. In fact, he went so far past handsome he was down the road and around the bend.

His doctor's coat was hanging open to reveal a worn denim shirt and a pair of cargo khakis. He was tan. Not overly tan, like one of those Jersey Beach freaks, or whatever that show was called—not that I ever watched it— but perfectly sun-kissed like he'd spent the weekend outside. Doing yard work. With his shirt off.

His hair was blond streaked with platinum, probably the result of a summer spent on a beach somewhere, and it was tousled into a disheveled "*I need a haircut, but I'm too busy wakeboarding and mountain biking to care*" look. When he raised his eyes off the manila folder full of my medical facts—height, last menstrual cycle—and, gulp—*weight*—I noticed that his eyes were the most crystal aquamarine blue I'd ever seen. They were the exact same color of a Tiffany jewelry box. And, as if I weren't ready to howl like a dog in heat already, when he opened his mouth to greet me, his deep voice positively oozed charm with its Southern accent.

"You must be Lexie. Hi, I'm Fletcher Haybee. How are you?"

"I… I… uh…"

My brain had shut off. I was sitting there, naked from the waist down, covered in a glorified quicker picker upper, staring at the best-looking man I'd ever seen.

"She's fine." Candace snickered.

The lovely doctor's eyes brightened. "Candace? What's up? Is this your sister?"

"Cousin. She just found out she's pregnant." Candace nudged me. "Say hello, Lex."

"Hello, Lex. Er, Dr. Haybee." I blinked a few times and focused on the tee shirt underneath his worn denim button down.

Holy hell, it was a vintage Aerosmith tee shirt! If there had been water in the examination room, he could have walked on it.

"Call me Fletcher." His accent made my toes, clad only in blue and white striped socks with dancing hippos on the heels (what was I thinking?) curl deliciously. "Any cousin of Candace and Brian's is a friend of mine."

I ignored Candace's knowing grin as I tried to put on my game face. Well, as much of a game face as I could have without *any pants on*. "You… you don't look like a doctor."

"Thank you. I take that as a compliment." He grinned and the corners of his eyes crinkled. I swear to God a ray of sunshine busted through the roof, illuminating him.

"He's the best OB in town." Candace announced proudly. "Remember when I had preeclampsia with Ellie's pregnancy and had bed rest?"

I peeled my eyes away from Fletcher. "Uh huh."

"Fletcher did all of the appointments in my last trimester at our house." She beamed. "How many doctors do house calls these days?"

Glancing back at Fletcher, who was nodding humbly, I replied, "Not many."

He laughed, and the deep, rumbling sound made the hair on the back of my neck stand at attention. "That's just one of the perks of being friends with your obstetrician."

I was staring at him. I couldn't help it. How did I miss this guy through all three of Candace's pregnancies? Why hadn't she dragged me to this office sooner?

Say when I wasn't pregnant and my face wasn't the same shade of grey as a gas station bathroom?

Fletcher put down my file and approached me. "Well, Lexie, it's nice to meet you."

"It's nice to meet you, too." We shook hands, and I bit the insides of my cheeks.

"My nurse tested the urine sample you left in the restroom, and as you know, you're pregnant. Congratulations." He tucked his hands into his pockets. "Otherwise, your white cell count looked good, and there wasn't too much protein in your urine, so that's great. Was this a planned pregnancy?"

I swallowed and ignored Candace's eyes probing the side of my face. "No."

His expression softened. "Do you want to discuss options? Are you planning to parent the child?"

"Yes. Of course." I tucked my hair behind my ears. "I always hoped to have children. Just didn't plan on doing it alone."

Fletcher appeared surprised. "Oh, you'll be a single mom?"

"Yes. Unless you'd like to marry me." I mumbled that last part.

"Excuse me?" he asked.

"Nothing!" I squeaked.

I fought the urge to slap myself on the forehead, and looked away from his bright eyes. There was something really wrong with me if I was this attracted to my obstetrician. I mean, within a matter of minutes, he was going to be looking at my crotch, for Pete's sake. And not in a *Fifty Shades of Grey* way, either. Argh.

"I'll have my receptionist give you some information about some local single mother support groups. That might be a great outlet for you." Fletcher made a note on my chart, then gestured to the papered examination table behind me. "Why don't you lay back, and I can do the examination."

"Oh, um, okay." I looked at Candace dumbly, who gestured for me to lie down. A wave of self-consciousness rolled over me.

The last time I'd been partially unclothed in front of a man, I'd been drinking overpriced merlot and watching made-for-TV movies. My buzz had made me feel invincible. I most certainly did not feel invincible on Fletcher's examination table. I felt unbearably naked, and suddenly aware of every ounce of cellulite and every freckle on my ultra-white skin. I wish I'd had the good sense to get a decent spray tan before coming to the obstetrician's office.

"It says in the medical records you had transferred that you had your breast examination just four months ago. So I won't need to do that today." Fletchers voice was soothing and calm, and would have made a normal woman feel relaxed as they lay there with their knees clamped together.

Unfortunately, I'm not a normal woman.

A plethora of off color jokes involving breast examinations came to mind as I lay there, his warm hands touching my calves. I'd always been the person that laughed inappropriately at funerals. During Speech 103 in college, when Professor Lidgerwood used the work rectify four times in one sentence,

I'd been the one to make cheesy jokes. When my mother passed gas during Easter services at church two years ago, I'd been the one with tears rolling down my face. The idea of Dr. Haybee giving me a breast examination was almost too much to handle.

"If you could just put your feet into the stirrups, that would be great."

I squeezed my eyes shut as he carefully guided my feet into the metal frames.

Candace leaned close to my face to whisper, "What's wrong?"

"Nothing." My voice came out tight since I was holding my breath.

"Are you uncomfortable?" she whispered.

"You could say that." I nodded, trying hard not to move any muscles from the waist down. The last thing I needed was to fart in Dr. Hottie's face.

Fletcher's head popped up between my knees, sending the paper towel fluttering. I scrambled to catch it and put it back down over my bits as he tilted his head to the side. "You okay, Lexie? Are my hands cold?"

I giggled maniacally, then snorted. "No. You're fine."

When his blonde head sank back out of sight, I turned my face to Candace and dropped my voice as low as it would go. "A little bit of warning would have been nice!"

She came even closer, bringing Aubrey with her. "Warning about what?"

I dramatically rolled my eyes from her face, to the area where Fletcher was gathering his speculum—and other such torture devices—and then back up again. "Him."

Candace's nostrils flared. "Sorry," she hissed. "I didn't think it would freak you out this bad."

"It's not freaking me out, I'm just—"

"You know, if you two keep whispering over there, I'm gonna start to feel self-conscious." Fletcher grinned at us from under my leg. "Now, Lexie, if you could just relax your knees a bit, that would be great."

Drawing a deep breath, I let my knees fall apart approximately three inches.

"That's great. Now a little more..." He drew out the word *little*, and patted my foot affectionately.

I looked up at the ceiling, and let my knees separate another two inches. Lord, how long had it been since I'd gotten a bikini wax?

"Seriously, Lex. Loosen up." Candace stifled a laugh. "You need to let the man do his thing."

"Could you put it differently, please?" I hissed.

Fletcher's warm hands went to my knees, which he gently pushed them apart, before settling down in my, er, *bits and pieces* quietly. Grimacing, I stared up at the ceiling and tried to ignore the humiliation creeping up on me. This was the least seductive moment of my life, making the day I had to help my mother shave her legs because she'd broken her wrist seem like a moonlit walk on the beach.

Candace snorted softly. "Sorry."

Once I was finally splayed like a turkey ready to be stuffed, Fletcher pressed on my lower abdomen. "Okay, now. Just relax. That's right. Now, I'm going to insert the speculum. Hold tight. It might be chilly."

The moment it hit my body, I yelped and scooted away from Fletcher's face. "Wow. Did you soak it in ice?"

"Just for you," he joked. His voice was muffled, which made it even more mortifying.

"Nobody likes an OB with a sense of humor." I caught myself clenching my legs together, then reluctantly let them drift apart again.

"No humor. Got it." His hands touched the backs of my knees carefully. "If you could scoot forward, that would be awesome."

"Right-o." I obeyed, dragging the tissue paper underneath me, resulting in a loud tear. As soon as the room went quiet again, my stomach growled noisily. It sounded like a caged animal.

Candace covered her mouth and looked away as she giggled.

Good grief, this is humiliating...

"Good job. You'll feel a tiny scrape now." He laughed politely when I jumped a second time. "You're doing fine, Lexie. Now I'm just going to check the shape of your uterus." I started counting ceiling tiles, and got to eighteen before he stood up from his rolling stool and pulled his latex gloves off with a snap. "Your uterus is just slightly tilted. That may make delivery complicated, but I don't anticipate anything serious."

I nodded and slapped my knees back together. Just because the good doctor's face had just been down there, didn't mean I needed to keep it out there for pictures and tours. "I remember my old gynecologist mentioning that once."

He made a note on my chart, then rolled a portable sonogram machine out from behind the examination table. "Why don't we take a look and do some measurements?"

I took my feet out of the stirrups and crossed my legs at the knees, and then the ankles for good measure. "You can do that?"

Candace chuckled. "Of course he can. That machine is for ultrasounds."

"No, I know that. But you can do an ultrasound on it already? Isn't it the size of a pea?" I watched as Fletcher plucked a bottle of blue jelly out of a warmer and approached me.

"It depends on how far along you are. It could be the size of a pea, or maybe even a grape. We'll take a look and see how many weeks pregnant you are, and then I'll show you a picture."

Pressing my lips together tightly, I didn't mention that I already knew exactly how pregnant I was, right down to the hour, what was playing on the television in the background, and what bra I was wearing. It was just classified information that I didn't want to discuss. Scratch that, *couldn't* discuss.

Fletcher rolled up the hem of my tee shirt, lowered the paper towel on my abdomen, and squirted a hefty dose of the jelly onto my skin. The moment the wand-like instrument touched my skin, the sound of static and a soft *whoosh whoosh* filled the room. Next to me, baby Aubrey hushed and Candace released a tiny gasp, before looking at me with tear filled eyes.

"It's real." She breathed. "This is really happening, Lex. You're pregnant."

"You didn't believe it?" I asked.

She laughed. "This just makes it all so real."

The whooshing sound filled my ears. "What is that sound?"

"That's your baby's heartbeat." Fletcher moved the wand, and the sound intensified. "Very strong. About one hundred sixty beats a minute." He turned the monitor screen around so that I could see what he was looking at. Fletched pointed at a dark shadow on the snowy screen that was the exact shape of a kidney bean, with a tiny flashing burst of white in its center. "You see here? That's the fetus, and that flash is the heart beating. You look to be about ten weeks and two days along."

The lights in the room dimmed and the only thing I saw was the kidney bean. No other sound in the room filled my ears except the soft thrushing of my child's heart, and without warning my own heart started to thud in unison. Every single cell in my body squeezed at the same time, and I forgot about Candace, Aubrey, the secret surrounding the baby's father, and even the hot doctor.

The only thing I could focus on was that flashing heart.

I loved my child. I loved it even though I didn't even know it. I loved it even though my entire life, my entire world, was changing from right side up to wrong side down. I loved it even though its father wanted nothing to do with it.

I was going to be a mother.

Chapter Three

Dinner at my mother's house was always an experience. From the time I was little, she collected Cabbage Patch dolls. The collection started out in my honor. She said she was gathering the dolls for my sake, her only daughter, her namesake—my full name was Alexandria Patsy Baump—but it became clear by the time I'd started junior high that the collection was hers and hers only.

Cabbage Patch Kids in every size, shape, and color, with every outfit imaginable. Some were preemies with tiny tufts of fake hair atop their plastic heads. Others were kids sporting scooters or skateboards. From a chef's hat and coat, to an astronaut, all of my mother's Cabbage Patch Dolls were dressed to the nines, and arranged on the wall-to-wall shelves of her living room as if they'd been frozen mid-activity. Tiny outfits of sunny yellow, bright blue, and varying shades of pink adorned their paunchy bodies, and a thin layer of dust covered each of their ornately styled yarn heads.

Most people in our small corner of Spokane knew Patsy Baump's house was not for the faint of heart. When you entered her house, you had to be prepared for tens of thousands of eyes to watch your every move, and to feel utterly creeped out as you used the bathroom while a horde of beady-eyed doll children observed you.

"Lexie, dear, you're late. What gives?" my mother asked when I walked into her house.

I'd been walking on air after my sonogram, putting the finishing touches on the pate squares I'd been making with a silly grin splayed on my face. So many emotions to sort through. Excitement and anticipation over impending motherhood. Trepidation about the big news I had to share with my family over a bowl of my mother's famous cheddar ham soup. And the surprising crush on my obstetrician I was now sporting, despite the fact that he was well aware I'd been too sick to shave my legs properly in weeks.

"Sorry." I pulled off my coat and threw it over a doll's head. "I worked late. I had a doctor's appointment this morning that I had to make up time for."

"Don't cover up Nathaniel's head." My mother plucked my jacket off of the yarn-covered head and patted it lovingly.

I forgot to mention that each of my mother's dolls had names. First and middle. And each of them had the last name of Baump. Naturally.

She frowned at me, her mouth pursing. "Why did you go to the doctor? Are you getting those headaches again? I told you to have a CAT scan."

"No. Not headaches." I hugged my mom and looked around. "Where is everybody?"

"They're around." She crossed through the living room to the kitchen where Corbin and Andrea were diligently chopping and sautéing. My younger brother, Darren, was furiously punching buttons on his phone, presumably texting some poor girl who would fall for his charm then get left in the dust within a matter of weeks.

"Who's your latest victim?" I bumped his chair as I passed.

Darren flashed a twenty-tooth grin and I rolled my eyes. He'd inherited the blond hair, blue eyes, and undeniable good looks that had served so many in my family well. His man-beauty was so dazzling that at times it was easy for even me to forget that at twenty-five years old, he was a college dropout who worked at a cell phone store in the mall and chased women who were barely old enough to have a legal drink. Darren had no intention of ever settling down, which added to the pressure my mother thrust upon me to remarry and procreate as quickly as possible. In my last birthday card, she'd suggested freezing my eggs.

Well, at least I had the procreation thing in the bag. That was something.

"Her name is Pandi, and she's a dancer." He announced this with pride. As if he were announcing he'd caught the Loch Ness Monster.

"What kind of a name is Pandi? Is she a large black and white bear?" I snatched a piece of stale candy out of the dish sitting on my mother's counter and popped it in my mouth, instantly inducing a wave of nausea. Fifteen-year-old ribbon candy was officially off the list of edible first trimester foods.

"No. She's stacked, though." Darren waggled his eyebrows and went back to his texting.

"Ugh. You're a pig." I flared my nostrils at him. "Mom, how did you manage to raise such a pig?"

"Breast milk," she announced definitively, stirring the pot of soup.

"Geez, Ma! We're about to eat." Darren twisted his handsome face.

I heard Corbin and Andrea snickering and poked them both on the shoulder. "Don't encourage her. I don't want to hear about Mom's boobs any more than the rest of you."

My mother gave me a pointed look over the top of the pink-lensed glasses. "Ha, ha, ha. Laugh it up, but it's a fact. He's the only one of you kids I didn't breastfeed. Now look at him. Completely unable to commit."

"I can commit," Darren said defensively. "I just choose not to."

Corbin looked up from the lettuce he was chopping. "So what kind of dancer is this Pandi-bear?"

Andrea raised an eyebrow at him. "I think we both know the answer to that."

"I'm with your wife on this one." I leaned on the countertop and snatched a piece of celery.

"She studied ballet. Before." Darren's phone beeped and he chuckled quietly at whatever the text said.

"Before what?" I asked around my bite.

"Before dancing in the cage at the Lusty Lass." Corbin nudged me.

"Would you two stop it?" My mother snapped a towel at us. "She could be *the one*."

"So you want Darren to marry a stripper, Ma?" Corbin laughed.

"It's honest work." She shook her head.

I poked my oldest brother in the ribs. "You just wish you moved as good as the girls who work at the Lusty Lass."

Corbin stared off in the distance dreamily. "That's the truth."

My mom and Andrea exchanged a smirk, and I rolled my eyes. Like me, Corbin inherited our late father's red hair and fair skin. Unfortunately for both of us, we'd skipped the rhythm gene as well, so it was inevitable that we were always the whitest and least coordinated people on the dance floor at every family wedding. Sad, really.

"I think you all need to support your little brother." My mother ignored the face Corbin made at me. "You never know. This Candi—"

"Pandi," Andrea corrected.

"Pandi," she said with a shake of her head. "Could be your sister-in-law someday—"

"Don't get ahead of yourself, Ma," Darren called.

"And since you aren't dating anyone, *Lexie*, someone has to give me grandkids." She hoisted the soup pot off of the stovetop and lugged it to the table, nodding at Corbin and Andrea. "No offense, dears."

My brother's and his wife's faces both dropped, making my heart clench. When my mother whisked out of the room, leaving behind the faded aroma of Red Door perfume, Corbin rubbed Andrea on the back. My hands instinctively went to my lower abdomen. It felt like something warm and glowing was nestled deeply in there. It felt wrong for my brother and his wife to crave parenthood as vehemently as they did, and I'd managed to stumble upon my pregnancy the same way others discovered that they'd found a crumpled twenty-dollar bill in the bottom of their washing machine.

"Come on," Andrea said, wiping her nose. She plucked the ceramic bowl of salad up and followed my mother's trail to the dining room. "Dinner's about to start."

We sat down around the table, Darren's thumbs furiously punching his phone while we all started passing the food around.

"Darren Kyle Baump, put that phone down and pay attention to your family," my mother barked from her spot at the head of the table. We all served ourselves and dug in.

"Mom, the soup is great as always." Corbin wiped his mouth with a napkin. "When are you going to share your recipe with me so I can make it for Andrea at home?"

My mother shifted in her seat, and she patted her blonde helmet proudly. Flattery got people everywhere with my mom. "It's a secret."

"I realize that." Corbin took another bite and closed his eyes. "But I'm thirty-five now. Don't you think I'm old enough to be trusted with the sacred family recipes?"

Andrea nodded. "Like the pumpkin cheesecake recipe."

I pointed my fork at my mother. "And the potato salad."

Darren stopped shoveling food into his mouth, and looked up from his bowl. "And the finger jello."

Corbin stared at him. "Of all of Mom's recipes, you want the one for finger jello?"

"Finger jello is awesome." Darren wiggled his eyebrows. "Jello shots, dude."

Rolling my eyes, I went back to my soup. "You're a child."

"No, I'm not." He shoved another bite in. "A child cannot legally drink. I, on the other hand, *can*." Darren focused his attention on me. "Why are you acting so old, anyway, Lex? It's not like you've got all these responsibilities to keep you home. You should come out with me and Pandi sometime. Do a few shots yourself and loosen up."

"I don't need to loosen up." I put my spoon down slowly. My stomach had turned into merry-go-round. Good Lord, was I ever going to be able to eat a meal without wanting to yak again?

"Yes, you do." Darren laughed. "You're wound tight. Seriously, come out with me this weekend. My friend, Spoons, thinks you're cute."

"Spoons?" Andrea chuckled. "Do I even want to know where someone gets the nickname of *Spoons*?"

Corbin choked on his soup. "I say go for it, Lex. Go out with Spoons, and let Pandi and Darren show you a good time."

"Do you have any friends with normal names?" I asked my little brother, who'd pulled his phone out again, and was texting under the table.

"Yes," he said. "Barry. Joe. Axel. Rosco."

Corbin, Andrea, and I all dissolved into giggles, and my mom just shook her head. "Your friends have terrible names," she sighed. "Lexie, did you know that Andrea and Corbin bought a new house to flip on the South Hill?"

The South Hill was one of Spokane's most coveted neighborhoods. With its hills, mature pine and maple trees lining the center of the roads in between the lanes, and turn of the century homes, I'd been dreaming about living there for years. "Really?" I asked, pushing my bowl back. "No kidding, guys? Where at?"

Corbin squeezed his wife's hand. "It's on Elm, and it is completely made of brick, with paned windows and a tiny courtyard out front."

"It's gorgeous. Apparently the owner died five years ago, and it's been empty ever since. His children finally decided to sell, since it's gone into such disrepair." Andrea grinned.

She and Corbin's reputation in the world of real estate around these parts was impressive, to say the least. The local realtors loved telling their buyers that they were selling a "Baump Home." The name was synonymous with exceptional quality and high-end finishing. No corners cut by Corbin and Andrea. They took pride in their work, and it showed.

"We're going to bring it back to life." Corbin nodded affirmatively. "The plan is to have it done in three or four months. Why don't you buy it, Lex? That should be enough time for you to put in notice at your apartment and arrange for financing."

"It's the perfect house for you." Andrea helped herself to more soup. "It's a buyers' market right now, you know."

My mother laughed breezily. "What? You want Alexandria to buy a house? On her own? Alone?"

Darren looked up from his phone. "That means the same thing, Ma."

"Hush." She scolded him. "Now, Lexie, you're not seriously considering this, are you?"

I gaped at her. "I just found out about it. I'm not seriously considering anything right now. Don't you think it's a good idea?" An image of the little flashing heart I'd seen on my ultrasound earlier, and my chest expanded. "I'm thirty. It's probably time I put down some roots somewhere."

My mother waved my words away like a fly. "Oh, shush. You're not even married."

My cheeks heated. "Last time I checked, they give home loans to single women, too."

"I know, but you wouldn't want to be a homeowner without a man around." She gestured all around her. "It's a horrible headache to have something need repair with no husband around to fix it."

"Oh, come on. You just call Pastor Irm to fix it," Darren said, not bothering to look up.

"I do not." Embarrassment pinked my mother's round cheeks.

My mother tried very unsuccessfully to hide that she was in love with the pastor, and had been for a long time. Yet she was on every committee the church offered that required her to work directly with the pastor, and ate dinner with him at least twice a week.

My brothers and I referred to it as evidence. She referred to it as stewardship. We *all* silently agreed not to discuss it.

"Well, we could help Lexie if something went wrong," Corbin said.

"That's right." Andrea smiled at me across the table. "What's the point in having two carpenters in the family if you don't use them?"

"But you didn't get your first house until you'd married my Corbin." My mother blinked a few times. "Would you really have wanted to do it alone?"

Andrea shrugged. "If that's the way my life had turned out, then yes."

My mom snorted. "It's ludicrous. Come on, Lexie. Find yourself a good man. Someone much more mature than *that Nate*, and settle down. You'll get a house and a gaggle of kids to care for."

I ignored the way she'd said my ex-husband's name like it was dripping in acid and burning her tongue, and smiled patiently at her. "Did you just use the term 'gaggle'?"

"Yes, I did." She took another bite. "Now, let's talk about you. What have you been up to lately, dear?"

All eyes rolled over to me, and I felt the sonogram pictures in my jeans pocket start to burn a hole. I was on the verge of dropping a double whammy on my family, and it was contributing to my nausea. My mother's reaction, which I was predicting would be exceptionally theatrical, would be nothing compared to the disappointment on Corbin's and Andrea's faces.

"Well, like I said when I got here." I swallowed, and avoided my mother's probing eyes. "I went to the doctor today."

"What for?" my mother demanded.

"That's all you have to tell us?" Darren rolled his eyes. "Seriously. Get out more."

"Can it," I hissed. "So anyway, there's something I need to tell you all."

Corbin leaned forward, resting his elbows on the tabletop. "Are you okay?"

"Jesus, Mary, and Joseph in Jerusalem, she's got cancer!" My mother pressed a hand to her ample bosom and choked on immediate tears. "I knew it. *I knew it.* When your dad had the aneurysm, I knew that it would strike one of you kids next. I just knew it."

"She didn't have an aneurysm," Darren pointed out. "She's sitting right here."

"Then it's cancer!" Mom bellowed.

Andrea jumped out of her chair and went to put her arm around my mom's shoulders. "Shhh, Patsy. Relax. Lexie hasn't even told us what she went to the doctor for."

"Or what kind of a doctor she went to see." Darren scoffed, grabbing another roll. "She could have gone to a woman doctor or something."

My mother yowled. "Ovarian cancer!"

My head flopped into my hands and I grit my teeth. "Seriously, Mom. I don't have cancer, all right? Can you take a breath and let me finish my damn announcement?"

Her tears immediately stopped. "There's no need for language."

"Just... everybody relax, all right?" Corbin touched my arm, offering a one-shouldered shrug, as if to say, *our mom...what a looney, right?* "Go ahead, Lexie."

Well, here goes nothing, I thought to myself, my hand going into my jeans pocket, and holding the picture underneath the tabletop the same way my brother had tried to hide his phone. "Actually, Darren was right. I went to the *woman* doctor."

"Really? Gross. Don't share that with us," Darren said around a mouthful of roll.

"Grow up," Corbin said in his most fatherly voice, which he'd been perfecting since our own dad's death thirteen years earlier.

"What's going on?" My mother dissolved into fake tears again. "Ovarian cyst? I've had three myself, and they're horribly painful. Endometriosis? Your Aunt Dory had that. Oh my word, I always knew one of you children would be sick, and I'd have to care for you. Don't worry, dear, I'll be here for you. You can move back into your room, and—"

I shook my head. "I'm not moving back in. I don't have an ovarian cyst or endometriosis, either."

"Well, for hell's sake, what's going on with you?" she demanded, pushing up her glasses and turning off her tears for a second time.

Darren sniggered. "No need for language."

"Hush." She swatted her napkin at him, and knocked a roll out of his hand.

Corbin took off his wire-rimmed glasses and rubbed his eyes. "I think we all just need to calm—"

"I'm pregnant."

My voice seemed to echo, despite the walls being lined with plush toys. Maybe it just sounded that way in my head. I couldn't be sure.

All sound, all movement, in the house ceased, and every single pair of eyes locked on my face.

Shakily, I brought the picture of my kidney-bean-like baby out from under the table, and placed it next to the pot of still-hot cheddar ham soup. It felt like my mother's house had slipped into a time/space continuum. Nobody moved. Nobody spoke. I was pretty sure nobody was breathing, either.

Darren was the first to break the unbearably uncomfortable silence. "Finally someone else is the family screw up." And with that, he stood up, tucked his cell phone into his pants pocket, and kissed the top of my mother's unmoving head. "Thanks for dinner, Ma."

As soon as the backdoor shut behind him, my mother blinked a few times, as if coming out of a trance. Her cheeks were the exact same shade of pink as her circa nineteen eighties glasses lenses, and her forefinger came down onto the tabletop with a definitive thump.

"Where did you get this picture?" she asked hoarsely.

"My obstetrician. Dr. Haybee." My eyes flicked over to Corbin, who'd put his hand over his wife's, and was now looking down at the remainder of his soup with an ill expression.

You're not the only one, buddy, I lamented silently.

"I thought you saw *my* gynecologist." My mother's voice was low and precise. "Nobody told me you'd switched."

I sat up straight in my chair and laced my fingers together. "No, Mom. I'm going to see Dr. Haybee through my pregnancy. Candace loves him, and he's friends with Brian."

"You're going to see him through…" She pressed her lips together. "Your pregnancy?"

One nod. Slow and steady. "Yes, Mom. My pregnancy."

Her eyes flicked to my unadorned ring finger. "Did you get married to someone and not tell me?"

I almost laughed. Almost. "Of course not."

"Who's the father?"

This was the first time I'd heard my big brother's voice since dropping the bomb, and it sounded positively deadly.

I looked at him. "There is no father."

"I'm not playing games with you," he repeated carefully, apparently in full-on protective older brother mode. "Who is the father?"

What next, the shotgun and a forced engagement? I straightened my shoulders and jutted my chin out. This was going to be a hard bone for my friends and family to stop chewing on. That much was clear already. "There is no father. He isn't in the picture. He won't be in the picture. You should erase him from the scenario completely. I have."

"He sure as hell will be, once I'm through with him," Corbin growled.

I did my best to return my big brother's icy stare. "No. He won't. And the subject is off limits from now on. *Is that clear?*"

We had a silent standoff lasting for around ten seconds before my mother stood up. Her chair fell backwards into a Cabbage Patch Kid wearing denim overalls. "Alexandria Patsy Baump! You mean to tell me that you're knocked up and not even going to marry the father!?"

"Yes." My voice was shaking. Tears started to fill my eyes like a clogged gutter. "That's exactly what I'm saying."

"What am I going to tell the Disciples of Christ Committee? Or the Bible study class? They're not going to let me stay in the presidency if I've got an unwed daughter who's having a child all alone! What kind of an example will that be?" She started pacing, knocking down two more dolls and not even bothering to pick them up. She was really upset with me this time. "What will Pastor Irm say? It's bad enough that you're divorced, now you're going to be some sort of single mother?"

"Mom, *you're* a single mother." My voice came out shriller than I would have preferred.

"Because my husband was taken from me by the good Lord, not because I exercised poor judgment on a lonely night!" she shrieked, throwing her arms out.

My head jerked backwards like I'd been slapped.

Andrea gasped, her first sound in a good five minutes.

"Okay, that's enough. Mom, sit down, so we can all talk about this." Corbin took his glasses off and rubbed his eyes again. "Aw, hell, Lex. I thought you were going to say you had cancer."

My mouth dropped open. "You wanted me to have cancer?"

Andrea jumped in, tucking her hair behind her ears. "Of course he didn't. I think we should start at the beginning. So…how far along are you?"

I drew in a shaky breath. "Ten weeks and a few days."

"And you'll raise the baby yourself?" There was a spark of jealousy in her brown eyes, but she kept it at bay and forced a small smile.

"Yes. I'm…" I looked at my mother, and my tears finally spilled over. "I'm happy. I know it's crazy, and I know it will be difficult. But when

Nate left me, and Marisol and I started the catering business, I honestly thought I would never be a mother." My hands went to my flat tummy. "This is my chance, you guys."

My mother watched me with a frown. "You have no idea what you're getting yourself into. You have no idea how hard it is to raise a child with two parents, let alone one. You're being foolish."

"You know what?" I stood up from the table, taking my picture back, and tucking it into my back pocket. "I'm ready to learn. I'm ready to be responsible for someone other than myself. And..." I wiped my nose on my napkin. "I really hope you'll all support me."

I looked down at Corbin and Andrea, who both looked like they'd fallen off their ladders at work and had the wind knocked out of their lungs. "I never meant to hurt you guys. I didn't plan for this to happen."

Corbin nodded. "I know, Lex."

I turned my gaze to my mother. "I'm gonna go now. I feel like I'm going to hurl, and I think you need some time to process this." I started towards the door, and nobody made a move to stop me. Just as I was about to turn the handle, I looked back at my mother, who was still standing at the end of the table with a hand pressed to her chest.

"I'm sorry, Ma."

Chapter Four

"Hey you! I didn't know you were coming." Candace held her front door open so I could enter, and I skulked past her with my head hanging low.

"Thanks," I mumbled. My nose was still stuffed from weeping as I drove the eight miles between my mother's house and hers.

"Hey, have you been crying?" She shut the door behind me. "What's wrong?"

"It's nothing." I crossed through her foyer to her kitchen amidst a chorus of cheers exploding in the next room. "I'm sorry. Do you have company? I can come by after work tomorrow."

Candace just shook her head and pointed at a chair. A tray covered in a variety of meats and cheeses rested on the table. "Sit down. You're always welcome here. Have a snack."

Eyeballing the meats, I tried not to inhale and sat as far away from the tray as possible. Another rouse of applause came from the living room. "Seriously. Did I come at a bad time?"

She rolled her eyes. "No. The Seahawks are spanking the Patriots. Brian and all of his friends are losing their minds."

"It's a miracle." I picked up a napkin and wiped my eyes. "When is Brian going to accept that the Seahawks suck?"

"I *heard* that." Brian's voice echoed in the living room, amidst the chatter of all of his friends.

"Sorry, Bri." I laughed.

"They're not sucking today." Candace sat down across from me. "So." She propped her chin on her fist. "You told your mom tonight."

I looked at her strangely. "How did you know?"

She shrugged. "Aunt Patsy called my mom. My mom called me. She was ticked off that I already knew your big news."

"Sorry to disappoint her." Aunt Dory liked to be the bearer of any and all juicy gossip. I looked at the platter wearily. "Can you move that?"

"You know, if you eat some protein, you'd probably feel better."

My nostrils flared. "I don't think so. Nothing makes me feel better."

"That just means you have a very healthy baby in there." Candace's eyes sparkled.

I smiled despite my roiling stomach. "Healthy or not, I'd like to be able to get through a meal. I couldn't even eat my mother's soup."

"What kind? Patsy makes such good soup."

"Cheddar ham." I closed my eyes and willed the memory out of my head. Even just remembering the smell made me ill.

"Oh, darn. That's good soup." She plucked a slice of summer sausage off of the tray and popped it in her mouth. "How long's it been since you've eaten a full meal?"

I thought for a moment. The days since finding out I was pregnant had started to blur together. I'd eaten. I was sure of it. I mean, so what if most of my bites were tiny tastes while I was preparing food at Sweets & Eats, to make sure I'd not over-salted the chicken salad, or made the crème brulee to sweet. That was eating, wasn't it? So what if every time I smelled anything resembling a cucumber, I ran to the restroom with my hand cupped over my mouth? I'd been eating. Sort of.

Oh hell, who was I kidding? It'd been weeks since I'd consumed a meal. Which was a real drag, considering how much I loved food.

"A long time," I confessed.

The men in the living room erupted in cheers.

"Here." Candace plucked a few pieces of each kind of meat off of the tray and placed them on a napkin for me. "Why don't you try to eat something, and we'll talk about how it went at your mom's place?"

I accepted her offering and nibbled on a slice of salami. "It went down in a ball of flames. You already know that."

She nodded. "Tell me what happened."

"Well, for starters, I think my family would have been happier if I'd announced I have cancer." I took another bite and chewed it slowly. "My mother cried. And accused me of having a one-night stand."

One of Candace's eyebrows rose high on her face. "Well, didn't you?"

I looked down at the meat in my hand. "No. Well, sort of. But not really."

"Good Lord, I can't take it anymore. Marisol and I are losing our minds." She balled her hands into fists. "Can't you *please* tell us who it was? This whole vow of secrecy thing is really making me nuts. Spill it."

Shaking my head, I took another bite. "No. It's not up for discussion."

She snatched a piece of ham off of the tray and chomped on it furiously. "Marisol thinks it was the president. She says that's the only reason why you would have to keep it such a secret."

I glared at my cousin. "The president? Really? And when in the world would I have had time to fly to Washington DC to have an affair with the president?"

Candace threw up her hands. "I don't know! Then the mayor. The mayor of Spokane? Or the governor of Washington State."

"Would you stop it, please?" I sighed, exasperated. "First off, the governor of Washington is a woman. You voted for her. And second, I don't even know the mayor. Now stop."

"Whatever. But don't think I'm letting this go."

"Oh, I don't expect you will." I forced a smile. "New subject."

She chewed her ham. "So once they knew you didn't have cancer, how did they take it?"

I shuddered. "The Patsy Baump drama was on high tonight. She said that she would be kicked out of the presidency of her church group."

"Which one?" Candace licked her fingers.

"Oh, I don't know. She's in about a hundred of them."

"True. Did she bring up Pastor Irm?"

I gave Candace a long look. "Doesn't she always bring up Pastor Irm?"

Her hand came down on the table with a slap, and she released a loud laugh. "I knew it! I told my mom Aunt Patsy would bring up Irm, and Mom said I needed to respect my elders."

"Why does everyone act like they don't see it?"

My brothers and I had all had plenty of time to get accustomed to the idea of our mother being interested in a man other than our father, but she preferred to play the martyr, carrying a picture of my deceased father in her purse the way a Catholic woman carries rosary beads. Everyone in the congregation saw the flirtation between my sixty-year-old mother and the seventy-year-old widower, Pastor Irmingham Jones. But when asked, my mother remained firm: she was a grieving widow, and would be until her last breath.

What a headache.

"So what about your brothers? Was Darren glad it was you who got pregnant instead of Panda?" Candace chuckled.

"Pandi," I corrected. "And yes. I think he'll enjoy being out of the spotlight for a while."

Candace's smile dropped. "What about Corbin and Andrea? How did they take it?"

Tears pricked my eyes. "That was the worst part. They looked so distraught. Andrea didn't talk for the first five minutes."

She covered my hand with her own. "I'm sorry. I know you never meant to hurt them."

Swiping my eyes, I popped the last bit of salami into my mouth chewed sadly. "I knew it was coming. I got what I deserved."

"What you deserved? Are you kidding? It's not like you did this on purpose." Candace eyeballed me. "Wait, did you?"

I put my hands up. "No. I didn't plan this at all."

"Well, even if you did, you don't have to make apologies for it just because Corbin and Andrea can't have kids. I mean, it's unfortunate they can't, but you can't avoid having your own children because you're afraid of making them feel bad. I don't think they'd want you to do that, anyway."

"No. They wouldn't." I dabbed at my eyes again. "They just looked so crushed. And my mom was pacing back and forth, chastising me for being unmarried."

"I expected that to happen, too."

"I know. I was just hoping she would surprise me." The rolling in my stomach returned and I pushed my napkin back. "It's like she's more concerned about her reputation at church than the fact she's finally going to get the grandchild she's been begging for since I was eighteen."

Candace grimaced. Being daughters in this family came at a price. Emotional perseverance. "She'll come around. She always does."

Sniffling, I nodded. "I hope so. Because once I saw that ultrasound…" The lump in my throat grew too big to ignore, so I stopped speaking.

Her fingers squeezed mine. "Pretty magical, huh?"

I looked up, my eyes spilling over again. We were going to need more napkins. "Yes. Just seeing that little heart flashing. It…" When I realized Candace's eyes were moist now, too, I knew I was in good company. "Everything just fell into perspective. This isn't a mistake. This is a miracle."

"That's beautiful." Her voice cracked and she pushed the napkin back over to me. "Come on. Try to eat a little more."

As soon as the odor of the salami hit my nose, my mouth began to water, and what little I'd eaten began crawling up the back of my throat. "Ugh," I moaned, covering my mouth. "No more."

As soon as Candace saw that my expression, her eyes widened. "Are you gonna get sick?"

"No." I wrapped my arms around my middle and sat very still for a heartbeat or two. "Aw, hell. Yes."

I bolted for the powder room right off of the kitchen, but halted when Candace shouted, "Wait! Not that bathroom! Quentin flushed a block this morning, and Brian has to fix it! Go upstairs, go upstairs!"

Bile filled my mouth, and I clamped my fingers down, trying to hold the vomit at bay as I charged through the living room. Frustrated cries of several men rang out when I temporarily blocked their view of the flat screen. I clambered up the stairs to the second floor bathroom, and was met by a commode tightly shut with a child lock. My body heaved forward as I fumbled with one hand to unlatch the lid, but it kept landing back down on the seat with a loud thunk. With each unsuccessful attempt, my stomach lurched, filling my mouth with vomit.

Lurch. Thunk. Lurch. Thunk.

This whole pregnancy thing was for the damn birds.

Finally the lid broke open, sending pieces of the plastic lock flying in all directions.

Woops. Guess I'll be replacing that later.

I buried my face in the porcelain bowl and relieved myself of everything I'd either tasted or eaten since the third grade. The sound of the football game raging downstairs was drowned out by my coughing and sputtering.

"You're trying to kill me, aren't you?" I asked my little kidney bean, my voice echoing against the dirtied water.

"You okay?" A deep voice asked.

I felt a warm hand touch my back, and I nodded, my forehead bumping against the seat. "Yeah. Just feeling a bit under the weather. Sorry to ruin your party, Bri."

"It's not Brian."

I lifted my head the tiniest bit. Crap on a stick, it was Dr. Fletcher Haybee—in all of his denim shirt wearing, tousled blond hair glory!

Fumbling to flush the toilet, I snatched a piece of toilet paper off the nearby roll to wipe my mouth. Leave it to Brian and Candace to invite the gorgeous obstetrician who just had his face in my junk over for a football game and cold cuts.

"I...uh...uh..." My mind was blank. Completely blank. I'd never been caught vomiting by a hot doctor before.

Fletcher knelt down and took hold of my wrist. "Having a lot of nausea?" He grew quiet and looked at his watch. It occurred to me that he was taking my pulse.

"If I didn't know any better, I would have thought my child hates me, and wants to slowly kill me from the inside out." I leaned against the toilet and blew my hair off my forehead. It felt like I'd thrown up at least two major organs.

He chuckled, the sound low and gravelly. It made my empty and twisted belly heat up like a fire pit. "Are you able to keep anything down at all?"

Sweat soaked the hair at the nape of my neck, and I suddenly realized how terrible I must have looked. Curse my ultra-white skin and freckles. Whenever I'd thrown up as a kid, I turned a pasty shade of gray, and my nose got splotchy and red.

I shook my head. "Not really. Although I ate a tic tac yesterday, and I don't think that came back up." I looked at the now clean water in the toilet wearily. "Though it may have just now."

Again he laughed, then put his finger under my chin to raise it. Fletcher's bright, aqua blue eyes searched mine for a few beats. "Your pulse seems all right, and your pupils aren't dilated. I think you're going to be fine."

"Great." Using another piece of toilet paper, I wiped the back of my neck off. "How long does this morning sickness last? And why do they call it morning sickness? Shouldn't it be called '*all damn day*' sickness?"

When he smiled, it showed a row of bright, white teeth. They were nearly perfect, with the exception of one of his canines, which was just slightly out of alignment. It was the most endearing flaw I'd ever seen. I was surprised at how squirmy he made me feel, considering I'd just finished puking my guts out.

"A lot of women get morning sickness all day long. The good news is, it should subside around twelve to fourteen weeks," he said. "My ex-wife got so mad at me when her morning sickness kicked in. She said it was a cruel joke from God."

Ex-wife? My ears perked up and I sat up straighter. Well, as straight as I could between the bathtub and the toilet. "You were married, Dr. Haybee?"

He sat down Indian-style across the bathroom rug from me. "Come on. Call me Fletcher."

"Oh, I don't want to be disrespectful." I looked down at my tee shirt and brushed at a wet spot on the chest. Dear Lord, I hoped it was water and not puke. I reached up to the countertop where the kid's toothbrushes were set up, grabbed the tube of toothpaste, and squeezed a dollop onto my finger.

He shrugged. "What's disrespectful about it? I'm going to deliver your baby. That's pretty intimate. We may as well be on a first name basis."

"Okay, then, Fletcher. Did anyone call you Fletch growing up?" I smiled before starting to scrub my teeth with my finger.

Rolling his eyes, he picked at a dark piece of lint on the fluffy white rug. "Yeah. It drove me crazy."

I rose up onto my knees, spit the toothpaste into the sink, and quickly rinsed my mouth out. "I can relate. Everyone has called me Bump for as long as I can remember. Geez, even my high school principal called me that."

"No kidding?" Fletcher grinned.

"Wish I were." I pulled my knees to my chest, and leaned against the cool porcelain of the tub.

"There's a certain amount of irony in that, you know." When I gave him a strange look, he nodded at my midsection. "Beings you're pregnant, and will soon have a bump."

"Thanks for reminding me."

"Don't feel too bad," he lamented cheerfully. "My last name is Haybee, and I went on to become an obstetrician. All my nurses call me Dr. Baby."

I giggled. "Dr. Baby?"

He blushed. "It's pretty stupid."

"I won't argue with that." I blew at a stray strand of my red hair. "So how many kids do you have, Dr. Baby?"

"Just one. A daughter. Martha." Fletcher's eyes sparkled when he said his daughter's name.

"Martha? That's beautiful. You don't hear that name very often anymore."

"Thanks. It's my mother's name. Have you thought of any names yet?"

I shook my head. "Ugh, no. I'm still processing the fact that I'm going to be a single mom." I chewed the inside of my cheek and hoped he wouldn't ask the inevitable question, but no such luck.

"Is the father involved? Will I be meeting him at one of your appointments?"

My teeth came down on the soft inner skin of my left cheek. "No." When his light eyes probed mine for a second, I added, "Let's just call this immaculate conception, okay, doc?"

His brow relaxed. "Hint taken."

"Good." I smiled, feeling some color return to my cheeks. "So how old is Martha?"

"She's nine, going on twenty-five." He laughed. "This morning she actually told me that someone my age should eat more whole grains."

"You're kidding." I pictured a little girl with blonde hair the same sun-kissed shade as his, preaching to him across the breakfast table.

"I wish I were." He leaned against the cabinet below the sink. "She's just looking out for me. I think she feels responsible for me. I don't mind. We're buddies."

This whole loving dad thing suited Fletcher, and I liked it. "How often do you see her?"

His eyes met mine again, and the corner of his mouth tugged upward. "Every day. Martha lives with me. She only sees her mom every few months. She's in the basement playing with Brian and Candace's kids."

Well, color me surprised.

The good doctor not only brought new babies into the world, but he was also raising one on his own? Fletcher Haybee was becoming more attractive by the second. Now, if there was only some way I could get his shirt off him, to check for a six-pack…

"Candace says you own a catering business," he said, interrupting my thoughts.

I nodded. "Yup. Eats and Treats. I started it with my friend, Marisol, after my divorce."

One of Fletcher's blond eyebrows tugged upward. "You're divorced?"

"My past is becoming very sordid, isn't it?" I hugged my knees. "My life isn't usually such a soap opera. In fact, for the past few years, my friends have been telling me to stop acting like an eighty-year-old."

His smile made my chest constrict. "You act like an eighty-year-old?"

"Well," I began. "I don't knit, and I don't own a bunch of cats. But I enjoy a nice evening in, watching some lovely television programs."

"The Lawrence Welch Show?" he teased.

"Do they even make that show anymore?" Tucking my hair behind my ears, I offered him a haughty expression. "No. But I have a weakness for the Food Network. Or any cooking competition show."

Fletcher's eyes widened. "Do you watch *Culinary Countdown*?"

I sat bolt upright. "I never miss an episode. They're all on my DVR right now."

"I love that show!" he exclaimed.

"Who do you want to win?" I demanded.

"I have no idea, but that Ralph has got to go. Did you see what he did to that pork loin last week? It was shameful." Fletcher shook his head in disgust.

"Wow." I looked down at my knees and tried to control my grin. I felt sixteen again. Talking to the star quarterback. "Do you cook?"

"Yes. But not very well." He sighed sadly. "Though Martha makes a mean omelet."

He was perfect. Like God had tailor-made my dream man, right down to the rock and roll tee shirts, then sent him down to Earth for me. My stomach roiled, and I grimaced. Since I was two months pregnant, meeting Fletcher right now was a horrible inconvenience. How sick in the head did I have to be, to feel attracted to my obstetrician? Talk about wrong.

"Hey, Lex. How are you feeling?" Candace peeked around the edge of the door.

She'd never been very good with vomit, so I wasn't upset she'd kept her distance while my stomach turned itself inside out. The last few times her kids had gotten the flu she'd wound up hurling at the sight of their little heads in the toilet.

I looked up at my cousin and realized how stupid I must have looked, sitting on her bathroom floor having a pow-wow with Fletcher. "Sorry I took so long. Dr…uh, Fletcher here has been talking me down."

She frowned. "I'm so sorry you're so sick."

I sighed. "Apparently it's par for the course."

"It really is." She leaned against the doorjamb, and looked down at Fletcher. "Did you check her out? Is she okay?"

"She's fine. Just a bit of '*all the damn time*' sickness." He winked at me, stood up, and offered me a hand.

I pretended that a bolt of electricity didn't shoot up my arm when I took it. "Thanks."

"You're a lucky girl." Candace slid an arm around my shoulders. "Your doctor was right here for a quick check up."

I glanced at Fletcher in all of his off-duty-doctor glory. My cheeks scalded. "Yup. Lucky. That's me."

"Come on." She led me to the stairs. "Let's go finish our talk. Thanks, Fletcher."

"Anytime." He drawled behind us.

Right as we started down the first step, I glanced over my shoulder, and he winked at me. "Ginger."

I stopped, stumbling slightly. "What?"

Was he giving me a nickname? Wasn't Ginger the hot chick on *Gilligan's Island*? That meant this was a compliment, right? My heart skittered in my chest like a tween girl's at a Beiber concert.

"Ginger," he repeated. "Ginger ale. Ginger snaps. Ginger root. Ginger seems to help with the nausea. A few of my patients have mentioned it."

"Oh." I blinked a few times, my fantasy fading. "Right. Thank you."

He returned to his game, and I followed Candace back into the kitchen. But so help me, for the rest of that football game, whenever the men burst into boos or cheers in the living room, I heard one voice above all the others.

I officially had a crush on my obstetrician.

Chapter Five

"I still don't understand why women do this on purpose."

Marisol stood next to a 4D diagram of a woman's uterus, her full lips pulled back into a pretty grimace. Though we were in an examination room at Fletcher's office, she wore oversized sunglasses that covered half her face, as if she were a celebrity in fear of being photographed.

Only she could make utter disgust look that good.

In the ten years since I'd met Marisol at a keg party in Brian's fraternity house, she'd not aged by one day. Her perpetually tanned skin remained smooth and supple, and her wide brown eyes remained crinkle-free and rimmed in abnormally long, dark lashes.

She was gorgeous, and received male attention wherever we went. Including in the obstetrician's office. When we'd gotten on the elevator, a man dropped his cell phone mid-conversation. She loved the attention, and often encouraged it for fun. Dating was a sport for Marisol. And if bedding men without the complication of feelings or emotions being involved were an Olympic event, she'd be a gold medalist.

Judging how she shuddered every time one of Candace's kids touched her, it was safe to say she wasn't exactly the maternal type.

"Oh, come on. Don't you think it would be cool to experience the miracle of childbirth?" And then I laughed.

She shuddered. "Ugh. No. You can't bounce back from that."

"Of course you can. Women's bodies are designed to go back to normal." I shook my head and shifted in my seat, the paper crackling underneath my jeans. At least this time I didn't have to be suffer through another awkward examination. Candace had promised that my naked-from-the-waist-down days were over for the next few months, and I was so relieved when she'd said it, I nearly cried.

There was nothing more awkward than knowing that hot Dr. Baby had seen my vagina, and would undoubtedly see it again. Repeatedly. And not for sexy reasons, either.

"Normal?" Marisol pushed her oversized sunglasses on top of her head. "Have you ever seen a baby being born?"

"Well, no." Suddenly I felt embarrassed. Should I have? Where could I get a hold of a video of something like that? I made a mental note to check YouTube later on. "You have?"

"Yes. It was horrifying." Her nostrils flared and she smoothed down her glossy hair. "We had to watch a video of a real birth in high school. It was their form of birth control." She stopped petting her ponytail and held her fingers up to form a circle big enough for a basketball to pass through. "Worked wonders on my class. No pregnancies that year."

"I'm sure it did." We looked at each other awkwardly for a beat. "So why did you tag along today?" I asked.

Marisol shifted so her back was to the plaster uterus. The light coming through the small window reflected off of her deep brown hair, and I touched my own short hair self-consciously. I'd taken extra care in picking my outfit for work that morning, knowing that I was going to be seeing Fletcher during my lunch break. I put on a dark pair of boot cut jeans, instead of my Levi's with a tear on the knee. I topped it off with silver shirt with beading around the neckline, instead of the usual novelty tee I sported. Marisol and I were doing some baking for a bridal shower we were catering this weekend, which meant getting covered in flour and frosting splatters. But today, I was careful to keep myself as tidy as possible.

Marisol brushed a fleck of lavender frosting off her sleeve. Oddly enough, even though we'd been working on the same cupcakes all morning, she'd effortlessly remained almost pristine. That was typical. She was couture, I was hand-me-down. She was put together perfectly, I was a hot mess.

"I'm here because Candace said your doctor is a hottie," she said in a bored voice.

Wait... what?

I looked down at Marisol from my perch on the table. She'd come to check out Fletcher? Nervousness plopped in my stomach and fizzled like Alka-Seltzer. Men were rarely immune to the beauty and blatant sexuality Marisol oozed. And I wanted to keep Fletcher to myself.

Not that I had a chance with him. He really was good-looking. Besides, he was my *obstetrician*. I was pretty sure he viewed our connection as nothing more than a doctor/patient relationship, despite that I was drawn to him like a moth to a porch light.

"You didn't come here to provide me with love and support?" I laughed nervously.

Marisol snorted. "Hardly." When she caught my frown, she quickly added, "I'm kidding. Of course I'm here to support you. But I'm also here to check out this baby doctor who apparently looks like a movie star."

The churning in my stomach sped up. "Oh. Well, he's all right. I guess."

Maybe if I feigned nonchalance, Marisol would lose interest, too. She was like a puppy, enamored until something newer and shinier came along to play with. The only distraction she'd ever focused on for an extended period of time was our business, and I was pretty sure that was only because there were no men involved.

"All right?" She pulled a compact out of her Fendi bag and began reapplying her lipstick. "Candace said you were falling all over yourself when he examined you."

My cheeks scalded. Curse Candace and her big mouth. "I was not. It's impossible to fall all over yourself when your feet are in stirrups."

"You know what I mean." She glanced at me, then went back to her lipstick. "You're attracted to him."

"No, I'm not. I mean, he's cute, I guess. But I'm not really into him."
I looked away, pretending to be fascinated with the black and white
photography framed on the walls.

Oh, look at that tree. That's a nice tree.

She blotted her lips together with a pop. "Why not?"

Not going after a hot, available man was a foreign concept to
Marisol.

I let one of my shoulders rise and drop casually. "I've got enough on
my plate, I suppose. I mean, in about six and a half months, I'm going to be a
single mom."

Marisol dropped her lipstick back into the bag. "I know. Can you
believe it? Like, *everything* will be on your shoulders. Food, shelter, clothes,
diapers. All of it." She laughed and shook her head. "I mean, holy shit, Lex."

The jealousy in my stomach dissipated and was replaced by a rock of
nervousness. Most of my thoughts over the past few weeks had been occupied
by the reality that I was embarking on the world's most difficult task
completely alone. I'd lost count of how many times Candace had proclaimed
her gratitude that Brian was a helpful, hands-on father.

This baby's father wasn't going to be helping with the midnight
feedings. Or anything else, for that matter.

"Of course, if anybody can handle it, it's you." Marisol pulled her
perfume from her purse, dabbed it on her pulse points, then offered it to me. I
shook my head. "You're very independent. I mean, look at you. When Nate
left, you could've totally fallen apart. Cried in your bed for a year. And
nobody would have blamed you."

I looked at the small window, and wished it opened. Talking about
my debunked marriage made me sweat, especially in a room the size of an
espresso shack with a plaster uterus taking up half the space.

"But you didn't do that at all," she went on, snapping her purse shut.
"You got back up, changed your name back to Baump, which I still think was

silly, considering the name Smith is so much less annoying than Baump. No offense."

I rolled my eyes. "None taken."

"You started a successful business with your gorgeous, amazing friend." Marisol gestured at herself. "And you've never looked back. Never taken him back for a pity hump, never—"

"Pity hump?"

"Yes. A pity hump. Come on, we've all had them." She waved her hand casually. "After the breakup. Too much wine. Maybe some made-for-television movies about couples finding love in concentration camps, or some such nonsense, and whammo! You wake up the next morning with no underwear on, a drunken striptease video on your cell phone, and your ex passed out on the other side of the bed."

"Good Lord, Marisol!" I slapped my hand over my mouth. "I take it that happened to you?" I asked from behind my fingers.

"Once or twice." She shook her head. "You're missing the point. The point is, if anybody can do this, it's you."

I smiled down at her gratefully. "Thank you. That means a lot to me."

"It should. You know I don't hand out compliments very often." Marisol laughed at her own joke. "Okay, seriously. Dr. Hot-to-trot really oughta consider changing the décor in here. That fake uterus is going to make me puke."

"For heaven's sake." I rolled my eyes. "You have one, you know."

"Yeah, but mine doesn't have a giant, big-headed baby bulldozing its way through it."

I eyeballed the uterus and crossed my legs. "Good point."

There was a swift knock at the door, and Fletcher's head of messy golden hair poked around the corner. "Lexie?"

When he spotted me, a grin spread across his face, and my heart flipped inside of my chest. "Hi, Dr. Haybee."

"Doctor?" He shut the door behind him. "I like to think we're on a first name basis, considering the fact that I held your hair while you vomited a few weeks ago."

"Okay. Hi, Fletcher." I caught myself giggling, and cleared my throat. Good Lord in heaven, he was so handsome. This time his white lab coat was unbuttoned over a wrinkled blue button down and a pair of dark grey slacks. The shirt was un-tucked, and open over a white tee shirt, making him look like adorably rumpled and casual.

"Did you try the ginger?" Happy wrinkles formed in the corners of his eyes.

I attempted to tear my eyes away from his, but found myself incapable. "Yeah, it worked. Well, a little bit. I'm getting tired of ginger foods now."

He patted my knee kindly. "Keep it up, and hopefully the nausea will subside soon."

There was a shifting of an overpriced handbag next to me, and I heard the click of Marisol's three-inch heels scrape on the floor. She'd worn her "low shoes" for work, and saved the five-inch platforms for her day off. She cleared her throat and nudged my leg, and I cringed inwardly.

Please let him be immune to Marisol's tractor beam.

Alas…he wasn't.

"Oh, hi." He blinked a few times as if the shininess coming off of Marisol was too bright.

My shoulders slumped when Marisol put out her hand demurely, tilted her chin downward, and gazed Fletcher through the veil of her long, dark eyelashes.

"Marisol Vargas," she purred.

Fletcher shook her hand. His eyes were locked on Marisol's heart shaped face and plump, full lips. "Fletcher Haybee."

"It's a pleasure to meet you. I've heard a lot about you." Marisol's words were like warm honey, all drippy and oozy-like. Cripes, if I listened to her much longer, *I* was going to wind up turned on, too.

She leaned forward in her seat just enough to show an innocent amount of cleavage, and Fletcher's eyes widened. "A pleasure to meet you, too. You're Lexie's friend, I take it."

"Business partner," I said flatly, watching as he succumbed to the power of Marisol's bust line. I knew I would rue the day I helped her recover from augmentation surgery.

"Oh, don't be modest." Marisol laughed, and I noticed how breathy she sounded now that Fletcher was in the room. Like she was going for a Marilyn Monroe thing. "We've been friends since college. We're practically family."

My jaw dropped, but neither of them noticed. Sure, Marisol was one of my best friends, but *family*? She'd long since declared that mine and Candace's family was crazy—not that she was wrong—and only came to family events serving alcohol. I loved Marisol, but it was the same way I loved my brother, Darren. Love, with a dash of confusion and irritation rolled in.

Fletcher grinned at me. "Well, any family of Lexie's is welcome here. It's nice to see she's got a good support system."

"That's me!" Marisol beamed, her grin wide and fetching. "I'm always here for our little single mama." She added a little pat on my knee for the effect.

I suppressed a scoff. When I'd asked her if she planned on helping me with the baby on occasion, she'd responded by making a gagging sound and announced, "*As long as it doesn't shit on me.*"

I focused on Fletcher's shirt to keep from pulling Marisol's glossy hair. We just needed to get through my appointment, get a new prescription for prenatal vitamins, then get back to Eats & Sweets. I squinted at the white tee shirt underneath. I detected some writing on the right side of the chest that indicated he was wearing another vintage rock tee. Possibly a Lynyrd Skynyrd this time. My pulse raced.

Fletcher and Marisol's laughter jolted me out of my fashion examination. When I looked up, she was holding his arm, laughing airily at whatever he'd said. He was grinning cheekily, obviously proud of himself for making the hot chick happy. Dear Lord, like a kid in a candy store.

"Oh, Fletcher!" she breathed. "You are so *funny*. Lexie, you didn't tell me he was *so funny*!"

Marisol was channeling her inner sex kitten today. Seriously, it sounded like she needed an inhaler. "I didn't know I was supposed to," I mumbled.

Note to self: do not *bring Marisol to anymore appointments.*

Fletcher tore his attention away from Marisol. "Well, Lexie, should we check that baby's heartbeat?"

"Sure." Laying down, I lifted up the bottom hem of my shirt. Fletcher scooped a hand-held Doppler off of the table, and looked down at my jeans. Though I couldn't be sure, I thought I saw a hint of color stain his cheeks.

"I'm gonna need you to unbutton your pants, please," he said politely.

"I'll bet you say that often, doctor," Marisol purred from her perch on a stool.

I slapped my forehead. "Good grief. Mar, take it down a notch."

She giggled. "I call it how I see it."

Now I was *certain* Fletcher was blushing. Looking up at the ceiling and wishing I were at least half as hot as Marisol, I unbuttoned my jeans and folded them down. "Will that work?"

"Perfect. Thanks." After squirting the blue goo onto my skin, he pressed the hand held microphone onto my lower abdomen and turned the instrument on.

Fletcher's face turned serious as he slowly rolled the microphone across my skin. I held my breath. After a few seconds, the familiar galloping sound of my baby's heartbeat filled the room, and his blue eyes lit up.

"There we go," he said. We listened for fifteen or twenty seconds, while Marisol picked at her nail polish in the corner. "It's at about a hundred thirty-five beats per minute."

"That's different from my last visit." My voice cracked. "Is that okay? Is he okay? Or she?"

Fletcher smiled down at me kindly. "It's just fine. The beats per minute will fluctuate from day to day, hour to hour. Just like we have relaxed times of day, and active times of day. Your baby does, too."

I nodded, relieved. "Thank you."

His blue eyes twinkled. "You're bonding with your baby."

My cheeks reddened. I was already talking to my baby in the mornings while I got ready for work. "I'm weird."

Fletcher put the Doppler down, fetched a tissue, and began wiping my skin off gently. My heart started to thrum inside of my chest like a truck engine, and I was sure he could hear it, but he didn't say anything. Instead, he just cleaned off my skin, then held a hand out to me. When I took it, he pulled me back into a sitting position, so that we were just half a foot apart.

"No," he said softly. "You're not weird. You're a mom."

My heart stopped vibrating and took flight. Well, that is until Marisol's face poked up between us, and she blurted, "He? You called the kid a *he*. What did that microphone do-hickey thing say?"

I blushed and buttoned my pants. "I just call it a he. It feels strange to refer to my child as an it."

"You're really getting into this whole motherhood thing." She snickered, then noticed Fletcher looking at her. "I mean, who can blame you? You know, creating life, and all that jazz."

Fletcher leaned against the table. "Life already has been made. Lexie's just forming the connection with her child that every mother gains. It's pretty cool to watch." He looked at me and winked.

Marisol nodded with false solemnity when Fletcher glanced at her, then rolled her eyes when he looked away. Oh, she was laying it on thick today.

As Fletcher started asking me questions about how I'd been feeling over the past few weeks, and of the results of my iron tests and urine dips, Marisol went into full-on flirt mode. By the end of my twenty-minute appointment, she was leaning into Fletcher so much her cleavage was practically resting on his elbow, and she'd actually referred to him as "big boy."

Twice.

I wasn't sure whether to laugh or cry when he watched her flip long, glossy brown hair. It felt like I was sitting in on an episode of *The Bachelor*, where I was just the poor schmuck who got to hold the bowl of roses.

When Fletcher patted me on the knee and announced he was going to go grab some prenatal vitamin samples for me, I jumped. When he excused himself from the exam room, Marisol practically jumped into my lap.

"Holy Hannah, he *is* hot!" she squealed. "Thanks for bringing me!"

I patted her back, wishing I had a knife. Then I mentally scolded myself for wanting to murder Marisol. "Oh, um, you're welcome. I'm glad you had fun."

"Fun?" She looked at her reflection in the stainless steel paper towel dispenser. "Dr. Hottie can give me a pap smear anytime."

I almost threw up in my mouth. "Oh good grief, Mar."

"What?" She reached into her blouse and adjusted her boobs. "He's absolutely gorgeous, and single. No wedding ring or tan line. I don't know how you can stand it." She caught my reflection in the dispenser. "Maybe you can't. Are you interested in him?"

I opened my mouth, then closed it again.

This was one of those pivotal life moments when I very well could have chosen to do what my heart wanted.

Just like when my ex-husband called me a week after packing all of his things and leaving me without so much as a note. I should have forced him to explain to me why the hell he'd left me high and dry. But I'd been afraid of his response. I didn't want to know what I might have done wrong. So rather than facing words I might not have wanted to hear, I'd said goodbye, hung up, taken out my contact lenses, and gone to bed, hoping his quarter life crisis would be over by the time my alarm went off in the morning.

Tell her. If you like him, tell her. She'll back off. She might be sort of trampy, but she's no man-stealer. If she knows you like Fletcher, she'll find a new leg to hump.

I shifted uncomfortably in my seat, feeling the waist of my pants brush against my abdomen. Fletcher had missed a spot of the jelly, and there was an area on my stomach that was still cold and sticky. My hand went to my belly, and my shoulders dropped a few inches.

I was embarking on the most difficult and life-altering experience I was ever going to have, and there wasn't any room for a romance.

Was someone who looked like Fletcher Haybee going to lust after me once my belly popped out and my ankles doubled in size? How about after the kid was here, and I was up all night breastfeeding until I was so tired my left eyelid twitched?

I watched as Marisol adjusted her blouse, smoothing it down over her tiny waist and curvy hips. That was the kind of woman Fletcher was going to want. Someone who could make red velvet cupcakes from scratch and looked like she could be a pro on *Dancing With the Stars*.

"No." I hated lying, especially to one of my best friends. But it was for the best. Right? "I… I'm not interested."

Her dark eyes lit up. "Really?"

"Really." I smiled falsely, and it gave me a headache.

"Why not? He's positively edible."

I shrugged and looked down at my midriff. "I've got enough on my plate, I guess."

"So you don't mind if I ask him out?" She petted her hair extensions like a cat.

"Nope. Go for it." I bit the insides of my cheeks.

"Yay!" She groaned, low and predatory. I wanted to cry. "He doesn't know what he's in for!"

"I've got an idea," I murmured, as the door opened again. Fletcher walked back in with an armload of vitamin packages.

"I brought you an assortment." He dropped them in my lap and smiled sheepishly. "You can take a new kind every few days until you find one that you like. I know that the iron in some of them can be hard for some women to digest."

"Thanks."

"Anything for you." He blushed, then put his hands in his pockets, rocking back on his heels. "Remember, you can call me anytime if you have a question or aren't feeling well."

We held each other's eye contact for a moment, and my stomach fluttered. "Okay," I said softly.

"So are we done with all of the medical talk?" Marisol purred.

Fletcher blinked a few times, then turned his gaze to her face. "It appears that way."

"Good." She giggled deeply and lowered her eyelids. On me, that would have looked like I'd taken a sleeping pill and needed a nap. But on Marisol, it looked sexy and delectable. "Let's get down to it."

Fletcher's eyes widened. "Okay."

"When are you going to take me to dinner?" Her fingers walked up his chest. My throat tightened and I pretended to be transfixed by the back of a vitamin box.

"I, uh, dinner?" His eyes flicked to me, then back to Marisol again.

Marisol tossed her hair again, knocking a pastel blue box out of my hand. It hit the door, landing on the linoleum floor with a smack.

"Well." Fletcher cleared his throat and shuffled his feet. He was really cute when he was uncomfortable.

"I love sushi. Or oysters." She grinned wickedly.

I imagined all of the things I'd heard about oysters being good for the libido, and suppressed a shudder. Fletcher, on the other hand, stared down at her as if he were caught in a tractor beam.

"Sushi is good." He offered Marisol a lopsided grin.

My stomach twisted.

"What time?" One of her perfectly arched brows rose.

Fletcher glanced at me, his cheeks turning a deep red. "Er, time?"

"What time are you going to pick me up?" Marisol moved even closer to him, and the front of her blouse brushed his doctor's coat.

"Oh." He laughed, and then coughed into his hand. "That. I'll—"

You've got to be kidding me. I slid off of the table, tearing the paper with my back pocket. When the two of them turned to look at me, I waved as I scooped my purse off the floor. "Sorry to interrupt. I have to use the restroom. I'll meet you in the lobby, Marisol."

As soon as the exam room door shut behind me, tears pricked the backs of my eyes. I made a beeline for the restroom. Anger, hurt, embarrassment—you name it, they were all there. I sat on the closed toilet seat taking deep breaths. The thought of Marisol and Fletcher getting their freak on after an evening of salmon skin rolls and oyster shooters was more than I could bear. It made me want to vomit.

In fact....

I dropped down to my knees, opened the toilet, and barfed. This was going to be a long pregnancy.

Chapter Six

As my Volkswagen bug rolled up in front of the dilapidated brick bungalow, my breath caught in my throat. Of all of the houses my brother and his wife had renovated over the years—and believe me, there were plenty—this one was going to be my favorite.

Arched doorways and paned windows. The tiny courtyard in the front yard was lined with a rickety picket fence covered in peeling white paint. The shingles hung off the roof and swung in the breeze like playground equipment, and the glass in the front window was cracked. Some masonry work was desperately needed around the front door, too, but it was the most adorable house I'd ever seen. Ten thousand times better than my one-bedroom apartment on the bottom floor of an old brownstone downtown.

"Are you gonna sit in that car all day, or are you gonna say hello to the pastor?" My mother's frosted head popped up outside my open window, the tiny bells on her cat sweatshirt jingling.

I jumped a foot off of my seat. "Mom, you scared me."

"Come on, now." She opened the door for me. "Get out before your legs cramp up. My legs swelled up to the size of tree trunks when I was pregnant, and I had Charley horse cramps every day."

My eyebrows rose high on my head. After finding out that I'd gotten myself knocked up, my mother stopped speaking to me for three weeks. It wasn't until Candace caught my mother after church and chastised her for turning her back on her only daughter last week that she'd finally come around.

My mother finally called to ask me to meet her at Corbin and Andrea's latest project for a picnic lunch and to chat. And by chat, I mean to listen to her explain why she'd decided to shun me for three weeks.

"It's nice to see you, too, Ma." I stood up and smoothed down the front of my shirt. Slamming my car door shut, I forced a smile. "I can't be swelling up yet, can I?"

My mother shook her head and glanced down at my ankles, which were covered with the ends of my jeans. "You might. Your jeans look tight. Are you retaining water?"

"No." I tugged at the waist of my jeans. "I'm barely over three months pregnant. My jeans are just starting to feel snug."

She patted her own ample tummy. "I blew up like a balloon when I was pregnant with you. Your father, God rest his soul, said I looked like John Candy."

"Thanks. I'll keep that in mind." Pastor Irm's bald head shone in the fall sunlight, and I dropped my voice to a whisper. "Why's he here?"

Mom beamed at Pastor Irm, who was admiring the nearly dead rose bushes underneath the front window. When he caught her staring, he waved.

"Hello, Lexie," he called.

"Don't be disrespectful," my mother hissed at me. "Wave at the pastor."

Obeying, I suppressed a snicker. "I didn't realize when you asked me to meet you here you would be on a date."

"Don't be ridiculous." She laughed nervously and adjusted the picnic basket in her hand. "I'm not on a date. Pastor Irm is just here to see the house and to wish your brother well."

"Sure." I stepped onto the sidewalk and faced her. "So what did you want to talk to me about?"

My mother's eyes roamed down to my belly. "Well, Candace and your brothers seem to think I've been too hard on you."

"They do, huh?" We walked slowly towards the house where the muted sound of hammering could be heard. "What do you think?"

She fingered her pastel pink collar. "I, well, I guess I was a little bit harsh."

"A little bit?" I looked at her pointedly. "Ma, you told Aunt Dory I had shamed the whole family."

"I was upset, Alexandria," she said loudly.

"Shamed the whole family? Really?" I stopped walking, and put my hands on my hips. "Ma, Darren has the words *Epic Win* tattooed across his chest. And *I'm* the disappointment?"

"Okay, okay. Fine." She shook her head. "I went too far. But, Lexie, I just want more for you."

"Families don't happen according to some grand master plan. My family is happening this way, and I need you to accept that."

"I do accept that." She pinched her lips together. "Now."

"I'm thirty years old. I'm completely independent. I own a successful business, and I donate to the Red Cross every year, just like you taught me." I watched my mother fidget in her spot for a second. "You should be proud of me."

"I am." Her mouth tugged down in the corners.

My hands went instinctively to my stomach. "You've been begging for grandchildren for years. Literally, for *years*. Now I'm giving you a grandchild, and you're spending half my pregnancy being disappointed."

She snorted. "Half? Please, dear. You're barely showing."

"You just said my pants were too tight."

"Well, they are. A little. When I was pregnant with Corbin, my butt grew to three times its normal size." My mother turned and wagged her fanny toward me. "Your father couldn't keep his hands off it."

I made a gagging sound. "Ugh, Ma, please."

"Regardless, I want better for you. I want you to have a house and a husband." She faced me again. "Being a single mom is the hardest thing you'll ever do."

"Besides burying you in the backyard," I mumbled, rubbing my forehead. I had a headache coming on, and still didn't know what drugs I could use without hurting my little nugget.

"Ha, ha, ha. Listen to me, young lady." She cut me a scathing glance. "I just saw this happening to you differently. You know, the husband, the house, the dog, the babies. All in the right order. Now look at you. You're thirty years old, divorced, living in a scuzzy apartment—"

"My apartment is not scuzzy," I yelped. "It's small. That's different."

My mom gave me a sideways glance. "Where are you going to put a baby in that place?"

"I don't know yet." I mumbled, looking up at the house longingly. "I haven't thought that far ahead. Maybe I'll buy this place once Corbin and Andrea are done with it."

She snorted. "Come on."

"Why do you have such a lack of confidence in me?" I asked.

Mom waved her hand, dismissing my question. "Listen, I've worked it all out." My mother put down the picnic basket and took me by the shoulders.

I cast a nervous glance over my shoulder at Pastor Irm, who was purposefully ignoring us. "What have you worked out, Ma?"

"I'm gonna help you through this." She smiled at me excitedly.

A wave of relief washed over me. Now we were talking. "You are? You have no idea how much I've wanted to hear that."

"Regardless of how it happened, this is going to be my first grandchild." Her eyes filled with tears, and she pressed a hand to the kitties again. "I can't wait to give him or her their first doll, and take it to Sunday school every week. I'm going to make a blanket, and help you with babysitting while you work."

"You are?" My eyebrows rose high on my forehead. Daycare was one of those issues that was keeping me up at night. Sure, the baby could come with me to work during the week, but finding care during events was going to be tricky.

"Of course," She said. "No sense in paying a sitter when you've got me. Especially with the hours you keep."

I resisted the urge to roll my eyes. In the catering business events were held on weekends and evenings. This meant lots of late nights up to my elbows in pate and champagne brie. "Wow. Thank you. That's a huge help."

"And I'll also make the baby clothes." She bent over to scoop up the basket and slowly ambled toward the house. "As soon as you know what it is, I'll get to work. I'll save you a fortune! I've been making doll clothes for years. How much harder could clothes for a real baby be?"

"Okay. But no miniature space suits, or presidential seals." I let her loop her arm through mine as we walked.

"Fine. But I will make bonnets. Girl or boy, a baby needs a bonnet." She pointed a finger at me.

"Oh, geez, I don't know. What if it's a boy? No boy is going to want to look back on his baby pictures and see himself in a bonnet."

"Tell that to the royal family," she chided. "Those boys wore bonnets and dresses, and they're plenty manly. That younger one's a ginger, like you. You should have had your baby with him. That would've been a cute baby."

I snickered. "I doubt Prince Harry is interested in procreating with me. Besides, my uterus is booked for the next few months."

She nudged me gently. "Well, will the baby's father have a fit if I put a bonnet on your baby?"

"I already told you—"

"Come on," My mom said with a deep sigh. "He's the father of my grandchild. Don't I deserve to know him?"

I turned to face my mom. "There's no one to know."

"So should I tell Pastor Irm that there has been a second coming?"

Rolling my eyes, I took the picnic basket away, and peeked inside. "Oh, tuna salad. Looks good." I said a quick prayer that I wouldn't be revisited by lunch later.

"Alexandria. Cut the crap." She snatched the basket back, and closed the lid. "Who got you into this situation?"

"I got myself into this situation. And good grief, Ma. Don't call my kid a situation."

"You know what I mean. I want to know who this man is, and why he is leaving you to deal with this all alone."

I jutted my chin out at him. "I'm doing this alone by choice."

She stared at me for a moment, then nodded firmly. "You and the baby will move back in with me."

I nearly swallowed my tongue. "I don't think that's a good idea."

"Of course it is," she said.

"What's not a good idea?" Corbin asked, coming out of the house with a tool belt hanging around his waist. He waved at the pastor. "Hey, Irm. How are you?"

"Fine, fine." The kind pastor folded his hands behind his back and meandered towards us. "You and the missus picked a gem this time."

Corbin kicked the brick steps proudly. "She will be when we're done."

"Corbin, dear, won't you talk some sense into your sister, please?" My mother hoisted the picnic basket from one arm to the other.

Corbin looked at me. "Hi, Lex. How are you feeling?"

"I haven't puked since Tuesday. That's a good sign." I jerked a thumb in our mother's direction. "Mom's been hanging around the dolls too much. She's lost her mind."

"I have not." She pushed up her pink-tinted glasses indignantly. "I just suggested that she move home with me."

Corbin stifled some laughter. "Gee, Mom, I don't know if that's such a—"

"Of *course* it's a good idea!" One of my mother's hands went to her soft hip. "Corbin, she's going to need my help, and her apartment is twenty-five minutes from my house."

For a reason, I thought.

"Well, Andrea and I are just ten minutes away from her. Lexie can call us anytime for help with the baby." Corbin brushed some sawdust off of his jeans. "She'll be fine. She can take care of a baby on her own, and we'll all be here to help."

I looked up at my big brother, and my heart swelled in my chest. For weeks now, I'd fought tears every time I pictured Corbin and Andrea's deflated expressions. Their unsuccessful attempts at starting a family were a sore subject in our family, as Andrea's pain was apparent every time she saw one of Candace's kids at a family get together.

"Really?" I squeaked. I sounded more like a kid sister than I had in a few decades.

Corbin offered me a one-shouldered shrug. "Of course. Andrea and I are psyched to have a niece or a nephew."

The hammering inside of the house stopped. Andrea appeared in the doorway, her hair pulled back from her face with a dusty bandana. "I heard my name."

Corbin put his arm around his wife and tucked her against his side. "I was just telling Lexie how excited we are to be an aunt and uncle. Oh, and get this, Lex. Darren said he's going to babysit for you."

"No, thank you." I pictured our younger brother sitting in a strip club with a baby seat next to him.

"Stop it. You're scaring her." Andrea's gaze turned to me, and she smiled sadly. "My reaction to your news wasn't great, and I'm sorry. We're very happy for you."

"And we'll be here for you every step of the way." Corbin finished for her.

"And to live vicariously through you," Andrea added with a sad chuckle.

Joyful tears filled my eyes. Stupid hormones. "Thanks, guys."

Pastor Irm's warm hands touched my shoulder and Corbin's. "It seems your family has recommitted themselves to each other, Patsy," He announced proudly. "There's nothing better than a unified family. Praise God."

My mother practically levitated. "Thank you, Pastor."

Corbin looked down at me. "Were we ever *un*-unified?"

I giggled, and my mother cut me a sharp look. "Praise God," she echoed. "Why don't we all go inside and start this tuna salad before it gets warm."

Following the line of people into the ramshackle brick bungalow, I looked around with a rueful smile. Just when I was starting to think that my family was entirely unsupportive of me, they pulled through. Now all I needed was to find a bigger place where my baby and I could live. A place with plenty of space to play and collect all sorts of oversized and noisy toys. And I needed to find a delicate way to make my mother understand that I would not be moving back in with her in the House of Dolls.

Chapter Seven

A few weeks later, I sniffed the cantaloupe and immediately placed it back on the pile.

Okay, cantaloupes are out.

My stomach keened, and I quickly pushed my cart away from the produce department of my favorite grocery store. That sucked. I hadn't managed to eat anything fresh since the day I'd found out I was pregnant. Which basically meant that I was walking around with my jeans unbuttoned on a carbo-load months in the making. Gazing longingly at the ripe hot house tomatoes, I headed toward the frozen foods section with heavy footsteps.

I had a lot on my mind. Ever since my lunch with my family at the brick house, I'd been trying to decide where I was going to live with my baby. As much as it pained me to say so, my mother had a point. I couldn't raise a baby in my current apartment. It was too small, and in its current state, I would have to put the bassinet on top of the refrigerator.

But I didn't have any money saved to put down on my own house. As much as I wanted to buy the brick bungalow that Corbin and Andrea were working on, there was no way I could manage paying for my half of Eats & Sweets *and* a fat mortgage. Oh, why couldn't I have a trust fund from my estranged Floridian father, the way Marisol did? Her house was perfect for a kid. Large corner lot, eat-in kitchen with granite counter tops, even a tree house in the willow tree in the back yard—built by the last owners.

The only thing about that house that was *not* conducive with children was Marisol herself.

"I miss you, my friends," I whispered to the tomatoes, as I lumbered past.

WHAM.

"Crap!" I yelped.

Sure enough, as if fate didn't already have the upper hand on me—as I was shopping with my pants open and a holey Creedence Clearwater Revival T-shirt on—I'd just tried to take out Fletcher Haybee.

"Lexie." He looked good enough to eat when he smiled at me.

Fletcher looked totally relaxed and informal. He wore a faded flannel shirt and jeans with stringy tears on the knees. If he'd not given me a pap smear just a few short weeks ago, I would have assumed Fletcher was a mechanic or a logger or something else incredibly manly.

"Doctor... er, Fletcher! Hi!" My voice came out entirely too shrill. As proof, an old lady glared at me from her motorized cart. Clearing my throat, I tried to lower my voice an octave or two. "What are you doing in my part of town?"

He held up a cream cheese Danish roughly the size of a bedroom slipper. "Word on the street is this place makes the best pastries."

The little mom and pop grocery in my neighborhood didn't exactly offer the most variety, but I was able to walk through a park to get there. Candace was always appalled that I was willing to pay more for their food rather than going to the local Super Foods to bargain shop, and Marisol never went with me because she said the place smelled like old people. This was false, unless all old people smell like hothouse tomatoes and homemade danishes.

"Word on the street is correct." I held my breath as another wave of nausea bum-rushed me. "The couple who own this place used to own a bakery in Ellensburg before moving here."

A line appeared between Fletcher's eyebrows. "You're still nauseous, aren't you?"

I waved a hand. "It's no big deal. Really, I...I've always wanted to go on an all carb diet, honestly."

He tilted his head. "I can prescribe something for it. Why don't you call my office tomorrow morning, and I'll see what we can do. I'm here for you, you know."

The light from the front store windows gleamed against his back, casting an angel-like glow around his body. If I heard correctly, a chorus of heavenly music sounded, too. Of course, that may have been my imagination.

"Thank you." I scanned the aisle for a point of interest that would continue the conversation. Great, I'd run into him in the dog food and feminine hygiene aisle. Curse this tiny store and their disorganized shelves.

I smiled. "So... the dog food aisle."

Fletcher looked around with a chuckle. "Yeah. I needed some kibble to go with my danish."

I laughed too loudly, and the old lady glowered at me again. *Get out of here, Grandma!* I thought to myself, before focusing on Fletcher's face again. "Well... do you have a big one?"

Fletcher's face reddened, and he coughed. "Do I what?"

I fought the urge to grab a box of Kotex to hide behind. "Uh, a dog. Do you have a big dog?"

"Oh, okay." His laugh was like butter melting over pancakes, making my carb-pit gut gurgle. "Yes. It's a big one. I mean, Martha and I have a Komondor."

"Isn't that a naval officer?" I asked, watching him pluck a ten-pound bag of dog treats off of the shelf.

"No." Again with that buttery laugh. I was finally starting to feel hungry. "That's a commodore. Our dog is a Komondor." Fletcher pronounced it slowly. Tucking the bag under one arm, he pulled his phone out of his pocket and turned it on. The screensaver was a picture of a lovely little girl with one arm thrown around the neck of the biggest dog I'd ever seen. The dog's hair hung to the ground in thick, white ropes, covering one of its eyes. It looked like a mop.

"Wow, look at that thing." I couldn't help but grin. It was so ridiculous looking, it almost didn't seem real. "What's her name?"

"She's a he," He informed me with a wink, stuffing the phone back into his jeans pocket. "And his name is Libman."

I snorted, then slapped a hand over my nose. Just at the end of the aisle, right beside the cranky old lady on the scooter, was a rack of Libman mops and brooms, their green and white labels gleaming in the sunlight. "That's the coolest dog name I've ever heard."

"Thanks," he said with a heart-stopping grin. "We've had him since my ex-wife left. He's gotten us through some tough times."

We started walking towards the dairy department, my hands fidgeting on the cart handle like a restless kid. "Your daughter is beautiful. She's got a great smile."

"Thanks. She's got her grandmother's smile." There was a hint of pride in his voice. "My mom was Miss Memphis about forty-five years ago."

"No kidding?" I raised my eyebrows. "Impressive. So you have pageantry in the blood?"

He chuckled and grabbed a box of crackers off of a shelf as we rounded the corner. "Yeah. I guess. I have one heck of a parade wave."

"So were you raised around here?" I pretended to examine the back of a can of spray cheese thoroughly.

"Nah. We lived in Tennessee until I was about fifteen. Then my dad transferred to Spokane." He said. "We lived on the north side. I went to WSU, then transferred to the U of W for medical school. How about you? Did you grow up around here?"

I nodded, putting the spray cheese back onto the shelf. "Uh huh. My whole family lives here. Well, not my dad. He died when I was a teenager."

I felt Fletcher's blue eyes on the side of my face. "Oh, I'm sorry," He said. "That must have been hard for you."

"It was." I picked up a box of saltine crackers, thought about it for a moment, then grabbed three more. "But I went on to college and now I own my own business, so I turned out all right. My youngest brother, though? Not so much." Dumping the crackers into the cart, I started strolling again. "He was only eight when it happened, and he never really matured much. He's still a giant kid."

Fletcher touched my elbow, redirecting me around a cardboard display. My skin flared with a prickly heat. "I have an older brother like that. Unattached, flighty, you get the idea."

"There's one in every family, right?" I smiled up at him. "So are you and Martha close to your parents?"

"Martha spends every day after school with my mother. They're currently making a quilt together."

"Oh, how sweet. I hope my mother does things like that with this kid." I imagined my mom quilting with my child. The image was quickly squashed by a vision of my mother dressing my baby up in doll clothes and propping him on a shelf. "Well, scratch that. She's a little bit…intense."

Fletcher grabbed a bag of coffee grounds. "Isn't everyone's mom intense?"

"Mine takes the cake." I raised an eyebrow at him. "She has a huge collection of stuff."

Crinkles appeared on either side of his eyes. "My mother collects bells. They're all over the house. Whenever you shut a cupboard or closet door, the whole house jingles."

"I can beat that," I challenged. "My mother's walls are lined with hundreds of Cabbage Patch dolls, and she has an entire filing cabinet filled with birth certificates for each and every one."

Fletcher released a low whistle. "Wow. Birth certificates. That *is* intense."

"Told ya." I tossed a loaf of white bread into the cart, looked up at Fletcher, then replaced it with a whole grain loaf. Didn't want the good doctor to think I wasn't nourishing my unborn child.

"Who's the father?" he asked. When I scowled, he quickly added, "Of the Cabbage Patch dolls? If *she's* the mother, who is the father?"

"My deceased father," I replied. "Though, I'm sure she'd have Pastor Irm be the father, if she thought she could get away with it."

"Who's Pastor Irm?"

We stopped next to the small display of fresh flower bundles, and I studied Fletcher as he examined a bouquet of bright yellow daisies. "Pastor Irm is the reverend in the church I grew up in. My mother's in love with him."

He raised his blue eyes to meet mine. "Are they dating?"

"No." I shook my head. "They're both widowed, and devoted to their dead spouses like a couple of martyrs."

"But she's in love with her pastor?" He picked up two bunches of daisies. One white, and one yellow. "Which ones do you like?"

Holy Hannah! Was he buying me flowers? I pointed to the white ones and started planning which vase I was going to put them in when I got home. "Yes. She has been for years. My brothers and I tease her all the time, but she won't admit it."

Fletcher put the yellow daisies back. "Why not? Will you and your brothers be upset?"

"Not at all." I laughed. "Actually, it would be a relief. Maybe if she found love, she would stop obsessing over our lives a little bit. Plus, it would be nice to see her happy. She's really lonely."

His smile returned. "Maybe she'll be happy when she has a new grandbaby to enjoy."

Nodding, I led him up to the counter, where a white haired woman started scanning my groceries. "I think so. Though she's none too pleased that her daughter is single and pregnant."

"Lots of single women have children," he said. "It isn't unheard of."

I offered him a one-shouldered shrug. "She's sort of old-fashioned. She still calls her answering machine the recorder-thingy, and keeps her remote control in a kitchen drawer, because she's afraid the laser will start a fire."

"Wow." Fletcher stifled a laugh. "Well, maybe she'll adapt with time."

"Here's hoping." I handed the old woman my debit card, and eyeballed my—er, *the*—flowers. Okay, so I had no reason to believe the flowers were for me, but I couldn't help myself. We were getting along so well. And when he'd touched me, it felt like being shocked by fresh laundry coming out of the dryer. "Either that, or she'll use it to guilt trip me into going to church with her every week for the rest of her life."

Snickering, Fletcher placed his groceries on the belt next to mine. "You're something else. Do you know that?"

That's good, right? I tried to present him with a flirtatious, over-the-shoulder glance, but it came off twitchy. "So, got a hot date tonight, doctor?"

His blue eyes rolled down to the flowers, and a lovely shade of red saturated his cheeks.

Ask me to dinner. Like… now. Ask me. I'll say yes. I swear I will.

"I, uh, well, yeah." He looked up at me, his gaze veiled with thick blonde lashes.

Blinking at him, I waited. This was the moment. My obstetrician was going to ask me to go get coffee. Or maybe even dinner. My stomach clenched. Would he ask me to dinner? And if so, would I have any pants to wear that closed over my belly?

Fletcher cleared his throat, jolting me out of my thoughts. "I do have a date. With…"

I stood up on my tippy toes without even meaning to.

"…Marisol."

Thump. My heels landed back on the floor, and I pressed my lips together. Though I couldn't be sure, I thought I saw Fletcher wince. It was quickly covered up with a sympathetic smile that bordered on sheepish. It was almost like he wanted me to high five him. *That Marisol, eh? She's a hot one. Can you blame me?*

"Oh!" My squeaky voice had returned. With a vengeance. "Right. So. That will be great. Or, fun. That will be great fun." I stopped speaking, but he just looked at me. The longer the pause went on, the more self-conscious I felt, so my words came even faster. "Yeah…so, Marisolwilllovetheflowers,I'msureofit.Supergoodfuntimes."

"You think so?" He handed two twenties to the old lady.

"'Course." I didn't bother to tell him that Marisol hated daisies. She said that they were cheap, and that if a man wanted to get laid, he'd better show up with flowers that cost at least seventy-five bucks.

We both grabbed our bags, and sauntered out into the sunshine. "Well," I sighed, forcing my face to smile. "Good luck on your hot date."

"Thanks." He looked at me for a beat longer than necessary. "Listen, it was really cool running into you like this."

My heart squeezed. I wanted to wrap myself around his leg and beg him to hang out with me listening to Elvis CDs and eating saltines all night. Instead of making out with Marisol on her overpriced Italian leather couch. But the nausea churning in my abdomen reminded me that having a raging crush on my OB wasn't exactly rational. "Agreed. Have… have a good night, Fletcher."

He waved, then strolled away, his backside practically glowing in his faded jeans. An image of those jeans crumpled in a heap on the hardwood floor next to Marisol's bed flashed through my mind. Shaking my head, I turned in the other direction and shuffled back to my Volkswagon.

It was me, Elvis Presley, and the saltines tonight. Alone.

Chapter Eight

"What the what?" Dropping the rubber spatula I'd been folding shredding zucchini into egg whites with, I pressed my palms to my pelvis.

Marisol looked at me from across the stainless steel prep table. "Something wrong with your girlie bits, Lex?"

I looked up at her. "Something, uh, tickles."

She shook her head, her glossy brown hair dancing. "There's an ointment for that, you know."

I winced. "No. Not like that. Like *inside*."

Her expertly-lined eyes widened. "Dear Lord, is it trying to get out? You're hardly even fat."

The glass door to the Eats and Treats kitchen swung open. "Hi, sorry I'm late." Candace flitted into the room in a pair of sweat pants and a tank top. "Aubrey cried when I left her with the babysitter, so I was late for yoga class. Then I didn't have a clean shirt, so I had to scrounge around the laundry room for twenty minutes."

Marisol nodded pointedly at me. "You see what your life is going to become."

Candace ignored her and dropped some bags onto the table. "Sorry I'm late for our lunch date. Which begs me to ask why in the heck am I bringing lunch to you guys, when you run a catering company?"

Marisol's shoulders rose and fell. "I didn't want to eat my own cooking."

"You're so weird," Candace scoffed. "I brought deli sandwiches. Lexie, I had no idea what to get for you, since the only thing that doesn't make you sick is—" She stopped speaking when she saw me my bewildered expression and my hands cupping my abdomen. "What? What's wrong? Are you all right? Are you having cramps? Spotting? Do you need to lie down?"

A snort came from Marisol's direction. "Chill out, Doctor-High-Strung, the little critter's just doing some Tae Bo."

Candace dove towards me. "You can feel it kicking? Really?" I nodded. "Oh, Lexie, this is so exciting!"

"I know, I can't believe it." Tears filled my eyes as another little tickle quickened inside of me. "Ah! There it goes again."

"Wait, wait, wait." Marisol put her spoon down and rested her hand on her hip. "Aren't you supposed to be huge before you feel it kicking? How many weeks along are you? Four weeks? Five?"

I frowned. "Fourteen and three quarters."

"I felt all of my kids when I was ten weeks along." Candace smiled smartly.

"Well, that pregnancy book said you don't feel the baby kicking until you're like halfway done cooking the kid." Marisol flicked a speck of zucchini off of her shirtsleeve. "I think you have gas, Lex."

"Since when do you read pregnancy books?" Candace asked, opening the lunch bags.

Marisol rolled her eyes. "Since that's all I can find around this place when I'm taking a break. All of the Cosmopolitan and People magazines are gone. Now all I can find everywhere is *What to Expect When You're Knocked Up*, or—"

"Expecting," Candace and I said in unison.

"Whatever. Anyway, so I've been reading it during my down time." Marisol took the sandwich Candace held out to her. "Thanks. And it says that you can't feel the baby kicking this early."

"Wait, it does not." Candace handed me a sandwich. "I read that book at least a dozen times. It says that it can be anywhere between twelve and twenty weeks. Usually the thinner the woman is, the sooner she feels it.

But I have a girlfriend who is heavy set, and she felt it at eleven weeks. It varies with every woman."

Marisol flared her nostrils at my abdomen. "I think Lex has to fart."

"I do not!" I took my sandwich from Candace, and tried not to smell it.

"Well, what does it feel like?" Candace asked.

Thinking for a moment, I opened my sandwich and peeled off every ingredient that was something I'd thrown up over the last three months. Lettuce, tomatoes, turkey, pickles, cheddar. I was left with a mayonnaise and sourdough bread sandwich. "It feels like flutters," I explained. "Like baby bird wings are flapping around inside of me. Way, way down low."

"Like baby bird wings?" Marisol cracked up. "You've got to be kidding me. Now you're just trying to wax poetic."

"Shush!" Candace turned so that her back was to our gorgeous Latina friend. "Ignore her."

I gasped. "There it goes again!"

"Fart, Lex!" Marisol cackled, biting into her bread.

Sticking my tongue out at her, I went back to my sandwich, my heart beating out of my chest. Even though I'd not had a period in four months, and even though I'd seen my little kidney bean's heart flickering on the ultrasound screen, this new experience was blowing my mind.

I could *feel* my child inside of me. Moving and dancing. Rolling and kicking. Growing and stretching. I'd created life within life—*me*, the nut with an ugly tee shirt collection and perpetual bedhead—and the gravity of that miracle pressed down on my chest like a boulder.

I nibbled on the crust of my bread. "This is really…"

Candace's eyes danced. "Amazing, huh?"

"It really is." Blinking back tears, I grinned at my cousin.

Marisol watched me with pointed curiosity, her arched brows pinching close together. "Dude. You're really into this whole pregnancy thing, aren't you?"

"I don't really have a choice, do I?" I swallowed my bite of bread. "It's happening whether I like it or not, so I may as well embrace it. This is a huge opportunity, Marisol. I never thought I would be a mother."

"I think you're going to be a great mother." Candace bumped shoulders with me, and bit into her own lunch contentedly. I could practically hear her planning future play dates in her head. It felt good to know that at least *one* of my best friends didn't think I was making a colossal mistake.

"Hey, speaking of huge opportunities." Marisol set her sandwich down, flopped into a nearby chair, and propped her feet onto the table. At least she had the decency to move a few feet away from the food we were preparing. "Or rather, lost opportunities."

Candace moved a chair across the kitchen, parking it right behind me. She pushed on my shoulders, forcing me to sit, then sat on the table between Marisol's platform heels and my nearly-untouched lunch. "What's up? Are you hearing the tick tock of your biological clock, too, Mar? Are you afraid to miss your opportunity?"

She gagged. "No. Not in the slightest. Have you seen what happens to your goodies when you push a kid out? Like, seriously? It's like Hamburger Helper afterward."

I pushed my sandwich away. "Well, I'm done."

"Sorry." Marisol waved a hand dismissively. "I'm talking about Fletcher."

Suddenly the Eats and Treats kitchen was stiflingly hot. My five-minute flirting session with him at the grocery store had haunted me for days, and it'd taken every bit of my strength *not* to ask Marisol how their latest date had gone. I'd been hoping and praying her silence meant he'd dumped her.

Candace perked up. "Oh, yeah? What's the scoop? What opportunity did you miss with him? Did he not call after your date?"

Marisol was aghast. "Be serious. They *always* call."

Damn. I blinked innocently at her, and prayed that my cheeks weren't as red as they felt. "So what's wrong then?"

"Is he terrible in the sack?" Candace asked. "I know how much you hate that."

I suppressed a snort. Candace wasn't lying. Marisol was very forthright with her opinions on her varying boyfriends', ahem, *bedroom skills*. If they didn't make her scream out swear words in Spanish, she didn't consider them worth her time. And though I couldn't believe what I was thinking, I hoped that Fletcher was terrible in bed. At least if he lacked certain talents in the bedroom, then I could go to sleep at night knowing he wasn't making Marisol bellow '*Ay caramba!*'

"That's just it." Marisol slapped her hand down on the metal table. "I wouldn't know!"

Gulping back a smile, I asked, "You haven't slept with him yet?"

She shook her head. "Three dates now, and he hasn't laid a hand on me."

"He hasn't even kissed you?" When Marisol shook her head, Candace's mouth twitched. "What a jerk."

"Don't mock me." Marisol narrowed her eyes. "This is serious. I wore my thigh high boots on our last date."

My stomach clenched. "What? I thought you said you went to the movies." When she just blinked at me, I added, "Who wears thigh high boots to see a romantic comedy?"

She looked at me like I was an idiot. "Last time I wore them we didn't even make it out of my house that night."

Shuddering, I focused my attention on the zucchini cakes I'd been assembling before Candace arrived. "Your life is one long-running episode of *Sex in the City*, do you know that?"

"Uh huh," she said proudly.

Candace polished off her sandwich, then brushed the crumbs off of her chest. "Just because he hasn't tried to nail you in a broom closet yet doesn't mean he doesn't like you, Mar. That means he respects you."

I washed my hands, chuckling. "Respect? What's that? Marisol doesn't know that word."

"Ha, ha. Laugh it up, preggo." Marisol took another bite of her sandwich and leaned back in her seat. "Okay. I get where you're going with this, Candace, but what if I'm not looking for respect?"

Candace sucked in a sharp breath, then released it slowly. "What woman *isn't* looking for respect?"

Marisol's dark eyes rolled upward. "Well, it's not like I want him to call me a whore and tell me to fetch him a beer, or anything. But what's wrong with adding a little bit of passion to the mix?"

"You'll get to the passion, eventually." Candace looked at me and shrugged. "Right?"

My throat clenched. I didn't want the passion between Fletcher and Marisol to ever happen. I mean, I loved my friend. I really did. She was funny and would run someone over with her car if I asked her too. But did I see Marisol with someone as sweet and patient as Fletcher? Did I see her as a step-mother for his daughter? No way! Marisol was the type of woman that young girls went to when they needed French kissing pointers, not life advice like what college to attend or how to get over a broken heart. Marisol was too bold, too crass for mother-daughter heart-to-hearts.

"I, uh, right," I said. "With time. *Lots* of time. Some couples wait years before bringing in the passion. You know, they say abstinence is the new sex."

Both Candace and Marisol gaped at me, and the kitchen fell silent. I heard a car passing on the road outside, and the clock across the room ticked quietly.

Marisol's mouth pricked upward. "Bold words coming from someone who's knocked up."

Candace slapped a hand over her mouth, giggling from behind her fingers. "Where did you that nugget of wisdom?"

Glancing down at my slightly protruding stomach, my cheeks burned. "I just heard it somewhere. What I'm trying to say is—"

"Oh, I know what you're getting at." Marisol stood up from her chair and walked around the table.

I watched while she started the sink and soaped up her hands. Did Marisol really know? Was she so in tune with me that she knew I fantasized about her boyfriend night and day? Wondering whether or not he'd watched the latest episode of *Culinary Countdown*, or what his favorite Elvis song was? Did he like my hair at my last appointment, or...

Oh, good Lord. I needed a life.

"What am I getting at?" I cringed, preparing myself for her answer. Humiliation was imminent.

Marisol dried her hands and faced us. "You don't want me to sleep with Fletcher, because you're worried that I'll wind up in a situation like yours." She gazed at me with a tilted head, and I just blinked at her. "You're so sweet. But I don't need you to be protective of me."

I almost laughed. She thought I was being protective? I felt Candace's eyes on the side of my head, but ignored her. "Oh, well, okay," I mumbled, going back to my work and praying I looked casual. I even added a yawn for good measure.

"Well, I think it sounds like Fletcher's being a gentleman." Candace slowly turned her focus back to Marisol. "Maybe you should adopt Lexie's logic, and take the slow road for once."

Marisol scoffed. "Please. I'll get him on our next date."

My stomach pinched. "How do you plan on doing that?"

She strutted back to the table. "I'm going to cook for him."

My head snapped up, sheer panic washing over me like a bucket of ice water. I was met with Candace's curious gaze. She frowned at me, but I didn't respond.

It was common knowledge that—if history served—Fletcher would be powerless to Marisol's lure especially after she cooked. She'd landed many a boyfriend with her Puerto Rican flan and braised short ribs. That, paired with her impressive cleavage, was a one-way ticket to Orgasm-ville, population: two.

Ugh.

My heart sank. Fletcher would be using one of Marisol's spare toothbrushes by the end of the week.

Marisol went back to her work, satisfied with having stunned us both into silence. I tried not to crush my zucchini into mush while Candace started cleaning up the bags and napkins from our lunch.

"So, while we're on the topic of abstinence," she finally said, tossing all of the garbage into the trashcan. "Lexie, you're really plugging away at this pregnancy."

"Yup." I didn't look at her. I couldn't. My hormones were all over the place, and I was already planning how I was going to go home in a few hours to have a good cry. Did I have any ice cream in the freezer?

"So, Marisol and I have been patient through this whole secrecy thing." She plucked a sliver of zucchini off of my cutting board and nibbled it. "But the novelty is wearing off. We need to know."

I raised my eyebrows at her. "Know what?"

"Who put the bun in your oven?" Marisol barked.

Candace grit her teeth together. "Was it Carl?"

"Who's Carl?" I asked.

"Brian and I set you up with him a while ago." She brushed a strand of her blonde hair out of her eyes. "Remember?"

I wrinkled my nose. "The one with psoriasis?"

Candace shook her head. "That was Odin."

Marisol snorted. "You went out with a guy named Odin?"

"Shut up," Candace scolded. "He's really sweet."

Marisol's eyes narrowed. "Was he a Viking with a horned hat?"

"I said shut up!" Candace turned her back to our gorgeous friend. "We also set you up with a guy named Doug. Was it Doug?"

"I didn't sleep with him!" I went back to grating zucchini with vengeance. "That date only lasted an hour and a half. He *cried*, and I convinced him to give his ex-girlfriend a call after he dropped me off."

She chewed her thumbnail. "Oh, right. They're engaged now, you know."

I closed my eyes. "Isn't that nice."

Candace snapped her fingers. "What about Kevin?"

My eyes popped open. "My landlord?"

"Yeah!" She grinned. "Your sink was clogged, and you said he stayed forever to fix it. Maybe you and Kevin had a little...*fling*."

"He's married," I cried. "Is that something you think I'd do?"

Candace frowned. "Well, no."

Marisol rolled some parchment paper onto a sheet pan. "Oh, come on. You've never been with a married man?"

Candace and I both gaped at her.

"No!" I yelled.

She shrugged. "To each his own."

"Seriously, your morality, or lack thereof, baffles me." Candace said over her shoulder, before facing me again. "A few months ago you said that a guy at your bank was flirting with you. Was it him?"

I put down my grater. "You think I slept with the guy from the bank, and just mysteriously forgot to mention it to either one of you?"

"Did you?" Marisol asked.

"Of course not," I snapped. "I tell you guys everything."

Candace looked over her shoulder. "It's true. She told us when she changed tampon brands last spring."

Marisol chuckled. "Guess she doesn't need those anymore."

I scowled at both of them. "No. I did *not* sleep with the guy from my bank."

"Then *who*, for Pete's sake!" Candace threw her hands out at her sides. "Lex, we've known the inner-workings of each other's lives for thirty years. Why in the world would you keep something like this from me?"

I didn't say anything. I just stood there, my eyes stinging. Time passed slowly with both of their heavy gazes fixed on my face, but still I said nothing. I didn't know what to say.

I mean, I wasn't loco. I knew that my baby hadn't been conceived via immaculate conception.

But if anyone—even my two best friends—knew how my baby had been conceived, they'd be so hideously disappointed in me. And I couldn't stomach that.

"Lex?" Marisol took her place at Candace's side. "Come on. This has gone on for long enough. Just tell us."

Candace's warm hand touched my arm, and I fought the urge to curl into her shoulder like I used to when we were little and we'd lie under the stars in our grandma's backyard together. I'd always been so afraid of the dark, and Candace had to talk me through each of our backyard sleepovers. "We won't judge you," she said softly. "I promise."

My throat clenched, and I slid out from under her touch. Grabbing my purse and denim jacket off of a hook across the kitchen, I walked straight toward the door. Pushing the glass door open, and letting a burst of crisp fall air into the kitchen, I mumbled, "I'm not feeling very well, Marisol. Finish up the zucchini cakes for me, will you?"

Chapter Nine

As soon as I let myself into my apartment that day, I'd fallen onto the couch and wrapped myself in the afghan my mother sewed for me after my divorce. (Because handmade blankets were apparently the cure for a broken heart.) Then I cried into the cushion for half an hour.

I'd never walked out of Eats and Treats like that. I'd never left Marisol to finish the work without me. And I was pretty sure that if I weren't four months pregnant and slightly crazy, she'd probably have followed me to my car to cuss me out. Luckily for me, I'd gotten away unscathed, and was now sobbing on the very piece of furniture where *The Incident* began.

Wiping my nose, I sat up and looked across my tiny apartment. Through the French doors beyond the kitchen, I could see my messily made bed, the patchwork quilt tossed in a haphazard pile over the pillows.

My red nostrils flared. That was where *The Incident* had ended. That day had been a rough one…

Marisol and had I spent that day in April catering a wedding reception with over four hundred guests, and by the time I'd stumbled into my apartment that night, my feet were throbbing so much it felt like there were subwoofers in my shoes. I'd ordered a large serving of chow mien from the local Chinese restaurant, then plopped down on the couch with one of the bottles of merlot Marisol sent home with me. We'd ordered too much for the reception, and now the Eats and Treats kitchen was bursting with the non-returnable wine that the bride and groom gave to us as a thank you.

I'd never been much of a drinker. I left the bar hopping and beer binging to Darren. But our clients had paid over fifty bucks a bottle for the stuff, so I decided it was better not to waste it.

I was wrong.

It probably would have been better to waste it. Or let Marisol take all the bottles home for her seduction supply. Because what happened next could only be blamed on two things:

Me and a bottle of fifty-dollar merlot.

Right around the time I poured my fourth glass, and the opening credits rolled on my second *Lifetime-made-for-television* movie about a woman finding love after losing her husband to cancer, a soft knock sounded at the door.

I sat up, brushing fortune cookie crumbs off my shirt, and looked around the room in a haze. The furniture blurred into the walls like a drippy watercolor painting, and I released a pungent red wine burp that made my eyes water.

When I passed the beveled mirror hanging next to the door, I caught a glimpse of myself. The hair on one side of my head was sticking out from laying on the couch, and there was mascara smeared underneath both of my eyes from weeping during the movie. (In my defense, it really was sad. Who knew that the chick from *90210* could make me cry?)

"Hello?" I called through the door. Even in my inebriated state I knew that I couldn't just open my door to any old riff-raff.

"Lex?"

The voice on the other side of the door made all of my major organs clench. For a split second, I thought I might throw up or pee my pants. Considering how much wine I'd had, there was a potential for both. I flipped the deadbolt and swung the door open.

"Nate?"

There stood my ex-husband. In all of his *dress-slacks-and-button-down shirt-even-when-it's-casual-Friday* wearing glory. His light brown hair was cropped close to his head, and on his face was the telltale "aw-shucks" smile. The right side of his mouth had always tugged up when he was up to no good.

It was *that* smile that had won me over at a fraternity party in college. It was *that* smile that he'd flashed when he popped the question Christmas ten years ago, while my mother wept nearby. And it was *that* smile he'd worn when we'd argued our way through weeks of divorce mediation. I balled my hands at my sides to keep from slapping *that* smile right off of his face.

"Hello, Lexie," he said.

I thought I smelled alcohol on his breath—or maybe that was mine. But when he swayed in place, I knew he was drunk. Placing myself in the middle of the doorway, I blocked his entry.

"What the hell are you doing here?" I hadn't seen Nate in two years, and before that, I'd only seen him from afar. Candace had stopped me from running a red light to hit him in a crosswalk once. "How did you know where I live?"

He grinned cheekily. "Your mom let the address slip when I called her."

"When did you call her?" I looked at the clock on a nearby table. "It's a quarter to eleven."

"A few minutes ago. Her number hasn't changed." He leaned against the doorjamb.

"Neither has her décor since 1985." I tried to fold my arms across my chest, but lost my balance, and braced myself on the door instead.

Leave it to my mother to inform the man who had abandoned me without so much as a second glance of what my new address was. She was probably sketching designs for my second wedding dress right now.

He chuckled. "Looks like I'm not the only one who was over-served tonight."

"Oh, please. You're one to talk."

Nate had been quite the drinker when we were in college. Ever the frat boy, he'd won many a game of beer pong, while Candace, Brian, and I watched in awe from the sidelines. It wasn't until we'd divorced that I'd realized what a red flag it was that my husband could drink a three-hundred pound trucker under the table.

I shook my head, making the doorway sway a bit. "Wait. You didn't answer my question. What the hell are you doing here?"

When I moved, Nate stepped into my apartment. Stretching his arms high above his head, he looked around the tiny space. His nostrils flared at the sight of all of the pieces of vintage furniture I'd kept in the divorce. His style was much more modern and streamlined than mine, a topic we'd always argued about. "I see your taste hasn't changed at all."

I slammed the door. "Why should it? You took what you wanted. I kept the leftovers, remember?"

His expression split into another grin when he spotted the lone glass of wine in front of the television. There was a woman crying on the screen. "Neither has your taste in entertainment."

Stomping over to the coffee table, I snatched up the remote and turned off the television. "Argh! Shut up. I don't even understand why you're here. Didn't you move away from Spokane a while ago?"

He shoved his hands into his pockets. "I went to Seattle, but my company downsized me back to Spokane." He hiccupped quietly. "I'm really beat. Can I sit down?"

The floor swayed again, so I flopped down onto one end of the couch. My lips were numb. "Fine," I muttered, gesturing at the opposite end. "Go ahead. But you can only stay for a minute."

I was too tired to argue with Nate. And even if I wanted to, I wasn't sure which one of them to argue with, as I was currently seeing two.

"Got it." He sat down opposite of me, and rubbed his eyes. "Sorry to barge in on you like this. Some coworkers and I had dinner and drinks at The Elm, and I was in no shape to drive. I heard you lived close, so…"

"You came to your ex-wife's apartment to sober up? Don't make a habit of it. I really can't stand you." When he looked at me with his infamous wounded puppy expression, I added, "I'll go make a pot of coffee."

"Thanks."

I walked as straight as my noodle legs would allow, and leaned against the counter while I poured grounds into the coffee maker. By the time I shuffled my way back to the couch, Nate had refilled my glass, and downed it like a triathlete chugging Gatorade.

"Hey!" I snarled.

"Sorry." He wiped his mouth with the back of his hand and put the glass back onto the table. "Oh, whoops. I was, uh, thirsty. Good wine, by the way."

"Oh-kay." I said slowly, sitting back down. "So you're back in town? Still working with the consulting firm?"

He nodded. "Yeah. And you're still doing the restaurant thing?"

"Catering."

"That's right." He slapped the couch cushion, sending fortune cookie crumbs flying. "You always did like cooking."

"Yup." I glanced at the coffee machine. "So, last I heard, you had a girlfriend."

"Yes!" His face went bright red. "Hilary. We live together. In fact, she'll probably be ticked that I came here."

"She wouldn't be the only one." Folding my arms across my chest, I narrowed my eyes. "Why didn't you call her to pick you up instead of showing up on my doorstep?"

He fingered something in his pocket. "It's…complicated. She actually kicked me out this morning. She says we need a break."

I eyeballed him. "Well, you're not spending that break at my apartment, that's for sure."

"I know." His glassy green eyes looked at me. "It's just that I've been meaning to call you. To talk to you."

"Oh, good Lord—"

He cut me off. "I've been thinking about you a lot lately."

When I rolled my eyes upward, the room dipped to the right. "Oh please, Nate, I—"

"Just hear me out." He scooted closer to me on the couch and put a hand on my knee. "I screwed up."

I jerked it away and reached for the wine bottle and glass. If we were going to have *that* conversation, I needed more of my fifty-dollar merlot.

He watched me, a smile tickling at his lips. "I never apologized."

My eyes reeled back to Nate's, blurring the room for a second. "You're apologizing? For what?"

He frowned. "What do you mean?"

I filled my glass right to the top, and took a healthy swallow. Or two.

You know, this drinking thing really did make all of your inhibitions melt away. Maybe Marisol wasn't such a lush after all.

"There's several things you could be apologizing for." I swallowed some wine, then burped into my hand. "Oh, well, let's see…packing up and leaving while I was at work? Emptying our checking account to get a bachelor pad overlooking the city? Refusing to answer any of my calls until after you'd filed for divorce? Sleeping with *my* divorce attorney? Twice. Only marrying me because your dad said that you wouldn't get your inheritance if you didn't marry me after four years of dating? Or lying to me about wanting to have a family?"

Nate's face paled. I guess he'd forgotten exactly how many things I had to be pissed off about. Silly him.

"I, uh, well," he stammered. "All of it, I guess."

The coffee pot gurgled in the next room. "No offense, but that was a blanket apology."

He shifted in his seat. "What do you want me to say?"

My temper started to boil the merlot in my gut. "You came to my house at almost eleven at night to talk, but you won't even acknowledge everything you did?"

"Okay, okay, okay. Easy." The end of Nate's nose had the red, shiny quality of a very drunk man. I doubted he would even remember all of this when he woke up in the morning. "Fine. Yes, I accidentally had a brief affair with your lawyer. That was wrong. I admit it."

I just snorted in response.

"And I took all of our money to get that apartment." He pointed a finger at me. "But if you remember, you weren't making as much as me back then, so technically most of the money was—"

I punched him in the leg. "Don't even finish that sentence."

"Ow. Geez." He rubbed his kneecap. "And not talking to you was immature, I admit that. But I was afraid of what you'd say." He looked past my shoulder at the TV screen. "Believe it or not, I felt bad for hurting you. When you started talking about having kids, I just panicked."

Wine apparently made me emotional, because hot, alcohol-tinged tears filled my eyes, and I crumpled right on the end of the couch. Covering my face, I squeaked, "Why didn't you tell me that you never wanted kids? Why did you let me marry you thinking that we would have the white picket fence, the family, and the whole stupid fantasy?"

"I'm so sorry." For the first time since arriving, Nate's voice softened. He sounded like the sweet kid I'd spent countless nights making out with in my dorm room. The kid who put a bread tie around my ring finger during economics class, promising me he'd replace it with a real one someday. The boy who'd touched me in the darkness of the back of his car, giggling about not getting caught by the R.A. "I never meant to hurt you. I just decided it was time to finally be true to myself. For the first time in my life, I didn't want to please anyone except myself." He took the wine glass from me and drank a gulp. "I know it was selfish. I apologize."

"Give me that," I hissed, taking my wine glass back and polishing it off. "So why did you apologize to me? Why now? Why not four years ago when you did it?"

"Because…" Nate's eyes lowered, and he dug something out of his pocket. His movements were slow and fumbling, like a tranquilized animal. When his hand emerged, he held a black velvet box. "Because of this."

I sat up straight so quickly that my stomach sloshed. "Whoa. Nate. No. This is… this is… I'm not…"

He smiled and blinked slowly. "It's not for you, Lex."

My heart slowed down to a normal pace, and for a split second, I was disappointed. Not because I wanted to be married to Nate. Oh, hell to the no.

But because I wanted to be married to *someone.*

I wanted to be loved. Treasured. Valued. Craved. But instead, I was a thirty-year-old spinster who was just a few cats shy of becoming the creepy lady in the building.

When Nate spoke again, his voice shuddered. "I want to ask Hilary to marry me." He reached out and grabbed the wine bottle, draining it into the glass and taking another drink. "I can't lose her."

I swallowed the thick lump in my throat, but it bobbed right back to the surface. "I… but I thought she kicked you out."

"She did." He opened the box and looked down at the ring. It was at least three times the size mine had been, and ten times as beautiful. Lucky cow. "Hilary said she wanted a commitment from me, and I panicked. But the moment I left, I knew that I was making the biggest mistake of my life. I love her. I want her."

"Does she want kids?" I snapped. I couldn't help myself.

He shook his head. "No. Neither of us do. Not ever. That's another reason why we're such a good match. We want the same things." He scooted closer to me, and put an arm around my shoulders. "But I've carried all of this guilt with me for years. Guilt over what I did to you. It just doesn't feel right starting a marriage with Hilary without apologizing to you for what I did to ours."

"You needed to clear your conscience?" My voice came out meek.

His chin rested on the top of my head. "Well, yeah. I'm sorry for what I did, Lexie. I guess I want your blessing."

I looked up at him incredulously. "My blessing?"

Nate half laughed. "It's just important to me."

I took back the glass, and polished off the merlot. Every angry and hurt feeling I'd stuffed deep down inside of me for years wriggled its way to the surface and kicked its way out, Chuck Norris style.

Before Nate could speak again, I was crying. Tears, snot, eye makeup everywhere, you name it. I fell apart.

"What's wrong?" His alcohol-soaked breath tickling my nose.

I realized how close Nate was now, but didn't move away. I don't know why.

"You knew I wanted a family," I wept, grabbing the front of his shirt in my hands and squeezing it. The first few buttons opened, and I leaned into him. "You knew it, and you married me anyway. Just to save face with your family. Or better yet, to make sure your dad didn't cut you out of your inheritance. You married me out of obligation."

He sighed. "I'm sorry, Lex."

I sniffled against his chest. "Do you know what it feels like to be rejected like that? To watch your dreams go down the toilet? Do you have any idea what it feels like to be looking down the barrel of the gun that is my thirties with no husband? No dating prospects? No baby prospects? No nothing?"

When I looked at Nate through bleary eyes, I thought I saw him staring down the front of my shirt, but ignored it. I was too caught up in the moment. Too emotional. Too *drunk*. "Now you want my *permission* to run off and marry someone else? A woman who already wised up and dumped you?"

He pouted. "As soon as Hilary sees the ring, she'll—"

"She'll what?" I sobbed. "She'll marry you, despite the fact that you're a selfish prick? I can't believe that you think you can make someone else happy, when your own wife wasn't important enough to make happy? Are you kidding?"

Nate cupped my cheeks and used his thumbs to brush away my tears. I heard him hiccup, but it was drowned out by the sound of the coffee machine gurgling. My head was swimming entirely too much to care.

"You are important enough." His voice was barely louder than a whisper.

I opened my mouth to respond, but the room swayed. It felt so good to be touched. So much so, that it almost didn't matter it was Nate who touched me. I closed my eyes and pretended it was someone—anyone—else.

His face moved closer to mine. "You *are*, Lex."

"I hate you," I told him in a feeble voice. All of my defenses were down. The department of reasonable thought inside my brain had officially shut down for the night, and I was running on autopilot.

Stupid, sloppy, drunk autopilot.

"I hate you so much," I whined. I wanted to forget. I wanted to feel something other than rejected. I brushed my lips across his skin, and Nate sucked in a sharp breath.

I don't know when the mood between us changed, but in an instant the oxygen in my living room thickened. It took more effort to breathe in and out.

When the end of his nose brushed mine, a shudder rippled through my body. I can't be sure if it was a shudder of disgust or desire, but at that moment I couldn't have remembered my own phone number. All I knew was it felt better than being sad. A whole hell of a lot better.

Nate's lips met mine with a fervency I'd not felt in years. It was an eager, desperate kiss between former lovers, with newness and familiarity all rolled into one. Only, Nate and I weren't becoming lovers again. We hadn't wanted *that* with each other in years. And the truth of the matter was, we didn't even *like* each other that much.

But, in that cloudy moment, I liked the way his lips felt on mine. I liked the way it felt when he nudged me onto my back, and gently pinned my hands above my head. I liked the way it felt when he kissed me so deeply my eyes rolled to the back of my head. I liked the way it felt to be *wanted* for the first time in months.

Okay, *years.*

I arched my back, pressing my body against Nate, and he moaned low in the back of his throat. The couch was rocking like a boat underneath me, and I gasped against his mouth.

"This is wrong." I said breathlessly as Nate fumbled with my shirt. The bubbling sound of the coffee machine echoed inside of my head, and everywhere on my skin that Nate's fingers grazed left trails of unsettling heat. "We shouldn't…this isn't okay…we—"

"It's okay, Lex." When Nate's mouth moved against my collarbone, I smelled a nauseating mix of alcohol and breath mints. "It's just like old times."

Just like old times. I giggled to myself. That sounded absurd. Old times with Nate seemed like an act. A farce I'd not been let in on until after he'd moved on to bigger and better things.

He pulled away from me, our lips separating with a loud slurp. "Do you?" He squeezed his eyes shut, then popped them back open a few times. "Want to stop?"

I needed to stop. I should have stopped. A smart woman would have stopped.

But did I?

Nope. I sure didn't.

"Shut up," I muttered, pressing my face to his again. Again, the couch swayed.

I don't know when we stood up, but when we did, my legs wrapped around his waist. My back slammed against the wall next to my bedroom door a few seconds later, sending a framed photograph of my parents at their fifteenth wedding anniversary crashing to the floor, and that's when I stopped using any sense of reason.

It was right around the time all the buttons on Nate's shirt flew in every direction. Not long after, my pants hung on the ceiling fan, and my brain shut off completely.

Chapter Ten

I didn't see the dog coming until I was flat on my back with a Tupperware container of fresh Kimmelweck rolls bouncing off my head. That's when I saw the giant mop of dirty white dreadlocks dancing as a sticky pink tongue lapped at my face.

I heard a little girl giggling. "Libman! Daddy, help me."

A hand pulled at the dog's collar, jerking him off of my chest. "Libman, heel!" Fletcher ordered. The dog the size of a Shetland pony backed off and sat obediently next to his leg. "Aw, hell. Lexie, are you all right?"

I took the hand he held out, and allowed him to pull me back up to my feet. A shockwave of excitement sparked from his fingers to mine, and then up my arm. His blue eyes widened when our skin connected, but by the time I was back on my feet, he'd righted his face back into its perfect smile.

Oh, how I dug that smile.

"Are you all right? Did he hurt you?" He placed his fingertips on my pot belly. "Did Libman step on you at all? How hard did you land?"

My pulse raced, so I moved away from Fletcher's touch. "It's all right. I'm fine. I was squatting, getting something out of the cooler, so I was practically already on the ground anyway."

I'd been digging through a pile of fresh fruits and vegetables, looking for the papayas Marisol had been unable to find earlier. We'd set up a tasting menu at the farmers' market in an attempt to drum up business before fall and winter, which were our slow months.

"Thank God." He turned his focus down to the massive, ropey dog at his side. "Bad dog. *Bad dog*!"

"Daddy, don't yell at him. You're hurting his feelings."

The sound of a small voice came from behind Fletcher's, and I blinked a few times to pull myself out of the handsome doctor's trance. There stood a little girl with long, wavy dark hair. She had the telltale smile of a nine-year-old, with some small teeth, and other larger ones growing in like mismatched Chicklets. Her eyes—the same exact shade of ocean blue as her father's—were wide and rimmed with an obscene amount of dark lashes.

In other words, she was as gorgeous as her father.

"He has to learn not to jump, Martha." Fletcher patted the dog's head and was rewarded with a grateful groan before Libman flopped to the ground and promptly fell asleep. "He knocked my friend onto her back."

"I'm fine. Don't worry about me." I stuck out my hand to the little girl. "Hi. How are you? Your dog is very special. You must love him very much."

Fletcher's mouth tugging into a grin. "Martha, this is Lexie Baump. She's one of my patients, and…" He paused and swallowed, letting his gaze linger on my face for just a moment too long. "My friend."

Martha put her hand in mine and we shook. "Nice to meet you."

When her hand slid from mine, I looked at her outfit. She'd obviously reached that all-important stage I remembered so well from my own awkward youth. Where wearing all of your jewelry and cute accessories at once is better than leaving something behind. Both of Martha's wrists were lined with jingling bracelets, and she had two oversized flowers pinned in her hair. Her neck was decorated with three necklaces, and two of her toes bore rings that may—or may not—have been intended for feet.

"Wow, Martha, I have to say, you're really gorgeous," I said. "All of that bling in this sunshine makes you sparkle like a pop star." I almost said "fairy" but then remembered that when I was Martha's age, looking famous was infinitely more important than anything else. I used to cry when people referenced my red hair to *Pippi Longstocking.*

She beamed. "Thanks. My dad says I look like Madonna." Her head craned as she looked up at her lovely father. "Who *is* Madonna, anyway?"

Fletcher's eyes closed at the same time my palm smacked into my forehead.

"Oh, child," he laughed. "I have failed you."

"You really have," I agreed. "What kind of father are you?"

His bright blue eyes popped open. "The kind who used to sing Pink Floyd to her in her bassinette."

Okay, so he hadn't failed her completely.

"Martha." I guided her over to my table, then I opened the container of rolls. "Madonna is an eighties icon. She practically reinvented pop music. She's like Lady Gaga. Times a thousand."

Martha's eyes widened. "Wow."

"I know, right?" I continued talking as I started slicing the rolls. "When I was a little girl, I used to wear tons of jewelry and lace gloves around just to be like Madonna. My mom thought I was nuts."

She handed me a roll to slice. "Were you?"

I pretended to think for a moment. "Well, maybe. A little."

Martha giggled. "My dad says I'm nuts. He also says I should play baseball, but I don't want to."

I made a face. "I'm not much of an athlete, either. He probably wants you to be a tomboy because he doesn't want the boys chasing you around."

Her little cheeks went a pretty shade of pink. "He says I can't date until I'm thirty."

"I'll talk to him." Giving her a conspiratorial wink, I offered her one of the berries that I was going to put on the rolls I'd already slathered in herbed cream cheese. "Want a strawberry?"

She took it and smiled. "Thanks."

"Anytime." I looked up at Fletcher, who was beaming at us. "What brings you guys to the market today, Fletcher?"

His smile tensed. Just a bit. "Well, Marisol said you guys were setting up a booth."

"Oh, okay." My heart coughed at the mention of Marisol. "She'll, um, be right back. She went to grab a mango."

She was still pretty sore about the fact that I refused to share who the father of my baby was with her. In fact, as she'd stalked away from our booth with her keys fifteen minutes earlier, Marisol looked over her shoulder and called, *"Your stomach is growing by the millisecond, and if I don't find out who the father is soon, I'm going to stop speaking to you. Serving appetizers with me all winter is going to blow if I'm giving you the silent treatment."*

"Oh, okay. I'll just wait." Fletcher's voice brought me back to the present. "Martha and I needed some produce, anyway."

I forced myself to grin up at Fletcher. "Well the market's the right place for that. What are your favorite vegetables? How about you, Martha?"

"Tomatoes. Broccoli. And corn." She rolled her eyes towards her father. "He hates all of them, and whines when I cook them."

My mouth dropped open. "Doctor Haybee, you should be ashamed of yourself. Didn't you tell me I needed more iron from leafy greens at my last appointment?"

"I did. But I'm a hypocrite."

"You totally are." I snickered, cutting into another roll. "I'll bet you don't take vitamins every day, or get a full eight hours of sleep, either."

"Wait a second. I do too take a vitamin." He winked, and my stomach tightened. Well, the stomach muscles around my ever-growing offspring. "But I'm lucky if I get six or seven hours of sleep."

"You might try eating some edamame. It has tryptophan." Apparently my flirt was set on high, because I tilted my head to the side and offered him a coy smile. "Or some spinach. That's a vegetable guaranteed to get you into bed." I bit my lip. *Did I just say that?*

Fletcher stepped closer. "I just haven't met a vegetable I like yet."

"That's because you haven't had my pasta primavera." One of my eyebrows arched, and the corner of Fletcher's mouth tugged upward. "It's been known to convert even the staunchest of vegetable haters into vegetarians."

"Really?" His voice had lowered by at least an octave, and he leaned forward with his palms pressed against the table. "You sound pretty confident about that."

My stomach whirled. The closer he got to me, the more my skin started to sizzle and pop like bacon in a pan. "Oh, I am."

Fletcher paused, and for a moment, all of the noise of the farmers' market melted away. Through the corner of my eye, I saw Martha's head bobbing in both directions, her gaze going from her dad to me and back again. My insides melted into goo, then churned inside of my belly.

He stepped even closer. "I find your cocky side very compelling." A smile was making his lips twitch and his eyes dance, and it was completely irresistible.

He's flirting with me. There's no mistaking it this time.

Fletcher's grin widened. Our faces were only a foot apart. "Listen, Lexie, I—"

"Hey, handsome. What are you doing here?" Marisol's voice shattered the moment into about eighteen dozen pieces that scattered all over the grass. The melted goo in my stomach hardened into a large, guilty block.

Fletcher tore his eyes from mine and stood upright. As soon as his attention was off of me, it felt chilly. Like when the sun slips behind a cloud.

"Hey!" He pulled Marisol in for a quick hug. "There you are. We were looking for you."

Marisol leaned in with her cheek pointed at Fletcher's face, but he released her and let his hands drop down at his sides without even noticing. My heart did a little victory dance, but I quashed my joy when I saw a flash of disappointment in Marisol's eyes.

Bad friend.

I went back to my work. Through the corner of my eye, I watched as Fletcher gently nudged Martha towards my gorgeous Latin friend. "Marisol, I want you to meet my daughter."

For the briefest of moments, Marisol's eyes widened and she appeared terrified. The nine-year-old in front of her was about as innocent and darling as tween girls came, yet Marisol's face paled as if Medusa snakes coiled out of Martha's skull.

Come on, I silently chided Marisol. Widening my eyes at my friend, I tried to remind her that Fletcher was watching. *Pull it together.*

It was really weird to want to help Marisol make a good impression with the man I wanted to desperately to make out with. Apparently, pregnant women had entirely too many hormones coursing through their veins, some of which actually affected their sense of reason. Case in point: lusting after your best friend's boyfriend. Who is also your obstetrician.

Oh, good Lord, I was going to hell. Where was Pastor Irm when I needed him?

The shock on Marisol's face melted away, and as quickly as she'd appeared startled, she sank into a warm, pleasant smile. Her manicured hand went out toward Martha, who appeared to be as enamored with Marisol's glamorous looks as much as her father was. "There she is. I'm so glad to finally meet you. I've heard so much about you, uh…"

Her brown eyes darted in my direction. I mouthed the name "Martha," then pretended to busy myself with the rolls. Good grief, Marisol didn't even know her boyfriend's kid's name? I still remembered his stupid dog's name, for heaven's sake!

"Martha!" she finished with a glorious smile. Twenty bright white porcelain veneers were enough to cover her flub, and both Fletcher and Martha broke into sheepish grins. "You're such a doll! Come on, let's go get a smoothie, hmm?"

My stomach clenched as Fletcher took Marisol's hand in his and laced his fingers with hers. His eyes were locked on her face like a tractor beam. I'd seen that look plenty of times. Men stumbled towards her, zombie-like, their eyes glassy and mouths slack. Apparently her powers were not lost on Martha, who was gazing up at Marisol's glossy hair and ample curves with an open mouth.

A flash of jealousy rushed through me, and I bit the insides of my cheeks to stifle it. I had no right to feel that way. Martha was *supposed* to like Marisol. Even if it meant forgetting how well she and I had gotten along a few minutes before. It didn't matter if Martha thought Marisol was infinitely more glamorous than I was. In a few months' time, I was going to have a child of my own to impress.

So why did it feel like I'd swallowed a boulder?

"Lex? Are you in there?" Marisol snapped a manicured finger underneath my nose.

I looked up. "I, oh, yeah. Sorry. I was concentrating."

Marisol blinked. "On the rolls?"

My cheeks warmed. "Yeah."

"Well, then," she said brightly. "Since you're having so much fun with that, can I sneak away to get a treat with Fletcher and Martha?"

My eyes flicked to Fletcher's face. His stare was locked on the side of Marisol's face. Crap.

"Sure!" I squeaked. "Go ahead. I've got this covered."

"Thanks, darlin'." The threesome—looking like a happy, and frighteningly lovely, family—walked away. Just as Fletcher and Martha rounded the end of the table, my friend wheeled around on her four-inch heel and flashed me the thumbs up sign.

Sighing, I went back to cutting the rolls, letting the crowd swallow the sight of her excitement up.

Well played, Marisol.

Chapter Eleven

"Ma, you bought enough. Stop. Seriously." I looked down at the bags hanging from my wrists and shook my head. My mother was nuts. For real.

She'd purchased five maternity shirts, and three pairs of maternity jeans for me. Surprisingly enough, they were cute, too. No circus tent frocks for me. But she'd also gotten the baby two Cabbage Patch Dolls. One boy and one girl. Dressed in matching overalls. With matching orange yarn hair.

It was a little much, and I wasn't sure I was going to be able to sleep with those dolls in my house, but I was trying hard to make our relationship work. I'd heard through Candace that she'd asked Pastor Irm, and the entire congregation at the church, to pray for her wayward daughter and her bastard grandchild. When I'd confronted her, she'd cried and asked me to forgive her.

After much introspection, and a few bowls of ice cream that came right back up, I forgave my peculiar mother and accepted her shopping invitation. She didn't know I secretly planned on leaving the pudgy-faced dolls in the trunk of my car. All she needed to know was that I knew she loved me, and I wanted us to get along. If it meant buying my unborn child creepy dolls with names like Angus and Petunia, then so be it.

"Oh, shush." My mom patted her hair helmet as she padded alongside me. "I want to spoil my daughter. Is there anything wrong with that?"

"No. I just don't want you to spend any more money on me." I gave her a sideways glance. "But I do love spending time with you."

She tittered and adjusted the gold cross hanging around her neck. "I enjoy it, too, dear."

"Listen, I know this is hard for you." I caught a whiff of soft pretzels as we passed a snack kiosk in the center of the mall, and my stomach rolled. "But I'm glad you're getting into the grandma thing. It's not so bad, is it?"

My mother's face lit up. "Goodness, no! I'm having a ball picking out baby clothes and blankets. And as you can see, I've already got her doll collection started."

"*Her* doll collection? So you think it's a girl?" One of my hands automatically covered my potbelly affectionately. I was really starting to show now. My stomach was starting to stretch the bottoms of all of my best vintage rock tee shirts. But I didn't mind. I spent most of my alone time talking to my baby and singing it classic Aerosmith songs.

My mom's smile widened. "I don't know what it is. Sometimes I think it's a boy, other times I think it's a girl. I just hope it's healthy and happy. You deserve a healthy child and a happy life."

Unexpected tears tickled the backs of my eyes, and I blinked a few times to keep from choking up in the middle of the mall. The last thing I needed to do was cry *again*. My hormones were so unpredictable, I'd actually cried while picking out a new lip balm at the pharmacy the other day.

"Aw, Ma. Thanks." I mumbled, my throat tight.

She looped her arm through mine. "You know that's all I've ever wanted for you, Lexie. A good job, a cute family, a lovely home." She paused for a beat. Then added, "A nice man to take care of you."

We passed a store whose window filled with lingerie in sizes I'd long since outgrown. "I don't need a man to take care of me."

She patted my hand. "Every woman wants a man to take care of her, sweetie."

"Well, sure," I agreed reluctantly. "Single, straight women do usually want a man to love them and care about them. But most smart women don't necessarily sit around praying for Prince Charming to show up and pay the bills. I've got a good job. My own business. I don't need a sugar daddy."

She stared at me through her thick pink-tinted glasses. "But you *want* someone to love you. And love the baby, right?"

I hesitated, and we passed through a gaggle of giggling teenage girls gathered around a cell phone. As soon as they were out of earshot, I replied, "Yes. Of course I do, but—"

"And the baby's father is out of the picture completely?" she pressed.

The ever-present nausea in my stomach quickly dissipated into irritation. I was so sick of this question. Really and truly. I'd only told one person who the father was, and that was the father himself, and it hadn't ended well at all. "Yes. I've told you that. He's gone. Over. The end. Not in my life whatsoever."

She paused right outside a shoe store. "Oh good Lord in heaven, you didn't use a sperm donor and a turkey baster, did you?"

"Ma!" I looked around to make sure nobody heard her. "Geez. No. What if I had?"

She pressed a hand to her ample bosom, and breathed a sigh of relief. "Well, I don't know. Let's just deal with the issue at hand, shall we?"

"What issue?" I stumbled behind her as she started walking again. "There's no issue."

"Well, honey, of course there's an issue." The needlepoint bunny rabbits along the bottom hem of the shirt danced atop her round bottom as she guided me towards a custom knife store. "You're pregnant and unmarried. I mean, I know, I know. You've got your little catering thing going on, and you've got the whole, you know, *girl power* thing happening. But you admitted it yourself. You want a man in your life."

I rubbed my eyes. I was suddenly tired. "Mom—"

"That's why I brought you here!" She gestured to a store where the door was decorated with faux grey blocks and silver suits of armor. The ornate black lettering above the door read *Round Table Cutlery*, and the clerks inside were dressed in Renaissance garb. It was the type of store I never would have gone into on my own.

Come to think of it, it wasn't exactly my mother's type of store, either.

"You brought me to a knife store?" I said flatly. "Why are you shopping for knives? And what does that have to do with me?"

Mom bounced in place. "Norman goes to church with me, which you'd know if you ever came to services anymore."

My blood chilled. "Mom, you didn't."

"Shush," she scolded. "He's a wonderful man. He owns his own business. He's forty-three, never been married, and absolutely loves kids."

"No, Ma. No. I'm not doing this." I tried to take a step backwards, but her grip was strong. We shuffled through the doorway, where a stout man in a court jester costume was rocking back and forth on his heels with an excited grin.

My mom's voice dropped to an unnecessarily loud whisper. "Listen to me, Lexie. This is your chance. Norman is a good man. He's agreed to take you out, and he doesn't even care that you're..." Her eyes flicked down to my stomach. "You know. Pregnant with another man's baby."

If the court jester, and all of his employees, couldn't hear what she was saying, they were deaf as doorknobs. I noticed large pit marks stained the shiny fabric underneath Norman's arms.

"He *agreed* to take me out?"

The moment I spoke, my mother's smile dropped. Norman's face turned red, and his eyes darted to the floor. Great. Now I'd upset the guy wearing a three-pointed satin hat with bells.

"What the hell are you thinking?" I hissed at my mother, squirming out of her grip.

"I'm just trying to help." She laughed nervously, and glanced at Norman. "She's hormonal. What are you gonna do?"

Thrusting the bags into her hands, I backed away. "This is humiliating."

"Lexie, dear, I didn't mean—"

I turned and walked out of the knife store, leaving my bewildered mother and her court jester behind. The soles of my shoes squeaked on the tiled floor as I hauled butt to the nearest exit. The hot prick of tears stung the back of my eyes. My mother had tried to pimp me out to a creepy man wearing a jester costume while managing his *knife* store.

Humiliation soaked my skin like sweat, and the cold fall air outside chilled me as I fumbled to unlock the door on my car. In the months since waking up with Nate in my bed, and an empty red wine bottle on the floor nearby, I'd suffered through more humiliation than one woman should have to endure within a year's time. I'd officially hit my humiliation cap for the year.

We shouldn't have done it. It had been a colossal mistake, and Nate and I both knew it. When I'd woken up and gasped that next morning, Nate sat bolt upright in my bed and jumped three feet away from me, toppling off the side of my bed. We'd gotten dressed with our backs to each other, mumbling promises to each other like *I'll never tell anyone this happened; this meant nothing;* and *I can't believe I did this.*

I'd announced—repeatedly—that I never wanted Nate to darken my doorstep ever again. An order he'd enthusiastically agreed to. And we'd vehemently avoided each other's eyes as we searched my apartment for Nate's missing left shoe.

It was a one-time mistake, I'd reminded myself for the rest of that day, and for several more afterward. *A terrible lapse in judgment that resulted directly from too much alcohol and too many Lifetime made-for-TV movies.*

And I'd meant it. I didn't want Nate. I hadn't wanted him for a long time. I just wanted *somebody*, and at that particular blip in time, Nate fit the bill. But I wasn't clinging to any sort of lost love reunited fantasy. In fact, the thought of being with Nate again made me feel like I was getting a migraine. I never intended to so much as speak to him again.

Until two months later.

Choking back a sob, I rested my head on the steering wheel of my car. How in the world did I think I was going to get through an entire pregnancy without telling everyone who the father was? My friends were ready to break up with me, and my mother was bribing men to "consider" marrying me. All I really wanted was for everyone to accept my immaculate conception story, and for my obstetrician to propose marriage to me.

I watched as a tear rolled off of the end of my nose, drop on my knee, and soak into my jeans. I'd reached a new low. Someone needed to write a country song about my life.

Tap, tap, tap.

Gasping, I jerked my head up so hard, it thumped into the headrest. There, standing outside my window in a battered leather biker jacket and jeans with holes in the knees, was Fletcher.

I bit the insides of my cheeks. Couldn't he, *for once*, look terrible?

I wiped my eyes on the end of my sleeve. Then forced a smile as I rolled my window down. "Fancy meeting you here, Dr. Baby."

"Likewise, Bump." His smile was wide and genuine, and shot a bolt of heat right to my core. "Are you stalking me now?"

Snorting, I glanced into the mirror to make sure my tears hadn't dragged any mascara down my face. "You got me."

"Hey." He knelt down so we were eye level. "You're upset. What's wrong?"

I forced a laugh. "Me? No. I'm fine."

He reached through the open window and put a hand on my shoulder. His cerulean eyes softened. "Nice try. Come on. I took a psychology class in college. Try me."

I sighed, and let a few more tears fall. What did I care about looking pretty and pulled together in front of him for? He was dating Marisol, the woman who could shave her head and wear a burlap sack and still look like a lingerie model. Who cares if Fletcher made my pulse race? He was taken. TAKEN.

"It's my mom. She…" I pressed my lips together and collected myself before finishing. "She ambushed me. She just tried to set me up with the owner of Roundtable Cutlery."

Recognition registered on Fletcher's whiskered face. "That medieval looking place? I went in there a few weeks ago."

I narrowed my eyes at him. "Got a big knife collection, Fletch?"

When he chuckled, the sound had a very dice-in-a-cup quality. It was lovely.

"Nah," he said. "I inherited my grandmother's silver collection. I was having it polished and sharpened. They did a good job." Pausing, his nostrils flared. "Wait. She set you up with the guy in the jester costume? The short one?"

"That's him." I rolled my eyes and suppressed a laugh of my own. "Seriously. He was sweating through his costume. It was horrible."

Fletcher's shoulders shook. "Satin's not a real breathable fabric, is it?"

"Nope." I picked at a loose piece of leather on my steering wheel. "Anyway, his name is Norman, and he's a small business owner who will apparently forgive me for having another man's baby. This is who my mother would like to see me marry. Preferably before my due date."

Fletcher's eyes flashed. "She doesn't want you to be a single mother."

"Not exactly," I said, my eyes filling again. "She'd marry me off to the postman if he were willing to tolerate another man's child."

"Tolerate?" He winced.

"It's okay." I felt a reassuring flutter deep within my abdomen, and my hands went to my belly. "I know I'm capable of caring for my child alone. I've never doubted that. Not for a second. I just wish everyone else believed in me, too."

The sound of a rumbling engine passed by while Fletcher scratched his chin thoughtfully. The quickening in my stomach subsided, and I suddenly felt very heavy and tired. Maybe, like my mother, Fletcher thought a baby needed to have a father, too.

Maybe he thought the way as Candace and Marisol did, like I owed it to everyone to tell them who the father was. To hold Nate responsible.

It seemed I would never make everyone happy.

Until Fletcher cleared his throat. "Well," he said, squeezing my shoulder. His touch lingered for just a beat or two longer than what was appropriate. "For what it's worth, I believe in you."

I turned my head and smiled at Fletcher. My first genuine smile of the afternoon. That was good enough for now.

Chapter Twelve

A few weeks after the mall debacle with my mother, the aroma of sautéed diver scallops filled my nose, and I braced myself for the rush of nausea that was sure to follow. I was getting so sick of wanting to ralph every time I smelled food. Or soap. Or an animal of some sort. Or, well, *anything*. Most women grew out of this phase of pregnancy at the end of their first trimester. Here I was, almost halfway through, and I still couldn't get through a day without barfing.

"Are you sick to your stomach?" Candace asked, coming around the kitchen island. Her blonde hair was pulled into a French twist, and she looked as fresh and pretty as ever, even though Marisol and I had her schlepping appetizers at a charity event.

"Actually, no." I shifted the scallops in the bubbling butter and smiled. My stomach remained calm. "I think I might be getting past the nausea now. The other night I ate a whole plate of food and didn't have to run to the garbage can once."

"That's great." She popped a grape tomato into her mouth. "So since you're consuming food again, that means Brian and I can invite you over for homemade eggrolls. We've been missing you."

I closed my eyes as my stomach wavered. Just the tiniest bit. "Okay. Soon. I promise. But don't mention eggrolls again."

"Right. Got it." She patted my arm, and I went back to basting the scallops. "Oh, the joys of pregnancy. Just wait until your libido goes nuts."

I gave her a sideways glance. "Excuse me?"

"Oh, man." She plucked a stuffed mushroom off one of the crystal platters and popped it in her mouth. I watched her chew and swallow, then she licked her fingers before explaining. "When I was about five, maybe six months along, I became *insatiable*," she said.

My jaw dropped as I used tongs to remove the scallops from the hot pan. I couldn't think of a time in my life when I'd felt less sexy. I felt gangly and scrawny everywhere except my potbelly, which was now starting to resemble a volleyball under my chef coat. I cared less about makeup and shaving my legs, and was more focused on finding my bed after a long day at work and making sure *Real Housewives* recorded on my DVR.

"You've got to be kidding me." I placed the scallops onto plates carefully dressed with saffron sauce.

"Nope. Not kidding at all." Candace winked at me. "Why do you think Brian keeps nagging me to have a fourth child?"

I threw my head back and released a burst of laughter. "So you're saying your husband only gets laid when you're knocked up?"

She handed me another tray of scallops to sear. "No. He gets lucky. Just not as much as when I'm expecting."

"Isn't it awkward?" I held my arms out in front of me, imitating the enormous stomach I would eventually have. "You know, logistically speaking."

Her cheeks pinked. "Not if you're inventive."

"Holy crap, Candace. TMI."

I placed the new scallops into the pan and the sizzling sound filled my ears. I couldn't imagine having sex while hugely pregnant. I could barely remember having sex before I got pregnant. The only time I ever felt, well, *randy* nowadays was when I was around my obstetrician. And frankly, that was both pathetic and wrong.

A few moments passed. Images filled my mind. Shaking my head, I asked, "So... inventive how?"

The kitchen door swung open, and Marisol emerged. Her white "Eats & Treats" apron was smeared with orange. "Okay, the carrot vinaigrette was a hit," she announced, dropping an empty tray onto the countertop. "But who in the hell brings a little kid to an event like this? Seriously?" Candace and I watched in amusement as she stomped around the island, brushing the fabric with a towel. "Dear Lord, I can't stand kids."

When I cleared my throat, Marisol's attention focused on me, and she smiled sheepishly. "Whoops. Sorry. Not *your* kid, Lex. I love *that* little nugget. You know that."

"Sure you do." I chuckled and turned over the scallops. "Good thing you're dating a guy with a daughter."

"No doubt," Candace snickered.

Marisol snorted. "Please. That kid thinks I'm amazing."

"You told me a few days ago that she rolled her eyes whenever you talked." Candace smeared some more saffron sauce on a row of plates.

Marisol's confident smile faltered. "Well, yeah. But just the other night I took her shopping, and she loved every second."

"Well, duh. You were buying her stuff," I blurted.

As soon as the words slipped out, I felt like a jerk. It was rude for me to point out that Martha only dug her when they were at the mall. Marisol was trying, really she was. But she'd never really connected with anyone too young to get into her favorite martini bar. Candace's kids didn't really like her, either. When Auntie Marisol came over she treated them like they needed to be dunked in a vat of hand sanitizer.

"Ugh, I don't want to discuss Martha anymore." Marisol sighed and tugged the apron off. "I finally date a hot doctor, and he's got a stinkin' kid."

Wincing, I looked down at the pan and tried not to get annoyed. I really liked Martha, and *not* just because her dad was as fine as the day was long. She reminded me of myself when I was a kid. Eager, girly, giggly, and saddled with the wit of someone much older. If *I* were dating Fletcher, Martha and I would be pals. Besties.

Wait. Stop. Inappropriate.

Silence fell over the three of us as Marisol put on a new apron. After a moment, Candace cleared her throat. "So, if you're looking for *inventive* ideas, Lex, why don't you hit up Marisol?"

"Whatever." I lifted the scallops out of the pan, arranged them on plates, then put new ones on to cook. The sizzling sound sent a cloud of aromatic air dancing around our heads. "She's never been pregnant. You have."

"Yes, but we all know she's been inventive." Candace wiped the edge of a plate with a towel.

"What? Me?" Marisol looked up. "Inventive how?"

"Inventive in bed," my cousin chirped.

"Candace!" I glanced at the kitchen door to make sure no one had heard.

"Oh, *that* kind of inventive." She smiled and adjusted her boobs in her blouse. "Yeah, I've got some skills, if I do say so myself."

Only Marisol could make being borderline slutty a source of pride. Of course, if I looked like her, I would probably walk around in a self-obsessed haze, too.

I laughed to myself. "Well, according to Candace here, I should be getting good and horny in a few weeks."

Marisol hopped on the counter and crossed her legs. "That so?"

Candace nodded. "That's what happened to me. All three pregnancies."

"Huh." Marisol readjusted her glossy brown ponytail. "The exact opposite of that happened to my hairdresser. She said that the idea of sex made her run to the bathroom to vomit until her head spun." She raised an eyebrow in my direction. "That sounds more like your style, Lexie."

I frowned I served the last batch of scallops. "Thanks."

Her hands went out defensively. "Hey, don't blame the messenger. I'm just saying you've been vomiting on an hourly basis for like five months straight. Now Candace has you thinking that you're going to turn into a nymph overnight."

"She might!" Candace exclaimed.

"Okay," Marisol conceded. "So what happens if she does? There's no baby-daddy hanging around. It looks like you're going to be all by your lonesome for some long nights, Lex."

I turned off the burner. "Ugh. Okay, you can stop there."

Marisol's shoulders suddenly sagged. "Of course, what business do I have bragging about my bedroom inventiveness, when I can't even get my boyfriend to lay a hand on me."

Candace tilted her head. "Is he considered your boyfriend if you haven't slept together yet?"

"I like to think so," Marisol snapped. "I don't know. This is unfamiliar territory for me."

My heart suddenly sprouted wings and took flight. I'd spent the better part of the last few weeks trying desperately to avoid thinking about Marisol and Fletcher in the throes of passion. Even the idea of them kissing made jealousy prickle at the back of my throat, so the idea of sex was almost too much to take.

"So you and Fletcher haven't messed around yet?" I asked.

Marisol's pretty face pulled into a frown. "Had sex? No, we haven't. And it's driving me crazy."

My mind whirled. *Victory.* Wait, wait. That wasn't nice.

"So why not?" Candace nibbled on another tomato.

"I don't know!" Marisol threw her hands in the air. "I've been giving him the signals. Hinting at staying in his place. Inviting him in for a drink. I've shown more cleavage on our last two dates than you see at the beach in August. I even dropped a condom out of my purse in his living room the other day. You know, the usual signs."

"Wow. Subtle," I commented flatly.

Candace's elbow poked my arm. "Marisol, it hasn't been that long. Maybe he's just shy."

"You've known him for years." Marisol's eyes flashed. "Does Fletcher seem shy to you?"

"Well, not particularly." Candace bit her lip, then added, "But Brian and I have never dated him. Maybe he's different with women."

Marisol snorted. "If different means he's taken a vow of chastity, then sure."

I sprinkled chives on all the plates. "Hey, what's wrong with a vow of chastity?"

Marisol hopped off of the counter. "This from the single pregnant chick."

My cheeks flushed. "Well, it's stupid to act like you're going to *die* because your boyfriend hasn't seen you naked yet."

Her hands went to her hips. "Relax, I was just teasing. Besides, Lex, if you looked like me naked, you'd want to share it with your hot boyfriend, too."

"Oh, Marisol," I said, scowling. "Beautiful *and* humble. What man could resist you?"

Candace put her hands up between us. "Okay, okay. Truce." She started filling a tray with plates. "Listen, Mar. I think you just need to relax."

"Relax? I can't relax. I'm sexually frustrated." Marisol picked up her own tray, and started muttering to herself in Spanish. She'd picked up the habit from her childhood nanny, who wound up becoming one of her many stepmothers.

"It's only been a month or two." Candace laughed. "Some people wait years to consummate their relationship. I think you just need to chill out. Let Fletcher take his time."

I helped Candace hoist her full tray onto her shoulder. "He's a father, for heaven's sake. Maybe he doesn't want his daughter to come out for cereal in the morning to find you in his kitchen wearing his button down."

Marisol thought about that for a beat. "Maybe if Martha weren't around, we could have some grown-up alone time."

"Exactly." Candace nodded. "Look, Fletcher's a guy. Eventually he's gonna want to do it. Give him some time, and I'm sure he'll arrange for you two to have a private date, and—"

"I've got it!" Marisol snapped her manicured fingers and grinned at us. "I'll get rid of the kid for a night!"

"Ugh, that's the stupidest thing I've ever heard." I plopped a plate onto Marisol's tray with unnecessary force. "Your hormones are out of control."

Marisol's brown eyes rolled down to my baby belly. "Come on, you aren't really trying to advocate chastity with me, are you? Now listen, I won't lock the little girl in a cage. I'll arrange for her to have a sleepover somewhere, that's all."

"What, are you gonna call Fletcher and ask for the names of Martha's friends?" I rolled my eyes. "Come on."

Candace glanced at me. "Well, Marisol, I suppose you could—"

"I've got it!" Marisol propped the other tray on her shoulder and winked at me. "Since you're so fond of the kid, Lexie, why don't *you* watch her for a night?"

"Me?" I blinked at her.

How was I going to get out of this one? There was no way I was watching Martha while Marisol laid her father. Sure, I wasn't exactly the portrait of morality right now. But that didn't mean I was going to help distract Fletcher's daughter while Marisol tried to pry his Levi's off.

"I don't think so." I wiped my hands on a towel. I could feel Candace staring at me.

Marisol sauntered towards the doorway, the tray balanced precariously on her shoulder. "Sure you do! Just the other day you said you're sort of lonely. You and Martha can order pizza, do your nails, watch a movie. She'll never have to know what's going on back in daddy's bed."

"Which will be X-rated debauchery, I'm sure," I said flatly.

"Heaven willing!" Marisol laughed and bumped the door open with her butt. "Thank you so much, Lexie. You're a lifesaver. This is going to be great."

She disappeared through the door before I could refuse again. For a moment, there was no sound in the kitchen, except the sound of my heart thudding in my chest. There was no way I could do this. I could barely get through my OB visits without begging Fletcher to dump Marisol. How was I going to hang out with his beautiful, innocent daughter while Marisol seduced him with her ample bedroom prowess?

I pressed my palms to my eyes and tried to rub the image out of my mind. "Oh, man. What the hell did I just agree to?"

"When are you going to tell her?" Candace came around the island and faced me.

"Tell her that I can't babysit?" My hands dropped. "I'm going to tell her as soon as she gets back in here."

Candace drew a long breath, then released it slowly. She was getting ready to use her *mommy voice* on me. "No, Lexie."

Plucking up the pan, and turning to the sink to rinse it off, I glowered down at the soapy water. "Ugh, what?"

"When are you planning on telling Marisol that you like Fletcher?"

Chapter Thirteen

I heard Fletcher's voice through the door, and suddenly my stomach was filled with a flock of rabid hummingbirds. Looking down at my form fitting black jersey shirt to make sure I didn't have any remnants from my lunch down the front, I took a deep breath to steady my pulse. Knowing I had an appointment with Fletcher today, I'd dressed in the scoop-necked shirt, silver hoop earrings, and dark grey slacks this morning. These were the nicest clothes I had that still fit.

Not that I was dressing to impress anyone.

Well, crap. Even I didn't believe that lie.

A swift knock sounded, and I sat up straight and threw my shoulders back. Wincing, I relaxed my spine. *I'm trying too hard.*

"Lexie." Fletcher strode into the room with cargo khakis and hiking boots sticking out from under his crisp white lab coat. Grinning, he grabbed the wheeled stool and rolled over to the examination table with a grin. "Just the person I wanted to see."

"Hi!" My voice cracked, so I cleared my throat. "Er, I mean, hi. So, you wanted to see me?" I felt jittery, and apparently that wasn't lost on Fletcher, because he chuckled as the tissue paper rustled beneath me.

Fletcher's eyes crinkled, and he plopped down on the stool. His chest and my knees were just two or three inches apart, and I felt a teensy shock of electricity pass between my body and his. "I saw on the appointment schedule you were coming today. I've been looking forward to it all morning."

"Oh. Me too." I crossed and re-crossed my legs at the ankle. Fletcher was so close to me, I felt like I was under a microscope. I'd not shaved my legs this morning. Could he tell? I'd also run out of fabric softener last week, and still hadn't bothered to buy more. My clothes didn't have their usual spring fresh scent. Shaking my head, I told myself to pull it together. When I thought about where his face was for most of the day, did the freshness of my laundry really matter?

"So did you make up with your mother?" When I looked at Fletcher strangely, he added, "After the big set up at the mall last week?"

"Right." My stomach sank. He'd seen me blubbering in my car. "Yeah. I haven't actually talked to my mom since that happened. I think she knows I'm angry with her, so she's keeping her distance."

"It's okay for you to tell her why, you know." He widened his blue eyes and my heart seized. "When I went through my divorce, my mother used to tell me how to take care of Martha. Every day it was something new. I wasn't dressing her right. I didn't comb her hair correctly. She wasn't eating enough protein. I mean, I'm a doctor, for Pete's sake. I know how much protein she needs every day."

"My mother would have taken it a step further and tried to get custody of Martha," I explained. "You know, for her own protection."

Fletcher laughed. "Sounds like your mom and my mom would make a good team. One of them could start with the second guessing, and the other could come in at the end to finish the job properly."

My eyes widened. "Let's never introduce them."

"Deal." He nodded. "But really, after a year of this, I had to sit her down and tell her I was Martha's father, and that I knew what was best for her."

"Did she believe you?" I couldn't imagine my mother believing me if I told her that. Hell, I already had told her, but she'd still convinced herself I was better off with a husband—*any* husband.

"Not at first." He shook his head. "When she argued that I'd never raised a child alone, I explained that the only way I was going to learn was by doing it alone, day in and day out."

I imagined my mother pressing a hand to her chest and hyperventilating at the thought of me parenting her grandchild alone. "How long did it take her to accept it?"

He thought for a beat. "A year or so." When my eyebrows rose high on my forehead, his hand squeezed my kneecap, sending tingles clear down my calf. "But once she saw with her own eyes that her granddaughter was flourishing, she relaxed. Now she trusts me just fine, and we've got a great relationship."

"I can't imagine having a great relationship with my mother." Fletcher's hand was still on my knee. I held my breath to keep him from moving it. An image of Marisol popped into my brain, but I quashed it with thoughts of Fletcher's butt in a pair of Levi's.

You're a bad friend, Lexie Baump, I told myself.

When Fletcher grinned, I noticed a dimple in his left cheek and decided I didn't care if I was.

"I just think you should sit your mother down," he explained. "And tell her that you are a strong, independent woman." He squeezed my leg for emphasis. My heart seized in my chest as Fletcher continued. "And that you don't need a husband forced upon you to be a successful mom. A marriage of convenience will not make you a good mother. *You* will make you a good mother. And with time, your mother will see that, like *I* do."

Stupefied, I opened my mouth, closed it, then opened it again. "You believe in me," I finally blurted.

Fletcher's eyes flicked down to his hand on my knee as if he just noticed it was still there. Rolling the stool back a few inches, he retracted his fingers and folded his hands in his lap. "I, um, I did. I do! Er, believe in you, that is."

"Thanks…" My voice trailed off and Fletcher and I sat there staring at each other for five seconds. Then ten. Then fifteen. His eyes bored into mine with an intensity that heated every inch of my skin.

"Let's get down to business?" Fletcher's voice cracked, so he cleared his throat. "Shall we?" I nodded, and he added, "Why don't you lie down and we'll measure your growth."

Blinking a few times to clear my head, I wiggled backwards on the table. As soon as I was laying down, I lifted the bottom of my shirt and started unbuttoning my jeans. Fletcher opened a drawer and took out a small measuring tape right as the sound of my zipper going down sounded. Opening my pants, I thanked God I'd had the good sense to put on a cute pair of lacy panties.

Fletcher turned back towards me, and his eyes widened. "Oh, it's not an internal examination!"

Mortified, I zipped my pants back up. "Um, sorry."

What was I *thinking*? Maybe next time I could hand him a whip and tell him I've been a bad girl. Fletcher looked away politely while I closed my pants. I noticed that the blush on his face had spread to his ears, which were now a lovely shade of fuchsia. At least he was as uncomfortable as I was.

Once my zipper was back up, his smile reappeared. Fletcher's fingers prodded my stomach a few times. "I'm just checking the size of your uterus," He explained, his eyes flicking from my belly, to my face, then back down again. "It's easy to find, since your stomach is still fairly small."

"Thank you," I said automatically. I wasn't sure if he'd meant it as a compliment, but every woman knows that if someone compliments your "small stomach," you thank them.

Fletcher stretched out the measuring tape down the length of my baby bump and nodded. "You're measuring at nineteen weeks and two days. That sounds right to you?" I nodded, staring at the side of his chiseled face. He really did have a nice profile. "How's the nausea coming?"

"It's getting better every day." I suppressed a shudder as Fletcher's fingers grazed the skin just below my ribcage. "I'm eating more and more at every meal. I should probably start watching my calories again."

I wasn't exactly sure why I'd said that. I was a caterer for hell's sake, I worked with, created, and *tasted* food for a living, and I'd never made any apologies for it. The small handful of men I'd dated since my divorce never seemed to care that I could order a tomahawk-cut Angus beef steak, cooked medium, and polish off every single bite of it. So why did I care if Fletcher thought I was one of those annoying count-every-calorie types?

"Actually, no." He put his tape measure back into his pocket, and pulled my shirt down over my stomach. His palms were sweaty. So were mine. "Right now, you're a little bit underweight for your height and body type. It's probably from all of the nausea."

Nodding, I tried not to think about all the random places around the city I'd vomited over the past few months. The restroom of at least four hotels where we'd been catering weddings; two garbage cans outside my food distributor's headquarters; once in my mother's lilac bushes; and countless times in the varied bathrooms at Candace's house.

"For the next few months I want you to eat an additional five to eight hundred calories every day." When Fletcher noticed that my eyebrows shot up (getting permission to gorge through the Thanksgiving and Christmas holidays was like finding the golden ticket), he added, "Once we put a little more weight on you, I'll have you meet with my nutritionist, and she can help you come up with a healthy food plan for you and your baby."

"Okay." I cradled my belly in my hands. "Does everything look all right?"

His face softened. "Yes. My nurse said that the heart rate was around one hundred sixty this week, and that's just where we want it to be. Your urine sample looked good, and your last round of blood work was clean as a whistle. Now I need you just need to focus on growing a healthy baby."

Fletcher held out his hand to help me back into a sitting position, and when I took it, a wave of energy danced between us. "Do you have any idea what it is? I mean, you know, from the measurements and urine samples, and stuff?"

He leaned against the examination table as I sat up. Once again we were just a few inches apart. "Unfortunately, no," he told me. Our fingertips were just a centimeter or two apart. "It doesn't work that way. We can only find out your baby's sex through an ultrasound, or an amniocentesis."

I pulled a face. "Amniocentesis sounds complicated."

"It is." He nodded. "We go into one of my procedure rooms, and while using an ultrasound to guide me, I insert a needle into your uterus and amniotic sac, then—"

"Whoa" I held out a hand. "Are you saying I have to have a giant needle jammed into my gut? You'll maim my baby!"

Fletcher put his hand on my shoulder and squeezed. "No. You won't have to have an amnio unless we suspect complications. Sometimes we do them in the case of advanced maternal age, too." I narrowed my eyes at him and he chuckled. "But you don't have to worry about that."

"Can we just schedule an ultrasound and never discuss that other test again?" I suggested, enjoying the way the ends of Fletcher's fingers massaged my shoulder as we sat there.

He grinned. "Deal."

We just sat there gazing at each other like idiots for a few seconds. After a silence that teetered on the edge of inappropriate, Fletcher drew a sharp breath, and let his hand drop. "So, uh, you can set that ultrasound up with my receptionist on your way out."

"Oh. Okay, thanks." I didn't want my appointment to be over yet. "So how's Martha?"

Fletcher dug into the pocket of his coat and pulled out his phone. "Check this out," he said proudly. The picture on the screen was Martha wearing a fluffy white cap on her head, and a dress with the biggest bustles I'd ever seen. "She's wearing her Halloween costume. She sewed it herself."

"No kidding?" I blurted. That kid had skills. "It's really great! What was she? A colonial woman?"

He pointed to the flag she was holding. "Betsy Ross."

"Of course!" I laughed. "It looks awesome. You should have brought Martha to my house for trick-or-treating. I was giving out full-sized candy bars, I'll have you know."

Fletcher raised an eyebrow. "I don't know where you live. If I'd known, we would have stopped by for sure."

"My building is in Brown's Addition, in the Mercer building. You a big chocolate fan, doctor?"

"That depends. What kind are we talking about?"

"Dark chocolate. My favorite."

Fletcher's eyes flashed. "Mine, too."

I dropped my voice down an octave and leaned in a bit. "Guess you missed out then."

"Seems that way."

I offered him a one-shouldered shrug. "I didn't get very many kids at my door, so I had lots leftover. I would've given you two."

"Okay, now you're just trying to rub it in."

"Is it working?"

"Sort of." His hand shifted on the top of the examination table, making our pinkies touch. It felt like his fingers were on fire. Or maybe it was me. "I not only missed an opportunity to get score some dark chocolate bars, but I didn't get to hang out with one of my favorite people, either."

He said I was one of his favorite people! My insides started to spin like propellers. "Are you just saying that because of the chocolate?"

Fletcher's eyes bore into mine. "Not at all. You know I like you, Lexie."

I opened my mouth to say something witty, but all that came out was a slow rush of air. "Is that so?"

Fletcher's hand covered mine on the table. "This is really inappropriate."

My mouth felt dry. "Because you're my obstetrician?"

"No." He shook his head back and forth slowly, and a lock of his sun-bleached hair dropped across his forehead. "Well, sort of. But mostly because of Marisol."

Oh. Her. A clump of cotton balls formed in my throat. "Right."

"Have you noticed?" He paused, and his bright eyes scanned the floor while he searched for the right words. After a pregnant pause, pun *intended,* Fletcher finished his sentence by gesturing between us. "Something here?"

My mind whirled.

Every gaze that lasted for a beat too long. Every touch that lingered for a millisecond longer than it should have. Every joke only he and I understood. Every shared smile.

Fletcher felt it, too. It wasn't just me being overly hormonal and horny like Candace said. I'd felt *something*. Something deep in my core that rattled my insides and left me reeling. Whenever Fletcher was around, I felt like I'd climbed too high on a ladder, and was on the edge of falling.

It was thrilling.

"Yes." My voice was hoarse. "I've noticed *something*."

"I thought I was going crazy." Fletcher's eyes dropped to my mouth. "Well, maybe I am crazy, because…" He paused and took a breath. He seemed to grapple with his words. "I want to kiss you."

At least thirteen million red flags popped up in my brain. Somewhere deep in my ear canals, I heard an alarm going off.

This just got real.

Fletcher wanted to kiss me. Which, in and of itself, was excellent. But Fletcher was with Marisol. Which, in and of itself, was not good. I loved Marisol. We'd been friends since college, and she'd been there for me through so much. And despite her faults, I'd always known Marisol loved me.

Fletcher's hand slid up my arm, coming to rest just below my shoulder. I heard the muted sound of a phone ringing somewhere in the office, and another sound I was pretty sure was my heart galloping inside of me.

"Lexie, I…"

I felt Fletcher's breath on my face as he started to close the gap between us.

My hand went up, landing on his chest. "I can't do this."

I stopped him just half an inch from connecting with my lips. It pained me to do it. I wanted Fletcher. I wanted him *bad.* But I wasn't going to stoop to this level.

Not today, anyway.

Chapter Fourteen

The place was perfect. It reminded me of a little dollhouse, with its window boxes and matching shutters. The curved front walk was lined with river rock, and the tiny courtyard outside the front door was decorated with a wrought iron bistro table and chairs. The comforting scent of chimney smoke filtered through the air from the neighbor's chimney, and I could hear kids playing in the leaves down the street.

I cradled my belly as I gazed up at the ivy-covered chimney, and the baby *thump, thump, thumped* me from within.

"This is gonna be our home, little one," I whispered as Corbin approached me from across the yard. His tool belt clinked against his legs as he walked.

"Hey, Lex. Come to see the progress?" he called. "What do you think? Wanna buy it?"

I bit my lip and forced an innocent smile. I wasn't ready to share my intentions with my oldest brother. Yet.

When I'd gone for my ultrasound a week earlier, I'd been both disappointed and relieved to discover that Fletcher was at the local hospital for a delivery. It wasn't that I didn't want to see him again—on the contrary, I wanted to see him again. *Often.* But now that our attraction to each other was out there floating around in the universe between us, it made being alone in a room with Fletcher that much more difficult.

I wanted him. And knowing he wanted me back was an odd mixture of exhilarating and terrifying at the same time.

After Fletcher's partner, Dr. Javornik, performed the sonogram, I went into overdrive. Every moment I wasn't working was now spent shopping for blankets, booties, little tee shirts, and sleepers. (All in varying shades of green and yellow, of course, since my little butterball decided to turn its back to the camera, refusing to reveal its gender.) All of my baby supplies were stacked in the far corner of my living room, partially blocking the doorway to the kitchen, and creating a hoarder-vibe I wasn't too fond of.

I'd also secretly started filling out loan applications to purchase a home. Well, not just any home. I wanted the brick bungalow Corbin and Andrea had fixed up. There simply wasn't enough room in my teensy apartment for a baby. The poor kid would have to learn to swing between the light fixtures in order to get from one end of the place to the other.

I looked past my brother's shoulder at the round stained-glass window in the middle of the front door, and my heart squeezed. I was going to buy it. This is where I was going to raise my child.

"I don't know," I lied, following Corbin towards the front door. "How much do you think you'll ask for it when it's done?"

"You'll have to talk to Andrea. She's the one in charge of numbers." The vibrating sound of bass shook the ground underneath our feet, Corbin and I turned around just in time to see a car roll past. "Oh, phew," Corbin sighed, running a hand through his copper hair. "I thought it was Darren."

I watched the car turn the corner down at the corner. "Are you avoiding Darren?"

He shrugged. "Darren showed up here last week and asked us for a loan."

My mouth dropped. "He actually asked you for money?"

Corbin followed my lead, and dropped his voice down to a whisper. "Yeah, Andrea and I both tried to call you afterward. Where have you been lately?"

"The mall," I confessed. When Corbin's eyebrows furrowed, I added, "Been doing a lot of baby shopping."

"Right." A moment of unhappiness that flashed in his eyes, but he quickly extinguished it. "Well, I think baby brother might have some big news soon."

My mouth dropped. "Did he get Panda pregnant?"

"No." Corbin shook his head. "But he's thinking about proposing to her."

I froze in place, my jaw ajar. Darren was going to ask Panda—er, *Pandi*—to *marry* him? As in for better or worse? As in a lifetime commitment? This from my brother who once admitted that he goes through women like tissues, and breaks up with them at the first sign of the dreaded "L" word. Now he was going to ask this girl to marry him?

My mother was going to have a heyday when she found out that my irresponsible baby brother was marrying this *Pandi* chick, while I was purposefully having a child out of wedlock.

"You're kidding." I followed Corbin through the front door, where we were met by Andrea spackling a wall.

"Not kidding. Apparently Darren's found the one." My brother smirked.

"Hi, Lex." Andrea put her tools down and smiled at me. "I see Corb here has shared the good news."

I blew her a kiss from across the room. "Ugh. He can't be serious. And asking you for ring money? Tacky."

"Yeah, well, that's Darren for you." Corbin lightly touched a patch of drying spackle.

"Be nice." Andrea elbowed her husband gently, and approached me. "I think it would give your mother something fun to focus on. Wedding planning will be a nice distraction, wouldn't you say?" She raised her eyebrows at me, and I caught the hint.

It was no secret that my mother was trying to marry me off to the first man who would have me, and quickly running out of time to do it. Maybe the fact that Darren and Pandi would be planning a wedding would help take her focus off of me.

"Yeah," I agreed. "Maybe you're on to something. Maybe we should all pitch in to buy Pandi a ring. A big one, so that she'll be sure to say yes."

"Are you nuts?" Corbin called across the room. "Darren can barely pay his cell phone bill on time. How can he provide for a wife?"

Andrea put her hands on my belly. "Maybe Pandi makes enough money for both of them."

"That's probably why he wants to marry her." Corbin pointed his hammer at the two of us. "Don't encourage this."

"Yes, dear." Andrea rolled her eyes at me and grinned. "Your belly is beautiful. How are you feeling?"

"I don't feel like my belly is beautiful, but thanks. I'm feeling really good now that I can eat again." I dropped my purse on the living room floor—which was covered in gleaming hardwood, by the way—and moved Andrea's hand. My baby was apparently taking up clogging, and preferred a spot underneath the right side of my ribs.

Andrea's eyes twinkled. "Any weird cravings? I had a friend who craved anchovies every single day."

I thought about the last few meals I'd eaten. They'd been interesting, to say the least. Now that my appetite was back with a vengeance, I was eating the most random meals ever. The night before I'd consumed a steak slathered in clam dip. And the night before that, I'd gorged myself on chicken wings dipped in bean dip.

I didn't want to admit such culinary sins to my sister-in-law, though. She and Corbin were on an ultra-healthy, macrobiotic diet because she'd read it helped with fertility.

"Some." I gestured to the coved arch that led to the hallway. "So show me around. This place is looking gorgeous. Probably my favorite Baump home yet."

"Thanks, sis." Corbin put down his hammer, and strode across the room. He grabbed Andrea's hand as he passed. "Come on, let's show her our favorite room."

Andrea smiled. "You're gonna love this, Lex."

We headed down the hallway, and I fingered the newly refinished built-in shelves that would someday house framed pictures of my baby and me. I peeked into the bathroom, where the new tile sparkled in the sunlight pouring through the window, and imagined myself giving the baby a bubble bath in the claw foot tub. The stairs at the end of the hall curved under the pitched ceilings, creating a fairy tale cottage feel as we approached the upstairs bedrooms.

Corbin explained all of the improvements he and Andrea had added to the bungalow over the past few months, but I scarcely heard his voice. I was too busy peeking in doors and envisioning myself rocking my baby in the corner, or hanging its clothes on tiny hangers in the closets. I loved the house more and more with each step we took.

"And this is our favorite room."

Corbin's voice tugged me out of my thoughts.

Andrea was standing proudly in front of a bay window that overlooked the maple tree filled backyard. It was adorned with a custom window seat adorned with handmade cushions. The cushions were covered in black and white toile, and on the underside of the seat was enough shelf space for at least two-dozen books. Through the window, you could see the entire Spokane city skyline, and the sound of the small rock fountain they'd built in the backyard trickled in through the open window. It was, in a word, *gorgeous*.

This was my baby's room.

Unexpected tears filled my eyes. "You guys, I…"

Andrea took hold of my arm. "Are you all right?"

"Damn these hormones." I laughed and wiped my eyes. "Yes. *Yes.* I'm fine. I'm just pregnant."

She slid an arm around my shoulders. "Good. Corbin and I were hoping this room would be a selling point, not make buyers cry."

"No, I'm chock full of raging hormones." I used the end of my coat sleeve to dab at my cheeks. "Candace says I'm supposed to be horny all the time, but all I want to do is eat and cry."

"Okay, that was more information than I needed." Corbin put his hands out. "I don't want to ever hear you talk about being *horny* again, is that clear?"

"Grow up, honey." Andrea guided me over to the window seat, and we sat down. "Your body is going through something major, Lex, and you're doing it all alone. I can only imagine how difficult it is."

I sighed. "It really is."

It felt good to let my guard down. As excited as I was to be planning my life with my baby, there was always a nagging feeling in the back of my mind at all times. I wasn't quite sure what it was. Worry, maybe? Just a tiny tickle in the back of my brain that occasionally reminded me that if the baby got sick in the middle of the night, there would be nobody there to calm me down. If the baby had colic and cried all night, there would be nobody there to relieve me long enough to take a nap. And that didn't even begin to cover all of the thoughts I'd had about attending school conferences and piano recitals alone.

"You know that we're here for you, right?" Corbin asked me, sitting down on a discarded tool box in the corner. "Mom is, too, you know."

When I shot him an *oh, please* look, he added, "In her own way."

"Corb and I can't wait to be an aunt and uncle." Andrea squeezed my hand. "We want to spend as much time with your baby as possible. Trips to the park, lunches at McDonalds, sleepovers, afternoons at the toy store, babysitting, you name it. We'll do it all."

Guilt pushed down on my shoulders. Though Andrea's words were sweet, the happiness didn't quite make it to her eyes. "I feel weird talking about how difficult it is to be pregnant alone when you two have been trying to get pregnant for so long. How selfish can I be?"

"No, Lex, no." Andrea's hands covered mine. "Don't worry about us."

"How can I not? You've been paying doctors thousands of dollars to do what I managed to do with just a bottle of wine, and—"

Corbin covered his face. "TMI, little sister."

"Right," I said quickly. "Sorry."

"Listen, Lexie," Andrea said. "We have something to tell you. It's not common knowledge yet, so don't say anything."

"Which means Mom doesn't know yet," Corbin explained. "So if you tell her that you knew first, she'll lose her cool."

"Got it." I nodded firmly.

They exchanged a glance, and then Corbin cleared his throat. "We've decided to adopt."

Elation filled my chest, and tears pressed against the backs of my eyes. "Ohmigosh! That's wonderful! Just incredible!" I jumped off of the window seat, and pulled both of them into a hug. "Details. I want details."

When we pulled apart, both my brother and his wife were beaming. For the first time in, oh I didn't know how many years, they actually looked *happy*.

"We don't know any details yet," Andrea gushed as Corbin held her tight. "But our application was approved, and we passed our background checks. We decided to adopt from Korea, because I traveled there after college and had such an amazing experience. Right now we're working on our dossier and getting our passports taken care of."

"We're hoping to be matched with a child within six months. Maybe more." Corbin grinned, and it was a mirrored image of our late father. My heart squeezed. "The waiting is the hardest part."

"This couldn't be happening to two better people." I fanned my eyes to keep from crying. "You two will make the most amazing parents. And my baby will have a cousin. I can't wait!"

Watching them holding each other while they discussed their future child was more than my hormonal heart could handle. Sure enough, I started to cry. I wanted to celebrate my baby with someone. I wanted someone to be standing beside me, rubbing circles on my back as I gushed about nursery plans and car seat options.

Out of nowhere, an image of Fletcher's smile popped into my mind, followed quickly with the memory of his mouth hovering so close to mine. My heart pinched, and I opened my mouth to speak, but only an odd sounding whimper came out.

Andrea was back at my side in an instant. "Are you all right?"

Nodding, I wiped my eyes on my sleeve. "Yes. I'm just a walking, talking hormone. It attacks when I least expect it. The other night I cried because I was out of jello."

Andrea laughed, but Corbin stepped closer to my other side. "No. There's something more. I'd know that sound you made anywhere. You made it every time you cried when you were a kid."

I sniffled. "I did not."

Corbin laughed. "Yes, you did. Something's weighing you down. What gives?"

I looked at them through my tears. "Have you guys ever wanted something so hideously inappropriate that you were embarrassed to say it out loud?"

Corbin frowned. "Everybody wants things. What is it? How inappropriate could it be?"

I covered my face with my hands, and spoke in a muffled voice. "I think I'm in love with my obstetrician."

There were a few seconds of silence, then Andrea giggled. She slapped her hand over her mouth. "Sorry. I thought you were kidding."

That made even more tears flow. "I wish I were."

"You're in love with your doctor?" Corbin repeated. "The guy who, um, you know." He gestured with his hand in a manner I hoped to never see from my brother ever again.

Andrea elbowed him in the gut. "Does he love you back?"

Shaking my head, I hiccupped. "I don't know. I doubt it. Well, maybe. He almost kissed me the other day at my appointment."

Corbin's eyebrows were high on his forehead, as he scratched the back of his neck. "Dude. You made out with your gyno during your appointment?"

"Please tell me your feet were *out* of the stirrups." Andrea tried to suppress a laugh by pressing her fingers to her mouth.

I rolled my eyes. "Ugh. Yes. Of course."

"I can't listen to this." Corbin turned towards the door.

"Wait!" Andrea touched my arm, and Corbin stopped in his tracks. "Didn't you tell me a few weeks ago Marisol was dating him?"

Chapter Fifteen

"Oh, honey, I'm so glad you came!" My mother's smile was wider than usual when she swung open the front door. I tried to ignore the set of googly kitten eyes staring at me from her pink sweatshirt when she pulled me across the threshold.

The only reason why I'd finally agreed to go to a family dinner at my mom's house was because Corbin, Andrea, *and* Darren had all texted me, begging me to call a truce with her. Plus, Corbin and Andrea were going to make their big announcement, and I didn't want to miss that.

Though I was really hoping I would be able to keep my hormones at bay while they were telling everyone the news.

I hadn't seen Fletcher in a while. We'd briefly spoken over the phone about my ultrasound results, but he'd kept the interaction short and to the point.

Never once did he bring up the fact that we'd almost turned my last OB appointment into an episode of *As The Word Turns*. Fletcher simply apologized for my unborn child's reluctance to turn the right direction during the sonogram, but that everything else inside of my uterus looked healthy as ever.

Now I just had to sit around wondering about the sex of my baby for the next four months. Oh, and whether or not my doctor loves Marisol or me more.

All in a day's work.

"Thanks for having me, Ma." I peeled off my coat and tossed it onto the couch. "What's for dinner? It smells—"

"JONAH!" My mother dove for the coat, and plucked it off an African-American Cabbage Patch doll. She fluffed his yarn hair affectionately. "Don't hurt the kids, dear."

"Sorry," I mumbled, walking around the corner to the dining room. I was greeted with a chorus of hellos.

Corbin was at the end of the table, with Andrea by his side. Across from him sat Darren, whose arm was slung around the shoulder of a tiny, buxom woman with eye makeup thick enough to cause permanent damage.

He brought Pandi to dinner, I thought to myself, nodding politely at her. This really was getting serious. Darren rarely brought his girlfriends home. She looked particularly uncomfortable sitting next to Pastor Irm, who beamed at me from his regular seat at the table next to Mom.

"Hi, guys. Sorry I'm late." I pulled out my chair, and noticed the small, unassuming man sitting next to Pastor Irm. His reddish gold hair was thin, and he'd attempted to grow a mustache, but since his hair was so thin, it just looked like he'd drunk orange Kool-aid. He offered me an anxious smile. When I sat down, the pastor nudged him with his shoulder and gave him an encouraging nod.

"So, um, Pastor Irm, is this your brother from Iowa you're always telling us about?" I unfolded the napkin onto my lap.

"Oh, no." Pastor Irm said happily. "My brother can't travel anymore because of his gout."

Darren snickered, and Corbin kicked him under the table. I barely noticed the commotion, because my head was buzzing. *This had better not be another set up.*

My mother brought a steaming pan of lasagna into the dining room, and plopped it down in the center of the table. "Kyle's a junior pastor at the church, dear. He's three hundred miles from home, and Pastor Irm thought he might like a home-cooked meal."

I breathed a sigh of relief. Not a set up. Pastor Irm would never do that to me. He may be a man of God who probably wanted to see me married, but he wasn't thoughtless. That much I could count on. Besides, my mom and I hadn't spoken in over a month. She wasn't dumb enough to tick me off again. "Well, welcome, Kyle. I'm Lexie. It's nice to meet you."

"You, too." A high-pitched giggle escaped his mouth. Through the corner of my eye, I noticed that Darren and Pandi were stifling laughter.

"So how's the baby doing?" My mother dished up square portions of Italian goodness. "It looks like that belly is taking over your whole body."

My face scalded. I thought I'd been keeping my weight gain under control nicely. With the exception of my round belly—which was now the size of a basketball stuffed under my vintage Kiss tee shirt. My mother had a knack for saying the wrong thing, and it was up to me to keep my temper in check. It wasn't her fault she was nuts. Living in a house with a thousand dolls lining the walls could really do a number on a person's psyche.

"Baby's fine." I plucked a piece of French bread out of the basket, then passed it to Pandi. She took it from me with the longest, sparkliest fingernails I'd ever seen. "Growing right on track, and wiggly as ever."

"Oh, are you feeling her kick?" Andrea's face lit up.

"Her?" Corbin forked a cheesy bite of lasagna. "Why are you so sure it's a girl?"

Darren pointed his slice of bread at me. "That there's a boy."

"How do you know?" Andrea teased. "It looks like a girl belly to me."

"Bullsh—"

"Watch it." My mother pointed her fork at Darren. "Don't you swear at my table."

"Sorry, Ma." His arm slid around Pandi's shoulders. I wondered if she was cold in her strapless party dress. Had my brother told her to dress for a night of clubbing, or was this how she always looked for family meals? "What do you think my sister's baby is, babe?"

Pandi shrugged, and her oversized hot pink earrings danced. "Like, I dunno. Right?"

Everyone stared at her until Corbin broke the silence. "Well, I think it's a boy, too, Darren."

"Should we start a pool?" Andrea offered.

I put up my hands. "Sorry, guys. I had an ultrasound a few days ago, and it was inconclusive. The baby wouldn't roll the right way, so all we could see was its back."

"Well, get another." My mother popped a bite into her mouth and chewed. There was a string of cheese dangling from her lip.

"I can't." I fiddled with the crust of my bread. "My insurance only pays for one ultrasound unless it's a high risk pregnancy. And I can't afford another one. Sorry, guys. It'll be a surprise for us all."

"Oh, I'll never make it." Andrea smiled up at Corbin. "There's so much waiting going on."

Corbin pressed a kiss to the side of her head. "I know, babe."

"What's going on with you two?" My mother asked, the cheese string wiggling. "Are you guys up to something? Are you sick? Who's sick? What is it? Cancer? Thyroid problems? Andrea, I thought you looked puffy."

Corbin shot our mother a warning glare. "Calm down, Ma. Andrea does not look puffy."

Andrea drew in a deep breath. She was a champ at tolerating my mother's occasional bouts with medical hysteria. Instead of throwing her hands up and storming away from the table, like I would have done, she reached into her purse and pulled out a brochure. "Actually, Patsy, Corbin and I have some news." She slid the glossy paper down the table, and my mother picked it up. "We've decided to adopt a child."

"No freaking way." Darren craned his neck to see the brochure. "Dude. That's so awesome, you guys!"

"You mean...you mean..." My mother looked up at Corbin and Andrea with tears in her eyes. Her thick eyeglasses magnified them as she quivered in her seat, the cheese string swaying precariously close to the brochure.

"Patsy, dear, let me." Pastor Irm reached over with his napkin and tenderly swiped the cheese away. My brothers, sister-in-law, and I all stopped eating to stare at the exchange.

Kyle cleared his throat. "This is excellent lasagna, Mrs. Baump."

"Thank you." My mother blushed. "So Corbin, I'm going to have *another* grandbaby?"

Corbin glanced at me and winked. "Sometime in the next year and a half or so, if everything goes according to plan."

My mother's squeal of joy would have broken the windows, had it not been muffled by all of the dolls. My brothers and I all put our hands over our ears, but Andrea just laughed and wiped away tears of joy with her napkin.

Pandi—just tuning into the conversation—looked up from her meal blankly. "Is this, like, a big announcement, or something?"

"Yes!" My mother bellowed. "Yes, Panda—"

"Pandi," Darren corrected.

"Whatever." Mom waved a hand. "Yes. Corbin and Andrea are going to adopt a baby. They can't get pregnant. So they're going to go to...go to...where is it you're going?"

"Korea," they said in unison.

"Isn't that just wonderful." Pastor Irm ate a bite of his lasagna with a smile.

My mother pressed the brochure to her chest. "They'll go to Korea together and pick out a baby."

"Well, it doesn't work quite like that," Corbin explained, sitting forward in his seat. "They'll pair us with a child, that's called getting a placement, and then—"

My mother shoved a bite of salad into her mouth and spoke around the greens. "Oh, I don't care how it happens, as long as you bring home my darling, sweet grandbaby. Do you know what it is, yet?" When they shook their heads, she winked at me. "It's just as well. Now we'll have lots of surprises to look forward to. But you'll travel to Korea, right? Together?"

"Of course." Corbin laced his fingers with Andrea's. My heart tugged watching them.

"I don't think either of us could stand to miss a thing." Andrea rested her head on her husband's shoulder. "We're just thrilled."

"I can imagine, dear. So am I." Mom gestured to me. "And I'm so glad you're going through this *together*. Instead of doing it Lexie's way."

I looked at my mom. "Huh?"

"Mom." Corbin frowned at her. "Don't."

"Don't be silly. I'm not coming down on her." My mom rolled her eyes at Pastor Irm. "I'm just saying that it's really special that Corbin and Andrea are going to pick up their baby together, whereas Lexie's going to deliver her baby all alone."

Darren glanced at Pandi. "All hell's about to break loose."

"No joke, right?" She tucked a strand of her long extensions behind her ear. Seriously, she sounded like she was stoned to the gills. Well, she was dating Darren, so it was a definite possibility.

I folded my hands in my lap, no longer hungry. "I won't be alone. Candace and Marisol will be with me."

"We will be, too." Andrea nodded.

"Of course," Corbin added.

Darren looked up from Pandi's cleavage. "Well, *I'm* not going to miss it, either. I'm gonna be the coolest uncle ever. I'll give him his first pocket knife, take him out for his first beer…"

"You think we can get the baby out of diapers before you get him drunk?" Andrea asked.

"Ha!" He pointed at her. "You just admitted that it's a boy."

Out of nowhere, Kyle released another one of his high-pitched giggles, and my mother shot him the look of death. "I see everybody else has been invited but me." Her voice cracked and Pastor Irm patted her hand.

"Wait, wait. We're losing focus." I didn't want to fight with my mother tonight. Not in front of the whole family. Not in front of Pastor Irm. And certainly not in front of creepy Kyle. "This is about Corbin and Andrea's big news."

"Great!" Andrea's voice was shrill. "You guys should meet the placement coordinator, he's the best—"

"I can see that you're mad at me, Alexandria." My mother's eyes bored a hole in the top of my head. "And I don't think you're understanding what I'm trying to say."

I put a hand up. "Mom, I got it. You don't need to explain. Can someone please pass me the salad?"

"It's just that your brother's baby will come into a home with *two* parents," she explained, wringing her hands around her napkin. "Which, we all agree, is what's best for the baby. Do we not?"

Exasperated, I let my palms drop onto the tabletop with a bang. "Yes. Of course. Two parents are better than one. Three parents are better than two. Good Lord, Ma, it's not like my baby is going to be born in a crack house full of prostitutes and pimps. We've been through this already."

"I didn't think it would be." Her voice started to quaver. I knew that once the tears started, I was going to have to leave. I was entirely too pregnant for my mom's tears. "But if I didn't admit that I wish you'd chosen a more traditional path I would be lying. And you know how I feel about lying, Alexandria."

My molars ground together painfully. "Your feelings about lying are slightly hypocritical, Mother, considering your crush on Pastor Irm."

Both Darren and Corbin looked down at their plates. Andrea covered her face. This was the untouchable topic we'd all declared off limits long ago. When Andrea met our family for the first time—aptly in this very dining room over a pan of extra cheesy lasagna eight years ago—she'd asked my mother how long she and Pastor Irm had been dating. My mother cried for a week, and referred to Andrea as "that woman" for almost a year.

"What in the *world* are you talking about?" My mother's eyes flicked between Pastor Irm and me.

Pastor Irm scooted his hand farther away from hers on the tabletop. "I, uh, think it's time to say grace. We forgot to bless the meal."

"Hold it, Jesus freak. I'm talking to my mother!" Pregnancy hormones flooded my body like a dam had burst somewhere between my uterus and my brain.

My mom gasped so hard, she nearly tipped her chair backwards, and Darren snorted. This was it. I was going too far, and I knew it. But the wheels had come off of the bus, and now it was careening out of control.

Corbin touched my arm. "Lex, why don't you sit down and—"

I jerked out of his grip. "No."

"You are being very disrespectful." My mother fanned her face. "You're breaking my heart, do you know that? You're rejecting everything I'm doing to help you. If you just gave me a chance, you'd be married before this baby even arrives. And then we could *all* take a breath of relief."

"You know why I haven't asked you to be there for the birth, Ma?" I hoisted myself out of my chair, and leaned over the table. I could feel warmth from my uneaten lasagna soaking my shirt over my belly. "Because you're insane. Certifiable. If you came to the birth, you'd probably bring a date for me. Then I'd be stuck entertaining some forty-something *loser* who can't get laid without an old woman's help all while I try to push my kid out!"

Kyle choked on his bite of salad.

Pastor Irm patted him on the back. "It's okay, son. She didn't mean it."

"Yes, I did." I snapped.

My mother craned her neck to look Kyle. "It's the pregnancy hormones, dear. They've taken over. When she's not expecting, she's really quite tolerable. You'll learn to love her eventually."

My eyes rolled from her, to Kyle, and back again. "Mom. You didn't."

She dabbed at her eyes with her napkin. "I was just trying to give you a little nudge."

Sighing, I brushed the cheese off of my now stained tee shirt, and nodded at my brothers. I couldn't believe this was happening again. When would I wise up to my mom's predictability? Good grief, the moment I walked in and spotted Kyle, I should have known. It was a setup, just like the sweaty guy at the mall. My mom was nothing if not consistent.

"I'm not so bad," Kyle's voice cracked. "I've got a real nice sedan. Four doors."

Is this what it had come to? I was so pathetic that I had to choose a life partner based on how nice his economy car was?

"I've got to go." I turned on my heel and charged for the door.

Chapter Sixteen

I didn't see anyone in my family for almost two weeks. Corbin and Darren seemed to understand why, but my mom? She was another story.

Twelve voice mail messages, varying from angry to apologetic, were deleted off my phone. I didn't want to hear anything else she had to say. There were only so many ways she could tell me I was disappointing her, and I'd already heard them all.

Her point sank in: I was a colossal failure. Got it.

But during my anti-family sabbatical, I'd been working on another plan. A plan that nobody, save for my unborn child, was aware of. And judging by the way he or she kicked when I talked about it, they were as excited about it as I was.

I was going to buy the brick bungalow with the window seat. I'd applied for a home loan, and by some miracle, or the lining up of at least a bazillion stars, I'd gotten it. Now all I had to do was present my offer to Corbin. I didn't have a realtor, but who needed one? I was offering full price, and I was his kid sister. More money for him if we didn't use one, anyway. It was a win/win.

I practically danced up to the front door of the bungalow. This was going to be amazing. It almost made up for the fact that Fletcher was probably out with Marisol at this exact moment, enjoying a sunny Saturday making out. Or more.

Tucking my loan paperwork underneath my arm, I poised my hand above the doorbell and took a breath. Here went nothing.

The door swung open unexpectedly, and I jumped, dropping all of the papers.

"Lex! What are you doing here?" Andrea appeared before me, just when the papers scattered at my feet.

"I came as a surprise," I told her, as we both bent down to pick up the papers. "I have something to show you and Corbin."

She glanced over her shoulder. "Isn't that nice? We have someone here right now, so can—"

I stood back upright. "Well, you can send them home, because when you hear what I've got cooking, you're gonna flip!"

Andrea's eyes flicked down to my belly. "What you've got cooking? Oh, my goodness. Did you have another ultrasound after all? Do you know the sex? Come on in."

Argh. Having a pregnant belly was like a one-way ticket to monopolizing every situation you're in, whether you like it or not. "No, I—"

Andrea stepped aside and called out. "Candace! She found out the sex of the baby!"

"Candace?" Wrinkling my forehead, I followed Andrea into the bright living room.

"Yeah, Candace and Brian brought someone over to see the house." Andrea stopped and put her hands on my shoulders. "Lex, listen—"

"Lexie!" The chorus of tiny voices was nearly drowned out by the thundering footsteps of six pairs of feet. Around the corner charged Candace's and Brian's kids.

"Oh, hey guys!" I bent down to press a kiss to each of their sweaty heads.

"Howdy stranger," Candace called, pulling me into an unexpected hug. My loan papers hit the floor again.

"Whoops. Uh, hi." I gasped for air as my cousin squeezed me. "What are you guys doing here?"

Brian grinned proudly. "Selling the house for Corbin and Andrea."

All the oxygen—or, what was left of it after Candace's hug—whooshed out of my lungs. "You did what?"

Candace put her hands on my belly. "Wait. Did Andrea say that you found out what the baby is?"

"Ten bucks says it's a girl." Brian reached in his pocket, producing a five-dollar bill. "Honey, do you have any cash?"

Candace shook her head. "You're wrong. It's a boy."

"You really think it's a boy?" Andrea's hands joined Candace's on my stomach. "I really think it's a girl."

"Ugh, would you two stop?" I wriggled out from under their hands. "Did you guys sell the house?"

Andrea's focus snapped back up to my face. "Oh, yeah. Listen, we need to talk."

"Why do you guys want to buy this house?" I stared, open mouthed, at Candace and Brian. They were foiling my whole plan. "There aren't even enough bedrooms for your kids."

Candace laughed. "Us? No, no, no. We love our house."

Brian threw his arm around Andrea's shoulder. "We're just helping out our cousins."

"What are you talking about?" I tried to look past the three of them. I could hear Corbin talking to someone in the kitchen. "Who's buying my house?"

Andrea chewed her lip. "Listen, I need to talk to… wait, *your* house?"

I bent down and scooped up one of my fallen documents. "I got a loan! I want to buy the house!"

Candace covered her mouth. "Oh, crap."

Ever cheerful Brian offered me a friendly smile. "Better luck next time, Lex. But hey, the good news is, your doc gets to live here. Small world, huh?"

Andrea winced.

"Fletcher came to see it a few nights ago, and made an offer today," Candace said. "Corbin's signing the purchase agreement right now."

Shivers danced across my skin, and I shuddered—yes, shuddered—at the mention of the good doctor's name. "F-fletcher's here?"

I wanted to do a happy dance, *and* throw myself onto the floor for a tantrum at the same time. Andrea's eyes screamed an apology as my brother and Fletcher entered the room.

"Hey, sis. You know Fletcher, right?" Corbin called, clapping Fletcher on the back. Andrea made a face at him, and his eyes widened. "*Oh, right. Of course you do.*"

Fletcher's cheeks reddened when he saw me. In true Fletcher style, his hair had been tousled into perfect bed head, and his low-slung faded jeans accented his vintage Elvis (*Elvis!)* tee shirt perfectly.

"Lexie." That was all Fletcher said. He shoved his hands in his pockets and stared at me.

"Fletcher." I tugged my denim jacket around my belly as best I could.

Now, let's get one thing clear: I was so grateful to be pregnant, and the thought of holding my baby in my arms soon was almost more than I could stand. But, if there was ever a time when I wished I could have my thin frame and flat belly back, this was it.

Fletcher's eyes grazed over my whole body, from my faded Chuck Taylor's to the bandana in my hair, leaving a trail of electricity behind as they moved. There was no denying the volt of energy surging between the two of us. Hell, if the lights had been on in the house, they would've blinked.

Brian cleared his throat, and I suddenly remembered that Fletcher and I weren't alone.

"So, um, Fletcher," he said. "Did you know Lexie found out the sex of the baby?"

Fletcher blinked a few times. "What? Did you have another ultrasound? I didn't see the scans."

When I shook my head, it felt like I was underwater. "No."

"She came to make an offer on the house." Andrea rubbed her forehead. "I feel so bad."

Corbin stepped forward. "You want to buy the house?"

"I, uh, yes." I held up a rumpled sheet of paper. "I got a loan. I didn't get a realtor. I knew you'd make more money that way."

"I didn't, either." Fletcher ducked his head. "Lexie, I'm so sorry, I had no idea you were interested in the house."

"Neither did I." Corbin pressed his lips together. "Why didn't you tell me?"

Tears flooded my eyes, and I opened them wider to prevent them from spilling. Curse these damned hormones. "I didn't want to say anything until I was completely certain. I came over as soon as I got the paperwork."

Candace took my hand. "Oh, honey, don't cry. It's okay. There'll be other houses."

The tears escaped, and slid down my face. I didn't want another house. I wanted *this* house. I practically saw myself holding my baby in the window seat upstairs, and making my morning coffee in the sunny kitchen. This was how I would prove to myself—and to my mother—that I didn't need a husband to take care of the baby and me, that I could do it on my own. Being a homeowner was the ultimate proof.

Andrea and Candace wrapped their arms around me, while all three men stood in an awkward semicircle. "No, no, no." I waved them away. "It's no big deal. I'm just tired. That's all. I'm just... I'm just..."

"Disappointed," Andrea finished for me.

Fletcher turned to Corbin. "I'm tearing up the deal."

"Wait." A look of panic flashed across my brother's face. "Lexie, are you serious? Are you sure you've got financing?"

Fletcher reached for the papers in Corbin's hand. "Listen, she's family, she—"

"No." I straightened my shoulders. "Ignore the tears. They fall at random, I'm telling you. I'm really fine with this. I promise. Fletcher—"

Saying his name gave a zap of hysteria right down into my core, and the baby flipped in my belly. "It's your house. I promise."

Corbin dragged a hand down the length of his face. "Argh. I don't know what to do."

Fletcher's bright blue eyes bored into mine. "I'm so sorry."

"You couldn't have known."

The air between us was heavy, and judging by the uncomfortable expressions on everyone's faces, they could feel it, too.

After an awkward pause that lasted entirely too long, Candace cleared her throat. When I moved my gaze to her face, she widened her eyes. We'd been close our whole lives, and I knew this expression to mean, *what in the world is going on with you?*

I shrugged. It was all I could do.

"Why don't we give Lexie and Fletcher a few minutes to sort this out," she offered, corralling everyone towards the door. "Kids, come on. Let's go look at the pretty landscaping Andrea did in the backyard."

The sound of a toilet flushing rang out, and then the kids toddled their way through the living room and out the French doors. Brian, Corbin, Andrea, and Candace followed, and when the door clicked shut, Fletcher and I found ourselves standing alone on the gleaming hickory floors.

Fletcher took my hand, and by gosh, the thrill shooting up my arm was practically lethal. "Lexie, take the house. It'll be a great place for you and the baby."

"No, it's perfect for you and Martha." I turned my palm so our fingers laced together. It was like our hands had been cut to match each other's. We fit together like puzzle pieces.

No, wait.

Fletcher was Marisol's boyfriend. Not mine. *Marisol's*. And Marisol was my friend. Good grief, I needed to rein it in.

"Where are your girls?" I asked, pulling my hand away.

"My girls?" A wrinkle formed between his eyebrows.

"Martha and Marisol." I stepped backwards to widen the space between us. He followed.

"Oh, right." He cringed. "They're getting pedicures today. Martha doesn't know I'm here. It's a surprise."

I forced a smile. What a lovely mother-daughter outing for Marisol and Martha. I wondered how Marisol was tolerating it. She usually got her pedicures at high-end salons that didn't exactly welcome children. Of course, they could be having the time of their lives, holding hands and gazing at each other in familial adoration. Jealousy pressed down on my shoulders.

"Pedicures sound fun," I squeaked.

He chuckled. "I'm trying to help them bond a little."

"Got it." Nodding, I pressed a hand to my belly. Both the baby, and my nerves, were going wild. And when Fletcher inched closer to me, it didn't help.

His cerulean eyes moved to my middle. "You all right? Nauseous?"

"No." I shook my head. "Just nervous."

His palm went to my stomach. "Baby moving? Sleeping okay? Eating enough protein?"

"Yup. Everything's good." I backed away from his touch. It felt too freaking good. Like something that could melt me right into a puddle on the floor if I let it.

"Good." We'd now moved into the hallway off the living room. Even though it was dimmer there, Fletcher's eyes still sparkled. "Listen, Lexie, I won't buy the house. There are other houses out there."

My heart twisted. I pictured Martha running across the front yard after getting off the school bus, a backpack bouncing on her shoulder, her dark curls flying out behind her. "Absolutely not. This is yours and Martha's home. I can feel it."

He looked around, his eyes scanning across the crown molding and refinished built-in cabinetry. The corners of his mouth pricked upward. "I really do love this house."

My palm covered his hand on my middle. "Then you should live here."

His eyes came back to mine. "You really think so?"

"Yeah."

And I meant it. I mean, I wanted the house. *Bad.* But I could see Martha cozied up to the fireplace with a cup of cocoa in the winter while Fletcher set up a freshly cut Christmas tree in the corner. It was the perfect house for them. "Maybe I'll buy the house next door, and we'll be neighbors."

"That would be great." Something flashed in Fletcher's eyes, and I couldn't quite put my finger on it. His lower lip pulled between his teeth while I was trying to figure it out. He looked so edible when he did that.

"So that's settled," I whispered.

Fletcher took hold of my upper arms and brought me against his chest. I could feel his heart galloping. "You really are something, Lex. Thank you."

I opened and closed my mouth a few times, but couldn't think of anything relevant to say. The scent that was so *him* flooded my senses, making my ears ring and my eyes slide shut against my will. He smelled like fabric softener, and minty toothpaste, and something else. Something musky and so, undeniably male it made my toes curl in my sneakers.

"I wish…" Fletcher's words petered out, and we were left in the dim hallway with silence all around us.

His hands started tracing circles on my back, leaving trails of tickling heat behind them as they went. I shivered beneath his touch, knowing I needed to put a stop to it, but wanting it to go on for at least another hour. Maybe two. Or possibly forever. The moment stretched out from three seconds, to five, and then to ten. I felt Fletcher's nose against my messy hair, and listened as he drew in a deep breath. The electricity between us was so strong, it nearly buckled my knees

"You wish what?" I pulled back and looked up at him.

"There's something between us," he whispered, his breath dancing across my lips.

I gulped. I wanted Fletcher. I'd wanted him for months. But this was wrong. *So* wrong. It was like I was at battle with *myself.*

"Yeah."

He pressed one hand to the small of my back and brought the other up to cup the back of my neck. I *loved* that. "I can't fight it," he mumbled, walking me backwards slowly.

The little redheaded angel on my right shoulder shook her head solemnly. *Tell him to fight it. Walk away, drive home, and eat some chocolate. That's the* right *thing to do.*

Fletcher brushed his nose across my cheekbone, and my heart started Irish clog dancing inside of my chest.

The little redheaded devil on my left shoulder joined in the dance. *Screw doing the right thing. Tell him to kiss you, and to make it worth your time!*

"Then don't fight it." The words came out of my mouth before I had any time to think about what I was saying.

That must've been the green light Fletcher was waiting for, because his lips were on mine before I could even process another word. They were full and warm, but surrounded by a glorious five o'clock shadow that made my limbs go weak and my eyes roll back in my head.

And roll back, they did.

Because when his head tipped to the side, and his tongue traced a path along my upper lip to encourage my mouth to open more, it was *over.* My hands dug into the back of his hair, tangling into his blonde locks, and securing his face to mine. His hand pressed my body into his even more, arching my back before sliding down my hip to my thigh, which he raised against his hip as we landed against the wall with a muted thud. An old painting swayed near the back of my head, but I didn't care as Fletcher's fingers kneaded gently against the back of my knee, and his teeth caught my lower lip with the softest of nips. His mouth moved down my jaw line to my neck, just below my ear, where his breath against my skin caused me to gasp—yes, gasp—as every nerve ending in my body hummed with utter awareness.

Self-control: gone.

Until we heard the French door in the living room open, that is.

"Hey, guys?" Candace called. "So who gets the house?"

Our heads jerked apart, and we gawked at each other with horrified eyes. His hand still held my leg against his hip, and the toes on my other foot were barely touching the floor.

"I..." His words stopped when Candace's footsteps came closer.

"Down!" I hissed, wriggling out of his grip. "Put me down."

"I'm sorry." He reached out to touch me, but drew back his hand instead.

Smoothing down my rumpled clothes, I pushed past Fletcher. Marisol's smiling face was scrolling through my mind like the newsreel on CNN. Today's headline may as well have been: *This just in: Lexie Baump is a horrible friend.*

"Lexie..." Fletcher grabbed for my sleeve, but I sidestepped him just as Candace came around the corner.

"Oh, there you are!" She giggled. "So did you two duke it out?"

I wriggled past her. I could still taste Fletcher on my lips, and dear Lord in heaven, it tasted *good*. "Nope. We worked it out like two adults."

Yeah, like two adults with their tongues down each other's throats!

"Well, that's good." She jumped out of my way. "Whoa. So who's the winner?"

"Me!" Fletcher blurted. His voice was loud and echoed in the hall, so he cleared his throat. "Me. We decided this would be a good home for us. For me and my daughter, that is. Not Lexie and me. Don't be absurd. I meant me and my daughter. Martha. Just us. And the dog. Libman will love the backyard, wouldn't you say, Lexie?"

"Yes." I didn't look at him. Couldn't. Did he have my lip-gloss all over his mouth? Because it certainly wasn't on my mouth anymore.

I was going to hell for certain.

"Well, that sounds just perfect," Candace said slowly.

"I've gotta go." He practically ran for the front door. "Do me a favor, Candace, tell Corbin the sale is still on. I'll be in touch with him soon."

"I, uh, sure. Bye." She watched him with raised eyebrows as Fletcher nearly walked into the door when it didn't open fast enough.

"See ya." Fletcher nodded in my direction. "Lexie."

I offered him a stiff wave, and he was gone in a flash.

Candace stared at the open door. "What's his problem?"

"I don't know! Seems pretty high strung!" My voice cracked like a pubescent boy.

Awesome.

"So do you." She folded her arms across her chest. "Okay, Lex, come clean."

Hysterical laughter bubbled to the surface before I could control it. I was busted. Caught in the act of betraying one friend by another friend. How poetic was that? I would lose Marisol's friendship, and Candace's respect, all in one giant swoop. Maybe we needed to call Brian inside. Make it a trifecta.

I tugged at my jacket a few times. "What? I mean, huh. I don't. I don't even… I, so, what was that supposed to mean?"

Candace's eyes narrowed at me. "Were you mean to him?"

Chapter Seventeen

Yet *another* two weeks passed, and I avoided everyone with the cunning stealth of a CIA spy.

Or something like that.

I let my voice mail pick up any calls not work related. I avoided stores where I'd seen Fletcher. And when Candace stopped by my apartment with homemade cookies and some refrigerator art made by her kids, I turned my television on mute and froze on my couch until she was gone.

As for Marisol? Well, it was hard to avoid someone you work with, but I certainly tried.

On my first day post-kiss, I'd slapped our work calendar onto the stainless steel prep table and explained that for the next few weeks—or at least until I got over my guilt for having sucked face with her boyfriend—I was going to handle most of the food work, and she was going to handle the business end of things. Marisol happily announced that it was an opportunity to wear all her expensive designer clothes and agreed right away.

I felt better spending my time in the kitchen cooking, baking, chopping, frosting, and slicing while Marisol was the face of the Eats & Treats. Her face was nicer to look at, anyway. My face was freckled, starting to get slightly puffy, and now carried the ugly weight of guilt. I swear I'd gotten thirteen new wrinkles since kissing Fletcher.

Speaking of Fletcher, I missed him.

Dear Lord, I missed him so much that if I closed my eyes and thought really hard, I could feel his hand holding the back of my knee again. I'd replayed those moments in the hallway so many times, it actually reeled inside of my mind like a ninety-minute feature film, complete with a soundtrack made up almost entirely of vintage rock.

That kiss, that one blessed kiss had rocked me straight down into my core. It knocked every other kiss I'd had in all my thirty years right out of the water.

I was planning to skip Marisol's upcoming birthday party. I had every intention of laying in my bed with a pint of mint chocolate chip ice cream and the remote, instead of dressing up and going out with friends to pretend I wasn't completely disgusted with my behavior and totally infatuated with Fletcher.

That is, until I got Candace's voice mail:

"Hey. I don't know why you're hiding under a rock these days, but I wanted to remind you about Marisol's birthday dinner Saturday night. We're meeting at Moon's Lounge at seven, and you agreed to bring the cake. Well, you did a month ago, before you decided to ignore everyone who loves you. Not that I'm bitter or anything. I just miss you, and I hope you're not having some sort of pregnancy-induced depression or something. You know I love you, right? I know you're overwhelmed, and that your mom's been really hard on you lately, and that you're probably really worn out. I want you to understand you're never alone, because I'm here for you. Okay? So anyway, I hope you'll decide to join us, and help me remind Marisol she's older than both of us! Ha! Love you, bye."

As awful as I felt about myself, and as stomachache inducing as a dinner with Marisol *and* Fletcher sounded, I couldn't deny how much my friends loved me. And besides, as wrong as it was—and believe me, I *knew* how wrong it was—I wanted to see Fletcher. If even from the other end of a table. I actually longed for him deep down in my heart where the ache after my divorce had been. It was so much more than a crush on my obstetrician. So much more than an acute need to get *laid*. So much more than a hormonal outburst caused by my gestating body. I loved him.

But I also loved my friend.

And so I bought a lovely black sequined dress just stretchy enough to mold over my round belly, and went to Marisol's party. Pairing the dress with a pair of bright red heels and a red flower pinned behind my ear, I thought I looked decent for a woman who was seven months pregnant.

Put on your game face, Baump.

"Lex! You came!" Candace squealed as I entered the private room at Moon's. She took the cake box out of my hands and pressed a kiss to my cheek. "You're radiant. How do you feel?"

I took a deep breath. "Feeling fine. Is everybody here?"

"Uh huh." She stepped aside and the room came into view. Moon's Lounge was a martini and piano bar in downtown Spokane that Marisol frequented, but I'd never been into. Now I knew why.

This place was posh, and I'd never been the posh type. Velvet covered chairs lined mahogany tables, and a chandelier the size of my Volkswagen Bug hung from the ceiling. One wall featured floor to ceiling windows overlooking the Spokane River, and the other wall bore windows that surveyed the rest of the lounge and the dance floor.

Everyone at the party was dressed to the nines. Members of Marisol's family—all extremely good looking—stood around holding wine glasses and mingling. A couple of our Eats & Treats venders and clients had shown up, and Brian was talking to Marisol at the end of a long table. Brian's navy blue suit offset Candace's silver shirtdress beautifully, and Marisol resembled a Victoria's Secret model in her flesh-colored lace cocktail dress. There was more gravity defying spandex employed with keeping her bosom on display than was legal, and I instantly felt self-conscious in my little black maternity number. If she looked like a lingerie ad, I probably looked like an ad for Gap Kids with a pillow underneath my dress.

"Look who's here, everyone." Candace dragged me towards where Brian and Marisol stood.

Everyone raised their glasses. "Lexie!" the crowd called, just as a tall man in a charcoal suit stepped out from between the vendors.

Fletcher.

The suit was tailored to perfection, and his tie was the exact same shade of azure as his eyes. His hair was gelled back from his face, and he'd shaved recently, because his skin was perfectly smooth. I briefly entertained the fantasy of sliding across the tabletop into his arms and running my hands down his jaw line.

I didn't. But I wanted to.

"Lexie," Fletcher said. His eyes were downturned at the corners, and he jammed his hands into his pockets. My name was heavy as it fell from his lips, so full of words we hadn't said. Things we needed to say, but likely never would.

Don't make it obvious. Be cool for once.

I took a deep breath. "Hey."

Keep it friendly, keep it casual. That was going to be my motto tonight. I'd seen Fletcher finally, which is what I'd been aching for. Now it was my job to be the friend Marisol deserved.

"Happy birthday, Mar! You look gorgeous!" I said cheerfully, turning to the birthday girl.

She grinned and ran a hand through her glossy hair. "Was there ever any doubt? Come here." Marisol pulled me into a hug. "Good to see you've cheered up some. You ready to party tonight?"

"Like a rock star," I said in a shaky voice.

Marisol squeezed my shoulder and leaned close to my ear. I could smell whatever cocktails she was drinking. "Did you see my boyfriend in a suit? Talk about fine, eh?"

I nodded, but wouldn't look. Couldn't. I could practically feel heat exuding from Fletcher's body to my own. "Oh, well, yeah. I guess."

"You guess?" Marisol threw her head back and downed the rest of her martini. "He's gorgeous. Now all I've got to do is get rid of all of his cheesy vintage tee shirts, and he'll be great. Oh, and get rid of that stinky dog. Then he'll be *perfect*."

He's perfect already! My heart thumped, and I put a hand to my chest. How could Marisol say that? I couldn't think of one thing about Fletcher that I didn't like, except that he was dating her.

I didn't like that. Not one bit.

"Mar, look at this cake Lexie made for you." Candace took hold of Marisol's hand and directed her attention to the opened cake box on the table.

Marisol gasped. "That's amazing."

I'd gone out of my way to make Marisol the best cake ever. It was red velvet, her favorite, and I'd fashioned it into the shape of a purse. Then I'd frosted and decorated it to look like an Hermes Handbag, complete with a little padlock-style trinket hanging from the zipper. It looked good enough to eat, or to stuff your cell phone and address book into.

And yes. I was kissing my friend's ass because I fell in love with her boyfriend. Cake was an acceptable apology for betraying a girlfriend's trust, wasn't it?

The crowd gathered around the pink box, oohing and ahhing over the exquisite detail. In a flash, I detected a flurry of heat dancing around my arm, and looked up to find Fletcher standing next to me. His face, like everyone else's, was pointed down at the cake, but his eyes were locked on me with an intensity sure to melt the fondant right off the cake.

How in the world could he look at *me* that way, when Marisol—and her phenomenal boobs—were in the same room?

Holding my breath so I didn't smell Fletcher's amazing minty-musky scent, I sidestepped away from the crowd and pulled out a chair on the opposite side of the table. I needed a cold drink. The room felt like they were pumping heat straight through the vent. Or maybe it was just me.

Either way, where the hell was the waiter?

"Well, nobody can eat this incredible cake until we've had our dinner." Marisol gestured to a waiter passing the window.

He practically dove into the room. "Are we ready to order?" His eyes never left Marisol's chest.

"We sure are, handsome," Marisol purred. She slid into her seat and crossed her legs slowly. "Why don't you tell me what's extra tasty tonight?"

"You mean besides yourself?" the waiter replied. The college-aged waiter beamed at Marisol.

Everyone at the table laughed, knowing this was typical Marisol behavior. I watched Fletcher for a sign of jealousy, but he just pulled out his chair and sat down. His eyes were locked on the table in front of him and he didn't appear tuned in to the party at all.

Candace plopped into the chair next to me. "Guess who Brian just spotted in the bar?" she whispered.

"Who?" I blinked at her, tearing my focus off Fletcher's downtrodden expression.

Candace's nostrils flared. "Nate. And some blonde."

As if on cue, the baby performed a double axel inside of my uterus.

"Ugh." I groaned, pressing my hands to my stomach. My ex-husband—and the father to my unborn child—was in Moon's at the same time as me. And my ginormous belly.

"I know, right? He makes me sick, too." Candace opened her menu with a snort.

I shrugged. "I guess it's a free country. He can dine wherever he pleases."

But I didn't *feel* nonchalant in the slightest. The last time I'd seen Nate was the day after I'd found out I was pregnant. I'd gone to his office in the middle of the day and forced his receptionist to allow me in.

He hadn't been happy to see me. That was all right. I hadn't been happy to see him, either.

"Dammit, Lexie, you have no right to barge into my office like this." *Nate blocked the doorway into his office. "In case you don't remember, you're not my wife anymore."*

I shoved past him. "In case you don't remember, you didn't mind the fact that I'm not your wife when you slept with me two months ago."

"Holy hell!" He peered out the door at the back of his receptionist's head. She was wearing a headset, and talking to someone on the phone, so she'd probably not heard. But I was still proud of myself for saying it out loud. Nate slammed the door to his office, and closed the blinds. "What in the world has gotten into you?"

I put up a hand. His question would have been so easy to make a dirty joke about, had it not been directed toward us. I shuddered. "I don't think you want me to answer that."

The look on his face practically dripped with disgust. Apparently our feelings were mutual.

"Listen." He lowered his voice and sat on the edge of his desk. I didn't sit down in the seat across from him. I was too fired up. It'd taken me four tries before I'd been able to get onto the elevator. "I understand that what happened between us might have brought up some feelings in you that you thought were forgotten. But that's no reason to start stalking—"

I closed my eyes and shook my head. "Don't flatter yourself, Nate. I don't want to be here anymore than you want me to be here. If I could afford a new one, I would douse my mattress in gasoline and burn it."

He flinched. "Ouch."

"Yeah. Right back atcha." I started to pace. "I'm not here for anything. I don't want anything from you. I don't need anything from you. In fact, you're the last person on God's green earth that I would ever come to for anything. Do you understand that?"

He nodded, his mouth pulled into a line.

I faced him, and put my hands to my stomach. I'd worn my work clothes, so I had my white chef's jacket on over a pair of ripped jeans. There were streaks of raspberry ganache on the jacket, and I'd pulled my hair back with a leopard print hairclip while I was making meringues that morning.

This sweet ensemble was accentuated by the fact that I'd been hurling for days, and my skin had taken on a sallow yellow color.

To say I looked like hell would've been an understatement.

"Nate, I'm pregnant." The words came out an octave lower than my usual voice, and then bounced around the office like a Ping-Pong ball.

Nate's eyes went from my face, to my stomach, then back to my face, then down to my stomach again. He didn't say anything. In fact, he didn't move at all. He sat frozen on the edge of his desk, with one hand over his mouth.

I'm sure he meant to make me feel like he was contemplating my announcement. But I knew better. He was crapping his pants. Right there in his corner office, in his three hundred dollar slacks.

Three minutes of painfully awkward silence passed. "Well, say something, for hell's sake."

His face was as white as the stack of documents on his desk. "It's… it's not mine."

I folded my arms across my chest. "Oh? Is that so? How do you figure?"

"Because we used a condom." He wiped a line of sweat off of his upper lip. "I remember."

I bit the insides of my cheeks so hard they throbbed. I didn't come to fight with Nate. I only came to do the right thing.

"No, Nate. We didn't," I said with metered patience. "You asked if I had any, and when I said no, you announced that you'd be careful. But like always, Nate, you were sloppy." Anger pressed down on me, tightening my skin.

He bounced off of the edge of his desk. "I wasn't sloppy! You were sloppy! How dare you blame this all on me!"

I pointed my finger at him. "You came to my apartment for a booty call!"

"Well you were the one who was trashed alone at home!" His face was turning purple.

"You woke up the next morning and vomited in kitchen sink!"

"You told me you were on the pill!"

"No, I told you I wished I was on the pill!"

He dragged his hands down his face. "Well, you—"

"All right, stop!" I backed away from my ex-husband. He was safer that way. "It was both of our faults. We both know it. We both caused this. Now we have to deal with it."

He raked his hand through his hair. "Hilary and I are engaged now. The wedding is in Hawaii this August."

Sympathy washed over me, dampening my anger.

I mean, Nate was a douche bag, there was no denying that. But, like I said, we'd both caused this, and he and Hilary had been temporarily broken up at the time. Nate hadn't meant for this to happen. Neither of us had.

"Listen," I said. "I don't need anything from you. I just felt like you needed to know. That's it. I just wanted you to know. To give you the chance to deal with it in your own way, I guess."

"Oh, no." Nate shook his head, and he straightened back up. "I'm not dealing with anything. This is on you, Lexie. Hilary cannot find out about this, do you understand me?"

"Why would I tell her?" I snarled at him, all of my sympathy fizzling away. "I don't even know the woman. The only thing I know about Hilary is that she has terrible judgment in men."

Nate's nostrils flared. "You're getting an abortion, right? You're taking care of this mess, correct?"

It felt like he'd punched me in the gut. I'd expected him to be a total ass, but to ask me to get rid of our baby? Unthinkable. "Yes. I'm taking care of this mess, Nate."

His eyes softened. "You're not keeping it, are you?"

"I..." I gulped. "This may be my only shot. I want to keep it."

He grimaced. "I won't own up to it. If you tell anybody, I'll lie."

I nearly laughed. Nate was so clueless. His reputation had been flushed down the toilet long before that drunken night. "There's a whole series of daytime talk shows devoted to proving who baby daddies are. If I wanted to, I could call Maury Povitch and get a DNA test. But your rep is safe, Nate. This baby is mine. Mine alone."

He turned away from me, and rested his hands on his desk. "Then I guess we don't have anything more to talk about, do we?"

I shuddered at the memory of my ugly conversation with Nate. I didn't want to think about that day ever again.

"So who's the blonde?" Candace's voice shook me out of my thoughts.

I looked at the wall of windows across the room, and shifted lower in my seat. I couldn't run into Nate here. Not tonight. "I don't know. Probably Hilary."

"I'll take the filet. Medium. Thank you." Candace said to the waiter, who was jotting down her order, while still staring at Marisol.

When she stopped talking, his eyes flicked to me. "And for you, ma'am?"

I wrapped my arms around my stomach self-consciously. Aw, hell. I'd become a *ma'am* overnight while Marisol was getting undressed inside our waiter's mind. "I'll take the crab soufflé and a pear salad, please."

He moved on to the next person and Candace leaned close to my ear. "So who's Hilary?"

I lowered in my seat another inch or two. If Nate walked past the glass wall to go to the restrooms, I was a sitting duck. There I would be, in all my pregnant glory.

"Hilary is his fiancée. They're getting married in Hawaii this summer."

Candace snorted, and slapped her hand down on the table. "Hey, Marisol." When our gorgeous friend looked our way, she said, "Did you hear that good ol' Nate The Great is taking the vows again?"

"Oh for the love of all things holy." Marisol offered us an exaggerated eye roll, and rested her head on Fletcher's shoulder. My stomach pitched. "Is he marrying the girl with the nose ring?"

I shook my head. "Um, no."

"Is it the one with the twin sister?" One of Candace's eyebrows rose high on her face.

Marisol leaned forward, but kept her arm across Fletcher's lap. "Holy Hannah, is it your divorce lawyer?"

Fletcher's eyes met mine. "Who's Nate?"

"My ex-husband." I held his eye contact and didn't look away.

"He slept with his divorce attorney?" Fletcher's frown deepened.

"Oh, no, no, no." Marisol waggled a finger in his face. "He slept with *Lexie's* divorce attorney. Twice."

"And their landlord." Candace took a sip of her drink. "Don't forget her."

I cringed. I'd forgotten about that one. Mother of all things beautiful, I'd procreated with *such* a bastard. Sweat pricked underneath my arms, and I shifted in my chair. Would it kill the waiter to crack a window, for Pete's sake?

"To Lexie's taste in men!" Marisol held up her glass and laughed.

Fletcher frowned. "Lexie, I had no idea...I'm so sorry."

Marisol nudged him. "Ugh. Don't be such a downer. This is a party, remember?"

"You're making fun of your friend." Fletcher scowled at Marisol. "Your *pregnant* friend, whose husband, by the sound of it, was a chronic cheater. It's not *nice*, Marisol."

My throat tightened, and the baby shifted in my belly. Fletcher was standing up for me. I wanted to stand up on the table and dance, but refrained.

That wasn't how one stayed incognito in a glass paneled banquet room. Fletcher's gaze left Marisol's and he smiled, bringing those gorgeous eye crinkles back.

Suddenly I had to use the bathroom. Bad.

Candace's eyes were wide. "Whoa. I didn't think about that. I'm sorry, Lex. Are you all right?"

Nodding, I pushed my chair back. "I'm fine. I just need to use the restroom."

Marisol pursed her lips and pouted for a few beats. "I think my boyfriend needs a drink. Waiter!"

The young waiter popped up out of nowhere, just as I slipped out of the room. Slinking right up against the wall like some sort of knocked up cat burglar, I sidled my way towards the restrooms—praying that I wouldn't run into Nate, or his...

"Oh! Excuse me!"

Too late.

I'd walked headfirst into Hilary as she came out of the restroom, in all of her thin, blonde glory.

"Sorry," I mumbled, trying to duck past her.

"Hey, wait." She touched my arm. "Aren't you Lexie?"

I looked up and offered her a feeble smile. "Guilty."

"I thought so." Hilary held out her hand. "We've never met formally, but I'm Hilary Paxton. Nate's fiancée."

I took her hand and shook it. My heart was hammering inside of my chest so hard it was difficult to hear what she was saying. "It's nice to meet you. Congratulations."

"Thank you." She beamed. "And apparently I should be congratulating you, too."

My throat sealed shut. I had no words.

And just when I thought that I was going to have to feign stomach problems to get out of the conversation, the door to the men's room swung open, and Nate emerged.

"Holy shit," he hissed, stopping in his tracks right in front of us. His eyes were the size of serving plates, and they bounced between his fiancée and my swollen stomach.

"Nate, don't be rude." Hilary swatted at his arm. "I was just telling Lexie congratulations. Did you know she was expecting?"

Nate's glare was positively lethal. He stared at me like I was a bug that needed to be squashed. Hard. "Nope. Congratulations, Lex."

"Thanks." I was going to throw up. Now I was sure of it.

"Better you than me," Hilary laughed, pressing a hand to her ridiculously flat middle. "I admire you. Pregnancy and motherhood. Whew! What a challenge. Good job."

"That's right, honey." Nate laughed, but no humor met his eyes. He looked repulsed by me. The feeling was mutual. "Come on, we've got to go. Everyone's waiting."

"Right," Hilary chirped. "Well, it was lovely to meet you, Lexie."

"You, too," I said.

"Goodbye now." Nate practically pushed his fiancé in the opposite direction.

I watched as they stalked away, and used the back of my hand to wipe away some of the sweat that was now covering, well, *all* of my skin.

This was a mistake. I couldn't do this. Seeing Marisol and Fletcher together, then seeing Nate with his fiancée, I felt like I'd been completely drained of all my energy. I didn't care about my pear salad, or even about Marisol's birthday anymore. I wanted to go home. I wanted my sweats. I wanted Chinese takeout. And I wanted the solitude of my little apartment. Stat.

Charging past the private room, I made a beeline for the exit, gasping in relief when I went through the door and the cool night air hit my skin. I already felt better.

"Where are you going?"

I heard the click, click, click of heels following me across the parking lot, and when I turned, I was surprised to see Candace *and* Marisol following me.

"What the hell?" Marisol held out her hands. "You're ditching me on my birthday?"

Candace bit her lip. "I saw Nate coming out of the bathroom. You ran into him, didn't you?"

I nodded, unexpected tears clogging my throat.

"Oh, honey." Marisol put an arm around my shoulder. "I didn't know you still cared about the bastard."

"You know, I agree. This is weird." Candace wrapped herself around my other shoulder.

I felt dejected. And empty. And just so damn tired of keeping everything inside. The secret was starting to rot inside of me. Seeing Nate—and the repulsed way he looked at me—only aggravated my condition.

Taking a breath, I moved out from under their arms. "Guys, I have to tell you something."

"Wait, I have something to tell you guys, too!" Marisol blurted

Candace nudged her. "Shut up. Lex is trying to speak."

I couldn't help but laugh. It was *so* like Marisol to interrupt. "Go ahead."

Marisol clapped her hands excitedly. "I think tonight's the night," She announced with a squeal. "Finally. Who waits this long for sex?"

My tears started again, and I covered my face. This night just got better and better.

Candace scoffed. "Oh, good Lord, Mar. Of course tonight is the night. It's your birthday. I'm sure Fletcher's going to give you a birthday present to remember."

I hiccupped.

"Oh, geez," Candace rubbed my arm. "Okay. Lexie's turn. Spill it. What do you want to tell us?"

My voice came out muffled from behind my hands. "I want to tell you who the baby's dad is."

And the floor was mine.

Chapter Eighteen

Well, as it turned out, Marisol's birthday did turn out to be a good night.

For me, at least.

When I'd gone into work that Monday morning, she'd come in with a scowl splayed across her pretty face and Spanish curse words spewing out of her mouth. Apparently Martha had gotten sick at her sleepover on Saturday night, so Fletcher cut the night short. There was no birthday present to remember for Marisol, unless she considered his gift of silver bangle bracelets the right present. But she didn't. In fact, she'd called his gift a poorly disguised cop out.

I would have treasured silver bangle bracelets from Fletcher like the Holy Grail, but whatever.

The news that he'd rejected her—even by default—was enough to lift my spirits as I settled into the last stretch of my pregnancy. And thank goodness I was almost done, because I felt like a moose.

For a while, I'd looked pretty cute, if I did say so myself. Through the miracle of pregnancy, I'd finally gotten the boobs I'd prayed for as a tween. My bra cups ranneth over, and every shirt I owned finally stretched gloriously across the front. (I'd always wanted that to happen.) And my stomach had taken on that darling little round quality that maternity models always had, just barely tenting their shirts, and accentuating how lovely and lean their arms and legs appeared.

But that phase ended as quickly as it had begun.

My face had started to puff up. Every day when I woke up and looked in the mirror, it seemed my lips or cheeks were fuller. If I kept going at the rate I was going, I was going to wind up looking like I was made out of pizza dough by the time I delivered.

But the swelling didn't stop there. Suddenly, my waif-like legs were becoming puckered and paunchy. I could press my finger into my white flesh, and the divot would stay for a good twenty seconds before my skin smoothed out. And my feet after work? Forget about it. Large, block-like squares of modeling clay that made lacing a sneaker almost impossible? Ugh. I was destined to wear flip-flops for the next two months. Fletcher's nurses said it was typical for me to swell during the last trimester, especially considering how many hours I spent on my feet. They said after a relatively drama-free pregnancy, it was bound to happen.

"Good afternoon, Lexie, how are you this week?"

The receptionist at Fletcher's office grinned at me from her perch behind the counter. Since I was in my third trimester, I'd started coming to my check-ups with the nurse more often, and the staff knew me by name.

"Fine, thank you." I tapped a silent tune out on the counter as she logged onto her computer. I would be lying if I didn't admit I was feeling a bit giddy about my appointment.

I mean, sure. I was puffier than the Stay Pufft marshmallow man, but the nurse wanted me to see *Fletcher* for a non-stress test today. Hooray!

Who would have thought that a test brought on by hypertension and edema could be so thrilling?

"Okay, I've got you all checked in," she told me brightly. "Dr. Javornik will call you back shortly."

"Thanks. Uh, what?" My heart stuttered.

The receptionist offered me a tilt of her head. I'm sure it was meant to be reassuring, but it kind of made me want to deck her. "Dr. Haybee marked all of your appointments until delivery to be switched to Dr. Javornik's caseload. I assumed he'd discussed that with you."

My face went beet red. I could tell because I could see my reflection in the mirror hanging on one of the walls. (Seriously, who put those in a gynecological office? What giant pregnant lady wants to look at her expansive figure in a gilded mirror?) "Um, no. He never told me. Can I… can I ask why?"

"Hmmm." The receptionist pressed a few buttons. "It doesn't say. I would imagine it's because Dr. Haybee's caseload is pretty heavy right now."

My mouth dropped open. Fletcher had broken up with me.

I mean, okay. I was fully aware that he and I were *nothing*, but in a sense, considering that this is the only way we got to see each other anymore, he'd dumped me.

Another head tilt from the receptionist. "I can see you're upset. And that's understandable. It's easy to get attached to your obstetrician over the course of your pregnancy."

I glared down at my hands. *Lady, you have no idea.*

"But I promise you," she said with a smile. "Dr. Javornik is wonderful. She's been in obstetrics for over thirty years, and she's quite popular with our first time moms. She's very gentle and reassuring. And she practices a lot of holistic medicine."

"I don't care how reassuring she is." I sounded like a pouty teenager, but I couldn't stop myself. My skin was tight, and my gut ached. My hoo-haw felt like a brick, and my feet were too fat to wear shoes. Plus, my heart had throbbed every single night since sharing that kiss with Fletcher. All I had to look forward to were my OB appointments, and now those were taken away from me.

I was a freight train, building up speed, one wrong comment from a total meltdown. "I don't give a flying monkey's *ass* about her holistic medicine. Do you hear me?"

One of the receptionist's eyebrows arched. "Oh-kay." She pressed a few buttons on the keyboard, frowned at the screen, then pressed a few more. "Listen, Lexie. It seems as though Dr. Haybee is booked solid for the next several weeks, and you really should have your stress test today."

I breathed through my nose. I was pretty sure my face looked like an overripe tomato. "Stress test. Got it."

She clicked a few more keys, refusing to look at me. "Let's get you in with Dr. Javornik for the test today, and then I'll speak to Dr. Haybee about what he wants to do with the rest of your appointments." I must have grimaced, because she added, "And don't worry. Our doctors do deliveries based on their on-call schedules. So depending on when you go into labor, there's still a good chance Dr. Haybee will be the one to deliver your baby."

"Fine," I grunted. It sounded more like the snuffling sound a pig makes, but hey, who cared at this point? I sure as hell didn't. Offering the receptionist a jerky wave, I shuffled off to the waiting area with a scowl on my face.

How *dare* Fletcher switch me to the other doctor? I mean, I was pretty sure he'd done it because we'd long since crossed some sort of line between doctor and patient. He'd said it himself: there was something between us. And it wasn't just a crush. It was more. So, so much more.

Tears stung my eyes as I sat squished into a tiny leather chair. I looked up at the ceiling to keep them from spilling. Was this God's punishment for what I'd done to Marisol? Or worse yet, was my mother right? Was God mad at me for getting pregnant out of wedlock with my douche bag ex-husband? Oh, dear Lord, how did one repent for that? Was it a few Hail Marys, and maybe a splash in a baptismal font? Or was more involved?

"Lexie?"

Jumping, I looked down to find Martha standing in front of me with a red, white, and blue starred backpack on her shoulder. Her long hair was pulled into two glossy braids with mismatched ribbons on the end. She was adorable like always, and my heart warmed despite all of the pain rattling around inside of my chest.

"Martha." I wiped my eyes on my sleeve. "How are you doing?"

She wrinkled her ski jump nose at me. "Better than you. Whatcha crying about?"

"Nothing." I forced a smile that was too wide to look natural. I probably looked terrifying.

Martha nodded knowingly. "Hormones?"

I laughed in spite of myself. Nothing got past this kid. "Yeah, you're right. What are you doing here?"

"My bus driver drops me off here every Thursday, then Dad takes me to karate." She dropped her backpack on the floor and settled down in the seat next to me. "You look pretty today."

The warmth in my chest started to spread. "Thanks, sweetie, but I'm pretty sure I look a little puffy."

She shook her head, making her braids swing. "Puffiness is normal. My dad says so. He also said you were pretty."

My stomach seized, and the baby kicked. "He what?"

One of Martha's shoulders rose and fell. "Yeah. The other night Marisol came over. She brought Thai food. Marisol was laughing because you have to wear flip-flops at work, and Dad told her to stop. Then he said you were pretty." She looked at me with a wince. "Marisol was pretty mad."

I bit my lip. It felt so weird to be completely torn between elated for me, and sad for Marisol. But I was. "Marisol's pretty beautiful. I don't think she's used to boys not telling her so."

"Oh, well." She swung her feet, kicking her backpack. "We ordered a pizza after she left. I hate Thai food. Everything's covered in peanut butter."

I laughed. "You've got a point. But there are some good dishes in Thai cuisine. I'll have to make you some."

"Sounds good." She played with the end of one of her braids. "But if you make that for me, I'll make you my world famous pizza."

I gasped and press a hand to my chest. "You make world famous pizza?"

"Uh huh." She nodded solemnly. "With pineapple and salami."

"No kidding?" Nudging her with my shoulder, I noticed that Martha smelled like strawberry lip-gloss. I loved strawberry lip-gloss when I was her age. "I should hire you at Eats and Treats."

"That'd be cool." She flashed her jack-o-lantern smile again. "Would you let me decorate cupcakes? I'm an expert decorator."

"Yeah?"

"Yup. I'm trying to teach myself how to make flowers."

"How's that going? It took me a long time."

She wrinkled her nose. "Not so good. My dad looked up a video on YouTube to see how, but we still couldn't figure it out."

I pictured Fletcher and Martha trying to construct frosting flowers together, and smiled to myself. "Keep practicing," I told her. "It takes time. But you'll get it."

"I hope so." Martha twisted a sparkly ring around her finger. "Because Libman's birthday is coming up, and I want to make a cake."

"Dogs can't eat sugar, silly," I reminded her. "It makes them sick."

"I know." She looked up at me with laugh. I noticed that her eyes crinkled in the corners when she smiled, just like her dad. "But my dad and I really like cake, so we always look for reasons to make it."

As if it were possible to love Fletcher anymore, suddenly I did. And I loved his daughter, too. Oh, what a sticky situation I was in. Those pesky tears tickled my eyes again. "So what else will you help me cook for Eats and Treats?"

Martha thought about it for a few beats, and her smile dropped.

I patted her knee. "What's wrong? Out of recipes already?"

"No." She sighed. "It's just that if I work with you at Eats and Treats, that'll mean I have to work with Marisol, too."

I half smiled. "Oh, Mar's not so bad once you get to know her. She can make a mean mole sauce."

"I wish my dad would break up with her." Martha propped her chin on her fist. "She's just so *grouchy*."

Part of me wanted to defend my friend, but the part in love with Martha's father wanted to let Marisol sink her own ship. She'd had months to forge a relationship with Martha, and instead of finding common ground, all I'd ever heard Marisol do was gripe. *That kid complains too much. That kid is always hanging around. That kid is always taking Fletcher away.* Fletcher was a father, and Marisol had had more than enough time to adjust to it. But her discomfort seemed to grow with every outing the three of them had.

I didn't say anything, so Martha went on. "She pretends I'm not there when my dad leaves the room. If I talk to her when he's not looking, she totally ignores me. Then when he comes back, she acts like everything I say is so cool."

Cringing, I shifted in my seat. I didn't even know what to say. But Martha didn't give me the chance to think of anything, because she threw her next comment out and my heart almost exploded all over the waiting room.

"I wish he was dating you!" she blurted, turning to face me. "You have stuff in common with him and you make him laugh. All he ever does when he's with Marisol is rub his eyes. He only does that when he's frustrated. You never frustrate him, Lexie. Plus, he said you like Elvis music, and *she* never lets him listen to it when they're together. I don't know why he met Marisol first. She sucks."

I didn't have the heart to tell Martha that Fletcher met Marisol after he'd met me, and that the minute he saw her, he was sunk like the Titanic. She was too beautiful and too charming *not* to date. Any resistance would have been futile.

"I hate her," Martha said in a wobbly voice.

I slid my arm around her small shoulders and pulled her to my side. "Shhh. Now don't cry. It's okay." I smoothed down her hair and closed my eyes. Holding Martha felt so natural to me. How in the world could Marisol not like this kid? "Listen, I know you and Marisol don't see eye to eye. And I understand why. Sometimes Marisol is sort of difficult to get along with."

Martha sniffled. "You got that right."

I rested my chin on her head. "But underneath it all, there is a hilarious and funny person who has been my friend for so many years I've lost count. She'll go to bat for me, no matter what it's for, and she'll win. Every time. You don't find that kind of loyalty in just any friend, you know."

Martha nodded, her hair tickling my nose.

"So even though on the outside Marisol is cranky, just remember that on the inside there is a person who will fight for the people she loves. No matter what. Maybe remembering that will help you to hate her less when she ignores you." Without thinking, I pressed a kiss to the top of Martha's head. "Okay, kiddo?"

A woman's voice rang out, tearing the moment in two. "Lexie Baump?"

I looked up at the nurse smiling at me. "I have to go. It was sure nice to see you."

"You, too." She forced a smile.

"You know what?" I dug in my purse, and yanked out a business card. "Here's my cell number. If you ever need some advice on how to navigate your way around Marisol, give me a call."

Her face lit up as she took the card. "Thanks!"

Hiking my purse up on my shoulder, I waddled towards the nurse. "I'm ready now," I told her, squeezing past her into the back of the office.

It was then that I realized Fletcher had been standing behind the receptionist across the room. His arms were folded across his chest, and a sad frown on his handsome face. God knew how long he'd been standing there, but I didn't care. I'd meant everything I'd said.

Chapter Nineteen

I looked at the tiny pocket-sized calendar resting on my passenger seat and released a colossal sigh. I was thirty-two weeks pregnant today, and it was time.

No, my water hadn't broken….

It was time for me to lay my grievances with my mother aside. Time for me to apologize to her for not speaking to her in a month. Time to forgive her for hurting me. And time for me to accept my mother, flaws and all.

The truth was, I was nesting.

My apartment had been scrubbed from top to bottom. Every article of clothing I owned, for myself *and* for my baby, had been washed, ironed, and folded to perfection. I'd assembled every piece of baby equipment and polished them until they gleamed. I'd even rented a carpet steamer, which I'd promptly used to sanitize my floors *and* drapes.

All that cleaning, and yet something still felt incomplete. I needed my mom. I *wanted* my mom. It was the same feeling I got every single time I got the flu. It didn't matter what age I was, when I was lying on my bed with a fever and the chills, I wanted my mom. Now I was about to have a baby. What woman didn't want her mother when she was thirty-two weeks pregnant and on the verge of becoming a parent?

Which is why I was parked in her driveway on a Saturday afternoon.

I hadn't called first. Mostly because I didn't know what to say, and because I was pretty sure my mother would cry.

I could never understand her when she cried over the phone.

Besides, her thirty-third, and final, message had left things open for my eventual return:

"Hi, Alexandria, it's your mother. Listen, I know you think you're going to be mad at me forever, and maybe you're right. But I want you to know that the moment you look at your baby, you'll understand why I do the crazy things I do. Because the love and protectiveness that a mother feels for her child is so overwhelming, it takes your breath away. That's why I keep trying to set you up. Because I would do anything to protect you from feeling overwhelmed and alone. That's all I'm trying to do. I mean, sure. I guess I went about doing it the wrong way, so sue me. But still. I only did it because I love you—and my grandchild—so much. I won't call anymore. I know I'm annoying you. But you know where I live, and the door's always open. Come see me when you're ready."

I looked at my mother's Buick in the carport. I was ready.

I hoisted myself out of my driver's seat and waddled up to the front door. This was it. Turning the knob, I pushed the door open a few inches. She never locked her doors. I'd been warning her how dangerous that was for years, but she'd always come back with, *Spokane's just fine! I* grew up *here, for Pete's sake!*

I hesitated in the doorway. I'd always just walked right in in the past, but things felt different now. Too much had transpired between us.

"Mom?" I called out softly.

There was no answer. Not that I was surprised. You couldn't have your house lined in stuffed dolls and not expect to have some soundproofing. I opened the door all the way. "Hey, Ma! It's Lex. Can we talk?"

My words sounded flat against the padding of all the Cabbage Patch dolls.

There was a dull thumping sound that came from the back of the house. She must be in the laundry room folding clothes. Her dryer had been purchased brand new by my father in 1988, and for as long as I could remember, the damned thing clunked like there was a clog lodged in the vent.

Muttering a curse word, I sidestepped a trio of dolls who watched me with painted on eyes. This place creeped me out more and more every time visited. It was going to be a struggle to bring my baby here for visits without wanting to sprinkle him or her with holy water afterward.

The banging sound stopped, and I halted. "Hello?"

I heard a muffled sound that could only be described as a wail.

My blood ran cold, and I strode through the living room. "Mom?"

It would figure that after all this time giving her the silent treatment, I would walk in to find her crumpled on the floor after a heart attack. How many times had Corbin and I discussed buying her one of those Life Alert things?

The bumping started again, increasing in volume and pace, and I took off in a run down the hallway. Holy hell, she was having a *seizure*! "Mom!" I bellowed, charging past the empty laundry room. "Mooom!?"

A groan rang out. A *deep* groan.

What the what?

I pushed her bedroom door open and wished instantly I hadn't. There was too much flesh and too much movement to process. Pastor Irm's black shirt and collar were tangled with my mother's lavender teddy bear sweatshirt on the carpeted floor. And my mother's giant beige bra with five hooks hung from the doorknob.

I heard my mother giggle—*giggle,* for crying out loud! I hadn't heard her giggle in at least twenty years.

And then I heard myself scream an obscenity that rhymed with "Holy trucking pit!"

Pastor Irm. And my mother. Getting their freak on.

Amongst the flesh, I saw two eyes pop open from behind thick pink tinted glasses. "ALEXANDRIA?"

I stood frozen. Couldn't move. Wanted to but simply couldn't.

Pastor Irm looked over his bare shoulder. "Patsy, what's wrong? I… oh, dear."

My mother's pale white legs started to kick on either side of the pastor. "GET OUT!"

My feet finally unglued themselves from the floor, and I ran face first into the doorjamb when I whirled around.

My mother's screams rang in my ears as I ran—nay, *sprinted*—back down the hall, and shoved my way through the front door. The sunlight assaulted my eyes as I tripped on the curb and dove across the yard.

"Keys, keys, keys," I muttered to myself, fumbling in the pockets of my hoodie. My hands were shaking, and I could hear the sound of Irm's groan echoing in my head over and over again. I shuddered as I yanked the keys out and tried unsuccessfully to press the unlock button. "Oh, son of a… I've got to get out of here."

Had they been doing the nasty for long? I racked my brain. How long had my mother and Pastor Irm been close friends? Ten years? Maybe more. Had they been having sex this whole time? I wasn't sure if I'd ever be able to go back to my mother's house, let alone eat dinner there again.

I dropped my keys on the driveway and raked a hand through my hair. They'd been bouncing around on my *father's* bed. Where else in the house had they done it? The kitchen? The dining room? Mother of all things beautiful, in front of all those dolls? It was enough to make me sick.

The screen door swung open and slapped against the house. "Alexandria, wait!"

I looked up and saw my mother. Her eyes were rimmed with red, and she'd pulled on her pink bathrobe. She held out her hands, and made a choking sound. "I'm sorry. I never meant for you to, I just, I'm so sorry."

My shock quickly morphed into anger. She'd been treating me like I was Satan's Mistress ever since I announced I was pregnant. Again, and again, and again my mother had made me feel like I was as horrible as someone sitting in a jail cell for murder.

And the whole time she'd been boinking Pastor Irm.

My mother started to come down the front steps towards me, but I put out my hands to stop her. "Don't come any closer to me."

My voice was shaking, but I took a deep breath and went on. No point in chickening out now. Not after what I'd just seen. "You've been so cruel to me. *So* cruel. And I came here prepared to apologize to you, just so that I could have you back in my life again. So that I could share this amazing experience with you. I've missed you, Mom. My whole apartment is ready for this baby, and the only thing that's missing is the grandma. I don't want to do this without you."

She didn't say anything. She just stood there crying.

I put my hands on my giant stomach. "Do you understand how much you've missed? You've missed most of this pregnancy because you've been so focused on marrying me off. You've missed experiences that I should have been able to share with my mother, because you were so focused on what a disappointment I am, or how much people are going to judge you because your pathetic daughter got knocked up. You treated me like I was some sort of slut."

My mother's hand went to her chest. "Lexie, I—"

"Shut up," I snapped. "You don't get to talk anymore. You don't get to decide what is acceptable or appropriate anymore. You don't get to judge me anymore. I just caught you in the act with your *pastor*. Who does that? What kind of a person treats their child like garbage, when they're doing the very same thing?"

I scooped the keys off of the driveway and unlocked my car. I knew I was going too far, but like everything else lately, I couldn't stop it. Couldn't rein it in. The hormones were a'ragin, and I had no control. "I'm so disappointed in you, Mom. *So* disappointed. Maybe it was best we weren't speaking, because I'm not sure I want you around my baby, anyway."

My mother covered her mouth, her shoulders bouncing. I slammed my car door, and fired up the engine. And as I peeled out of the driveway and sped away from the house, I realized that I was crying, too.

This was not how I'd seen my day going.

Chapter Twenty

"Mommy, I have to peeeeeeeee!"

Candace rolled her eyes at me and we followed her daughter, Ellie, through the thick crowd. Laughing, I pressed a hand to my back. "Slow down," I huffed. "Do all four-year-olds have to go to the bathroom this often?"

In the hour I'd been sitting with Candace, Brian, and their kids at the *My Little Pony LIVE!* concert, we'd made three trips to the restroom, and it was only intermission. Given the saccharine sweet music played at ear-damaging decibels, and an entire convention center filled with preschool-aged children and their tired parents, my head hurt as much as my puffy feet did. I was starting to question whether my own child would *ever* need to see a concert and was leaning heavily toward no.

"Unfortunately, yes." Candace stepped around a little boy who was splayed on the floor, crying. His mother looked like she wanted to cry, too. "You should have seen the kids when we went to see *Disney on Ice* last year. Ellie had a total meltdown and threw up on the guy in front of us."

Snorting, I stumbled when the little boy started to flail. "Whoops, sorry." I told his mother, before scrambling to catch up with my cousin at the restroom line. "Slow down. Wait for me."

She glanced over her shoulder at me. "You're moving pretty slow these days, Lex."

"Thanks for pointing it out." I scanned the line. It was at least ten people long, and that didn't include the people waiting *inside* the bathrooms. "Nice. I'll deliver this kid before I get to a toilet." A skinny woman behind us grimaced, and I caught a glimpse of it in the corner of my eye. "Sorry. Just kidding."

I'd only come here to get out of my apartment. Every time I was alone, memories of seeing my mother's dance of passion a few days earlier came rushing back. And when I started to get depressed about the absence of my mother in my life, it reminded me of the fact that I'd not seen or spoken to Fletcher in more weeks than I cared to mention.

That's usually when the tears started, and the boxes of individually wrapped snack brownies came out. Even my maternity clothes were starting to feel too small.

"So." Candace looked at me for a few seconds. "My mom called me the other day."

"Oh, yeah? How's Aunt Dory doing?" I chewed my thumbnail and danced in place a little. The baby was pressing against my bladder, and I was about two minutes from bursting.

"She said that you and your mom had another argument," she said.

I avoided my cousin's eyes. The last thing I wanted to do was tell that I walked in on my mother screwing Pastor Irm. If I told, my Aunt Dory—and the rest of my family—would know within the hour. "Yeah, we did."

"Did she try to fix you up again?"

"No."

"Well, what was it about?" Candace was fishing for more information, but I wasn't giving in.

First off, talking about it would just make those horrifying moments come alive inside of my head again. There wasn't enough therapy in the world to get over seeing Pastor Irm's bare butt in my mother's dim bedroom. And second, no matter how much my mother did to hurt me, I still felt protective of her. Aunt Dory would have a heyday with this information, and it would kill my mother to find out that everyone knew she wasn't the chaste widow anymore.

I forced a smile. "Just typical stuff. You know my mom."

"Yeah." The line between her eyebrows told me she was concerned. "Hey, have you heard from Marisol lately?"

Heaviness formed in my chest. Marisol had been quiet at work lately, and most of our conversations had consisted of work details only. What event we had coming up, who was in charge of making the quiche, and which one of us was going to make a run to the restaurant supply store. There had been times when I'd wanted to ask her if she needed to talk. But I'd swallowed back every question. I didn't want to hear about Fletcher. I didn't want to know if they'd slept together, or if they were having problems. It was all too much to handle. Too much to hear.

"Um, no." I moved forward with the line. "She's been pretty quiet, and keeping herself busy lately."

Candace frowned. "I wonder if she and Fletcher are doing all right?"

"I hope so."

And it was true. I was practically ready to pop out a baby, and I looked more like Opie than a lingerie model on a *good* day. Marisol was the right choice for Fletcher.

"Fletcher seems distracted." Candace danced in place holding Ellie's hands. "He came over for the game the other day and barely knew who was playing. When Brian asked what was wrong, he said he had a lot on his mind. Then he did something sort of weird."

I pretended to be enthralled with Ellie's hair bow. I didn't want to hear about anything that Fletcher did, because I would probably turn it into something to think about and obsess over for days.

"Mommy, pick me up!" Ellie held out her hands. "Mommy! Pick me up!"

Candace swung her daughter onto her hip, and leaned in close to me. "He started asking about *you*."

The baby sucker punched me in the bladder and I leaned forward. "Seriously, is this line moving at all? Oh Lord, I have to pee."

The skinny woman behind us groaned. "We *all* do, lady."

"Well, you're not eight months pregnant, are you?" I snapped.

Candace put her hand on my shoulder. "Did you hear what I said? Fletcher was probing Brian for details about you."

I waved a hand, and ignored the swirling feeling I felt in my chest. "Whatever. He probably wanted to check up on my pregnancy."

"I don't think so." Candace shook her head. "I think there's something you're not telling me."

"Nope. You know all." Biting my lip, I silently asked God to empty the bathroom. If we kept talking about Fletcher, I was definitely going to wet my pants.

"Come on, Lex, things between the three of us girls have weird for weeks," Candace said. "And now Fletcher spends all of his time with Brian asking about *you*?"

I pressed my lips together and avoided her eyes.

She groaned and went on. "What's Lexie's ex-husband like? Why did Lexie leave dinner the other night? What was Lexie like in college? What are Lexie's hobbies?"

"I like piña coladas and getting caught in the rain." Laughing at my own joke, I moved forward with the line.

"Come on." She snorted. "You have to admit it, it's odd. And oh, holy hell. Speak of the devil."

"What?" I followed her line of sight and my eyes landed smack dab on Fletcher. He was walking hand in hand with a frowning Martha. In an instant, I broke out in a sweat. "Oh, crap, crap, crap!"

Candace stared at me. "What is wrong with you?"

I turned so my back was pointed at Fletcher. "Screw me running."

"Not now," she hissed. Then she waved. "Hey, Fletcher. Over here!"

I looked over my shoulder. Martha spotted me and made a beeline towards us. "Lexie!" she cried happily, putting out her arms.

"Hi, Martha." She fell against me for a hug. This kid fit against me as much like a puzzle piece as her dad did.

Stop thinking like that.

Fletcher stopped walking a foot or two away from us. When he spoke, his eyes stayed locked on mine. "Hi guys. Fancy meeting you here."

Candace looked between Fletcher and me a few times. "What brings you to the *My Little Pony LIVE!* concert?"

Martha pulled away from me and wrinkled up her nose. "My dad thinks I'm five years old."

Fletcher put a hand on the top of his daughter's head. "I bought the tickets on a coupon website and thought she'd like it."

"I'm not a baby anymore, Dad." Martha wriggled out from under his hand.

He offered us a shrug. "She asked for a pony doll a year ago. I didn't realize the concert would be so passé."

My heart swelled. Fletcher looked so cute when he was sheepish. Especially when he was sheepish in a vintage plaid shirt and old Levis with holes in the knee. He was the only doctor in town who looked like he moonlighted in an auto garage.

"What were you thinking, Dad?" I teased, letting my guard down.

Fletcher's eyes lit up, and a spark jolted between us. "I was trying to impress her. Guess it fell flat."

I opened my mouth. Then closed it. Then opened it again, but nothing came out. There was so much I wanted to say to Fletcher. Words upon words stacked up on the tip of my tongue, but they all sat there, unmoving.

I could feel Candace's gaze on the side of my face. Finally, one sentence came out. "You switched me to a different doctor."

Fletcher nodded, squaring his shoulders. "Thought it was best."

I shook my head. "I don't want Javornik. I want you."

Fletcher gulped, making his Adam's apple bob. "I thought it would help."

Candace's head popped up between us. "Why would it help? Why was it best? What's going on?"

"Mommy, the line is moving." Ellie pointing a chubby finger.

"Go on, Lex, you can go first." Candace nudged me. "You have to pee really bad."

"No, just go without me." I didn't even look at her. I knew I was being rude, but that stupid tractor beam thing was happening with Fletcher again. I hated it. And loved it. But mostly hated it.

She looked down at Martha and held out her hand. "What about you, Martha? Do you need to go?"

"Yes, please." She looked up at Fletcher. "Wait here, 'kay?"

He finally looked away from me. "Got it. Right here. Thanks, Candace."

My cousin narrowed her eyes at Fletcher. "Uh huh. It seems as though you two need to talk."

"Right. I suppose so." His cheeks reddened.

"Oh, good Lord, would you guys make up your mind?" The woman behind us growled. "Some of us really have to go!"

I swung around. "Then get in there you impatient cow!"

"Whoa." Fletcher took me by the elbow. "Please excuse us."

I let him lead me across the palatial building, stopping at a row of windows that overlooked the Spokane River. I pulled my arm away.

"Feeling a little touchy lately?" he asked.

I sighed. "I guess."

"You know, a lot of women will get a hormone surge in the last trimester, and it can make them—"

"Can you just be Fletcher right now, and not Dr. Know It All?" I snapped.

He stifled a laugh. "Okay."

I pressed a hand to my forehead. It was really hot in this place. Or maybe I was just a beached whale and I got overheated every time I *moved*. "I'm sorry. I just haven't seen you, or spoken to you, in so long. And things are just so weird between us. And between Marisol and me, and aw, hell. I don't know."

"I get it." Fletcher's mouth tugged downward. "It's been rough for me, too. I haven't seen Marisol lately. I've just been doing some thinking. Sorting things out."

I swallowed back the lump in my throat. "I'm trying to give you and Marisol space. But then I run into you two together, and all of my feelings come back. I move backwards about ten spaces."

"Me, too," His hand came up to touch me, but dropped. "I thought if I moved your case to Dr. Javornik, it would help. But now I just miss you more."

"I thought my feelings would dissipate, but they're just getting worse." I pushed my hair back from my forehead, and fanned my face. "I hoped it was some sort of hormone surge, and that I wasn't stupid enough to fall for a guy who isn't even available. But every time I'm around you… whammo. I can't look at anyone else or form coherent sentences. I'm losing it."

This time Fletcher's hand did capture mine, and his thumb started to stroke a path from one side of my knuckles to the other. "I thought the same thing. I thought if I avoided you, I would get over whatever it is I'm feeling." He pulled my hand, bringing me an inch or two closer.

I should have pulled my hand back. A responsible woman would have pulled her hand back. But did I? No. No I did not.

"Lexie, what I feel for you is strong." Fletcher's eyes bored into mine, and I was pretty sure I was going to burst into flame soon. "It crosses every line that I, as a doctor, have. It's completely unprofessional and inappropriate. I have no right to want you, not only because I'm dating Marisol, but because I am, or was, your *doctor*. But when I'm with you, all I want is to be touching you. And when I'm not with you, all I can do is think about where you are, who you're with, and whether or not you're happy or sad or smiling or crying. And when I see you with my daughter…"

Fletcher stopped speaking. We were now close enough to each other that I could have stood on my toes and pressed a kiss to his neck. After a beat, he cleared his throat. "Let's just say, Lex, my feelings for you scare me."

"I'm scared, too," I whispered. "I've got so much baggage. My mother's sleeping with her pastor, and I'm pregnant, and—"

"I don't care about baggage," he whispered. "None of that matters."

It didn't make sense. I was eight months pregnant, red-faced, sweaty, and puffier than someone with a peanut allergy who ate a Snickers bar. My hair was a complete mess, and if you stared at my stomach through my tee shirt for long enough, you would see it shift and move like a scene from the movie *Aliens*.

But the way he was looking at me filled me right up to the brim with joy. Fletcher was beaming down at me like I was the most gorgeous, traffic-stopping supermodel he'd ever laid eyes on. He looked at me like I'd just told him he'd won a billion dollars. I'd been waiting my whole life to have a man look at me like that. Nate never had. Neither had anyone else, for that matter. Fletcher's gaze felt like the warmest sunshine on the most perfect spring day, and I never wanted him to look away.

"What do I do?" His voice was soft, and the crowd around us was thick, but I could still understand him. I would have been able to recognize his voice from ten miles away.

The lump in my throat won over, and my eyes filled up with hot tears. He was dating Marisol. "I don't know."

"I can't pretend I don't have feelings for you anymore." He took hold of both of my shoulders. "I don't want to fight it anymore."

He's dating Marisol.

Heat started to creep up the back of my neck. "And yet you're still dating my friend." Fletcher's mouth pulled into a guilty line, and I went on. "If you feel so much for me, and nothing for her, then why are you still stringing Marisol along?"

Fletcher's head hung, his forehead touching mine. "I don't know. I thought that…" His voice petered out.

I waited and took a shaky breath. "You thought she was too hot to just give up on."

"No." He raised his head and looked me in the eye. "Falling for one of my patients, especially one about to become a single mother, is unethical. You're emotionally fragile. If I tried to pursue you now, it would be taking advantage of you at your most vulnerable point."

"Wait." I pushed Fletcher's chest and moved him back a few inches. "You're still dating Marisol because I'm *emotionally fragile*?"

Fletcher grasped my hands. "No, wait, I—"

"There you are." Candace called. Her eyes widened at the sight of Fletcher's fingers enveloping mine. "I, um, are we interrupting something?"

"Yes," Fletcher said at the same time I said, "No."

"Daddy, what are you doing?" Martha asked, putting her hands on her hips.

I turned back to Fletcher. I wanted to tell him that I didn't care what he'd done with Marisol—or anyone else, for that matter. But I wasn't an idiot. At least not all the time, anyway.

"I'm sorry, Fletcher." I pulled my hands away, and shoved them into my pockets. "But that's the biggest pile of bullshit I've ever heard in my entire life."

His mouth dropped open. I stomped past Candace, pulling on the sleeve of her blouse as I went. I heard Fletcher say my name, but ignored it. I had too.

"Intermission is over." My voice shook. "Brian's probably wondering where we are by now."

"Oh, uh, okay." She scooped Ellie up, and followed me. Once we were a good fifty yards away, she grabbed my arm. "What the heck was that about?"

I didn't stop walking until I got to our section. I was afraid if I could still see Fletcher and Martha, I was going to dissolve into a sobbing mess, and Candace was going to have to scrape me off of the floor with a shovel.

"We kissed," I blurted.

Candace gasped. "Just now?"

"No." Shaking my head, I covered my eyes. "A long time ago. At the house he's buying from Corbin. But it started before that." When I opened my eyes, tears slid down my face. "I'm in love with him, Candace."

Chapter Twenty-one

"I think Fletcher is going to break up with me." Marisol's voice was flat and defeated.

I nearly swallowed my tongue.

It'd been twenty-four hours since I called Fletcher out at the *My Little Pony LIVE!* concert. And I'd come to my Lamaze class—where my friends were acting as dual coaches—prepared for a punch in the face from Marisol. But instead, she'd walked in with slumped shoulders, and plopped down on the floor with a thump.

"What makes you say that?" Candace asked nervously. Her blonde eyebrows were so high on her forehead they practically blended into her hairline. She knew the whole story now and was begging me to come clean to Marisol. But I refused. It was up to Fletcher to make this right now.

Why? Because I was pregnant and moody and "emotionally fragile," that's why. Oh, and also because I was a total chicken.

"He called and asked me to come by his place tonight after," she gestured to the rest of a class, "this thingy. Whatever it's called."

Our teacher, a tall woman with a long silver braid running down her back, walked by and touched Marisol's shoulder. "This class is called Prepared Labor and Natural Birthing. Welcome, friend."

Marisol made a face. "Whatever. When do they start serving alcohol?"

Candace swatted at her. "It's not a cocktail party."

"It should be." She scanned the room. "Look at this place. It could use an upper, if you know what I mean."

There were women—all round and ready to drop a baby at any minute, just like me—sitting in varying stages of relaxation. Some were between their husbands' or boyfriends' knees, breathing peacefully while they rubbed circles on their backs. Others were lying on their sides on a beanbag or pillow, while their men kneaded their feet lovingly. The mood in the room at the learning annex was as relaxed and calm as a bathtub filled with warm water and bubbles.

In my corner of the room, Candace was on my left, texting Brian, who was unable to get the *Sesame Street* DVD to work. And Marisol was on my right, checking her eye makeup in a compact mirror. I was the only single mom in the group.

Awesome.

"This environment is conducive to the environment you'll want to bring your baby into," the silver haired lady said as she sauntered around the room. Her fingers touched Marisol's shoulder as she passed. "Speak softly. You don't want your baby coming into a world full of noise and confusion."

Marisol glanced up at her. "Me? Oh, no, it's not *my* baby. It's hers." She jabbed her thumb at me and shuddered. "I'm just here to help with the old heave-ho and all that."

I closed my eyes. This was my support system? "Marisol, please."

She laughed at her own joke. "Come on, loosen up, Lex. You'll be so drugged out you won't care what I call it."

"I delivered all of my kids naturally," Candace announced.

"Yeah, well you're a freak of nature." Marisol rolled her eyes.

"I'm sorry. She knows not what she says." I held out my hand to the teacher. "I'm Lexie Baump. This is my first child, and I haven't decided on natural or medicated childbirth yet."

Marisol elbowed me. "Oh, be serious."

The teacher shook my hand. "I'm Maureen. And I hope to convince you that you're capable of bringing your child into the world without medication. We're going to teach you primitive methods that have been used by natural mothers for centuries."

"Primitive is right." Marisol snorted. "I'm definitely going to need a cocktail."

Candace put her arm around me. "You can do it, Lex."

Maureen beamed down at us. "It's so nice to see modern families like yours having children. I do hope you'll enjoy the class."

She walked away, and I slapped a hand on my forehead. "That's what we look like? A couple?"

Candace giggled. "It is *very* modern."

"Then who's Marisol?" I gestured at our friend, who was lying back on the provided pillows with her eyes closed.

"She's our girlfriend." Candace said, matter-of-factly. "We're polyamorous."

"Sweet." I ignored the aghast stares from the other moms.

We watched Marisol for a beat, her ample bosom rising and swelling. Most of the men in the room were staring at her, but that was because she'd come to Lamaze in a short skirt, and was now curled up like a kitten on the floor. "This isn't exactly the place for a nap, you know."

"Oh, take it easy on her." Candace dropped her voice low, so that only I could hear it over the sound of the instrumental music Maureen had turned on. "She's gonna get dumped in a few hours. Let her rest up."

I bit my lip, hope and shame coiling together like smoke in my chest, making everything feel tight and uncomfortable. "Do you think so?"

"Well, it's not like you don't want it to happen." Candace raised an eyebrow at me.

"I don't. I just. I don't know what I want to have happen," I hissed. I was so torn. When I walked away from Fletcher at that concert, I'd secretly hoped he would show up at my apartment later that night, single and completely unattached, with an engagement ring in his pocket. And possibly wearing nothing but his Elvis tee shirt and a smile.

But I also wanted Marisol to be happy. And there were times—amongst her gripes and whining—when it seemed as though dating Fletcher made her happy. Who was I to take that away from her?

"Well, you'd better figure it out pretty quick," Candace whispered, as Maureen took her place at the head of the classroom. "Because when Marisol meets up with him tonight, I can almost guarantee you that things are gonna get sticky really fast."

"What? Who's sticky?" Marisol pushed herself up next to me and rubbed her eyes. "Ugh. I'm so tired. I'm bored, too. How long does this class last?"

"In a hurry to get to Fletcher's?" Candace fished. I shot her a dirty look, but she just shrugged innocently.

Marisol ran her hand down her hair, frowning. "No. Not especially. Just in a hurry to get it over with."

I picked at a loose thread on my jeans, not wanting to sound to obvious. "Well, how do feel about breaking up with him?"

She waved a hand. "It doesn't matter. I mean, our food rep asked me out last week, so I'll probably set something up with him. I've been kind of keeping him in my back pocket."

"Larry asked you out?" I gaped at her. She was the only person who would line up backup boyfriends, just in case her current one didn't pan out.

"I didn't really want to go, but he'll be a nice distraction." Marisol sighed. "I just don't like getting dumped. I really thought that Fletcher and I had chemistry, but—"

"Welcome to Prepared Labor and Natural Birthing, everyone." Maureen held her arms wide and scanned the crowd. "It's my goal to make you all feel at home, at peace, and enveloped in a hug from Mother Nature—"

"Oh, wow. This really is pretty granola," Candace whispered.

"But what?" I asked Marisol, ignoring as Maureen described the breathing techniques we would be practicing in class.

She dropped her voice low. "Oh, you know what I mean. When I met Fletcher, our physical connection was hot. I mean, *hot*. I really thought we were going to make sparks together."

I felt like I was going to be sick.

"But after a month or so, it was clear that his mind was somewhere else," Marisol explained. "The only reason I stuck it out was because he's a freaking doctor. A hot one, at that. I mean, have you seen his ass in a pair of jeans, Lex? Good Lord, it makes me want to go to confession!"

Had I seen Fletcher's butt? Um, yeah. I'd seen his butt. In my head, I'd made movies about his butt.

I cleared my throat. "Um, well, I guess it's nice."

"Nice?" Marisol widened her eyes at me. "Give me a break. He's got the kind of body that could turn a nun into a whore."

The woman next to us shushed us.

Marisol turned to her. "I *know* you didn't just shush me."

"Ladies, focus." Maureen scolded us. "Repeat after me... hee, hee, hooo... hee, hee, hooo."

"The first time we messed around, I couldn't get enough of him, you know?" Marisol went on. I bit the insides of my cheeks to keep from screaming. "I couldn't get his shirt off fast enough. And the pants? Forget about it."

"I thought you hadn't slept together," I said through grit teeth.

Candace nudged me. "Not the time."

"We haven't. And now we won't. Probably." I winced, but Marisol didn't take notice. "We made out, I guess. But every time we got close, his daughter would need something. Or his phone would ring and it was the hospital. Or he..."

My eyes bugged out of my head. "He what?"

Her brows knit close together. "He would pull away. Say he needed to be somewhere. Find some excuse to avoid sex."

"Yes!" When Marisol wrinkled her nose, I added, "I mean, *yes*. I understand. That would be really tough."

"Exactly!" She threw her hands up. "I mean, how long am I expected to go without getting laid?"

The woman sitting next to Marisol scowled at us. "For heaven's sake, would you talk about this later?"

Candace mouthed the words, *shut up* at us.

Maureen stared down at us with a double-chinned frown. "You'll never bring your baby into this world naturally if you don't know how to choose your focal point."

Marisol and I breathed like obedient students.

Once Maureen moved to the opposite end of the room, she leaned close to me again. "But it wasn't just the ass, you know? When Fletcher and I were together, there was hope. Does that make sense?"

I shook my head. "What do you mean?"

"Fletcher made me feel like settling down might not be so bad," she said. "I would watch him with his kid and it got me thinking. Maybe the whole monogamy, husband and kids, white picket fence thing really *is* all it's cracked up to be."

I gaped at her. This was *not* the Marisol I'd been friends with since college.

She raised her eyebrows. "What? I can't want domesticity?"

"No, no. You can." My voice cracked. "I just never thought I'd see the day. I didn't realize Fletcher brought that out in you."

That complicated things. It wasn't like I was surprised by the way he made Marisol feel. Hell, seeing Fletcher in faded Levi's would've made a *tree* ovulate. But the thought that Fletcher's familial appeal was now making *Marisol* ovulate? She deserved to have a life with someone. She deserved to have kids, and dogs, and the American dream. But why did it have to be Fletcher she wanted it with?

"I didn't realize it, either." Marisol picked at her nail polish. "I just hoped that if I stuck it out long enough, we'd finally gel, you know? Maybe I'd finally figure out how to connect with his kid—"

"Martha." I looked down. "Her name's Martha."

"Whatever." She shook her head. "Then maybe he and I could find some common ground, because Fletcher really is great. And we'd be even more great if he'd finally let me get him into bed—because we all know once he's in bed with me, all bets are off."

The woman next to her sneered, while her husband nodded enthusiastically.

Marisol turned her body so that she was facing me. "I could never get through to him. I had to initiate all of our dates. I had to call him. I had to remind him to take me places, and to invite me to things. It's like I was the guy in the relationship. Can you even imagine?"

"All right, everyone. Cleansing breath." Maureen pressed a hand to her stomach and demonstrated her deep breathing. "In and hold, and out and relax. Good job. Everyone join in."

The group all sucked up air in unison, except Candace, Marisol, and me.

"Wait a minute," Candace leaned forward so she could see Marisol. "You mean to tell us that you've never planned a date, or pursued a guy before?"

Marisol offered a nonchalant shrug. "No. Have you?"

Candace pinched the bridge of her nose. "Oh, good Lord."

"The worst part is, I think Fletcher is seeing someone else." Marisol pulled her knees up to her chest and wrapped her arms around them. "He's always distracted, his mind always seems to be somewhere else, and he just can't focus on *me*."

Heat crept through the collar of my shirt, scorching the skin up the sides of my face to my hairline. Fletcher hadn't been focusing on Marisol, because he'd been thinking about *me*. And I couldn't even begin to explain how backwards that felt. But oh Lord, it felt *good*.

Candace's elbow jabbed my arm.

"Ow." I rubbed my puffy arm. "What was that for?"

Candace mouthed, *Tell her.*

Shaking my head, I pressed my lips together. I couldn't admit to Marisol that the woman Fletcher had been obsessing over was me. I couldn't admit that we'd kissed. She'd never forgive me. I wasn't even sure I'd forgiven myself.

"Now, I want everyone to lay back between their partner's legs." Maureen grinned at the group. "We're going to practice feeling each other's breaths. Bring your bodies in unison to help your child enter the world."

I looked from friend to friend. "Who wants the honors?"

"That's my cue." Marisol pushed herself to her feet. "Smoke break."

"Come here, Lex." Candace watched her go. The rest of the class slid into position and proceeded with unifying their bodies and all that. "She's smoking again?"

I grunted as I sat between her knees. "She must be stressed out."

Candace started to drum a silent tune on my back with her hands. "I wish she knew about you and Fletcher."

My chest clenched. "Why? He's already dumping her. And I already feel awful."

"She'll find out eventually, you know." Candace stopped talking for a moment while Maureen passed by. "I mean, eventually you and Fletcher are going to want to go public with your relationship. She'll be hurt if she finds out through the grapevine and not from you. You're in love with her ex-boyfriend, Lex. An ex-boyfriend she apparently actually cared about."

"Yeah, what's up with that?" I craned my head to look at my cousin. "For the first time in the history of *Marisol*, she starts contemplating domesticity with the one man in the world I can't imagine my life without?"

"Shhh!" The woman next to us pressed her finger to her lips.

Candace turned my shoulders, forcing me to face forward. "Listen," she whispered. "I know Mar is hard to take. And I know she'll probably be over this break up by the end of the week. But I also know she'll be devastated when she finds out that you didn't have the decency to tell her that you're with him yourself."

"She may never have to know," I hissed.

"Come on, Lex. Don't be dumb." Candace rested her hands on my shoulders. "You aren't going to spend the duration of your relationship in your teensy apartment."

"Of course not," I mumbled. "Fletcher's buying a house."

She sighed. "You're better than this, Lex. Lying by omission is as bad as lying, and you know that."

Candace's words sat in my ears, prickling and burning me from the inside out. I knew she was right. I wasn't stupid.

"Husbands and life partners, rub circles on mom's back." Maureen announced, demonstrating the motion. "Remind her how much you adore her. Remind her of your passion and devotion."

Candace went back to patting out a tune on my shoulder blades. "My passion and devotion to you doesn't change the fact that you need to come clean. I won't keep a secret like this from her forever."

I looked around at all of couples. All of the women had their eyes closed, and their mouths were all pulled into O's while they huffed and puffed. My life was so grossly different from all of these other moms. What I wouldn't have given to be sitting there with a loving, devoted husband, instead of my know-it-all cousin—who was completely, annoyingly *right*.

"I can't do it," I finally told her, letting my face drop into my hands. "I can't bring myself to tell Marisol."

A pair of platform pumps appeared in front of me.

"Tell me what?"

Chapter Twenty-two

Sure enough, at ten o'clock that night—long after I'd gotten home from my Lamaze class and slid into my favorite flannel nightgown that provided plenty of room for me, the baby, and possibly an Oldsmobile—the call from Marisol came.

"He actually had the audacity to use *the line* on me, Lex. The line all guys use when they're dumping a woman. It's not you, it's me, he says."

She hadn't even given me a chance to say *hello* yet. She'd just launched into her tirade as soon as I picked up the phone.

"I'm so sorry," I said. And I was.

I didn't know when I would hear from Fletcher. The only thing I allowed myself to focus on was that my friend was upset. "I'm sure it really *is* him, and not you."

Marisol had no idea how right I was. At least she didn't know I'd made out with Fletcher. At least, I didn't think so.

"No kidding it's him." She sniffled. "I've never been dumped in my life. Freaking loser."

My mouth dropped open. "Marisol, are you crying?"

I hadn't witnessed her crying since 2007, when she found out Valentino had stopped designing clothes.

"No." I heard the sound of a tissue being yanked from a box. "I'm just... I'm... checking to see how you were. You looked pretty tired after your what's-it-called tonight."

"Lamaze class." Rolling my eyes, I settled down on my couch and pulled a blanket over my legs. "So what else did he say?"

"Oh, well, apparently he bought a house from Corbin. Did you know that?" Marisol's voice was letting lower by the second. She didn't get squeaky and high pitched like typical chicks do when they cry. She grew progressively more pissed off and dangerous. Like a hand grenade, just waiting to go off.

I winced. "Um, yeah. I just assumed you knew."

"Well, you would think!" She yelled. "I was dating him, for hell's sake. But, nooooo. Why would he tell me? Or invite me over to see it? Or ask my opinion on wall color?"

"You're mad about wall color?"

"I'm mad because he dumped me!" Marisol shrieked. "I mean, he's moving next week, and hasn't even asked me to help or to even *see* the place, and that speaks volumes about what he thinks of me. Not to mention, despite my efforts tonight, the guy won't sleep with me. I'm insulted!"

"Oh." My heart did a happy dance. I took a sip of a nearby glass of juice to celebrate. *I'd like to propose a toast…*

"He's gay. He's *clearly* gay. I mean the writing is on the wall."

Choking on the juice, I slapped a hand on my chest. "So, um, did Fletcher say anything about, you know, anyone?"

I was pretty sure I was safe. Marisol hadn't started cussing me out in Spanish yet.

"Of course not," she said, sighing. "He's acting all noble, like he's doing the right thing. But I'm not new to this rodeo. I know he's seeing someone else. Or at least thinking about it."

My stomach clenched. "You do?"

"Yes, and when I find out who it is, guy or girl, I'm going to drive to that cow's house, and—"

My doorbell rang and I jumped so high I dropped the phone. "Marisol? You still there?"

"Was that your doorbell?"

Scrambling to put the phone back up to my ear, I peered through the crack in my curtains and gasped. *Loudly.* There, on my doorstep, was Fletcher. "Um, I gotta go."

"You're hanging up on me?" She demanded. "I'm in *need*, here."

I looked down at my nightgown and grimaced. I looked like Ma on Little House on the Prairie, minus the night bonnet. "I'll call you right back."

"What!? You've got to be kidding me! You're—"

I didn't hear any of the Spanish words she'd started to yell, because my thumb slipped and I hung up.

"Be right there!" I called, looking down at my reflection in the mirror. I looked horrible.

The doorbell rang again. Moving quickly was definitely out, as I'd fallen asleep sometime between the seventh and eighth month, then woken up a slovenly animal with two left hooves. Once I was on my feet, I shuffled towards the bedroom. There was a pair of sweat pants and a tee shirt on my bed, and at least if I were wearing those, I wouldn't look eighty-three years old.

The doorbell rang a third time, and I skidded to a stop.

"Lexie?" A muffled voice called. "I'm sorry it's so late. It's me, Fletcher." He cleared his throat. "Fletcher Haybee."

Stifling a giggle, I yanked a cardigan off of the back of a chair and tugged it on over my nightgown. I unlocked the chain and swung open the door. "I know who it is."

A smile slowly spread across his face. "Lexie."

"Fletcher." I leaned against the doorjamb and pulled my sweater around my body tightly. It was clear he'd had had a rough evening. His face was covered from even more whiskers than usual, and there were circles under his eyes. "I was on the phone with Marisol."

His mouth pulled into a line. "She left my place a while ago."

I drew in a breath, then released it slowly. "She's upset."

"Yeah." A line appeared between his eyebrows. "I screwed up. Hurt two women who didn't deserve to be hurt."

I raised an eyebrow at them. "Two?"

He shuffled on the welcome mat. "Can I come in?"

Stepping aside, I took inventory of my tiny apartment. The deep red walls were covered with silver frames filled with black and white food photography, and my charcoal grey couch was covered in a discarded red fleece blanket. Fortunately, there were only a couple of lamps on, so the empty ice cream cartons and several discarded dirty socks lying around were hardly noticeable.

"I didn't know you were coming." I brushed some cookie crumbs off of the front of my nightgown. "I look terrible."

Fletcher shook his head. "You're beautiful."

My heart raced. Hell, it didn't just race. It performed the Indianapolis 500 inside of my chest. "Thank you."

He turned in a circle, taking everything in. Suddenly I was very aware of the fact that I had a bookshelf filled with vintage cookbooks and collectible Elvis figurines. And next to that, there were my AC/DC figurines and autographed Steven Tyler picture. I was a geek, and there was no denying it. If he went into my bedroom and saw my extensive tee shirt collection, the veil would drop completely.

"This place is so you." He leaned close to a framed photograph of Julia Child on the wall. "Eclectic. Like you."

I fanned my face. "I wasn't expecting you."

He faced me. "I owe you an apology."

"No, Fletcher, you—"

"You were right." Fletcher put his hands in his pockets and started pacing. There wasn't much room in my living room to do it effectively, so he looked like he was turning in circles. "I didn't break things off with Marisol sooner because she worked on paper."

I must have looked like I was ready to throw a lamp at him, because he stopped and held his hands out. "Just hear me out. I didn't mean that the way it came out. I meant Marisol wears expensive clothes and drives a BMW. She gets her nails done, and gets a spray tan once a week, even though she's

Hispanic. She acts like every other doctor's wife I've ever met since medical school."

I frowned. "Candace doesn't do that."

He shook his head. "But most of them do. Marisol looked the part. She was single, available, and walked the walk."

A lump started growing in my throat. "You're not scoring any points with me."

"I mean she fit the bill." Fletcher exclaimed. "And, more importantly, she wasn't my patient."

"Oh."

"The woman I'm crazy about is about to have a baby. A baby I was responsible for delivering." His shoulders sagged, and he looked down. "Do you understand how unethical my dating you would be? I would have lost the respect of my staff, not to mention Brian and Candace. They told me you'd been through so much. That you deserved to finally have some happiness in your life after being hurt so badly. Once they told me that, I…"

He raked a hand through his blonde hair, setting it on end. "I promised myself I would forget about all of the feelings I had for you. I would pretend I wasn't having a heart attack whenever you walked into the room. If I just gave it some time, and tried harder with Marisol, or, hell, *anyone else*, eventually my feelings would go away."

"I felt the same," I confessed. "I thought it was hormones. I thought it was some pregnancy-induced crush. I kept thinking that if I just stayed away from you, my feelings would disappear, and everything would go back to normal."

"What the hell is normal, anyway?" His green eyes bored into mine.

"Look at you." I gestured to his faded jeans and open leather coat. "You're gorgeous and smart. You're a doctor, for Pete's sake, and don't even get me started on how amazing Martha is. You're supposed to have the hot wife on your arm. Marisol is exactly that. I'm just *me*."

Fletcher took a step closer to me. "But I like just you."

I looked down at my nightgown. "I look terrible. I—"

"You look beautiful to me. You always do."

I gestured over my shoulder at my open closet just beyond the bedroom door. "I wear jeans and tee shirts, unless I'm meeting a client. And even then, I carry casual clothes in my car, so I can change as soon as the meeting's over."

Fletcher's eyes locked on mine. "I graduated from medical school wearing a Beastie Boys tee shirt. My ex was furious."

I didn't look away. "I don't like to cook. When I get home after work, all I want to do is put my feet up and watch the DVR, so I eat frozen dinners and ice cream."

He didn't look away, either. "I like to cook, but I'm not good at it. Martha bought me a pink apron that says *Kiss the Cook* for Christmas last year, and I wear it. Often."

"I wear my hair short because when it grows past my chin I look like Carrot Top."

"I use more hair products than most women because I have so many cowlicks on my head. When I first get out of the shower, I look like Buckwheat."

I stifled a giggle. "I drink coffee with a straw because I don't want to stain my teeth."

"I used to be anti-gun before I had a daughter." A smile tickled the corners of his mouth.

"I can't tan. I've tried, and all that happens is I burn, then I peel, then I'm as white as I was when I started. Marisol and Candace tease me because I'm so white, I'm practically translucent."

He smiled widely and pointed to a row of three perfectly straight, white teeth on the upper right side of his mouth. "You see these teeth here? They're a bridge. I knocked the originals out trying to learn how to skateboard in college. I fell and cracked myself in the face with the board. I never tried skating again after that, but I still have the board hanging in my office because it looks cool."

A flurry of butterflies cropped up in my stomach. I think I loved him even more. "My mother's certifiably insane. Her house is filled with dolls that watch your every move, and I'm pretty sure she has full on conversations with them when nobody else is there."

"My mother owns DVDs of every Denzel Washington movie ever made, and says if she dies, she wants to come back for one day as Denzel's wife."

I grinned. "I never learned how to swim."

"I'll teach you." He took another step towards me. "I spent hours playing Dungeons and Dragons as a kid."

"My ex-husband said I was frigid."

"My ex-wife said I was immature."

Suddenly the room was uncomfortably warm. Damn these pregnancy hot flashes, or maybe it was just the fact that we were headed into uncomfortable territory. But I had to keep going. He deserved to know it all.

"He's the father," I said hoarsely, putting my hands on my belly. "The biological father, I mean."

Fletcher's lips pulled into a line. "I wondered after your response at the birthday party." He sucked in a pull of air and released it slowly. "Are you two still involved?"

"No. Absolutely not." Shaking my head, tears flooded my eyes. "I can't stand him. We can't stand each other. He wants nothing to do with me, or the baby, and I'm glad. It was one of those late night, pity party, too much to drink sort of things I wish I could take back. Except that…" I looked down at my middle as the baby shifted within. "Then I wouldn't have this little guy. And I don't think I could live without my baby."

Fletcher's eyes warmed. "I think you're going to be a great mother. Sometimes the best things come out of our worst mistakes."

"You're a great father." The tears won, and spilled over. "Martha is amazing. She's witty and sweet and creative. She's the kind of kid I hope my baby will grow up to be like."

He beamed, and it was lovely to see. His blue eyes reflected the light from a nearby lamp, and the weight of his gaze covered my skin in warm goose bumps. "I'm so sorry I got us into this mess."

"I know," I whispered, wrapping my arms around myself to hide my trembling. "I'm just sorry I met you at such a weird time in my life. I'm sorry I'm so huge and pregnant, and I'm—"

"Shh." Fletcher put his finger on my lips. "Don't apologize. Not to me. You're perfect." Fletcher stepped closer, and we were barely a half-inch apart. The heat coming off his body made my head swim. "I want to be with you, Lexie Baump. I want it to be you, me, Martha and your baby. All together. I want us all to become a family. I want the American dream, or nuclear family, or whatever the hell you want to call it. I want it all with *you*."

I should have said something, but I couldn't. This was happening. I mean, *really* happening. I opened my mouth, then closed it.

Blank. My mind was blank.

He cringed. "Do you want those things, too?"

Nodding, I croaked my reply. "Yes."

His hands went to the wall behind me, trapping me between his arms. His nose traced a line across my forehead, then down my temple. I could hear his baited breath, his heart beating—or maybe that was mine—and my eyes fluttered shut.

"I want—"

I didn't let Fletcher finish. My hands went to the sides of his face and my lips were on his in an instant, and we clicked into place like puzzle pieces once again. His hands slid down the wall to my waist, which he grasped. Pulling me against his body, his hands trembled with a fervency that rattled my ribs, and set off an electrical buzz inside of my head.

Fletcher tilted his head to the side, deepening the kiss and tickling the edge of my teeth with his tongue. I snaked my hands down his chest, gripping the worn cotton in white-knuckled fists and yanking him closer. Earning an appreciative growl, I dragged his full lower lip between my teeth before pulling back to gaze into his deep pools of azure.

"I'm lightheaded," I whispered.

"I want you," he replied.

"Okay." I brought his mouth back to mine, arching my back. For a moment, I didn't care I was hugely pregnant. I didn't care that I'd already washed all of my makeup off, or that my legs felt like hairbrush bristles. All that I cared about was that Fletcher was here with me.

I may as well have been the hottest woman in the world. Fletcher's heavy-lidded gaze told me that in his eyes I was.

His lips traced an invisible line down my neck to my collarbone, where one of his hands stroked a fiery line across the skin at the neckline of my nightgown. One of the buttons popped open, and his mouth came down on the newly exposed skin, setting fireworks off in my head and making my gasp. The second button opened, and his hand pressed against my heart, feeling the thrum of my heartbeat through my flesh.

"Lex."

"Don't talk." I dragged my nails down the front of his shirt and tugged the hem upward. Fletcher's breath caught.

His lips brushed mine again, just a whisper of touch, sending shockwaves down my spine. When his fingers grazed down my side, lightly tickling the flesh, my toes curled inside of my socks. I opened my mouth to speak, all of my language skills evaporating into thin air, leaving me with just one word.

"Bedroom."

Blinking, Fletcher's neck straightened and he faced me with a bewildered expression. His lips, still slick from our kiss, parted. "Lexie."

I leaned forward to kiss him again.

His hands grasped my shoulders. Holding me at arm's length, he stepped back from my body. "No. Stop. Slow down."

My jaw dropped. "Huh?"

He brushed a strand of hair back from my face, and cupped my cheeks. "I can't do it this way."

The baby kicked me in the bladder, and I was suddenly reminded of the circumstances. Eight months pregnant. Flannel nightgown. Hairy legs. No makeup. "Oh," I mumbled, tugging the sweater closed over my partially unbuttoned nightgown.

"Hey," Fletcher put a finger underneath my chin. "Look at me."

"No, it's okay. I totally get it, I mean, look." I forced a laugh that came out entirely too loud. "It's cool. I swear."

"Wait. Hold on." Fletcher pulled me against his chest when I tried to duck out of his grip. "Lexie, look at me." I looked up and he smiled warmly. "Believe me, *I want to.*"

He pressed a kiss to my forehead and my heart squeezed in response. "I want to be beautiful for you," I told him.

"You already are." He rested his forehead against mine. "But this isn't how I want this to happen."

This time my laugh was genuine. "This isn't one of those vampire movies, Fletcher. You don't have to be virtuous. I know I'm super pregnant, and it's probably not such a turn on."

"It's not that." He leaned in and pressed another kiss to my lips. "It's just that I want something substantial. I want to get to know you, and—"

"You've given me a pap smear. How much more do you want to get to know me?"

"Not funny." Fletcher's face reddened. "I mean I want to do this properly. I want to take you on a date."

I giggled. Being around Fletcher made me feel like an excited teenager being hit on by the quarterback of the football team. Or, rather, a *pregnant* teenager. "Okay. A date, then."

He grinned, and the crinkles in the corners of his eyes made an appearance. "Awesome."

I touched his lips lightly with my own. "Where are we going for this date? Judging by my size right now, a buffet would be lovely."

"Stop it." He shuddered—yes, *shuddered*—when I kissed him. He laced his fingers with mine, and walked me over to my couch. "I don't know where we're going yet. But I'll figure it out. We'll go on the date of the century in a couple of weeks." He sat down and pulled me onto his lap.

"A couple of weeks? Why so long?" I asked. I wasn't sure if I would make it that long before our first date. Why didn't he just ask me to walk on hot coals while he was at it?

"My brother is flying in tomorrow help me move into the new house and spend some time with Martha." Fletcher stroked his fingers up and down my leg as we sat there, and I almost forgot that I was probably squishing his legs. Almost. "And then next weekend we're all headed to Arizona for a family reunion. We do it every few years."

I nodded. "Sounds like fun."

"I wish I could buy you a ticket to go with us. My mother would love you. But it's too dangerous to fly this late in your pregnancy. Doctor's orders." He touched his finger on the end of my nose, making my stomach whirl. "Plus, I want to keep you to myself for a while. Maybe I'll come over with some Chinese takeout while my brother is here."

"Mmm, sounds awesome." I closed my eyes and pressed my face into his hand, drawing in his scent. "That constitutes a first date, doesn't it?"

He grinned and shook his head. "Nope. You deserve more."

I pouted. "When will you get back from Arizona?"

"Two weeks." His hand curled around the back of my neck, pulling me down for another kiss. We pulled apart with a smack and he winked at me. "I traded a month of on-call time with Dr. Javornik to do it, but I haven't seen my brother in over a year. This will be our first time together with the whole family in three. I'll try to sneak away while my brother is here, so I can see you, but the minute I get back, it's you and me."

I nodded and brought my mouth to his again. I had no idea how I was going to get through the next two weeks. Now that I had Fletcher, I didn't want to let him go.

Plus, that buffet didn't sound half bad.

Chapter Twenty-three

"Lex, someone's here to see you."

Marisol's eyes were narrowed, and I immediately thought Fletcher had come into Eats & Treats to see me. He'd already surprised me with ice cream late the other night, leaving Martha home with his brother while he snuck away to see me.

Marisol still didn't know he and I were together, but that hadn't stopped me from tiptoeing around her for the last week. I was extra careful not to mention his name, even though he was in my thoughts—and his name was on the tip of my tongue—all the time.

While I was worried about the state of our friendship, I wasn't all that concerned about her broken heart. She'd already gone on three dates with our food distributor, and judging by the hickey she'd come in with earlier, I was pretty sure they'd gone to bed together. Sure, Fletcher had bruised Marisol's ego, but her ~~sex~~ social life wasn't suffering in the slightest.

"Who?" My heart leapt into my throat.

"Who do you think?" She folded her arms across her chest.

It'd only been a week since Fletcher had left my apartment in the middle of the night after the best make-out session I'd ever experienced in my life. In those seven days, ten hours, and thirteen minutes since he'd pressed one last kiss to my lips before disappearing into the night, we'd had ice cream once, emailed each other twice a day, talked on the phone at least once a day, and I'd long since lost track of how many text messages we'd exchanged. We were getting to know each other more than I ever realized was possible. For instance, I now knew about Fletcher's lucky socks, which he'd not washed since his senior year of college when he'd scored a one hundred percent on a physiology exam. And he knew that I keep all the stickers off of my produce, and that they decorate the inside of my plate cupboard door.

I also knew he'd been thinking about me night and day since parting ways, and that his brother accused him of being high while they were painting his new living room. And Fletcher knew I was sleeping with one of the throw pillows off my couch, because it still smelled like him.

Oh yeah, I had it bad. We both did.

I brushed flour off of my apron, and tried to smooth down my hair. I'd been making homemade fettuccine for the past two hours, and looked about as limp as the noodles I was cutting. "Oh, geez. I'm a mess. Send him in."

"Him?" Marisol's eyebrows rose. "Sorry to disappoint you, love. It's your mother."

My shoulders sagged. "Oh."

I didn't want to see my mother. I'd already seen too much of her and Pastor Irm. I wasn't sure what to say after the things I'd said outside her house that day. As gratifying as it should've been to discover my mom was a giant hypocrite, I didn't feel good about it at all. She'd still lied. She'd still judged me more harshly than anyone else I knew. And she'd still broken her promise to accept me—and my baby—time and time again.

"You sure you want to see her?" Marisol had never been my mother's biggest fan. "I can send her away."

I narrowed my eyes at her. "You looked like you would enjoy doing that entirely too much."

She shrugged. "Eh. It's been a boring afternoon. Some Patsy drama would pass the time. Who did you think it was, anyway? You looked entirely too excited for you to think it was your mother at the door."

Heat saturated my neck and face, and I wondered if my feelings for Fletcher were obvious. Marisol could usually sniff out one of my crushes like a bloodhound finds a steak.

It was just a matter of time before I was going to have to confess my big secret to her, because things with Candace had become increasingly strained. She'd told me, in no uncertain terms, that she wasn't going to keep a secret from Marisol, no matter how good the reason was. I'd promised that as soon as Fletcher and I went on our first official date, I would take Mar to lunch, sit her down, and explain that Fletcher and I were dating.

The baby kicked me in the back, and I grunted in pain. "Ugh. I was excited because I thought it was the stork."

"Ha, ha, ha." Marisol sauntered towards the front of the shop. "I'll send her back. Gird your loins."

I stood next to the stainless steel table I'd been rolling noodle dough on and smoothed down the front of my apron. As the door opened, I noticed I'd left out my knife set and quickly tossed it into a nearby sink of water. The last thing I needed were any weapons lying around. My mom wasn't a violent woman, but until a month ago, I'd not considered her a sexual woman, either.

"Alexandria."

I looked up to find my mother standing across the table from me. She was wearing a baby blue sweatshirt with dancing kittens across the bosom, and a pair of stonewashed jeans that were an inch or two too short. Her graying blonde hair had been ratted and teased into a perfectly round helmet, and a chain of pink beads held her glasses on her head. Her eyes were rimmed in red, and she was wringing her hands as she waited for me to respond.

I took a deep breath. "Hi, Mom."

She looked down at my stomach. It'd gotten so big that my apron strings barely tied behind my back. "You look so cute," she said with a tiny smile. "You're glowing."

Snorting, I brushed a strand of hair back from my forehead and secured it with a barrette. "That's usually code for *you look sweaty and gross,* isn't it?"

"Oh, don't be oversensitive, you—" My mother cut herself off, took a breath, then said, "What I mean to say is, you look beautiful, dear." Her eyes flooded, and she fanned her face. "I can't believe my baby's having a baby."

My heart swelled. "You're going to have two grandbabies, as soon as Corbin and Andrea get a placement."

She nodded. "I'm a lucky woman."

I fidgeted with a spoon. "What brings you by today, Ma?"

Her eyes fell to the floor. "I can't believe I've missed so much."

"What do you mean?"

"I should have been with you at your appointments," my mom said with a sigh. "I should've been picking out booties and layettes with you I should have helped plan your baby shower. I should have been the one to buy your baby a crib, or a stroller, or one of those new-fangled front pack thingies."

I swallowed. While I honestly wasn't sure what a layette was, I understood where she was going. In my mother's quest to make me an honest woman, she'd missed the bulk of my pregnancy. Now I was on the verge of delivery, and I'd experienced almost every pregnancy milestone sans my mother. It sucked. Really sucked.

"I know." My voice was quiet. "I've really missed you."

"I missed you, too." She pushed up her glasses.

"You can come to my shower," I offered. "Candace is throwing me one next week. I want you to be there."

"You do?" Her eyes filled with hope. "Oh, Lex, I was so wrong. I judged you so harshly. I epitomized the kind of person I never thought I'd be."

Nodding, I swallowed back the ball of emotions tickling the back of my throat. My instinct was to go around the table, wrap my arms around my mother, and tell her that it isn't her fault, and that I'm sorry. Ever since my dad died, my brothers and I had treated her with kid gloves, but I wouldn't do it today. She'd hurt me so badly.

"You were really rough on me, Ma." I told her, my voice cracking.

My mother squared her padded shoulders at me. "I will never do that to you again. Not ever. I accept you, and your baby, just as you are right now."

Shaking my head, I tossed the spoon into the sink. "I don't know. It's hard to believe you. You've promised me that before."

"I may screw up from time to time," she said. "Because I'm not perfect. As you well know. But I promise you that I'll try my hardest, and that I'll always apologize when I do something stupid." She sighed. "You've been through so much over the last few years, with the divorce and starting your own business. And you've done it all without the help of a man, Alexandria. This whole time I'd been watching you, assuming you'd be happier and more successful if you had a husband to take care of you. When the truth was you were doing more with your life *without one*."

My mouth dropped open. She got it, she really did. "Thank you," I croaked.

I hoped this was real, and that my mother wasn't going to parade in some random guy from her church five minutes from now. I examined her face. She looked serious. Her brow was furrowed, and her lips were pulled into a line. She only made that face when the truth was being spoken, or when she was listening to Pastor Irm's sermons at church.

Ew. Pastor Irm. Not a great visual.

"I want you to know I'm proud of you." My mom's chin started to quiver. "I want you to know that I love you, and I know you're going to be an amazing mother. You're so determined and diligent, you won't even need help. The rest of us are going to have to beg you to let us come over to relieve you."

"I don't know about that." I chuckled nervously. "I'm a little scared to be alone. But not so scared that I don't think I can handle it. Just scared enough to feel anxious to tackle it."

"You were always that way." My mom shook her head and smiled. "If your teachers told you there was a test coming at the end of the week, you wanted to take it on Wednesday. You didn't want to wait. You weren't scared. Just determined. Sometimes when you were little, I thought that determination would be the death of me. But I can see it serves you well now."

"I still need you," I blurted. When my mom looked at me with a face full of hope, I shrugged. "A girl needs her mom, you know? I mean, I could do the single motherhood thing alone. I know I could, if I had to. But I don't want to do it without my mom around." My shoulders sagged now. "I just want you to accept me the way I am. Don't try to improve me. Just let me improve myself."

She nodded and wiped a tear off of her cheek. "It's a deal. I promise this time. I really do."

"I know." I reached out a hand and took my mother's across the table. It felt great to feel her soft fingers around mine. I could feel the promise of a new relationship in her grip, and I actually believed it. "And, I promise to accept you the way you are, too."

She nodded and wiped her eyes again. "Of course you do, dear."

"No, Mom, listen." I gave her hand a gentle shake. "Look at me."

She looked at me with a cringe. She knew where I was going next.

"You're, um, you know, *with* Pastor Irm." It wasn't a question. It was a statement. Stating the obvious, if you asked me. But that was my intent. Throwing the absolute truth out between us, and letting it lay on the tabletop like a big ugly mess we couldn't ignore.

Ten seconds passed. Finally, she nodded so subtly it was almost unperceivable.

My stomach turned, and the baby shifted. This epitomized uncomfortable. I felt like a parent giving their teenager the sex talk, instead of a grown woman discussing her mother's sex life.

"Ma, do you love him?" I already knew the answer to that question. My mother had been in love with Pastor Irm for years. We all knew it. Just because we pretended like it wasn't happening didn't make it untrue.

My mother released my hand and patted at her hair self-consciously. She opened her mouth and released a high-pitched giggle. "I do. Oh, Alexandria, I've been wanting to talk about it for so long!"

I covered my mouth and laughed. "I knew it. That was the worst kept secret I've ever heard. You love him, and he loves you. It's been clear for years."

She beamed. "I haven't felt like this since your dad and I were dating."

I came around the end of the table and looped my arm in hers. "I'm happy for you. I really am."

"You're not upset?" She asked. "I always thought that you and your brothers would be upset if you though I was replacing your father."

"It's not replacing Dad." I led her to a small table and chairs where Marisol and I sat during breaks. "If it makes you happy, I'm all for it. Corbin and Darren probably feel the same way. We only want you to be happy."

Her cheeks were pink as she grinned at me. "Do you really mean it?"

"I do, Ma. In fact, I have something to tell you. But it's a secret." I bit my lip, words dancing at the end of my tongue, threatening to fall off. I lowered my voice to a whisper "I think I may have found myself someone who makes me happy, too."

Chapter Twenty-four

The door to the examination room swung open, and the moment Fletcher stepped in, it felt like the room flooded with sunshine. His blonde hair was mussed, and his white coat was unbuttoned over a denim shirt and wrinkled khaki pants. He wore a grin so wide and unabashed I literally felt my insides squeeze.

Actually, I'd been feeling my insides squeeze all afternoon. Stupid Braxton-Hicks contractions. But the point was still clear: Seeing Fletcher two days earlier than planned was a wonderful treat. Ten bazillion times better than a chocolate mousse filled cupcake.

He shut the door and grinned at me. "Lexie."

I gripped the edge of the examination table until my knuckles went white. What a treat. I'd expected to get Dr. Javornik-the-wonder-hippie to check on my baby. Fletcher and I were going on our first official date in exactly forty-seven hours, right after my baby shower at Candace's house, and after two weeks apart, I was more than ready to see him.

"Hi," I whispered, suddenly shy. "I thought you weren't coming back from Arizona until Saturday morning."

Fletcher stepped closer, resting his clipboard on a nearby stool. His warm hands touched my knees softly, sending an exciting tickle dancing up my legs. "I called to check on things in the office, and my receptionist mentioned you had an appointment today. I flew in early so I could catch it."

My head felt light. The squeeze in my stomach flexed, then released. He'd flown all the way home to see *me*? "I'm glad."

He smiled and his eyes crinkled. "Me, too. Are you sure it doesn't make you uncomfortable?"

"Why would it?" I relished the way he looked at me. It was like being under a heat lamp.

"Because we're together." He moved closer so he stood between my knees. His hands wound themselves around my middle, settling on the small of my back. "I'm going to let Dr. Javornik do your examination, but I'll be nearby. I can step out and handle some dictation while you're speaking with her."

"You don't have to do that," I said quickly. "I mean, you can stay with me, you know, for moral support. You won't even have to put on gloves to do that."

He brushed his knuckles down my arm. "You sure you won't mind? It won't bother me to wait outside."

"No. Stay. You can watch Dr. Javornik in action."

"All right. Maybe she'll teach me a thing or two."

"Hey." I pursed my lips, trying not to grin like a kid caught with candy. "You said we're together. That's very presumptuous, doctor."

"Is it?" His nose brushed mine. "I missed you."

"I missed you, too," I whispered. "I was afraid you'd changed your mind."

"About what?"

"About me." I ran my hand through his hair.

He turned his face into my palm and drew in a deep breath. "Don't think that's possible."

"So the date is still on?" I closed my eyes as Fletcher pressed light kisses along my cheekbone.

"Buffet dinner, then a movie, then dessert overlooking the river," he said.

I giggled. "Perfect."

"You smell so good." He cupped my face. "Have you always smelled this good?"

My chest swelled. "I'm wearing the same perfume I always wear."

"That's it." He snapped his fingers. "When I met you at that first appointment, you smelled like this. It hung in the office for a long time after you'd left, and it drove me bonkers."

Oh good Lord, how I loved this man. "How's Martha?"

He hesitated. "I told her."

My eyes widened. "You told her about us?"

"Yeah." His eyes shone. "I asked her what she thought about us dating, and she danced around the room."

"I might have danced around the room a little, too," I confessed. A pain rolled through my lower belly like a wave, spreading to my back. I sucked in a sharp breath. "Especially after we kissed."

His grin widened. "I can neither confirm nor deny that dancing took place when I got home."

The pain in my belly was going away now, but the twinge in my heart remained. "I'm going to tell Marisol now. I was waiting until after our first date."

When I paused, Fletcher finished for me. "To see if we still wanted each other?"

I nodded.

"Well, I'm here, aren't I?" He leaned in and brushed his mouth against my ear. It sent a flurry of shivers sliding down my spine. "How about you? You still in?"

My eyes rolled back. Just a little. "Abso-freaking-lutely."

"Then it's time to tell her." He played with a strand of my hair. "I should be with you when you do it."

"No." I swallowed. It was getting really difficult to concentrate with Fletcher's mouth so close to mine. "This is my responsibility. I can do it."

"You just call me, and I'll be there." His breath tickled my ear. "There's no reason you have to do this—or anything—alone again."

My mouth found his, and a whirl of hysterical joy rushed through me, setting every hair on my body on end.

We kissed and kissed, and it was glorious. I'd been afraid that the spark between us would've shrunk during our time apart, but I was wrong. It was alive and well. And I *couldn't wait* until our date.

After about five minutes of very teenager-ish making out, the door swung open, and Dr. Javornik appeared. "Hello, Lexie, how are... oh!"

Fletcher and I pulled apart, our faces red and swollen. "Sorry." Fletcher stepped back and smoothed a hand down the front of his coat. "Sorry, Bev. I guess the secret's out then. Lexie and I are dating."

Dr. Javornik's eyes widened. "Clearly. And how long has this been going on?" Her eyes flicked down to my belly.

"Not long," I said quickly.

Fletcher took my hand and laced his fingers with mine. "Long enough. Lexie would like me to keep her company during the examination. Is that all right with you?"

"Of course." Dr. Javornik nodded, a smile teasing the sides of her mouth. "You know the nurses are going to have a heyday with this, don't you?"

Fletcher pressed his lips together. "I expect they will, won't they?"

Patting my knee, Dr. Javornik smiled kindly. "You'll live. Now, how about we get down to business. How are you feeling, Lexie?"

The baby wiggled deep within me, setting off another cramp that rushed to my spine, then receded. "Doing all right, I suppose. I've been cramping a lot lately."

The doctor flipped open my chart, while Fletcher rubbed circles on my back. "Cramping is normal in the last weeks of pregnancy, but we'll do a quick internal check to make sure you're not dilating," she announced. "Your non-stress test last week looked good."

I nodded. I'd been having those tests on a weekly basis for four weeks now. They were a pain in the butt, but I'd been happy to get the weekly ultrasounds. I'd even decided to leave the baby's sex a mystery, much to Candace and my mother's frustration. But so much about my pregnancy had been unorthodox. It felt good to leave this one last detail alone. One last surprise for me to keep, when so much of my life was right out there in the open for all to see.

"Overall, I'm feeling okay." I leaned back on the table, as Dr. Javornik started to feel my belly. "I mean, I'm a bit worn out, I guess. But I assume that's what's to be expected when you're eight and a half months pregnant and working full time."

"That's true." She smiled.

"How's the swelling in your feet?" Fletcher interrupted. "Are you putting them up at night? Drinking the water like I told you?"

"Yes, doctor. I'm putting my feet up." I rolled my eyes at him. "Isn't Dr. Javornik doing this examination?"

"Right." He sat on the stool next to my head. "Old habits, and all that."

"Anyway, the swelling is—" I gasped as another cramp ripped through my abdomen, shooting into my back, and down into my bum.

"You all right?" Fletcher touched my cheek.

"Hmmm." Dr. Javornik's hand's covered my stomach. "That's a strong contraction you're having. Your uterus is rock hard."

I tried to reply, but all that came out was a mangled whimper. These cramps were really starting to tick me off.

Fletcher stilled next to me. "Want me to get a monitor?" he asked in a low voice. Dr. Javornik didn't answer. She just watched me as I grimaced my way through the cramp.

Finally, I caught my breath. "Okay, when you warned me about these practice contractions, you never said they'd make me want to die."

"Sometimes they can be pretty rough," Dr. Javornik agreed. "There can also be pain when you bend or twist, because of all of the ligaments being stretched in your midriff. But I think you're having some contractions, young lady."

"How long have you had them?" Fletcher asked me.

I sucked in a breath of air as the pain wore off. "I don't know. A couple days."

A line appeared between his eyebrows. "How far apart are they?"

My eyes searched Fletcher's face for some sort of reassurance, but all I could see was complete seriousness. He was in doctor mode now. My new boyfriend was nowhere to be found. "I don't know. I haven't been paying attention. A minute or two, I guess."

"Any back pain?" Dr. Javornik's hands moved around my middle.

I thought for a moment. "Well, yeah, I guess. It usually starts in the front, down low, then sort of radiates upward before shooting to my back."

Fletcher stood up. "What do you think, Bev? Should I get the—"

She frowned. "Yes, please."

I watched her expression as my pain receded. Panic was starting to creep up on me like a shadow. "Is something wrong?"

Dr. Javornik patted my leg reassuringly. "I'm sure everything's fine. We're just going to take a quick peek to make sure this isn't preterm labor."

"Wait," I blurted. "I thought this was normal. Fletcher, what's going on?"

"I'm sure it is." He bent down and pressed a dry kiss to my forehead. "Dr. Javornik just wants to be sure." Fletcher darted out of the door before I could ask him anything else.

"Is the pain in the perineum area at all?" Dr. Javornik asked.

"My what?" When she glanced downward, I laughed. "Oh, *there*. Um, yeah. That's where the worst of it is."

"Uh huh." Her lips pressed together, just as Fletcher charged back into the room pushing a portable sonogram machine. "Have you had any discharge?"

I felt my face heat. There was nothing I wanted to discuss less in front of my new boyfriend that I'd not even gone on my first date with yet than *discharge*.

"I, um, well—" Again my words stopped, and I froze in place while my abdomen morphed into cement again, and gripping pain flashed through my body. I opened my mouth to keep talking, but no words came out. Just a high-pitched squeal of air. Part of me felt embarrassed, but the pain was too strong to care. I was locked into place.

"Lex?" Fletcher took my hand. "Squeeze my fingers. It's okay."

I obeyed, closing my eyes. These weren't Braxton Hicks contractions anymore, that much was clear. And if they were, then real labor was going to freaking *kill* me. The pain in my back made me want to go lay down in traffic. After a minute, the pain started to subside, and I released a long, ragged breath. When I opened my eyes, Dr. Javornik was watching me closely, with her watch poised under her chin.

"Man," I said breathlessly. "That one hurt like a mother fu—"

"That wasn't even two minutes between contractions," Javornik warned us sternly.

"Fletcher, I'm starting to freak out."

"Everything's fine," he told me. "I'm right here."

Dr. Javornik opened the door and called out into the hallway. "Hey, Joni?"

A heavy set brunette came into the room. "Yes, doctor? Oh, hi, Dr. Haybee. I didn't know you were—" Her words stopped as soon as she saw Fletcher's hands covering mine. "*Oh*. I see. Hi, Miss Baump. How are you today?"

I tilted my head upward. It was the nurse who'd helped Dr. Javornik conduct the stress test the week before. Waving awkwardly, I called, "Um, I don't know. Good, I think."

Dr. Javornik ignored out small talk. "She's having some contractions."

"They're a minute twenty apart, and lasting for forty-five seconds, give or take," Fletcher added, staring down at his watch.

"He's just being protective, I'm okay." I suddenly felt embarrassed. I didn't want to be *that* patient. The one who made a big deal over nothing. Candace made Brian take her to the hospital four times before Ellie's labor really started. What if I just had something simple, like gas? Marisol and I had made broccoli quiche the other day. What if I just needed to cut a giant fart? Oh holy crap, what if I did it while Fletcher was in the room?

"Protective?" Joni's eyes flicked to Fletcher. He shook his head.

Dr. Javornik turned on the sonogram, and lifted up my shirt. "Let's just take a little peek here."

"I think I'm just having some tummy trouble." My voice was starting to get high pitched as panic set in. I couldn't be in labor. I wasn't ready. "I had some quiche yesterday, that—"

Joni slipped a blood pressure cuff onto my arm. "I'm going to need you to lay back, Miss Baump. All right?"

Fletcher's grip on my fingers tightened when Dr. Javornik squirted the blue goo on my skin. "Have you felt the baby move recently, Lex?"

"I…uh…yes." My eyes went from Fletcher's frowning face to Joni's. "Just a few minutes ago."

"BP is 167 over 120," Joni called.

"I changed my mind." I used my elbows to push myself back up. The thin paper underneath me crinkled. "I don't think it's a big deal. I—"

What happened next *was* definitely a big deal. There was another cramp, this one worse than all the others, and it shot straight into my spine like a bullet. I yelped, jumping off of the table an inch or two, then felt a tearing sensation deep within my core. The pain was bigger, so much bigger, than anything I'd felt before.

Warmth soaked my pants. Black splotches appeared in my line of sight. A shrill ring filled my ears. *Mother of God, I'm going to die right here on this table!*

"Where's that ultrasound, Bev?" Fletcher's voice was loud, and it cut through the ringing in my ears like a beacon, bringing me back to reality.

I opened my eyes, flinching when the light hit my retinas. Sweat had piqued on my forehead and underneath my arms. I'd fallen back into a laying position on the paper, shredding it with the waist of my jeans in the process.

"What the hell is going on?" I growled.

Dr. Javornik's mouth pulled into a thin line when she brushed her hand against my jeans. Her knuckles were covered in bright red. "She's hemorrhaging."

My head popped off of the table. "I'm what?"

Fletcher moved away from my side, to peer down past my belly. His eyebrows knit together, and he pulled the metal stirrups out from underneath the table with a sharp clack. "Possible abruption," he muttered, pulling the door open all the way. "Nancy, we need ambulance transport, please. Stat."

"Stat?" My head swam. I'd watched enough medical dramas on TV to know that stat was never good. "Fletcher?"

"You said you felt the baby move a few minutes ago?" Dr. Javornik felt my stomach, gauging the position of my baby.

Nodding, tears filled my eyes. "Yes. What…what's wrong?"

"It's going to be fine." Fletcher's hand touched my face, but his eyes stayed locked on my nether region. "You're having some bleeding."

"*Some* bleeding?" My voice cracked. I didn't know much, but I knew enough to know that bleeding while thirty-six weeks pregnant wasn't good. I tried to push myself up. "Is my baby okay?"

Someone spoke from outside the examination room. "Ambulance is coming, doctor."

"An ambulance?" I croaked. "Those are really expensive. I can drive."

Joni appeared on my other side. She used her hands to gently push me back on the table, then guided my feet to the stirrups. When I moved, I felt a gush. The paper beneath me was soaked. "It's all right, Miss—"

Gasping, I gripped the edge of the table when another contraction barged through my body like a Mack truck with no brakes. I curled around myself, groaning.

"Her name is *Lexie*." Fletcher said tensely, his voice cutting through the haze around me. I focused on his face and forced myself to keep my eyes open.

Joni touched Fletcher's arm. "Are you okay, Dr. Haybee?"

"Yes," he snapped. I'd never seen this side of Fletcher before. His face was pale, and his movements were swift and concise. A far cry from the ultra-casual, gentle man I'd been kissing just moments before. "We need underpads. Quickly."

"Got 'em," Joni announced, pulling them from a drawer.

"Thank you." Dr. Javornik tugged latex gloves on with a snap. "And Joni?"

She stopped moving. "Yes?"

"We'll need to do an internal exam. She needs to be undressed from the waist down." Dr. Javornik moved the wand on my stomach. "Someone needs to alert the hospital that we're coming in."

"Right." Joni nodded, returning to my side. "Lexie, we're going to get these jeans off of you, okay?"

I opened my mouth to protest, but the pain halted every word in the back of my throat.

"Just breathe. In and out, in and..." Fletcher's directions faded away as Joni began peeling my clothes off of my bottom half. He craned his neck to look at the screen on the sonogram machine over Dr. Javornik's shoulder. "There's a heartbeat, Lex."

I whimpered, sweat rolling down my forehead into my eye.

Dr. Javornik's lips pursed as she scowled at the fuzzy orangish screen. Muttering under her breath, she moved it from one side of my belly to the other, then down close to my pubic bone. Lower, lower, and lower it went until her movements stopped. "There it is."

Fletcher squinted as he watched the screen. His face was pale. "Shit," he whispered.

I started to ask what he was talking about, but another contraction tore through my groin like a chainsaw, ripping me in half. I cried out, and Joni shut the exam room door. Everything in the room started to blur and spin, and I reached out for Fletcher, unable to make words while my uterus hardened into marble.

Dr. Javornik dropped the wand, and did an internal examination. The pain increased so suddenly that I saw spots of light, and arched off of the table. Everywhere I looked there were blue absorbent pads soaked and splattered with blood. Squeezing my eyes shut, I tried desperately to block out the images.

"Call… Candace…" I managed to hiss.

Someone came to my side and took my hand. I didn't know who. It didn't matter. I couldn't think straight anymore. It felt like I was drowning in the pain, too locked into place to do anything but sink.

"Abruption," Dr. Javornik's voice cut through the mayhem. "Joni, call Valley General, tell them to prep an OR."

Fletcher cupped my face. It was all I could do to open my eyes and look him in the eye. "The baby's still okay for now. But the placenta detached from the uterine wall, and you're bleeding heavily."

I nodded, gritting my teeth. Fletcher's head started to waver, as my eyes unfocused again. Finally, some words came to the surface. "Going to…get….sick."

Joni showed up on my other side, placing a long plastic bag under my mouth. "Right here, dear."

Turning to my side, I unloaded the contents of my stomach, and felt another gush between my legs. Suddenly I was chilled to the bone and shaking, despite the sweat dampening all of my skin. I wiped at my mouth and closed my eyes again to block out the gripping dizziness that took over my body.

To say I was scared would've been an understatement. I was terrified. But the pain had me so gridlocked I couldn't articulate any of that fear. I just had to lay there and wait for whatever hell I was in to be over...

"Six centimeters," Dr. Javornik announced.

"Transport is here." I don't know who said it, but the voice echoed in my head.

Fletcher appeared again. "Joni will call Candace."

"Thank you..." I was nauseated again, but too weak to roll over. Another gush of warmth. "Please get the... baby out safely... please don't... let the baby..."

My eyes got too heavy to hold open anymore. Blackness filled my peripheral vision. Everyone's voices sounded like they were at the end of a telephone connection a thousand miles away. The room was cold. My arms jerked as I shivered. I wanted to go home. I wanted my mom. I wanted to sleep.

The last voice I heard was Fletcher's. "I'll ride with her."

And then the blackness swallowed me.

Chapter Twenty-five

Sleep. Blissful sleep.

"…gonna need an immediate cesarean."

Sleep…

"Two pints of O-positive."

More sleep…

"…fetus will need corticosteroids."

Am I dreaming all of this?

"Lex, everything's going to be fine. I'll be with you the whole time."

I want to talk back to Fletcher. But I'm just so tired.

"All right. Count backwards from ten…"

Ten, nine… what comes after nine?

I don't remember anything about the birth. Just blips of sound in between hazy, slovenly dreams filled with muted voices and beeping machines. I was asleep, but still just aware enough of the noise in the ambulance and operating room to turn it all into an acid-trip type dream.

Fletcher rode in the ambulance with me, and I thought I'd heard the sound of my mother calling my name as they pushed my gurney through the double doors leading to the operating room.

I'd been prepped for surgery upon arrival. No time to stop. No time to think. No time to process what was going on around me. Just bam, bam, bam. And then nothing.

***

"Lexie?" I heard Fletcher's voice. He sounded far away. "Lex, honey, can you open your eyes?"

I didn't want to answer. I wanted to sleep. I hadn't slept this good in so long. How long had it been?

"Lex?"

I tried to open my eyes, but the lids were apparently made of lead. Once. Twice. Third time was a charm.

The light flooded my pupils and I flinched as Fletchers' face came into focus. I could hear the dull sound of phones ringing out in the hall, and a soft beeping sound right next to my head. Looking around, my eyes rolled shut again, and I had to force them to open back up. The room I was in was decorated in pale pinks, with vertical blinds that partially blocked a view of the night skyline.

"What?" My mouth felt like it'd been lined with carpeting. I tried to sit up, but my arms and legs felt like sandbags. Groggy did not begin to cover how I was feeling. It felt like I'd been hit and dragged by a truck, and then thrown into a lake. Where I promptly sank to the bottom.

"What time is it?" I croaked.

Fletcher sat down on a stool next to me, and held a straw close to my mouth. "It's six-thirty. Stay down. You just had major surgery. It's too early to get up yet."

Six-thirty! I'd missed the whole day. When I sucked on the straw and cool water filled my mouth, I nearly groaned in appreciation. I don't think water had ever tasted so good.

"Better?" he asked.

I nodded, then looked around the room. There was an IV pole with several bags, including blood, hanging from it.

"S-surgery?" I noticed there was an oxygen tube hanging down from my nose, and flinched. "What the—"

"Shhh, relax." Fletcher dragged his hand down the length of his face. He looked exhausted, and was wearing light blue scrubs. "You had a placental abruption. The placenta detached from the uterine wall, so Dr. Javornik did a C-section. I sat in on the procedure. You lost a considerable amount of blood, so a transfusion was necessary. She was able to save your uterus, though."

"A transfusion?" I tried to reach for Fletcher, my hands heavy as they dragged across the sheet. As my fingers raked across my middle, realization settled in over me like a dark, dense cloud, pressing me into the bed like a vice grip. "W-where's my baby?"

"Looks like someone woke up!" A cheerful nurse in baby pink scrubs strode into the room with a thermometer in hand. She patted Fletcher's shoulder. "You've been here all afternoon, doctor. Don't you want to take a break?"

Fletcher shook his head. "No, ma'am. I'm fine."

"Fletcher," I said, my voice louder now. "*Where's my baby?*"

"In the NICU." His smile was gentle, and the crinkles around his eyes returned. "Lexie, you have a son."

"A son?" Something washed over me. It wasn't quite cold, but it left my skin peppered with goose bumps.

He nodded. "His lungs were slightly underdeveloped, so the neonatologist expects him to stay for a few days, to a week at most. But he's as strong as an ox, and is the loudest kiddo in there."

Suddenly—despite the fact that I was covered in tubes and wires, and my body felt buried in sand—the room seemed brighter. *I had a son.* And he was going to be okay. My face crumpled, and when I went to cover my face, I bumped my oxygen tubes. "Oh my gosh, oh my gosh."

"Here, let's get rid of that." He unwound the tubing from around my ears, and set it on the table next to the bed.

"I'm sorry. I'm just… I just…" My voice sounded strangled. Tears flowed from my eyes, snot dripped from my nose, and I had no control over it. It was too much to handle, too much to process.

I was a *mother.*

I choked on another sob. "S-sorry."

Fletcher leaned in and wrapped his arms around me. Pressing a kiss into my matted hair, he whispered, "Don't be sorry, Lex. You did such a good job. He's perfect." When he pulled away, I realized there were tears in his eyes, too. "Five pounds, eight ounces. Twenty-one and a half inches. And a head of red hair, just like his mom."

"His APGAR scores were good," the nurse added, sticking a thermometer into my ear. When it beeped a few seconds later, she surveyed the results, then looked at Fletcher. "Temp is 101."

"We just gave her acetaminophen. It should come down within a half hour or so, so check her again in thirty minutes." Fletcher glanced at my IVs. "And make sure to stay on top of her hydration."

The nurse jotted Fletcher's instructions down on a small notebook. "Got it. Anything else? How's her bleeding?"

Fletcher's thumb stroked across my knuckles. "I checked it just before she woke up, and it looks normal. We'll need to try to get her sitting up in the next few hours. Possibly get her into a wheelchair so that she can go see her son."

"He can't come to my room?" I slurred. I reached for the straw, and took another drink of water to alleviate my cotton mouth. "I wanted to room in, and breastfeed, and—"

"All in good time. He's in the NICU for now, and it's for the best. They're taking good care of him." Fletcher brought my hand to his face to kiss it. Through the corner of my eyes I noticed that the nurse was watching us with pointed interest. "You've had a hard day. Let's get you up and moving, and I'll take you to check out your son's awesome hair."

"So he's a ginger?" I laughed groggily. "That figures."

"He's as gorgeous as you are." He wiped away my tears with the pads of his thumbs, and pulled his phone out of his pocket. "I took pictures for you."

I wept as he scrolled through the photos. There, in all of his brand-spanking-new glory, was my son. His skin, though streaked with blood and cheesy vernix, was porcelain white. In the few shots where his eyes were open, they were the same dark blue I recognized from my own baby pictures. And sure enough, there were wet, reddish curls standing up off of his head.

My heart swelled so much, I thought my chest would crack open. My son looked nothing like Nate. He was a Baump, through and through, with a nose like Corbin's, lips like Darren's, and round, dimpled cheeks like my mother's. My joy was inexplicable.

After we'd been enjoying pictures for an hour, I was moved to the post-delivery floor, and I heard Candace's voice ring out from the doorway. "Has someone woken up?"

Fletcher, who'd remained by my side, stood up and grinned. "Yup. She just saw pictures."

"Hi." I waved lamely. "Come on in."

Candace gestured down the hall. "Come on, guys! She's up!"

My family lumbered into the room like a herd of elephants. Corbin and Andrea were both carrying enough stuffed animals and balloons to welcome every baby on the entire floor. Candace and Brian closely followed, their eyes wandering to my hand, still laced together with Fletcher's. Next came Darren and Pandi, who was once again dressed for a nightclub, in snakeskin short shorts and a tube top. Maybe it was the morphine, maybe I had the buzz of new motherhood, but I didn't even care that she looked like a streetwalker.

Last to enter the room was my mother. She came in with Pastor Irm, and for the first time in, like, *ever* they were hand in hand. As soon as our eyes met, she started to cry, and I reached for her.

"Alexandria," she sobbed, bending down to envelope me in an embrace. I drew in her scent of Jergen's lotion and cookies. "I'm so glad you're okay."

"Dr. Javornik did an excellent job today," Fletcher announced.

"I hear you never left her side," Candace told Fletcher, coming around the bed to hug him. "Guess you must care about my cousin an awful lot."

Fletcher's cheeks reddened. "Looks like my secret's out."

Candace wiped a tear from the corner of her eye. "It's about time."

Brian punched Fletcher in the shoulder. "You could have told me."

My mother sat on the edge of the hospital bed. "*This* is your special someone?"

Darren narrowed his eyes at Fletcher. "Dude. Are you a doctor?"

"Yes, sir." Fletcher nodded. "Obstetrics and gynecology."

"Your gynecologist is your baby daddy?" Darren cracked up. "Damn, Lexie, you know how to score free health care, huh?"

Corbin whacked him on the back of his head. "Shut up."

"Don't mind us, Dr. Haybee." Andrea explained. "We're a motley crew, but we mean well."

"Thank you." His hand found my shoulder and squeezed. "But call me Fletcher."

"Thank you, Fletcher." My mother's voice shook. "For saving my daughter. And my grandson."

Fletcher ducked his head humbly. "It's my pleasure, Mrs. Baump."

"Oh, call me Patsy." My mother fiddled with the lace collar on her kitten sweater. "And this is, um, my special friend." She gestured for the pastor to join her by my bed. He obeyed, and grinned when she slid her arm under his. "Pastor Irmingham Hollbrook."

The whole room went silent. Darren and Corbin's eyes were so wide I would have laughed, had I not been in such shock myself—and still a little stoned. Andrea and Candace both slapped their hands over their mouths to suppress their giggles.

Fletcher shook Pastor Irm's hand. "Good to meet you, sir."

"Thank you, son." Pastor Irm looked down at me. "Congratulations, Lexie."

I bit my lip. "I didn't call Marisol. We had an event this evening. Oh, crap."

Candace rubbed my leg. "I called her, and she called in some help from your food rep. She's going to come see you as soon as she's done. I think she was little relieved she didn't have to be your labor partner."

I laughed. "Guess it was her lucky day."

"You'll, you know, talk to her when she gets here, right?" Candace raised an eyebrow at me.

"Yes. Of course." I nodded, pressing my lips together tightly. Mine and Fletcher's feelings were public now, no use in keeping it a secret from Marisol anymore.

"So, like, if you and the doctor are together, then, like, are you two getting married?" Pandi asked, shuffling on her platform heels.

I pulled out of my mom's embrace. "We haven't even had our first date yet. Give us some time."

"Oh, I think this constitutes a first date," Brian pointed out. When everyone's attention turned to him, he offered us a shrug. "I'm just sayin'."

Andrea laughed. "He's got a point. I think sitting by someone's side while they're cut open constitutes a date."

Corbin put an arm around his wife. "I agree. That may have taken care of dates one, two, *and* three."

Fletcher scratched his hand across the back of his neck. "Let's just focus on getting Lexie healthy again. Then we'll decide what constitutes a first date."

My mother nodded happily. "That's a fine plan. Now, tell me about my grandson."

I looked around the room. "Haven't any of you seen him yet?"

Everyone shook their head, and Fletcher offered me a small smile. "I thought you should meet your son first."

Tears filled my eyes yet again. Man, I thought pregnancy hormones were rough; they had nothing on these post-partum hormones. I couldn't believe this man cared about me. *Me.* Geeky, gawky, mouthy me, with the crazy red hair and a flat chest.

I glanced downward. *Whoa.* Not so flat-chested right now.

Fletcher pulled his iPhone back out. "Do you mind if I show them now, Lex?"

Shaking my head, I squeezed my mother's hand. "Please do."

Mom looked at the screen and squealed. "He's so beautiful."

The room filled with the sound of oohing and aahing. Pastor Irm picked up the box of tissues and started passing them around, as everyone—including both of my brothers—were sniffling.

"Corb, he has your nose!" Andrea squealed.

My mother wiped her nose. "He's the loveliest thing I've ever seen."

"Omigosh, Lex." Candace clapped her hands. "What's his name? What's his name?"

I took a breath. I'd had my son's name picked out since the day I found out I was pregnant. "Ian," I announced in a wavering voice. "His name is Ian Alexander Baump. His middle name is after Dad." I looked at my mom, who dissolved into tears and rested her head on Pastor Irm's shoulder. "And Ian, because it means *a gift from God*."

Well, that did it. Everyone was blubbering now. There was something about hospitals, new babies, and emergency C-sections that really brought out the emotion in people. When Brian started scrolling through the pictures again, everyone crowded around for a second look, and Fletcher sat back down at my side.

"Lexie." He sighed happily, taking my hand in his. "Congratulations, my dear Lexie."

"Thank you so, so much," I whispered.

"I need to tell you something." He leaned close. "Something important."

"What?" My pulse spiked. I guess I was kind of edgy. Too much excitement for one day. "What's wrong?"

"No, no. It's good." He chuckled. "I think."

I took a deep breath. "Okay."

"I think…" Fletcher leaned forward and pressed his lips to mine. When he pulled away, he swallowed hard. "I think I love you."

I closed my eyes, utter and complete joy filling me right to the top. "I love you, too, Fletcher."

"What the *hell*?"

I looked up just in time to see Marisol come to a stop at the end of my bed. She put her hands on her hips, and tapped the toe of her four-inch knee high boot, glaring at us with utter and complete contempt. "Well this explains *everything*, doesn't it?"

Chapter Twenty-six

Fletcher stood up. "Listen, we didn't mean for you to find out this way."

"You've got to be kidding me." Marisol gaped at Fletcher.

Everyone in my family turned around at the same time.

"Mar, come and see these pictures of the baby," Candace offered with a nervous laugh.

"Not now." Marisol turned her gaze to me. "Lex, really?"

Fletcher frowned. "This isn't the time or the place, Marisol. Lexie's just had major surgery, and has yet to see her son."

She shook her head. "Listen. I'm really glad you and the baby are all right. I've been worried sick about you all day."

"He's beautiful," I said weakly. Fatigue was starting to settle in on me like a lead blanket. "You should see him. Brian, show her the phone."

Brian went to hand her the phone but she swatted it away. "I don't want to see," she snapped. "I want an explanation."

I tried to sit up. "Listen, I—"

Fletcher came around the bed to face Marisol. "This is all my fault."

I pushed the button on my bed to sit myself up more. My whole body felt heavy and disconnected. "No, Fletcher, it's not."

Marisol put her hand up to stop him. "That's bull. You told me there wasn't anybody else."

"Awkward," Darren sang. Corbin's hand connected with the back of his head again, and Darren's smile disappeared.

"At the time, there wasn't." Fletcher looked down at me, his eyes softening. "I've had feelings for Lexie for months. I should have been honest with you about them, but I didn't think I would ever act on them. And I didn't, at least, not until the very end of our relationship."

"Excuse me?" Marisol blinked a few times.

"We never meant to hurt you. Or keep anything from you." Fletcher's shoulders slumped. "I hate myself for putting yours and Lexie's friendship in jeopardy."

Corbin stepped forward. "Um, guys? This has been a long day for Lex. Can you take it out in the hall or something?"

"He's right." Fletcher reached for Marisol's arm. "Why don't we go get a cup of coffee, and I'll explain."

"Go to hell," she snarled, before turning her focus back to me. "Lex, why don't you try to explain? I'd prefer to hear this from my *friend*."

Candace stepped to Marisol's side. "Why don't we *all* head down to the cafeteria?"

Corbin held up the phone. "Fletcher took pictures. Would you like to see?"

Not one to pass up a dramatic moment, Marisol tossed her hair wildly. "Just like a proud father, huh?"

My mother gasped. "Lexie, is the doctor the father?"

"I, uh." I turned to look at my mom, and thought I saw tracers. I was suddenly more tired than I'd ever been.

"His name is Fletcher," Darren corrected. "Duh."

My head swiveled in his direction. Again with the tracers. How much pain medication had I had?

"Hush." My mom sniffed.

"They're getting married." Pandi put a hand full of extra long fingernails on her hip. "Right after their first date."

Marisol gawked at me. "You're getting *married*?"

"I'm not getting married." I gestured down at my deflated stomach. "Mom, I was pregnant before I met him."

"This is ridiculous." A muscle in Fletcher's jaw twitched. "Marisol, let's step outside."

She looked up at him with a glare. "Drop dead."

"You know what?" Candace put her arm around Marisol's shoulders. "Let's go to the cafeteria. This is getting out of hand."

"Out of hand?" Marisol folded her arms across her chest. She looked completely flummoxed. "I'm just trying to wrap my head around my friend and business partner kissing my ex-boyfriend. How many times did that happen while we were still together? Huh?"

The room went silent, and I heard the faint cry of a baby somewhere on the floor. Like a comedy movie, everyone's eyes grew round and wide, then fixed their gaze on random spots around the room.

Well, everyone except Darren and Pandi, who'd started to kiss, oblivious to the soap opera unfolding all around them.

The quiet in the room stretched from a few seconds to a full minute. Corbin, Andrea, Candace, and Brian all seemed to hold their breath, waiting for the you-know-what to hit the fan. Fletcher laced his hands on top of his head and released a long, guttural sigh.

"Marisol," he began.

I started to cry. Again. The air in the room felt thick and heavy, and it was all I could do to keep my thoughts straight. "I never meant for it to happen, I'm *so* sorry."

Her brown eyes widened. "Really?"

Marisol's voice cracked, and my heart jerked inside of my chest. I never wanted to hurt her. She'd been my friend for a decade, and despite all of her annoying qualities, Marisol would've taken a bullet for me. What I'd done to her, no matter how strong my feelings for Fletcher were, and no matter how much I loved him, was wrong.

"Mar." I tried to sit up, but the tubing on one of my IVs got caught, and I yelped in pain as it pulled on my flesh.

Fletcher darted to my side and unwound the tubing. "You okay?" The guilt on his face was clear, as the corners of his mouth were pointed downward, and his brows were bound tightly together.

"You fooled around with Fletcher while I was dating him?" Marisol asked me, her damp eyes reflecting the soft light in the room.

"I'm so sorry," I told her, choking on the words. "But how was I supposed to know you were that serious about him? It's not like you've ever been serious about anyone before."

"That doesn't make it okay," Marisol yelled, her voice wavering. "It's against the friend code. You know that."

"I do." Nodding, I rubbed my eyes. "And it's not like I thought what I felt for Fletcher was *okay,* but you fleet from one guy to the next so quickly. It never occurred to me that—"

"I knew from the beginning I had feelings for Lexie," Fletcher interrupted me. "I shouldn't have ever gotten involved with you."

"And for the record," I said. "Candace has been telling me for weeks to let you in on the secret!"

Candace slapped her own forehead and groaned.

Marisol's eyes darted to Candace. "You knew about this?" When she opened and closed her mouth, offering no explanation, Marisol groaned. "You're my oldest friends. Lexie, we're in business together. I trust you with everything. Or, I *did.* "

"It wasn't like that," Candace said, trying to reach for her hand.

Marisol hid her hand behind her back. "Don't touch me." She pulled her purse up on her shoulder and raised her chin at me. "I don't even know what to say. I don't think I can forgive you for this."

My mouth dropped. I'd expected anger, not exile. "Wait, I—"

She turned on her heel, and darted from the room. Candace offered me a knowing glance, then charged after her, calling her name.

I felt like a terrible friend, even in my still-partially-stoned-and-disoriented state. This wasn't how *I* treated friends. This wasn't how *I* conducted myself. I'd hurt someone who'd been by my side through college, my divorce and the building of my dream company, and I'd just obliterated her confidence. Crumpling, I pulled my blankets up around my face and gave into my emotion while everyone looked on. My family's gaze was heavy as I sobbed. All their love and support from just minutes ago had melted into awkwardness and judgment. Two emotions I was just plain tired of.

Fletcher bent down at the side of my bed. "Lexie, it's okay. She'll come around." When I didn't respond, I heard him sigh. "I'll talk to her. It's my fault, anyway."

I hiccupped. "She's my friend. My business partner. I knew better than to be the kind of woman who would try to steal a man. No man is worth breaking up a friendship."

Fletcher flinched. It was microscopic, so I barely saw it, but it was there. "If I had to do it all over again, I would have been with you seven months ago. I'm sorry."

I didn't say a word. Maybe it was the guilt. Maybe it was the sheer heaviness of what had happened that afternoon. Maybe it was hormones and a system still filled with morphine and whatever drug they give a person to numb their whole freaking body. But I turned my head away from Fletcher on the pillow instead.

"I need to think," I whispered.

"Lexie," my mother said softly.

"What?" Fletcher swallowed. "I… okay. So I'll come back in a few hours, and then we'll go see Ian."

"No." I closed my eyes, trying to block out my mother's disappointed gaze. My thoughts were to jumbled. Too discombobulated to add hers in the mix. "I need some time. Give me time."

"Time." It wasn't a question. Just a statement. I heard Fletcher stand back up. "All right. Time it is, then."

The room once again went silent. After a few seconds, I felt Fletcher's lips press to the top of my head. "You know where to find me when you're ready."

With the squeak of his shoes on the linoleum floor, he left the room. And when I opened my eyes, I discovered my family had filed out behind him. Only my mother remained, so I steeled myself for her opinion. Surely she had one.

Instead, she crossed the room and covered my tube-filled hand with her own. I curled into her soft body and wept, letting it all out. Not holding a thing back.

"I'm sorry." I cried into her sweatshirt.

But Fletcher couldn't hear that. He was gone.

Chapter Twenty-seven

Ian and I came home seven days later.

He was the perfect baby. Nursing like a champ, sleeping in between feedings, and doing this ridiculously cute smiling thing while he snoozed that made my uterus contract and my eyes immediately flow like a sprinkler system. Logically speaking, I knew he was just a typical baby. Eating, sleeping, pooping—you know, it was all in a day's work. But the new mommy part of my brain convinced me that Ian would one day lead nations, cure cancer, and possibly even fly. Yes, he was *that* amazing.

And I adored him. He was the most incredible thing I'd ever done. My greatest mistake with the most excellent result ever. Sure, I'd spent the last eight and a half months hurling, growing, aching, crying, and suffering through mood swings that would have killed a lesser woman. But every time I heard that glorious squeaky cry, and felt Ian nuzzle into my neck as I burped him, I knew with everything inside of me that he'd been preordained to be *mine*. Ian was the new man in my life.

And as for the other man in my life?

Well, I hadn't seen Fletcher since he walked out of my hospital room.

Even though I'd been distracted by learning how to care for Ian and recovering from surgery, Fletcher was never far from my thoughts. I thought about him as I fed Ian at night. I thought about him as I watched the cars rolling by on the highway through my window. I thought about him whenever someone in a white coat rushed past my door. My heart ached for Fletcher as much as it swelled with love for my son. He was the yin to my yang, the sparkly jumpsuit to my Elvis. I wasn't quite sure what to do with myself without him, and I'd only really *had* him for a couple of weeks.

There were times when I swore I heard his voice in the hallway, discussing other patients with the nurses, and I'd silently prayed for him to come into my room. But he never did. Dr. Javornik performed all of my postpartum care.

Fletcher had left the ball in my court. When I was ready, I knew where to find him. And so far I hadn't been ready.

Marisol never came back to the hospital. Candace had gone to see her at Eats & Treats several times, but Marisol was unwilling to bend. I'd kissed Fletcher while they were still together. I'd broken the friend code.

It weighed on me. And the weight was so heavy. Every visit from friends and family felt empty without Marisol gliding into the room, announcing that she would never have children and that the nurses needed makeovers.

Between Ian, Fletcher, and Marisol, I'd shed more tears this past week than I had in my entire existence.

"Okay, let's get you inside." Andrea shut off her car engine, and unbuckled her seatbelt, bringing me out of my thoughts. We were outside of my little brownstone building, and my mother was grinning like Cheshire cat at my apartment door.

I smiled. "I'm home. With my *son*."

"I know." She squealed happily and clapped her hands. My sister-in-law needed to be a mother. *Soon*. "Can you believe it?"

Shaking my head, I unbuckled my own belt. "No. It's very surreal. Last time I left my apartment, I was headed to an OB appointment."

The image of Fletcher coming into the examination room and kissing me scrolled through my mind.

I needed to call him. I wanted to call him. Really, I did. But the fact that I'd lost Marisol over him made me feel so dirty. I didn't deserve him. Not if it meant I couldn't have my friend, too.

Hot tears made my eyes swim, and I bit my lip. I didn't want to cry. Not again. I'd already cried twice on the way home from the hospital, and I only lived fifteen minutes away. "Hey," I said to Andrea in a falsely cheerful voice that sounded very cartoonish. "Will you carry Ian's car seat in?"

"Of course." And almost as though Andrea was sensing my impending tears, she rubbed my shoulder. "Let Corbin help you out of the car, okay?"

Nodding, I opened my door. My older brother was waiting dutifully on the curb. I wasn't allowed to lift anything heavier than Ian for the next few weeks, so my mother, brothers, and Andrea were taking turns staying with me. I couldn't tell who out of the four of them was the most excited. I was just grateful. Only time would tell how grateful I would be in a few days when my tiny apartment felt even punier with a constant array of helpers around.

"Come on, Sis." He held out his arm, and I grabbed it.

He hoisted me onto my feet, and I groaned when the incision area on my abdomen ached. "How many Cabbage Patch Kids has mom put in my apartment?"

Corbin snorted as we shuffled slowly up the sidewalk. "Just a couple. I think at least one of them is for Ian. The rest just came to keep her company."

I stifled a laugh and waved at my mom. It wasn't her fault she was crazy. And things with her had gotten much better since she came clean about her relationship with Pastor Irm. She'd stopped trying so hard to make us all perfect and finally accepted us for who we were. The same way we'd started accepting her.

"I swear to you, if I come out of my bedroom and see one of those dolls staring at me in the night, I'm going to lose my cool."

Corbin squeezed my arm. "Just text me, and I'll come over to relieve her for a day or two, okay?"

"Got it." I looked up at him. "Thanks, Corb."

"You're welcome." He paused, and we halted on the cracked walk. "I have a secret."

"What secret?" I asked as Andrea walked right past us with the baby. My mother was practically salivating, waiting for her chance to hold Ian. I'd always considered her to be a pretty intense mother, but I'd not yet seen what the first grandchild did to a person. "Spill it, Corbs. It's on the tip of your tongue, and you know it."

He grinned, and for an instant it reminded me of our father. "We got the call."

I blinked. "What call?"

"*The* call." He bounced in place a little.

I gasped. "They paired you with a child?"

Nodding, my brother's eyes filled. "She's almost two, and living in an orphanage in Gyeonggi."

"I don't know what you just said, but I'm so happy for you." I threw my arms around him. "Ouch. Okay, no hugging just yet."

"There will be plenty of hugging when she arrives." Corbin took my arm again and we resumed walking. "Don't tell Andrea I told you. She wants to wait until the whole family is all together, and Darren and Pandi are bringing dinner over tonight."

"Darren and Pandi?" I snickered. "Hope you like Funyuns and beer."

"Sounds good to me," he said with a contented sigh. "So, have you called him yet?"

"Called who?" I played dumb, even though I knew Corbin was way too smart to fall for it.

"Cut the crap." Corbin looked at me with a frown. "He loves you, you love him. He helped to save your life and Ian's. What's keeping you from picking up the phone and calling Fletcher?"

"Marisol." When I said her name, my voice cracked.

"I see." He drew a deep breath and we stopped walking again. "Listen, I don't know Marisol as well as you do, but isn't she sort of a serial dater? Hasn't she, er, been around the block a few times?"

"She has." I shook my head. "But that's not the point. She really liked Fletcher, even if he didn't feel the same way back. She was actually starting to consider a more traditional life."

"Like fidelity?" He rolled his eyes.

I nudged him, tugging at my incision. "Ow. No. Well, yes. But other things, too. Like family and marriage. Things that would center her. I mean, not that you have to be married to be centered. But Marisol can't live like a horny twenty-year-old her whole life."

"Why not? Darren does." Corbin laughed at his own joke. "Okay, sorry. I see your point. So when she was dating Fletcher, she fell in love."

I bit the inside of my cheek to keep from tearing up yet again. "Not quite that. But she was headed in that direction, I think. But Fletcher didn't feel the same way towards her, because he had this weird magnetic pull to me."

"You can't be held responsible for Fletcher not loving Marisol." Corbin sighed. "It's not your responsibility to put your life on hold for the sake of your friend."

"You're right," I conceded. "But I had no business flirting with him, and going out of my way to see him, and…"

"Making out with him?" Corbin offered. "Good grief, Lex, you didn't go to bed with the guy."

"Ugh. I know." I rubbed my eyes. "But had there been a bed there, and had we been alone, I don't know what would have happened. Or if either one of us would have pulled the brakes."

"Everyone loses control. You should have seen Andrea and I when we were dating. Mom's couch will never be the same." Corbin winced. "Do you have any idea how uncomfortable this is to discuss with my kid sister?"

"Shut up. We're adults." I laughed, and a tear—or two—spilled over. "I know everyone loses control, but losing control with a guy who's dating one of your best friends is completely wrong."

"Who also happens to be the man who loves you?"

"Yes, but—"

"No buts." Corbin faced me. "I've seen you get hurt, repeatedly, by your ex-husband, who also left you high and dry with no money in your bank account and no self-esteem. You picked yourself back up, got a business loan, started your own successful company, and slowly put your life back together. All without a man." His frown melted into a proud smile. "You don't spend your time searching for a new husband like so many women do. You don't jump from bed to bed. You aren't a serial dater. You spend most of your time alone, and you're completely okay with it. Andrea and I have been so impressed with you. You're a hero."

My mouth was open. I was in shock. My family wasn't exactly prone to spontaneous bouts of openness and affection. I started to reply, but Corbin kept talking.

"You're right," he said. "You and Fletcher were wrong to kiss while he was still with Marisol, and for that you have to ask your friend to forgive you. And then you have to accept her decision. If she decides never to forgive you, and to remain pissed off until the day she dies, that's something you have to live with." He put his hands on my shoulders. I could see my mom and Andrea staring at us through the front window with curious expressions "But know this. I wouldn't trade my years with Andrea for anything. *Anything*. My time with her, and our love for each another, is the best thing I've got in my life. She builds me up, brings me back to earth, encourages me, calls me on my BS, laughs at all of my jokes, keeps me warm on the darkest nights, and nobody—*nobody*—can love me the way that she does. She's my whole world. And my kid sister deserves the same."

Well, crap. I leaned forward, until my face was against my brother's chest. My tears soaked his jacket, and he wrapped his arms around me. "Oh, kiddo," he sighed resting his chin on my head. "Don't give up the person who loves you like that just because you feel guilty. In this one instance, you really can have your cake and eat it, too. Do you understand that?"

"Yes." I sniffled. I did understand what Corbin was trying to explain. I didn't know what I was going to do with it, but I'd heard him loud and clear. I deserved love as much as anybody else did. "Thank you, Corbs."

He released me. "You're welcome."

"Hey!" Our mother's voice rang out from the doorway. "Don't make her cry. She just had a baby. Why are you picking on your sister?"

Corbin put his hands up. "I'm not, Ma."

"Sure." She leveled him with a disapproving stare, then held her hands out to me. "Get your nipples in here, dear. The baby needs to be fed."

"Oh, good Lord." Corbin cast a pleading glance at his wife, who was bouncing Ian on her shoulder in the doorway. "Can you keep my mom at bay?"

"Not a chance," Andrea giggled.

I took my mother's hand and let her guide me into my apartment. Corbin was right. I *did* deserve the kind of love he and Andrea had. And I would consider what he'd said about having my cake and eating it, too.

* * *

The doorbell rang, jolting me out of sleep. I'd been sleeping on the couch, curled up with Ian, for a couple of hours since Andrea and Corbin left. "I'll get it," I mumbled, looking around in a daze.

"You stay there." My mother got out of the nearby rocking chair where she'd been grooming one of her dolls while QVC played quietly on the television. "That little one is going to wake up hungry soon, so enjoy the peace."

Pressing a kiss to Ian's head, I drew in a deep breath of his irresistible new-baby scent. "Okay, then."

When she opened the door, a burst of cool air swept into my apartment. I heard my mother say, "Oh, it's you. I'm so glad you came."

Pastor Irm, I thought to myself, smirking and pulling Ian even closer. I knew she wasn't going to be able to go much longer without seeing her Boy

Toy. I was actually starting to get used to seeing them together, and as weird as it was to admit, they were pretty cute.

"Thank you, Patsy. Candace told me that Lexie's home now."

My eyes popped open. I knew that voice. That deep, sultry tone. The slight Latin accent that made men fall all over themselves.

Marisol was here.

"Lexie, you have a guest." My mother came around the corner, wringing her hands. She mouthed the words, *It's Marisol.*

My still puffy stomach flip-flopped, and I struggled to sit up. Ian was snoring in my right arm, so I used my left arm to try to smooth down my hair, which was likely standing in all directions.

"I, um." I didn't want to do this now. I didn't want to see the person who hated me most in this world. I was too hormonal. Too emotional. "I don't know if this is a good time."

"Oh shut up and let me in. It's the least you can do." Marisol breezed past my mother and stood before me, a giant blue and white floral arrangement in her hands. It looked like it could have easily cost a few hundred dollars.

My mom's eyes darted between Marisol's face and mine a few times before announcing, "I'm going to go check on the minestrone."

And with that, she darted into the kitchen to fiddle with the soup she'd made. What a chicken.

A second passed. Then two. Then three. Marisol finally wiggled the arrangement. "Well, *here.*"

"Oh, sorry. Just set them on the coffee table." She put them down with a plunk, then folded her arms across her chest. The arrangement was almost the same width as the table. "Wow," I breathed. "That's gorgeous. Thank you."

"Oh, get over yourself. They're for Ian." She rolled her eyes and looked around, clearly uncomfortable.

I swallowed. I deserved her bitchiness. "Do you want to sit down?"

Marisol sat down stiffly. She watched Ian in my arms for a few moments. He was starting to wake up, and was squirming and unfolding himself from his bean-like position. "He really is something, isn't he?" she finally said. "He's so tiny."

I beamed down at my baby. "I'm pretty fond of him."

"Well, it's a good thing, huh?" She laughed and fiddled with her earring. "Because the return policy on those things is a real pain."

I avoided her eyes. It was difficult to apologize to someone when they were notorious for saying the absolute wrong thing.

Marisol shifted in her seat, then cleared her throat quietly. "So, Candace says we need to talk."

I brought my eyes back up to hers and sighed. "She's right. We do."

"Well then." Marisol blinked a few times. "Let's get this over with."

Don't let her annoy you, I reminded myself.

"Mar, I'm so sorry." My voice cracked.

There was no turning back now. Sure, I wanted Fletcher with all of my heart. But without Marisol's forgiveness, it would never feel right. I had to at least *try* to right my wrong.

She leveled me with an icy gaze. "Are you, now?"

"I should have told you from the beginning that I had feelings for Fletcher." I ran a shaky hand through my messed up hair. "I knew the first time I saw him that I liked him. I figured you were better for him, since you're so beautiful and glamorous, and—"

"You see, that's what ticks me off about you!" She threw up her hands and pushed herself out of the rocking chair. "You're constantly putting yourself down, and sticking me on some sort of pedestal. It's insane. And annoying. I mean, don't you see yourself?"

I looked down at my stained tee shirt and the plastic hospital bracelets around my wrist. There were still sticky patches on the tops of my hands from my IV tape. "Um, yeah. Why?"

"You're beautiful," she thundered. My mother peeked around the corner, then disappeared. "You've got natural beauty I could never have. You can wear a pair of jeans and a fifteen-year-old tee shirt and still look hot, and I have to have laser treatments just to have two eyebrows. You make being attractive look effortless. Don't you understand how hard it is to be friends with you? To work alongside you? *Of course* Fletcher wants you and not me. I'm like a yippy poodle with manicured claws and a diamond-studded collar. You're like a loyal golden retriever that fetches sticks and rolls over to let him pat your belly."

"Whoa," I said quickly. "We never slept—"

"That's not what I meant." Marisol frowned. "The point is Fletcher isn't a poodle kind of guy. He's a golden retriever kind of guy. Have you seen that horse he calls a pet?"

"Libman is awesome." I stood up from the couch, groaning when my stitches pulled. "I don't even know what to say. I never knew you felt that way. You're always so confident."

Marisol stopped pacing and faced me. Her nose was red. "Don't you get it? I'm not confident at all. I'm so petrified that nobody is going to notice me that I spend all of my time monopolizing all of the attention everywhere I go. You? You just walk into a room and people notice you. It's effortless for you."

"Mar—"

She made an odd whimpering sound and covered her mouth. I froze, unsure what to do. Seeing Marisol cry was like spotting a unicorn.

"Of course he wanted you," she cried. "You two were made for each other."

I put up a hand. "Okay stop right there." When she silenced, I took a deep breath. "Everything your saying is shocking. But the bottom line is I screwed up. I did something wrong, and I should have known better. Whether we were made for each other or not, kissing him while you guys were dating was horrible. I want to be with Fletcher, more than anything. But not if it means losing your friendship."

Marisol was crying now, her tears dragging her makeup down her pretty face. I bent down to put Ian in his cradle at the end of the couch, then reached for my friend's hands. When she didn't pull away, my heart did a victory dance. "I'll never do anything like this to you again. I'm sorry."

Marisol's head sunk down onto my shoulder. "I forgive you," she sputtered into my shirt. "But only if you forgive me."

I put my arms around her and squeezed her tight. "What the hell for?"

She pulled back and looked at me. Her face was a hot mess for the first time in, well, *ever*. "For being so obnoxious. For making you feel inadequate. For sleeping with anything that walks. No, wait. I'm not sorry for that."

"Stop. Okay. I forgive you." I heard Ian starting to stir in his little bed, and a shockwave jolted straight through my body into my boobs. "I need to feed him, I—"

"Oh, no you don't." Marisol squeezed me even tighter. "You need to listen to me, Lex."

I blinked at her. "W-what?"

"You freaking love him," she said with conviction. "Go to him. Profess your feelings for him. Get freaky with him. Get on one knee and ask him to marry you, or something, for Pete's sake! But don't sit around ignoring him because of me."

Chapter Twenty-eight

Once Marisol and I finished having our come-to-Jesus moment, and I'd fed Ian—an act Marisol deemed both barbaric and utterly compelling at the same time—we sat down on my couch with steaming bowls of minestrone to plan out how I was going to woo Fletcher.

Sure, we'd already declared our love for one another, and experienced more together than most couples would go through within their first year. It felt like we'd been a couple for ages already, and we'd not even gone on our first date. Bloody, emergency C-sections followed by full-on family blowouts had a tendency to do that to a couple.

And then there was that little detail of my sending Fletcher away. And not wanting to see him. And not returning his calls. Or texts. It was especially inconsiderate of me since Fletcher had flowers sent to my apartment. *Three times.*

Yeah, it was no surprise to me that Marisol told me I needed to do something big.

"You're gonna have to eat some crow, my dear," my mother had said as she rocked Ian in the corner.

"Mmhm. She's right." Marisol nodded. "You've got to show Fletcher that you're in and not going anywhere. Go big or go home."

And so I spent the next few days planning.

Okay, *fine.* A week. But it wasn't my fault.

Every time I walked past a mirror, my heart would crash into the bottom of my flabby stomach. My lips were covered in fever blisters, something I'd not had since junior high school, but the trauma of Ian's delivery had unearthed them once again.

My skin, usually white as snow and perfectly clear, was covered in angry, red zits. And my boobs had taken on lives of their own. My breasts had grown to twice their size and now resembled overheated volleyballs, and my stomach wiggled like pudding when I did even the simplest things—you know, like *breathing*.

I wanted Fletcher to desire me. I wanted him to not only love what was inside of me, but I also wanted him to crave the outside, too.

I know, I know. I was putting the women's movement back a few paces with my post-partum induced insecurities. But I couldn't help it. I wanted to be a sex goddess, but when I looked in the mirror, I saw Quasimodo with wet stains on my tee shirt where my nipples were.

"Get over yourself," Candace said as she cradled Ian in her lap.

Marisol nodded in agreement from behind her compact mirror. They'd come to see me (i.e., the baby), and were none-to-pleased when Marisol jacked my phone and discovered *no* outgoing calls to Fletcher in my call log.

"You're blowing it," my cousin continued. "He's called Brian every day since the delivery to check on you. Brian says he sounds terrible. He's sick with worry. You're killing him."

"And look at these text messages!" Marisol piped in. "I see you're still ignoring them. Seriously, I get the whole playing hard to get thing, but this is plain stupid."

"I know." I covered my paunchy middle with a throw pillow. "I'm just trying to get a grip on my hormones before I see him. Maybe drop a few pounds."

Candace frowned at me. "Are you joking?"

I looked down at my lap.

"This is asinine. He loves you, Lexie." Marisol gestured to the vases of roses, lilies, and tulips arranged around my living room. "And you're ignoring him."

"Have you seen me lately?" I adjusted one of the nursing pads in my bra. "The constellation of Orion is on my face, and my stomach looks like an angel food cake dough that didn't cook long enough."

Marisol rolled her eyes. "Listen, he may love you and all, but a guy like Fletcher isn't going to wait around forever."

Candace shot her a look. "Marisol—"

"No, I'm serious." She closed her compact with a click, and dropped it into her purse. She then held out her arms. "Okay, give me the kid, and I'll explain what the hell I'm talking about."

Candace stood up and placed Ian in Marisol's waiting arms. She'd actually gotten pretty good at holding Ian. The first time she'd done it, he had been suspended in her hands at arm's length away from her body. Now she actually cradled Ian close to her body—though she still faced him outward, in case he exploded. It'd only taken one spit-up incident to convince Marisol he was a ticking time bomb.

"There we go." She started swaying slowly. "Listen, I'm not saying Fletcher's going to replace you. He doesn't seem the type. Frankly, he strikes me as the type who would just pine away for you for the rest of his life. He's loyal like a bird dog, that one. But other women?" Marisol scoffed. "They'll be on him like white on rice. No woman is going to leave a catch like Fletcher Haybee alone for long. I'm not saying it's right, I'm just saying it's true."

I let her words marinate for a few moments. I hated to say it, but Marisol was right. When it came to knowing the ins and outs of conniving women, it was definitely her wheelhouse. "I'll call him as soon as I can get myself together," I said. "As soon as I can shower on a daily basis."

"Wait a minute." Candace's hand came down on the arm of the rocker. "Lex, he sees women in your current state all the time. Women who've just given birth and their skin is broken out. Women whose stomachs haven't gone back to normal yet. He doesn't care how you look right now. He cares how you're doing."

"I just…" My voice came out jagged, and I cleared my throat. "I want to be beautiful for Fletcher. I don't want him to see me like this."

"Good Lord, you are such a moron." Marisol spoke so loud that Ian jolted in her arms. "Oh, sorry." She dropped her voice to a whisper. "Lex, he saw your vagina with one of those speculum thingies in it."

"Geez!" Candace leaned forward to cover the baby's ears.

Marisol smirked. "Come on, you bled all over Fletcher's office. He saw you with your abdomen cut open and your guts spilling out. He kissed you in your hospital room while you were so stoned you were practically drooling, and he's practically beside himself waiting for you to contact him."

A tug pulled in my heart. "I can't even give Fletcher what I want to give him. I'm not even allowed yet. And if I were, all I have to do is *think* about Ian, and I leak all over the place like a deranged dairy cow."

"So double up on the nursing pads," Candace said.

"And everything makes me cry," I continued. "Literally everything. Yesterday I realized I was out of butter and I cried for forty-five minutes. The hot water in the shower ran out this morning, and I wept like I was at a funeral. I can't even imagine what an orgasm would make me do. I may never stop sobbing. And in case you haven't figured it out, that's not exactly sexy, guys."

Marisol snorted. "You can say that again."

"Hush." Candace used one of Ian's receiving blankets to swat at her. "Lexie, do you think that's what this is all about? Sex?"

I opened and closed my mouth a couple of times, before finally croaking, "Well, in part."

"This isn't just a lust thing. This isn't just a romp." Candace threw her hands up. "We've known him for a few years now, and never in that time has he expressed anything more than a passing interest in a woman. His focus has always been on his daughter and his practice. This is the first time we've ever heard him say he loves a woman. The first time we've seen him wrecked over a woman. When I had each of our kids, I was a mess. You know that. My hair fell out, I got terrible psoriasis on my shoulders and back. My entire body completely rebelled against me, and I looked like I'd been hit by a truck and then dragged for a few blocks."

I nodded. "I remember."

"So do I," Marisol agreed, giggling. "You were a horror movie."

"Gee, thanks." Candace snapped. "What I'm trying to say is, Brian adored me. He treated me like the most beautiful woman in the world. He never complained that he wasn't getting *laid*. He never griped because I wasn't wearing fancy lingerie. We got to know each other more in those months than we had in the years we'd been together before. We got reacquainted in here." She pointed to her head first, then tapped her chest. "And *here*. And that's what you and Fletcher have the opportunity to do. Do you understand that?"

I got it. Deep inside of my heart, something slid into place with a satisfying click, and everything I'd been grappling with for weeks—months, if I wanted to be technical—made sense. Sure, it was unorthodox to fall in love with my obstetrician, a man who happened to be dating one of my friends. But now I'd been given the opportunity to pull the reins, to slow things down, to let mine and Fletcher's feelings mature into something real, and grand, and permanent.

"Fine." I reached out my hand and smiled at my two best friends through watery eyes. "My phone is next to you, Marisol. Will you please hand it to me?"

She shifted Ian to one arm. "Check it out. One hand."

Candace closed her eyes. "Oh holy crap, no tricks. Just give her the phone."

"Yeah, yeah, yeah." She tossed my phone across the room. "Are you calling Fletcher?"

"No." I offered them a smile. "I'm calling a travel agent."

***

Fletcher's receptionist looked up from her computer and smiled. "Lexie, how are you? I didn't know you were on the schedule today."

I put down Ian's car seat, and tugged at my jacket. I'd dressed in my most forgiving clothes, and sported a lot of black in the hopes of disguising my still puffy exterior. Today it needed to be all about the inside. "I'm not actually."

Her smile widened. "It's good to see you. The last time we saw you, you were on a stretcher. I think your two-week post op appointment is tomorrow, isn't it?"

"Yes." My stomach spun at the memory of all of the panic—and blood—in the office that day. "By the way, I'm sorry I scared you all."

"It was actually pretty cool," she admitted. "Usually we don't get to see any excitement. That was the first time we've almost had an in-office delivery."

"That's me. The rule breaker." I shuffled in place a bit. "I wondered if I could speak with Fletch, er, Dr. Haybee?"

"Well, he's got back to back patients this afternoon, so—"

The receptionist was interrupted when Dr. Javornik came up behind her with a file folder. "Oh, hey there, Lexie! What a nice surprise. How are you feeling?"

"Hi." I waved awkwardly. "Great, thanks."

"How are the hormones? Feeling uneven?" She brushed a strand of her long grey hair back from her face.

Tears sprung in my eyes. Why? I didn't know. Like I said, it didn't take much.

"That's normal, dear. They'll fluctuate for a few months now." Dr. Javornik nodded as she spoke, seemingly agreeing with herself. "How's your flow? Slowing down? What about your incision area? Keeping it clean?

I bit the insides of my cheeks to keep from crying. I really needed to get Fletcher to the waiting room, otherwise I was going to chicken out. I'd already sat in the parking lot for twenty minutes before finding the guts to come inside.

"Lexie came to speak to Dr. Haybee," the receptionist informed Dr. Javornik. "But since he's busy, maybe you could see her, and—"

The doctor's eyes widened. "You'd like to see Fletcher? Oh, let me go get him."

Doubt started creeping up on me like an annoying shadow. "I can just come back."

"No, no, no!" Dr. Javornik yelped, making Kelly jump. "He'll be so happy to see you. I'll tell him that you're here."

As she bustled off, I felt every set of eyes in the waiting room settle on me. Fixing my eyes on Ian's car seat, I waited with my arms folded across my chest. Part of me wanted to run back to my car, where a box of tissues and a breast pump were waiting. But I refused. This was it. I had to put on my big girl panties and push forward.

I sat down on the edge of one of the leather chairs and swallowed down my fear. I loved Fletcher. He loved me. This should've been the most natural thing to do in the world.

So why did I feel the need to throw up?

Ian started to squirm and grunt in his car seat, and a couple of nurses peeked at me with excited grins. I could practically smell their anticipation, and sweat prickled underneath my arms. Good grief, was everybody in this place waiting for me to come talk to him? Nothing like trying to right a wrong with an audience.

Ian's grunts started to morph into whines, so I rocked his car seat. "Shhhh…" I said quietly, trying to ignore the nurses gossiping in hushed voices about me.

…Apparently, he's crazy over her…

…had me order flowers for her. Three times…

…broke his heart…

I leaned forward and put my face in my hands. This was a bad idea. Ian's cries were getting louder, despite my rocking, and I could feel the all-to-familiar rush of warmth through my chest.

Oh, no, I thought. *Not here.*

"Shhh, it's okay, honey," I cooed.

Then the inevitable happened. My son released one of his freakishly high-pitched screams that cut right through me, deep down into the marrow in my bones. Before I even had time to process what was happening, two warm circles of wetness formed on my shirt.

"Oh, shit…" I hissed, opening my jacket and looking down. Sure enough, Bessie the cow had returned. *Double breast pads, my ass!*

"Lexie?"

The deep voice sent an electrical current through my body, right into my core.

Fletcher.

Pulling my jacket closed, I stood up and saw Fletcher striding towards me, his white jacket flapping out behind him. His worn, plaid button down was untucked, his jeans had a hole in the knee, and as always, his blonde hair was tousled to utter perfection. He was the only doctor I'd ever met who looked perpetually seventeen. Doogie Howser had nothing on Fletcher Haybee.

"Hi." My voice came out squeaky. Not that I was surprised. I'd just soaked through my bra, two breast pads, and my shirt right in front of a group of gaping onlookers. What was next? Peeing my pants?

"Why are you here?" He stopped just short of touching me. Instead, he put his hands in his pants pockets and rocked on his heels. His eyes roamed to where I was clutching my jacket around me like we were standing in the middle of a hurricane. "Are you all right?" His eyebrows pinched together. "How's your healing? Is the incision all right?"

"No, everything's fine." I wanted to reach out and touch him. I wanted to pull him against me and press my lips to the side of his neck. Dig my hands into his hair and lose myself in him all over again. But the last thing I wanted to do was soak him with breast milk. Talk about unsexy. Ugh. "I just came to talk."

"Okay." I saw his Adam's apple bob when Fletcher gulped.

My eyes darted to the nurses behind the front desk watching us. They all pretended to be busy with random things when my eyes met theirs, but I wasn't stupid. This had become a sideshow. I took a breath and held it, willing my nerves to take a rest.

Finally, I opened my mouth. "Listen, I—"

Ian released another scream, this time even louder than the last. Another gush, and not only had I drenched through my shirt, but my jacket and the sleeves that were folded across my chest.

"Oh, dear God, no," I moaned, my face crumpling.

Fletcher's arms were around me in a flash. "Lex, what's wrong? Talk to me."

I glanced down at Ian, who'd settled himself back to sleep. What a punk.

Pushing against Fletcher's chest, I tried to move away, but his grip was strong. And it felt *so* good. Forgetting about the wet mess, I leaned into Fletcher, drawing in his scent and letting it fill my body with familiar warmth.

"I'm sorry. I'm so, so sorry," I mumbled into his jacket. "I should have called you. I should have talked to you. First I wanted Marisol to forgive me. Then once she gave me her blessing, I couldn't get over what a sloppy mess I am right now. Then I almost wussed out in the parking lot, and I had to walk to the door twice, and..."

I looked up at him. He was watching me, his blue eyes patient as I babbled. Actually, babbling didn't begin to cover it. Once I'd started speaking, it was like releasing the air from a balloon. One giant whoosh, and everything was out.

"I would pick up the phone to call you, then pass the mirror in my bedroom and see myself. Or I would go to text you, and the baby would cry and I would start to cry, too. I cry all the time, and for no reason. It's insanity."

Fletcher's eyes crinkled. "That's natural, you—"

"Let me finish." I sniffled. "I was worried that if I was with you right now, while I'm such a wreck, and so rumpled and tired all the time you would get turned off. I want to be beautiful for you. To be sexy for you. To be everything you deserve. But right now functional is all I can manage. I'm lucky if I get a shower before five o'clock at night. Yesterday, I found a popsicle stick in my hair."

Fletcher stroked the back of his hand down the side of my face. "I don't care. Don't you get that? Even if all I can do is hang around with you in your pajamas while you feed the baby, that's what I'll take. I just want to be with you. I want to get to know you. I want to know what your middle name is and what your major in college was. I want to know all of you, not just the physical you. Instead of pushing me away, we should be using this time to learn everything there is to know about each other."

Nodding, I felt my eyes spill over. Again. "I cry. All the time. About everything."

"Sweetie, it's normal," he said. "Your body's been through a traumatic experience. Sometimes it can take weeks, even months, to level out. If crying at random is your worst trait, I'll take it. Besides, if you let Martha and me help you with Ian, you might get showered sooner, and find more reasons to laugh instead of cry."

I blinked up at him. Seriously, was he too good to be true? "You're incredible. I don't deserve you. Or her."

He shook his head. "You do, Lex. And we're the lucky ones, to be getting you and Ian."

"And you don't mind waiting?" As soon as I said it, I heard the hiss of whispers coming from where the nurses were standing.

Fletcher pressed a kiss to my forehead. "As much as I want you, Lex, and believe me, I do, I've waited this long. What's a bit longer?" I opened my mouth to respond, but a weird choking sound came out, and I dissolved into tears again. "Silly girl," he said, rocking me back and forth. "As if I'd mind. You're worth waiting for. Don't you know that I love you?"

"I love you, too." My voice was barely audible as Fletcher's finger caught my chin, bringing my face up to his. *This is really happening.*

"I've never felt like this before. It's like I've known you my whole life." His eyes danced, and the end of his nose tickled my own. "You're amazing, Lexie Baump. And funny. And sexy. I cannot imagine wanting another woman ever, ever again."

I thought I heard one of the nurses sigh, but forgot about it the moment our mouths met. His lips—so soft, yet surrounded by his delicious five o'clock shadow—molded themselves to mine, then nudged them open. When his tongue tickled my own, I tilted my head to the side and threw my arms around his neck. A rumble sounded deep in Fletcher's chest, as he held me against his body tightly, lifting my feet off of the floor.

The only reason we stopped making out was because the waiting room filled with the sound applause. We pulled apart, looking around while all of the nurses and expectant mothers around us clapped.

"I forgot about them." He laughed and rested his forehead against mine before bringing me back down to the floor. "Go big or go home."

"That's my motto, too." I grinned, wiping my cheeks. "I love you, Dr. Baby."

"I love you, too, Bump." Fletcher pressed another lingering kiss to my mouth, making the receptionist giggle.

I reached into my jacket pocket, and pulled out an envelope. "Which is why I got us these."

"What's this?" His arms loosened and when he took it from me, I noticed that there were wet spots on the front of his shirt. *Oh, snap.*

I covered my face with my hands. "Fletcher, your shirt…" Wincing, I glanced down at my son, who was stirring in his sleep again. Bessie the cow was going to have to feed the baby. Stat.

Fletcher's cheeks reddened, and he tugged at his white coat. "Believe me, in my line of work, this is not the oddest thing that has wound up on my shirt."

"Ugh. TMI." I nudged him. "Open the envelope. I planned our first date."

One of his eyebrows cocked upward. "So your emergency C-section didn't constitute a first date?"

"That's what Candace said."

"Kidding." Fletcher tore open the envelope and pulled out six tickets.

Two airline tickets to Tennessee, two tickets to a Rolling Stones concert in Memphis, and two admission tickets in Graceland. His blue eyes widened to the size of half dollars, and one of his palms landed with a slap on his forehead. "Is this? What the? When? How?"

I'd used my savings to create the perfect first date for us. And in three months' time, we would be whisked away for a weekend of gold lamé and rock and roll. "Will you go out with me, Dr. Baby?"

"Will I ever." He cupped my face, letting the tickets fall to the floor with a flutter. "You're amazing. I'd be a fool not to marry you today."

My insides whirled like a top. "Let's get to know each other first. And then I'd be a fool not to say yes."

Again our faces crashed together, and the room exploded into cheers. This was it. Dr. Fletcher Haybee, OB/GYN was mine. And I was his. I couldn't believe how lucky I was to have found the one person who—

Ian's scream cut through my inner monologue, and the two of us dissolved into laughter. I couldn't ignore him much longer, otherwise we would both need new shirts.

"Duty calls," I whispered against Fletcher's lips.

"Here, let me." He bent down and started to unbuckle Ian's straps, soothing words coming from his mouth like honey while I looked on.

When Fletcher lifted Ian out of the seat, his eyes blinked open. His red cheeks faded back to his normal shade of porcelain as Fletcher held him in his arms. As if on cue, the room hushed and then my son offered Fletcher his first wide, unabashed, toothless grin.

"Come on, Lex." Fletcher said, winking at me. "You can feed him in my office."

We were a family now.

The end.

Epilogue

Fletcher

"Are you ready, babe?" I poked my head in the door of the restroom and looked around.

Lexie turned on her heel and put her hands on her hips. The taffeta of her dress swished when she moved to shut the door. "Fletcher, shame on you! You know you're not allowed in here. Get out!"

"Fine." I put up my hands and backed away slowly. "By the way, you look hot."

I heard her laughing as the bright pink door shut with thump, and strode back out to the waiting room of the Elvis Chapel of Love with a bounce in my step.

When I came around the corner, I was met with a motley crew of anxious looking faces. Brian, Candace, and their kids; Marisol, and her latest flavor of the month, some day trader named Doug. Darren and his newest girlfriend, Yvette, who was even denser than Pandi had been. Corbin, his daughter, Rayna, and a pregnant Andrea, who'd discovered her pregnancy while in Korea for the adoption. And Martha, who was bouncing Ian on her hip like a pro.

And then, of course, Pastor Irm, who approached me with a reassuring smile. "They kick you out of the bathroom, son?" he asked, straightening my bow tie.

I could hear the sound of classic Elvis music being played in the nearby chapel, and hoped the chaplain remembered the list of music I'd slipped to him upon our arrival. These Baump women could be so picky about their tunes.

"Sure did," I replied, giving Irm a clap on the shoulder.

I actually really liked the guy. He was kind and seemed to make Lexie's mom happy. I didn't even mind his sermons, even if Lex had to nudge me every few minutes to keep me awake.

In the six months since Lexie showed up at my office with tickets, much had changed.

She and Ian moved into my brick bungalow, and we spent our nights together eating dinner around the table as a family, renting movies, and taking turns folding laundry. Lexie became the mother Martha had never had. She became her girl scouts' leader, spent every Sunday afternoon giving Martha cooking lessons, and read with her every night. They're tighter than tight, and Martha recently started calling Lexie mom—something that tugs on my heart every single time I hear it.

And as for Lexie's son?

Well, all it took was one gaze into those wide eyes and one glimpse of his head of red curls, and I was sunk. I considered him my son from the moment I lifted him out of his car seat at my office that day, and officially adopting him two months ago was tied with Martha's birth as the second best moment of my life.

What was the number one moment?

That would be when Lexie and I found a small chapel in Memphis where we were married just hours before the Rolling Stones concert. We spent our first night together after having been married for seven hours, scoring backstage passes from a bouncer, and watching Keith Richards make love to his guitar like the petrified God he is.

It was amazing. Everything I imagined it could be after a year of knowing Lexie and fantasizing about taking her to bed. Well worth the wait. She was every bit as sexy and I'd known she would be. And the best part of our impromptu honeymoon? We spent the next morning touring Elvis Presley's shag-carpeted palace. That was the icing on the cake.

Oh, wait. You thought I was at the Elvis chapel to get married to Lexie?

Nope. We'd been married for three months already. Actually, I was getting ready to stand next to Irm while he and Patsy took the vows. They finally decided to make it official after years of keeping their love a secret. Lexie and I offered to help throw them a big wedding, but Patsy and Irm declined. Since they'd both been married and widowed, and news of their relationship had been met with mixed reviews by the congregation at the church, they decided that small and simple was the right way to go.

Getting Patsy to agree to an Elvis wedding? Well, that'd taken some convincing. But Lexie—and her brothers—were relentless. It was the lure of Vegas buffets and slot machines that finally won her over. Plus the dry Vegas heat was good for Irm's arthritis.

"Okay, we're ready."

I heard Lexie's voice and turned around. Patsy stood in a white dress and some sort of net thingy over her face. She was already crying, and her cheeks were the same shade of pink as her bouquet of carnations. She looked unbelievably happy, and judging by the gasp next to me, Irm was beyond happy with how his bride looked.

But my eyes didn't stay on my mother-in-law for long. It was hard not to notice my wife at her side. Her copper-colored hair was pinned back from her face on one side with a clump of white flowers, and her dark pink bridesmaid dress hugged her slender build in all the right places. Lexie's long neck curved beautifully as she leaned close to her mother to whisper words of encouragement, and I had to make fists at my sides to keep from grabbing her and burying my face in her hair.

I loved Lexie with everything inside of me, and it seemed like my feelings for her doubled, even tripled, every day. Our life together was the stuff dreams were made of, and I wouldn't trade one second of it for all the money in the world. Our little family was perfect.

After all, we were Baby & Bump.

Acknowledgments

There's nothing in this world more important to me than my family. My husband, my kids, my brothers & their families, my mom, and my motley crew of mismatched friends. They're all part of what makes me who I am. I really tried to create that same feeling in Lexie Baump's world. This plethora of people, who all bring their own brand of chaos to the table, but all support and love her in their own way. I hope I succeeded.

The idea for *Baby & Bump* came from a Facebook comment someone left on my page one day. A girlfriend (Hi, Tanya!) made a remark about how awkward it would be to have a hot obstetrician. That one random comment turned into an idea in my head that grew and grew and grew until Lexie Baump and Fletcher Haybee had become real people to me. I owe Tanya, and all of my Facebook fans and friends, a huge debt of gratitude for all of their awesome feedback and support. All of my best book ideas come from all of you, and your interesting lives.

A big, fat thanks also goes out to my beta readers (and friends), Jess McCallan and Katie Fox, because if I didn't make you guys laugh and beg for more stories… then it would be back to the drawing board for me. A good author is nothing without feedback, suggestions, and room to grow. Like I always say, the minute I stop listening to feedback is the day I give it all up, and become a podiatrist. Which would be awkward, considering how much I hate feet.

At the risk of sounding melodramatic, *Baby & Bump* really wouldn't be worth a second glance without the critique, feedback, support, and wicked editing skills of the *incredible* Meggan Connors. Seriously, I gave up on this book at least a dozen times. True story. But Meggan never did. Every time I came back to it, she just smiled, read it, and offered me tips, and then patted my head affectionately when I quit again. You know, she and I have come a long way from that pitch fest group at ECWC all those years ago, and our relationship has evolved from writing acquaintances to full on friends. She listens to me gripe about my weight, and she laughs when I send her inappropriate pictures of men in kilts. Meggan's the real deal, folks, and I'm pretty lucky to work with her. Thanks, Meggan.

As always, I have to thank my five darling little monsters. Without each of you, I wouldn't have muddy shoes to pick up or a bazillion loads of laundry to fold. I wouldn't be fat, and I wouldn't have an extensive knowledge of all things Star Wars and Disney XD. But I would also be half the person I am today. So I'm pretty lucky, eh?

Half the reason I write romance is because I am living a romance novel every day. I mean, sure… my nerd and I spend most of our time fighting over the remote, listening to mind-numbing tween music all the time, and laughing at the idiocy of 80's movies, but nobody loves me the way he does. And nobody accepts me the way he does. It's so weird, it's almost as if my husband *likes* the fact that I can't ever shut up and I laugh at my own jokes. Thanks for being my own romance hero, old man.

I hope you all enjoyed the first book of the *This & That Series*. It was a joy to write… even if I did start and stop about twelve times. Stay tuned for Marisol's story next!

~Brooke

Apples & Oranges
Book 2 of the This & That Series

One broken four-inch heel, two sweat marks on a Micheal Kors cowl neck blouse, three chipped fingernails, and a broken down BMW 3 Series convertible. Not exactly a fun way to top off my debunked luncheon with my mother.

"*Inútil pedazo de mierda de coche,*" I hissed as I hiked across the busy street.

A woman pushing a stroller in the crosswalk glared at me. "Nice language."

"How was I to know you'd understand?" I snapped. It wasn't my fault she'd heard me calling my car a piece of you-know-what. Besides, who walked their baby around in ninety-degree weather? "Buy a minivan, breeder."

A car honked their horn at me, but I ignored it. The "walk" sign had long since started flashing red, but I couldn't move any faster, thanks to my busted shoe. Add in the fact that I'd left my iPhone under the napkin at the restaurant so I couldn't call for a tow, and the unseasonably warm May weather was making my most recent blow-out worthless, and my surly attitude was multiplying. Being forced to walk to the nearest auto shop was the icing on the crap cake that was my day.

I didn't *walk* places. I drove places. Walking was what tree huggers did because they thought car exhaust was the devil. The only time I ever walked was when I was cooling down on the treadmill after a work out, which usually involved my gorgeous trainer, and in that case, I didn't mind. But in ninety-degree heat with a messed up shoe? *I minded.*

By the time I hobbled into the first garage I'd come across in this sketchy neighborhood—because when do cars ever break down in nice, gated communities with manicured lawns and luxury cars parked in the driveway?—I resembled a limp piece of lettuce. My hair was flat, my clothes were wrinkled and soaked, and I was pretty sure I'd sweated most all of my makeup down into a bronze ring at the base of my neck.

Limping past the door of the corrugated metal shop with a red roof, I headed straight for the open double garage doors. There was no time to chitchat with some sort of dimwitted receptionist, and there had to be some grease monkey underneath one of these pieces of crap. I'd just spent forty-five minutes across a table from *my mother,* and if that wasn't enough to put someone on edge, I didn't know what would. My stomach dropped as I passed the mirrored glass door. I never went in public looking like this. *Ever.*

"What can I do for ya?"

Jumping, I tripped over a crack in the cement, and stumbled into the garage. Standing before me was a kid, likely in his early twenties, with a prominent nose and dark, shaggy hair. His coveralls were oil stained and greasy, and he was peering up at me from underneath the hood of a beat up truck that looked like it should've been laid to rest a decade ago. It was clear he was going to be gorgeous one day, once he'd gotten the chance to grow into his Mediterranean features, but for now he was sporting the awkwardly cute appearance of someone who knew not the full extent of his capability. I remembered those days.

"Yeah. I need help." I said, tugging off my other shoe and tossing both of them into a nearby trashcan with a thunk. The back of my blouse was completely plastered to my skin.

His eyes widened. "Hey-yo. I can help you. What seems to be the problem, pretty lady?" Standing upright, his head whacked into the truck hood. He blushed and rubbed his tousled head sheepishly. "Ow. Sorry."

I would've laughed, had I not been on the verge of heat exhaustion. When his eyes roamed from the top of my head, down to my toes, and back up again, I added, "Is it take your son to work day today?"

Years and years ago, I'd left the seventh grade in May with the body of a pubescent boy, then returned in September with the body of a Playboy model. I'd inherited my mother's fondness for surgically enhanced boobs, and my father's Cuban good looks, and whether I liked it or not, men took notice. My mom eventually took me shopping, introducing me to the fun of lingerie shopping and four inch heels, and by the time I was sixteen, I'd grown fond of the leering stares and the way I could control men with the flip of the hair or the jut of a hip. Now that I was in my thirties, I used my inherited looks to my advantage for everything from lowered insurance premiums to free mochas. Hey, you work with what you got, right?

The kid in the coveralls smirked. "Yeah, right. My dad doesn't work here."

I raised an eyebrow. "You're what? Sixteen? Seventeen, kid?"

"Nineteen," he replied with a grin.

"Tempting, big guy." I lifted my dampened hair off of my neck, and his eyebrows rose higher on his forehead. "But really, the sign says family owned and operated. Who runs this place?"

He straightened his shoulders. "Who says I don't? Want a tour?"

This kid was persistent, I had to give him that. But I didn't do the cougar thing. Not with boys *that* young, anyway. The youngest I dated was twenty-two, a full decade younger than me. I'd only done that because Candace had declared it inappropriate and morally wrong, and, well, I couldn't let her win that argument, could I? We'd only gone out a few times, before I realized I was in competition with the guy's Xbox, and that wasn't gonna fly. I stuck to my own age bracket, or older, now.

"I'll pass on that tour." I pulled my wallet out of my handbag, then slid my platinum card out of his worn slot. "But seriously, my car's broken down on Manito Boulevard, and I need a tow."

He laughed. "That sucks."

"Sure does." This kid was getting on my nerves. Pressing my lips together, I glanced at his embroidered nametag. "So… *Trey,* do you think you could find someone to run out there and get it?"

Trey put his hand on the edge of the truck and leaned back casually. It slipped, making him stumble, then right himself with a grin. "I might be talked into it."

I tilted my head to the side. "Are you joking?"

Now, normally I enjoyed being flirted with as much as any girl— maybe even more—but today I wasn't interested. Not only was this boy out of my preferred age bracket, but I was also an hour late getting back to work the day before a three hundred guest wedding, and I still had to get someone to tow a car that I'd signed the lease on thirteen months ago.

He shook his head. "No, ma'am."

Aggravation crept up the back of my sticky neck like a spider, so I put my hands on my hips and leaned closer to the kid. He gulped. "Listen up. I've got a dead car holding up traffic out there, and a business partner who will fillet me and serve me up with capers if I don't get my ass back to work. Understand?" He nodded, so I went on. "So how's about you call your tow truck guy and let me borrow a phone, m'kay?"

Trey furrowed his dark eyebrows at me. "You don't have a phone?"

"I left it at a restaurant, okay?" I snapped, wiping my brow. "Seriously, would it kill you guys to air condition this place?"

"Too expensive," growled a low voice from the back of the shop, making Trey stand up straight and tuck his hands into his pockets like a good boy. "There's a recession going on. Or haven't you heard?"

Snarling, I peered around the edge of the truck. "How long have you been over there?"

There was a scraping sound as a creeper rolled out from underneath a Honda Civic. "Judging by those fancy shoes you threw away, I don't imagine someone like you understands the concept of a recession."

"Excuse me?" I snapped.

"That's my uncle." Trey's voice cracked, and he covered it up with a cough. "We're business partners."

There was a scoff from underneath the Honda. "Hey, Trey, why don't you stop flirting with the woman and tell her whose name is on the lease?"

Whoever it was under that Civic, he needed a throat lozenge. This uncle's voice sounded like he'd been gargling with broken glass for a decade or so. With a labored (or was that annoyed?) sigh, a man stood up and ambled towards me.

"Oh, my," I said under my breath, dropping my hair and smoothing down the front of my skirt.

This guy was appealing. And by that, I meant *straight shot of heat right to the center of my belly hot.* He was tall, taller than me in a pair of four inch Jimmy Choo's, which meant around six feet, and that was enough to make me want to turn a backbend right there on the cracked cement floor.

"You are, Uncle Demo." Trey pronounced the name like *Thee-mo,* the traditional Greek dialect rolling off his tongue like butter.

Oh, they're Greek? I thought to myself as this Demo character sauntered towards me with a scowl. His dark eyes were hooded with thick black eyebrows, and a trimmed five o'clock shadow decorated the bottom half of his face. His dark hair, peppered with silver strands above the ears, was dampened at the nape of his tanned neck, and stood in all directions. His coveralls were undone down to his waist, then tied in a knot at his hips, and all that he wore on the top half of his body was a white wife beater that practically sang next to his dark olive skin.

Demo, proprietor of Triple D's Garage, was a bonafide Mediterranean stud. Not that I ever dated the work-by-the-sweat-of-his-brow type. My mother called dating men like that "slumming it," but I wouldn't go that far. I just didn't find the rough hands, scarred skin, covered in sweat thing to be hot. No, I usually stuck with doctors, lawyers, and executive types. The kind that wore suits made out of Italian wool and drove cars as nice as min, or better. The kind who spent their days immersed in paperwork and strategy meetings, not axle grease and transmission fluid.

Hey, I'm not stupid. I knew it was shallow, but the apple didn't fall far from the tree, I supposed. Squaring my shoulders, I turned my attention away from the horny kid and onto his buffed up relative. Maybe sticking with the guys in suits was overrated. My friend Candace always said her ophthalmologist husband, Brian, was at his hottest when he was mowing the lawn shirtless. Maybe she had a point. Slumming it couldn't be that bad, when guys like this were up for grabs.

Apples & Oranges: Book 2 in the This & That Series
Coming soon from Brooke Moss

"I write because if I don't...my head will explode, and ruin the drapes."

♥

Brooke writes complex, character-driven stories about kismet, reunited lovers, first love, and the kind of romance that we should all have the chance at finding. She prefers her stories laced with some humor just for fun, and enough drama to keep her readers flipping the pages, and begging for more. When Brooke isn't spinning tales, she spends her time drawing/cartooning, reading, watching movies then comparing them to books, wrangling five kids, mugging on one hubby she lovingly refers to as her "nerd", and attempting to conquer the Mount Everest of laundry that is the bane of her existence. Brooke is also an avid Autism Awareness advocate, and a passionate foster/adoptive mother, who loves to share her experiences with anyone who will listen. Find Brooke elsewhere on the web at www.brookemoss.com